SHADOWS

By John Saul

SHADOWS

JOHN SAUL

LINDA GREY
BANTAM
BOOKS

NEW YORK · TORONTO · LONDON · SYDNEY · AUCKLAND

SHADOWS

A Bantam Book / July 1992

All rights reserved.
Copyright © 1992 by John Saul.
Book design by Stanley S. Drate/Folio Graphics Co. Inc.
No part of this book may be reproduced or transmitted in any
form or by any means, electronic or mechanical, including
photocopying, recording, or by any information storage and
retrieval system, without permission in writing
from the publisher.
For information address: Bantam Books.

Library of Congress Cataloging-in-Publication Data

Saul, John.
  Shadows / John Saul.
    p.   cm.
  ISBN 0-553-07474-1
  I. Title.
  PS3569.A787S5   1992
  813'.54—dc20   92-1317
                                                    CIP

Published simultaneously in the United States and Canada

Bantam Books are published by Bantam Books, a division of
Bantam Doubleday Dell Publishing Group, Inc. Its trademark,
consisting of the words "Bantam Books" and the portrayal of
a rooster, is Registered in U.S. Patent and Trademark Office
and in other countries. Marca Registrada. Bantam Books, 666
Fifth Avenue, New York, New York 10103.

PRINTED IN THE UNITED STATES OF AMERICA

BVG   0   9   8   7   6   5   4   3   2   1

For all my friends on Lopez Island
And especially:

Larry and Rita
Ron and Jennifer
Robert and Christopher
Jon and Barb
And—last, but certainly not least—
T.A.

SHADOWS

PROLOGUE

Shadows.

Timmy Evans woke up in shadows.

Shadows so deep he saw nothing.

Shadows that surrounded Timmy, wrapping him in a blackness so dense that he wondered if the vague memory of light that hovered on the edges of his memory was perhaps only a dream.

Yet Timmy was certain that it was not merely a dream, that there was such a thing as light; that somewhere, far beyond the shadows in which he found himself, there was another world.

A world, he was suddenly certain, of which he was no longer a part.

He had no idea what time it was, nor what day, nor even what year.

Was it day, or night?

He had no way of knowing.

Tentatively, the first tendrils of panic already beginning to curl themselves around him, Timmy began exploring the blackness of his shadowed world, tried to reach out into the darkness.

He could feel nothing.

It was almost as if his fingers themselves were gone.

He put his hands together.

1

Instead of the expected warmth of one palm pressed firmly against the other, there was nothing.

No feeling at all.

The tendrils of panic grew stronger, twisting around Timmy Evans like the tentacles of a giant octopus.

His mind recoiled from the panic, pulling back, trying to hide from the darkness.

What had happened?

Where was he?

How had he gotten there?

Instinctively, he began counting.

"One."

"Two."

"Three."

"Four."

The numbers marched through his head, growing ever larger as he listened to the voice in his mind that silently intoned the words that meant the most to him in all the world.

The same voice he remembered from the suddenly dim past, when there had been light, and sounds other than the voice that whispered the numbers to him in the silence of his mind.

Even then, before he had awakened in the shadows, only the numbers had truly meant anything to him.

It had always been that way, ever since he was very small and had lain on his back, staring at an object suspended above his crib.

The numbers on the blocks hanging from the mobile had meant something to Timmy Evans.

Though he had been too young to have a word for the mobile itself, the memory of it was clear.

"One, two, three, four."

The object, brightly colored and suspended from the ceiling on a string, turned slowly above him, the voice in his head speaking each numeral as his eyes fastened on it.

"One, two, three, four."

Later, he'd seen another object, on the wall high above his crib.

"One, two, three, four, five, six, seven, eight, nine, ten, eleven, twelve."

Timmy Evans had learned to count the numbers as the hands on the clock pointed to them, though he had no idea what the clock was, nor what purpose it served. But he would lie in his crib all day, his eyes fixed on the clock, saying each number as the hand came to it.

When he'd learned to walk, he'd begun counting his steps, saying each number out loud.

Counting the steps that led down from the front porch of his parents' house.

Counting the cracks in the broken sidewalk that separated his yard from the street.

Counting the panes in the stained-glass windows when his parents took him to church, the pillars that supported the church's high ceiling.

Counting the slats in the venetian blinds that covered the window of his room at home, and the neat rows of vegetables in the little garden his mother planted in the backyard.

Counting everything, endless numbers streaming through his mind.

Numbers that meant something.

Numbers that meant order.

Numbers that defined his world.

The numbers filled his mind, consumed him.

They were his friends, his toys.

He put them together and took them apart, examining them in his own mind until he understood exactly how they worked.

Multiplying them, dividing them, squaring them, and factoring them.

Even as he'd grown up and begun to talk of other things, the numbers were always there, streaming through his mind.

Now, in the terrifying darkness into which he'd awakened, he began to play with the numbers once more.

Timmy began with a million.

He'd always liked that number.

A one, with six zeros after it.

He multiplied it by nine hundred and ninety-nine thousand, nine hundred and ninety-nine.

Then multiplied the total by nine hundred and ninety-nine thousand, nine hundred and ninety-eight.

He kept going, the numbers in his head growing ever larger, occupying more and more of his mind.

And yet the shadows were still there, and though he tried to concentrate only on the numbers, never losing track of the total, the shadows and the silence still closed around him.

He moved the numbers into the space in the back of his mind where he could keep them going with half his mind, and used the rest of his mind to try once more to figure out where he was, and how he'd gotten into the shadows.

School.

He'd been at school before he woke in the shadows.

A nice school. A school he liked, where the other kids were almost as good at numbers as he was.

A pretty school, with a big house set on a broad lawn, shaded by the biggest trees Timmy had ever seen.

Redwood trees.

He'd never seen trees that big before his parents had brought him to the school.

Nor had he ever had friends before.

Friends like himself, who could do things with their brains that other children couldn't.

But now something had happened to him.

What?

He tried to remember.

He'd been in his room.

His room on the third floor.

He'd been asleep.

And before that, he'd been crying.

Crying, because he'd felt homesick, missing his mother and father, and even his little brother, whom he didn't even really like.

He'd cried himself to sleep, wondering if everyone was going to tease him the next morning, because he'd burst into tears in the dining-room, and run out, and up the stairs, slamming his door and not letting anyone in all evening.

Then, sometime in the night, he'd awakened and heard something.

Heard what?

Timmy couldn't remember.

He concentrated harder, and a memory—so fleeting it was barely there at all—stirred.

A rattling sound, like the old elevator that went from the first floor all the way up to the fourth floor.

Then—nothing!

Until he'd awakened in the shadows.

Awakened, to find that there was still nothing.

Once more, he tried to reach out, but his body refused to respond, refused, even, to acknowledge the commands his mind issued.

Paralyzed!

His entire body was paralyzed!

Now the panic that had been entangling him in its grasp gripped him with an irresistible force, and he screamed out.

Screamed out—silently.

He tried to scream again, when out of the shadows, lights began to shine. Brilliant lights, in a spectrum of colors he'd never beheld before in his life.

Sounds, too, burst forth out of the silence that had surrounded him from the moment of his awakening, a cacophony of achromatic chords, layered over with the screeches and cries of the damned souls of Hell.

The sound built, along with the blazing lights, until Timmy Evans was certain that if it didn't stop, his eyes would burn away, and his eardrums would burst.

Crying out once more, he tried to turn his mind away from the sights and sounds that assaulted him, to turn inward, and bury himself among the numbers that still streamed through the far reaches of his consciousness.

But it was too late.

He couldn't find the numbers, couldn't make sense of the gibberish he found where only a few short seconds ago the order of mathematics had been.

Then, as the sensory attack built to a crescendo, Timmy Evans knew what was happening to him.

Just as he realized what was happening, the last moment came.

The lights struck once more, with an intensity that tore through his brain, and the howling cacophony shattered his weakening mind.

In a blaze of light, accompanied by the roaring symphony of a thousand freight trains, Timmy Evans died.

Died, without ever remembering exactly what had happened to him.

Died, without understanding how or why.

Died, when he was only eleven years old.

Died, in a manner so horrible no one would ever be told about it.

The first day of school was even worse than he'd thought it would be. Part of it was the weather. It was one of those perfect days when any normal ten-year-old boy would rather be outside, poking around in the desert that surrounded Eden, searching for horny toads and blue-bellies, or just watching the vultures circling in the sky, then maybe going to hunt for whatever had died.

But Josh MacCallum wasn't a normal ten-year-old, and it didn't seem as though anyone was ever going to let him forget it.

Not his mother, who was always bragging about him to her friends, even though she could see him squirming in embarrassment every time she went on about how he'd been skipped.

Skipped.

Like it was some kind of terrific thing, something he should be proud of.

Except it wasn't neat—it wasn't neat at all.

All it meant was that you were some kind of freak, and when you came into the room on the first day—the room where you didn't know anybody because all the kids you'd gone to school with last year were in another room in another building—they all stared at you, and started whispering and rolling their eyes.

It had started even before he got to school that morning, when

7

he'd tried to talk to one of the guys who was going to be in his new class.

"What's Mrs. Schulze like?" was all he'd said that morning as he'd run into Ethan Roeder on his way out of the ugly little row of apartments they both lived in.

Ethan had barely glanced at him. "What do you care? All the teachers *love* you, don't they?"

While Josh's face burned with the rebuff, Ethan yelled to a couple of his friends, then took off without even a backward glance. Josh had struggled to hold back his tears. For one brief moment he'd felt a burning urge to pick up a rock and throw it at Ethan, but in the end he'd just thrust his hands in his pockets and started trudging by himself through the dusty streets toward the cluster of sun-baked brown buildings that was Eden Consolidated School.

Eden.

Even the name of the town was a crock.

He'd figured out a long time ago that the name of the town was just a publicity stunt, thought up by some developer to fool people into thinking there was something here besides cactus and dirt.

It was like Greenland, which he'd read was just a big sheet of ice, named Greenland by some long-gone huckster in the hope that people would move there.

Well, they sure hadn't moved to Eden, even if it was in California.

The town looked as lonesome as Josh felt, and as he'd approached the school that morning, he'd thought about just walking on by, and straight out to the freeway five miles across the desert, where he might be able to hitch a ride to somewhere else.

Los Angeles maybe, where his father was living.

Or at least had been living the last time Josh had heard from him.

The urge to keep on walking hadn't lasted any longer than the urge to throw a rock at Ethan Roeder, though, and Josh had gone into the middle school building, found Mrs. Schulze's room, and finally gone in.

It was just like what had happened the last time he'd been skipped.

He'd stayed outside until the last possible second, and when he finally slipped through the door, hoping to sink unnoticed into a seat in the last row, Mrs. Schulze had spotted him and given him a too-bright smile.

"Well, here's our little genius now," she'd said. Josh cringed at the word, wishing he could disappear through a hole in the floor, but his wish came no closer to coming true than any of the other wishes he'd fervently sent out over the years to whatever powers might be looking after him.

If there were any powers looking after him, which he'd decided he doubted, despite what they told him in Sunday School every week.

He'd stared straight ahead as the rest of the kids, all two years older than himself, had turned to gaze at him. He hadn't had to look at them to know the expressions on their faces.

They didn't want him there.

They didn't want him getting perfect scores on all the tests, while they could barely answer the questions.

It hadn't been so bad until two years ago, the first time he'd been skipped a grade.

Back then—and it seemed like an eternity to Josh—the rest of the kids were his own age, and he'd known them all his life. He'd even had a best friend back then—Jerry Peterson. And no one seemed to care that Josh always got the best grades in the class. "Someone's gotta be a brain," Jerry had told him more than once. "At least it's better that you're it, instead of some dumb girl."

Even then, when he was only eight, Josh had known better than to point out that if the smartest kid in the class had been a girl, she certainly wouldn't have been dumb.

And then he'd gotten skipped the first time. By the middle of the next year Jerry had a new best friend.

Josh didn't.

Nor had he found one, because when you're nine, a year makes a big difference. All the boys in his new class already had plenty of people to pal around with. And they sure didn't want a "baby" hanging around.

For a while he'd hoped that maybe someone new would come

to school, but that didn't happen either—people didn't come to Eden; they went away from it.

Now he'd been skipped again, and the kids in his class were two years older than he, and the boys were a lot bigger.

Now, as his teacher's voice penetrated his reverie, he could feel them watching him, feel their smoldering anger.

And hear their snickers as they realized he hadn't been paying attention to the teacher.

His mind sped, instantly replaying Mrs. Schulze's all-but-unheard question. "Come now, Josh," she'd said. "Surely you remember the date of the attack on Fort Sumter?"

"April twelfth, 1861," Josh blurted out. "Two days later, the garrison at the fort surrendered, and the Civil War began."

The snickering died away, but Josh felt angry eyes fixing on him from all over the classroom.

What was so wrong with being smart? It wasn't his fault he remembered everything he read, and could do algebra in his head. And it wasn't as if anybody else had been able to answer the question. He hadn't been waving his hand in the air like some kind of kiss-up! Besides, he'd spent most of the summer reading books about American history, and the questions the other kids hadn't been able to answer at all had seemed pretty easy to him.

So it was going to be another endless year of being bored in class and lonely outside of class.

When the noon bell finally rang, Josh busied himself with his book bag until all the rest of the kids were gone, then slid out of his seat and started for the door. Before he could escape, the teacher's voice stopped him.

"Josh?"

He stopped, but didn't turn around. He could hear Mrs. Schulze's heavy footsteps coming down the aisle toward him. When he felt her hand on his shoulder, he once again wished the floor would open and the earth would swallow him up.

"I just wanted to tell you how happy I am to have you in my class this year," Rita Schulze said. "I know it's not going to be easy for you—"

Before she could finish, Josh spun around and stared up at her, his stormy eyes brimming with tears. "No you don't," he said in a voice that trembled with emotion. "You don't know if it's going to be easy or hard. And you don't care, either! All you care about is that I can answer the stupid questions!" His voice rose as he lost control of his tears. "And that's what they are, too—stupid, stupid, *stupid*!" Jerking away from the teacher, Josh turned and stumbled into the mercifully empty hall, then ran toward the boys' room at its far end.

Five minutes later, his tears dried and his face washed, he emerged from the boys' room and uttered a silent sigh of relief when he found the hall empty. He went to his locker, put his book bag inside and took out the brown paper bag containing his lunch. He was about to close the locker when he suddenly changed his mind and burrowed a hand into the bottom of his book bag, fishing out the copy of *Les Miserables* his mother had given him last week. Though he knew the cover wasn't real leather, he still admired it for a moment, with its ornate gilt border surrounding a fleur-de-lis pattern.

Since he already knew he'd be sitting by himself in the cafeteria, he might as well try to read a few chapters.

In the cafeteria, he joined the tail end of the lunch line, silently moving forward until he was able to pick up a carton of milk, then edging toward the cash register. "Well, look who's here," Emily Sanchez said, smiling warmly as she rang up Josh's purchase. "Seventh grade already. Next year, I wouldn't be surprised if you're headin' for high school!"

Josh managed a slight nod of his head, and held out his hand for the change from the dollar bill he'd given Emily. As she put the coins into his hand, Emily leaned toward him, her voice dropping to a whisper. "Any of them kids give you trouble, you let me know, okay? They ain't so smart as they think they are, right?" She winked conspiratorially, but Josh didn't see it, his flushing face already turned away as he hurried toward an empty table in the far corner.

No one spoke to him as he threaded his way between the tables, but he could feel them watching him.

He sat down with his back to the room, determined to ignore

the rest of the kids, and opened his bag to pull out the peanut butter sandwich and small container of cottage cheese that invariably made up his lunch.

"I know it's not interesting," his mother had explained to him over and over again whenever he'd complained of the sameness of it. "But it's good for you, and it's all I can afford."

And so he'd eaten it, day after day, through one school year after another. Today, though, as he contemplated the sandwich in the heat of the cafeteria, he wasn't sure he was going to be able to choke it down.

Indeed, as he took the first bite, chewed it, and attempted to swallow it, it stuck in his throat, and he was finally only able to dislodge it by taking a long swallow of the milk. Opening the book, he began reading, and soon was lost in the tale of Jean Valjean, who was just then stealing a set of silver candelabra from the kindly priest who had taken him in.

Josh turned the pages rapidly, his eyes skimming over the text, taking in every word as he felt himself sinking deeper and deeper into the story. And then, with no warning at all, the book was snatched out of his hands. Startled, he looked up to see Ethan Roeder smirking at him, the book held just out of his reach.

"Watcha readin', smart-boy?" Ethan's mocking voice grated on his ears.

Josh shoved his chair back, rising to his feet. "It's just a book. Give it back."

"Why should I?" Ethan danced away, holding the book out of Josh's reach. "Whatcha gonna do? Call a teacher?"

"Just give it to me," Josh pleaded. "It's not anything you'd like anyway!"

Ethan Roeder's mocking sneer turned angry. "Says who? You think I'm too dumb to read it?" Keeping the book away from Josh's frantic efforts to snatch it back, Ethan opened it.

For the first time, he realized the book wasn't in English. "Holy shit," he cried. "The little creep's reading some other language."

"It's French, all right?" Josh wailed. "It's what the book was written in. So give it back, okay?" He reached for the book once more, but Ethan was too quick for him.

The older boy grabbed Josh's arm, squeezing hard, his fingers digging into the younger boy's flesh. By now the kids at the next table were staring at the confrontation, but none of them made a move to help Josh. Panicking, Josh glanced around wildly, searching for a friendly face, for someone who would help him. But no one moved. In that instant, as he realized that he was totally alone, something inside him snapped.

"Leave me alone, you asshole," he yelled. Jerking hard, he pulled his arm free, then picked up his chair and swung it at Ethan. The bigger boy ducked, then grabbed one leg of the chair and twisted it out of Josh's hands.

Frustrated, Josh groped behind him, felt the carton of milk and closed his fingers on it. As Ethan's fist drew back to smash his face, Josh hurled the milk at him. From another table a wave of laughter erupted as the white liquid cascaded over Ethan's face and ran down his shirt.

"Jesus," Ethan yelled. "What did you do that for?"

"Why can't you just leave me alone?" Josh snatched his book up from where it lay in a puddle of milk on the floor. He tried to wipe the milk off the already wrinkled pages of the book, but it was too late.

He'd had the book less than a week, and it was already ruined.

"Look!" he yelled. "Look what you've done to my book!" He hurled the damp volume at Ethan Roeder, and was about to fling himself on the bigger boy when a booming voice rang out from the door.

"All right, break it up!"

Arnold Hodgkins had been principal of Eden Consolidated School long enough to know how to put a quick end to a disruption in the cafeteria. Now he strode from the door, wading through the crowd gathered around the two boys, one of his thick hands clamping hard on a shoulder of each of the combatants. "That'll be enough! Got it?"

Josh winced as the principal's fingers tightened on his shoulder, but he said nothing.

Ethan Roeder, though, glared angrily at Josh. "I didn't do anything!" he cried out, his voice quivering with fury. "He started it!

We were just sitting here, and he threw milk all over me! Look at my shirt! It's soaking!"

Josh's mouth dropped open at the magnitude of the lie, but before he could say anything at all, one of the other boys, José Cortez, moved in next to Ethan. José and Ethan were buddies. "It's true," José said, his eyes burning into Josh as if daring him to challenge his words. "Ethan didn't do nothin'. Josh just went nutso. He's crazy!"

Josh's eyes darted from one face to another, praying that some-one—*anyone*—would tell the truth. But all the kids gathered around Ethan Roeder were his tormentor's friends, all of them kids from his own class. Kids who already hated him.

His eyes searched further across the cafeteria, and finally fixed on Jerry Peterson, who was standing up on a chair at a table next to the far wall, straining to see the action on the other side of the room and report to his friends what was happening.

Two years ago Josh had been at that table himself, sitting next to Jerry, giggling at whatever joke his best friend might be telling.

Now, Jerry hardly even seemed to see him. Their eyes met for a quick instant, but then Jerry looked away, jumping down off the chair, disappearing behind the crowd of bigger kids who surrounded Josh and the principal.

"Well, what about it?" he heard the principal demanding. "Is that the way it happened?"

Josh shook his head miserably. "I was just sitting by myself, reading. Ethan grabbed my book and wouldn't give it back."

"Oh, Jeez," he heard Ethan groan. "What would I want his stupid book for? I just asked him what he was reading, and he went apeshit, just like he always does!"

"That'll be enough!" Hodgkins snapped, the look in his eye telling Ethan not to press his luck any further. "Roeder, you and Cortez clean up this mess. And no backtalk! MacCallum, you come with me."

Josh nodded, but said nothing. His head down, he followed the principal out of the cafeteria, already preparing himself for the lecture he was going to get about disrupting the cafeteria.

The first day of school this year, he decided, was even worse than the first day last year.

And it wasn't going to get any better.

"Chili up, no tears!"

Brenda MacCallum heard the shout from the kitchen, but acknowledged it with no more than a quick nod of her head as she tried to keep up with the changing orders of the four men who were impatiently ordering lunch. Not that she could blame them for their irritability, but was it her fault that Mary-Lou had called in sick that morning, leaving just herself and Annette to deal with the lunch rush? Still, the slow service wasn't the customers' problem, and she held her temper carefully in check as one of the men changed his order for the third time. But when Max's voice—etched with sarcasm this time—came again, his demand to know if she'd suddenly turned deaf combined with the heat of the day to snap the thread of her nerves.

"I hear you," she yelled back. "But I've only got two arms and two feet."

"More like one of each, given the service around here," one of the men muttered.

Brenda clenched her jaw, firmly checking the words that hovered on the tip of her tongue, and turned away, heading for the kitchen. Only another forty-five minutes until the noon rush was over. Forty-five minutes until she could find the time to sit down and drink a cup of coffee while the feeling came back into her feet. As she passed the cash register, the phone beside it started ringing. But Brenda ignored it, moving on to the pass-through to slip the order onto the wheel and pick up the three bowls of chili that were still steaming under the warming lights.

"God damn it, Brenda," Max growled. "You think the customers want their food stone cold?"

"If they want food, they don't come here in the first place! And don't yell at me—I'm not the one who called in sick."

Max opened his mouth as if ready to fire back at her, but then seemed to decide it wasn't worth it. And he was right, Brenda reflected as she balanced the three bowls of chili, a basket of stale sourdough bread, and a dish of grated cheddar cheese that was rapidly turning orange, on her left arm, while she picked up the limp salads with her right. This was not the day to push her, not after this morning, when she'd all but had to force Josh into going to school, and tend with the baby's colicky stomach as well.

As she threaded her way to the table where three women—with whom Brenda had gone to high school only ten years ago—waited for their lunch, she caught sight of herself in the mirror behind the soda fountain, and her heart sank.

Though she was the same age as the three women who were waiting impatiently for their chili, she looked at least ten years older. Her hair, once a luxuriant mane of naturally blond curls, had darkened into a drab, limp mass that looked as if it hadn't been washed for a week, even though she'd shampooed it this morning right after Josh finally left for school.

Her face had taken on the first lines of middle age, although she was still only twenty-eight. Which, she ruefully realized as she delivered the chili to her three former schoolmates, was nobody's fault but her own. After all, it had been her decision to marry Buck MacCallum, even in the face of her mother's objections, as well as those of everyone she knew. But back then, Buck had been as handsome as she was pretty, and she'd been too young to see anything beyond his well-muscled body and his thickly-lashed brown eyes.

Eyes, she'd quickly discovered, that never missed a pretty face—and some not so pretty ones, too.

Within a year of Josh's birth, Buck had taken off, bored with Eden, bored with pumping gas and fixing carburetors at the Exxon station, bored with her. So she'd come to work for Max, waiting on tables and struggling to make enough to support herself and Josh.

And then, a year and a half ago, she'd run into Charlie Decker for the first time since high school, and thought her problems were over. Charlie had flattered her, told her she didn't look any different than when she'd been the homecoming queen nine years earlier. He promised to take her and Josh to San Francisco as soon as a deal he was working on came through.

They'd made plans to get married, and when she'd become pregnant, Brenda hadn't worried at all.

Until she'd called Charlie in San Francisco to tell him the good news, and a woman had answered the phone.

A woman who turned out to be Mrs. Charlie Decker. The woman who had occupied the position for six years.

And who told her that if she wanted Charlie, she was welcome to him, because Brenda was the third goddamn tramp who'd called in the last year, wondering when that no-good son of a bitch was going to come and get her.

Shaking, Brenda had hung up the phone and put Charlie Decker out of her mind. No point in even telling him about her pregnancy. When Melinda was born, she'd given the little girl Buck MacCallum's last name, figuring if it was good enough for herself and Josh, it couldn't hurt Melinda, either.

But that was when the ends had finally stopped meeting, and she'd had to go on food stamps to keep their stomachs full.

The sound of Annette's voice broke through her reverie just as she was putting the last of the order down in front of her old schoolmates. "What's *wrong* with you, Brenda?" Annette was demanding. "Can't you hear me? It's Arnold Hodgkins, and he says he has to talk to you *now!*"

The three women at the table glanced inquiringly at her. Brenda's heart sank. *No,* she told herself as she started toward the phone. *Not yet. Not the first day. Please?* But her heart sank further as she heard the school principal's voice on the phone.

"Hello, Mrs. MacCallum." The three words were freighted with a note of tired resignation that told her the whole story.

"Oh, Lord," she sighed. "What's Josh done this time?"

"He started a fight in the cafeteria," Arnold Hodgkins replied. "He claims it wasn't his fault, that he was just sitting there reading a book, and that everyone else was picking on him."

"And the rest of them say he just freaked out," Brenda finished for him, already knowing what was coming. She'd hoped that after the trouble last year, it would be over with, that by following the school's recommendation to skip Josh into the next class, he'd be challenged enough to stop relieving his boredom in the classroom with constant troublemaking and displays of temper. Well, so much for that hope.

"I think you'd better come down here," Hodgkins was saying. "He's not talking at all, and he's refusing to go back to class."

Brenda scanned the packed tables of the café, then noted the time once more. She could see Max glowering at her from the kitchen. Catching her eye, he nodded meaningfully at the orders that were piling up beneath the lights in the pass-through.

She weighed her options, then made up her mind.

"Mr. Hodgkins, I can't come right now. It's the middle of the lunch hour rush, and one of the other girls didn't come in. Max is already glaring at me, and if I take off, he'll fire me. Can't you put him in the library or something? Just for an hour?" Her voice had taken on a plaintive note, and she instinctively turned away from the dining area and the eyes of the women who had once been her friends.

Blessedly, the school principal seemed to understand. Almost to her surprise, she heard him agree. "All right. I'll keep him in my office. But try to make it within an hour, would you? I've got a meeting with the head of the school board, and I don't intend to be late."

"Thanks, Mr. Hodgkins. I'll get there within an hour, I promise."

She hung up the phone and hurried toward the pass-through,

where Annette was trying to cope with the backlog of orders. Max was hunched over the grill, his back to her.

"Trouble?" Annette asked.

Brenda nodded, then spoke to Max. "I'm going to have to take off for an hour after we get through lunch. It's Josh . . ."

Max glanced sourly up from the griddle where he was tending to a dozen hamburgers. He shoved his spatula at one and flipped it with a violent slash of the wrist. "How come he always has problems on my time?"

Brenda took a deep breath, wanting to snap back that Josh was only ten years old, that all kids have problems, and that this particular problem was cutting into her day just as much as it was his. Unless, she reflected darkly, he was suddenly planning to pay her for the hour she would be gone. Now *that* would be a first. But she said nothing.

Finding this job hadn't been easy; finding another would be even harder.

Annette, sensing her distress, smiled encouragingly. "Hey, take it easy. You can have a couple of my hours tomorrow night, and it's not like the tips are heavy after lunch. Do what you have to do, and screw Max, right?"

"Right," Brenda agreed, her lips twisting wryly as she picked up another batch of orders and started toward a table next to the window. But screwing Max wasn't the answer, because Max wasn't the problem.

Josh was, and right now she hadn't the slightest idea what she was going to do about it.

At one-thirty, with all but two of the tables empty and reset for the after-school crowd of teenagers, Brenda took off her apron and hung it on one of the hooks at the end of the kitchen where the lockers were. Max's perennially angry eyes fixed on her as she started for the door.

"You plannin' to wear my uniform on your own time?"

"It's only an hour, Max. It's not like I'm taking the afternoon off to go dancing." She glanced down at the pink nylon dress with a too-short skirt. "And if I were, I wouldn't go wearing this crummy thing."

"That 'crummy thing' cost me fifteen bucks," Max growled. "An' I don't have to provide uniforms at all, you know. If that kid pukes on it—"

"Oh, for God's sake, Max! Can't you be a human being for even five minutes? Josh isn't sick, he's just—" She floundered, searching for the right words, but Max cut in before she found them.

"Yeah, yeah, I know. He's just too smart for his own good, right? 'Cept it seems to me if he was so damn smart, he'd learn to keep himself out of trouble. You just get back here in an hour, understand?"

"Okay," Brenda replied, taking his dismissal as tacit permission not to bother changing her clothes. She hurried out the back door, the midday heat instantly making her break into a sweat that caused the nylon dress to cling clammily to her skin, and slid behind the wheel of her nine-year-old Chevy.

The engine ground disconsolately when she turned the key, and Brenda swore silently. "Please, please," she murmured, twisting the key over and over again, and resisting the urge to press the accelerator to the floor. "Just this once, don't give up on me."

Just as the battery was about to give out, the engine caught, coughed grumpily, then began chugging. Keeping her foot on the gas, Brenda reached back and cranked down the rear windows, then leaned over to the one on the front passenger side. It was permanently stuck in the closed position, but she always tried anyway, on the theory that miracles do happen now and then, and one of them just might befall her ruin of a car.

No luck.

She backed out of the parking space into the alley, and a moment later was on Main Street, heading out to the school. Eden Consolidated, a group of mock-adobe buildings was huddled on the edge of town. Beyond it was nothing but an arid expanse of desert, eventually broken by mountains dimly visible through the constant haze of smog that drifted out from Los Angeles, two hundred miles away.

Brenda drove slowly, wanting to take a few minutes to collect herself before she had to face Arnold Hodgkins. As tempting as it was to feel sorry for herself, she resisted. She suddenly had an image of herself in an old Bette Davis movie. What was the name of it? She couldn't remember. The one where Bette was a waitress in a crummy café in the desert, and there wasn't even a town around it, not even one as worn-out as Eden. And Davis had never had so much as a single romance, except with a poet who didn't really care about her.

At least I've been in love a couple of times, Brenda reflected with the innate honesty and black humor that had gotten her through some of the worst moments of her life, even if they were rats. And I've got a couple of kids who definitely aren't rats! In fact, one of them's a genius, for all the good it does any of us right now. And we're not starving, and we have a place to live, and things could be a lot worse.

Almost to her own surprise, she found herself humming as she pulled the car into the school parking lot and made her way to Arnold Hodgkins's office. But her composure deserted her as she spotted her son slouched in a chair in the corner of the principal's office, his large dark eyes, as heavily lashed and deep as his father's, staring sullenly up at her.

"Well, look at you," Brenda said. "Sit that way much longer, and you're going to get a hunchback."

"Who cares?" Josh replied, making no move to correct his posture.

"I do, for one," Brenda told him. "And until you sit up properly, I'm not going to listen to your side of the story."

Josh made a face indicating that he didn't think she was going to listen to him anyway, but straightened up in the chair.

"It was Ethan," he said. "He started it. All I was doing was reading *Les Miserables,* and he came up and grabbed the book away from me. He wouldn't give it back, so I threw my milk at him."

Brenda's gaze shifted from Josh to Arnold Hodgkins. "What does Ethan Roeder have to say about it?"

The principal shrugged, and waved Brenda into a chair. "Just what you'd think—that he didn't do anything. According to Ethan,

Josh had no reason to throw a carton of milk on him." He shook his head helplessly. "Unfortunately, I'm not sure what I can do, since the rest of the children all back up Ethan's story."

"That's ridiculous," Brenda broke in. "Ethan's two years older than Josh, and at least twenty pounds heavier and three inches taller. And I don't care what other problems Josh might have, he's not stupid. He wouldn't pick a fight with someone as big as Ethan!"

The principal's hands spread in a gesture of frustration. "Mrs. MacCallum, try to calm down. I'm not taking sides—I'm simply reporting what I was told by the other children. Nor is it the first time there have been reports of Josh behaving with unprovoked violence." He paused, then went on. "Unfortunately, this is not the only episode you and I need to discuss today."

Brenda hesitated, her indignation blunted. "You mean there's more?" she asked.

Hodgkins chewed uncomfortably at his lower lip. "Rita Schulze was here during lunch hour. It seems she had a little run-in with Josh just after the morning session ended."

Brenda's eyes moved back to her son. Josh squirmed in his chair. "She wouldn't leave me alone," he complained. "Every time she asked a question, she made me answer it, like I'm some kind of freak or something. All the rest of the kids were staring at me, and talking about me, and—"

He fell silent as he read the anger in his mother's eyes.

"So you were rude to your teacher, and threw milk on Ethan? Is that it?"

"No!"

"Don't lie to me, Josh. I want to know what happened."

"I'm telling you, Mom! I didn't do anything!" Josh's eyes flicked around the room, as if he were searching for some avenue of escape, and Brenda reached out, taking his chin in her hand, forcing him to look at her.

"Is that the truth, Josh?"

Silently, Josh nodded. After a moment Brenda let her hand drop away and turned tiredly back to the principal.

"What are we going to do?" she asked. "It was the same thing last year. Bill Cooley was always holding Josh up to the rest of the class, like they should all be as smart as he is. It wasn't fair to them, and it sure wasn't fair to Josh."

Arnold Hodgkins's gesture of helplessness expanded. "It's a difficult situation," he admitted with obvious reluctance. "But—"

"But you shouldn't have skipped him again," Brenda cut in, her voice rising to an angry crescendo. "You should have left him with his class."

Hodgkins shook his head doggedly. "That's not the problem! Not the problem at all! The problem, when you get right down to it, is that we just don't have any programs for kids like Josh. The school's too small, and the resources too limited."

Brenda MacCallum stared at the principal. "So what am I supposed to do? Take Josh out of school? It's not my fault this place can't deal with him."

Now Hodgkins leaned forward, picking up a pamphlet from his desk. "I didn't say it was your fault, Mrs. MacCallum, and if I implied it at all, I'm sorry. But the facts are the facts. There isn't much we can do for Josh here. He needs special programs, with specially trained teachers, and he needs to be with other kids like himself." His eyes fixed on the pamphlet, which had arrived on his desk only last week, along with a computer-generated "personalized" letter suggesting that perhaps Josh MacCallum might be a candidate for the school the pamphlet described. Initially he had dismissed both the letter and the pamphlet, certain that the solicitation had been stimulated by nothing more than the centrally scored IQ tests all the Eden children had taken last spring. But after the incident in the cafeteria, he had studied the brochure more closely.

Brenda, still dazed by the principal's last words, stared at him. "What are you saying? You think I should just pick up and move? You think I *can* just pick up and move? And even if I could, where am I supposed to go? How am I supposed to find the kind of school you're talking about?" Before she could go on, Hodgkins handed her the pamphlet.

It was from a place called the Barrington Academy. A sketch of a large mansion surrounded by a broad lawn studded with towering pine trees was printed on the heavy buff-colored paper. She stared at it quizzically, then looked up at Arnold Hodgkins. "What's this? It doesn't look like any school I've ever heard of."

"It's not," Hodgkins replied. "It's a private school designed for gifted children. It's up north at—"

But Brenda MacCallum didn't let him finish. She was already on her feet, her eyes blazing. "Private school?" she demanded. "Where am I going to get the money for private school? I'm a waitress. I get minimum wage, plus tips, and let me tell you, in Eden the tips aren't much! Since Melinda was born, I've even had to go on food stamps!" She paused to fight back her tears, then, summoning what dignity she could gather, went on. "I'll have a talk with Josh, and make sure that from now on he behaves himself. I would appreciate it if you made sure the rest of the kids around here—and the teachers, too—stop making him feel like some kind of freak! Come on, Josh."

Arnold Hodgkins rose out of his chair and started around the desk. "Mrs. MacCallum, wait. There's a lot more we need to talk about. If you'll just calm down—"

But it was too late. Brenda, clutching Josh by the hand, was already halfway down the hall. For a moment Hodgkins considered going after her, but decided that in the woman's present mood, there was nothing he could say.

The problem of Josh MacCallum could wait, but the president of the school board could not.

———

Brenda drove silently along the ragged edge of Eden toward the decaying building in which she lived, feeling Josh's anger radiating toward her, but doing her best to ignore it. When Josh finally spoke, she knew she had to respond.

"You didn't have to talk about me like I wasn't even there," he said.

For a moment Brenda thought she might cry. She reached out and squeezed her son's knee. "I'm sorry," she said. "I guess I just got so mad at Mr. Hodgkins that I forgot you were listening."

"Well, I was. And I heard everything you said. And it's not fair, Mom. I didn't do anything at all."

Brenda took a deep breath. "I'm not saying you did, sweetheart. But if all the other kids—"

"They're all liars!" Josh shouted, his anger bursting forth. "How come no one ever believes me? It's not fair!" He reached into the book bag, jerked out the book he'd been reading in the cafeteria, then began ripping its pages out, one by one. Rolling down the window, he flung the pages out into the desert breeze. Brenda could see them fluttering behind the car.

"Josh! What are you doing? Do you know how much that book cost? I had to order it special from Los Angeles!"

"I don't care!" he shouted. "I hate the book, and I hate school, and I hate Mrs. Schulze and Mr. Hodgkins and everyone else! I hate it all!" With every furious sentence, he yanked another page from the book and flung it out the window, until he was pulling them out by the fistful, filling the area behind the car with a storm of white. "And I hate you, too," he yelled. "I hate everybody and everything!"

Brenda reached over and snatched what was left of the book out of his hands, tossing it into the backseat. "Well, let me tell you, buddy-boy, right now I'm not too crazy about you, either."

For a moment she thought she was going to slap her son. Then her gaze settled on the open window by his side.

For the first time in two years, it was wide open.

The little miracle had actually happened.

As Josh stared at her in amazement, Brenda threw her head back and began laughing out loud.

A moment later, though, her laughter choked off, then died. As the reality of her life, and the life of her son, closed back in on her, she began to cry.

The miracle of the open window, she decided, was just too little.

What she needed was a much larger miracle.

But where would it come from?

3

Brenda pulled the car under the sagging carport behind the apartment house and wondered for the hundredth time whether it would be better to call the landlord about peeling paint yet again, or simply organize yet another work party among the tenants to paint the building themselves. Bill Roeder might even be able to do something about the sagging beam under the carport—a post, or something.

"This place sure is a dump," Josh remarked, almost as if he'd read her mind.

"It could be a lot worse," Brenda reminded him. "There are millions of people who don't even have something like this to live in."

They climbed the stairs to the second floor, and walked down the sun-drenched walkway to the apartment at the south end. The location was a mixed blessing at best; though the apartment had windows on three sides, it also was exposed to the sun on those same three sides. By four o'clock in the afternoon the rooms had usually taken on the less attractive aspects of a pottery kiln. Still, the rent was cheap, and though she was constantly looking, so far Brenda hadn't been able to find anything better.

As she slipped her key into the lock and pushed open the door, she was relieved to find that Mabel Hardwick, the downstairs neighbor who had volunteered to watch Melinda while she put in her hours at the café, had remembered to pull the drapes over the windows, reflecting the worst of the heat back out into the desert. The room, though relatively cool, was gloomy, however, and Brenda immediately moved to the draperies on the east wall and pulled them open. The light flooding in and the grinding sound of metal against the curtain rod awakened Mabel, who had been dozing on the sofa, the television droning a few feet in front of her.

"Oh!" the elderly woman gasped, stifling a yawn and self-consciously heaving her bulk into an upright position. "Brenda! What are you doing—" As she spotted Josh standing silently just inside the door, she clucked sympathetically. "Oh, dear. Didn't you even make it through the first day?"

Though Josh flinched—even Mrs. Hardwick clearly thought that whatever had brought him home early from school must have been his fault—he said nothing. Before Brenda could explain the truth of the matter, Melinda, who had been sitting in her playpen staring at the television set, caught sight of her mother, climbed unsteadily to her feet and began to wail.

"It's all right, sweetheart," Brenda soothed, picking up the little girl and cradling her against her bosom. "Mama's here now. Everything's going to be fine."

Melinda, the routine of her day unaccustomedly disturbed, only howled louder. Carrying the baby on her hip, Brenda went to the refrigerator, pulled a bottle out and put it in the microwave.

"You just sit down and let me do that," Mabel Hardwick said, pulling herself to her feet. "I shouldn't've been dozing in the first place, but you know how it is when you get to be my age." She started toward the tiny kitchen that was little more than an alcove off the living-dining area, but stopped when Brenda shook her head.

"Why don't you just take a few minutes for yourself, Mabel. I don't have to be back at work for another half hour." A tiny little lie, but if she took an extra fifteen minutes, Max might not even notice. "Besides, if you're going to have to look after both kids this afternoon, you'll need a little breather."

Josh, who had followed the older woman into the kitchen, rolled his eyes. "Aw, come on, Mom. Mrs. Hardwick doesn't need to come back. I can look out for Melinda myself."

"Really," Brenda observed darkly. "I can't even trust you to make it through the first day of school without getting thrown out, and now you want me to trust you with your sister?"

Josh's mouth dropped open and he felt his eyes fill with tears, but he turned away quickly, instinctively refusing to let either his mother or Mrs. Hardwick see the pain he was feeling.

"Great!" he muttered. "If I can't do anything right, I just won't do anything at all!" He stamped across the room, disappeared into the short hall that separated the two small bedrooms and one tiny bath from the living room. There was a crash as the door to the room he shared with his baby sister slammed shut.

═══

Josh threw himself on his bed, burying his face in his pillow.

It wasn't *fair*! None of it was. Not what Ethan Roeder had done to him in the cafeteria, or Mr. Hodgkins not believing his side of the story, or his mother making him come home from school, or any of it. Why didn't they kick Ethan out? He was the one who'd started the fight!

And why wouldn't his mother let him take care of Melinda? It wasn't like he was a baby anymore. Lots of kids his age stayed home alone while their moms worked.

It was Melinda.

She didn't trust him with Melinda.

He sat up, glaring malevolently at the crib that occupied the opposite corner of his room.

It wasn't even his room anymore. Now it was Melinda's room, too, and it seemed more and more like it was *just* her room. His eyes darted over the floor, fixing angrily on the littered toys.

Maybe he should just open the window and throw them all out onto the dirt next to the building.

He picked up Melinda's favorite toy, a teddy bear that he himself had chosen for her right after she was born, and started toward the window. But even as he began to open the window, he had already changed his mind.

None of what had happened was Melinda's fault, he decided. She was just a little baby. Why should he punish her?

He took the teddy bear to the crib and laid it on its back next to the pillow, so that it would be there for her the next time Melinda was put in her crib. Then he straightened out the blanket, carefully tucking it in so that the bear was nestled under the covers, only its furry head poking out, its shiny eyes looking up at him.

The neatness of the crib—the simple orderliness of it—somehow made him feel better. Without really thinking about it, he started picking up the rest of Melinda's scattered toys.

Her alphabet blocks seemed to be everywhere. As he gathered them up he arranged them precisely on the brick-and-board shelves that served as not only his bookshelves, but her toy box as well. He put them carefully in order, leaving gaps for the letters he hadn't yet found. When he was done, they were all there except for the C and the N. The C turned up under the bed, and he finally found the N stuffed down into the toe of one of his own slippers. The blocks arranged, he began picking up the large pieces of a simple jigsaw puzzle, putting them back in their cardboard frame and setting it up so it leaned against a wall. He moved on to the picture books and crayons that seemed to be strewn everywhere.

Finally finished with his little sister's belongings, he began on his own, a haphazard heap of possessions that littered his side of the room.

Methodically, he started over, sorting through the various junk he'd collected, putting every item back exactly where it belonged.

As he picked a dirty shirt up off the table by his bed, his gaze fell on the hunting knife his father had sent him for his birthday last year.

No, not last year.

The year before.

Last year there hadn't even been a card.

He picked the knife up, staring at the blade. He wondered where his father was right then, and what he was doing.

Did he even remember that he had a son named Josh? Or did

he have another son now, another boy, whom he played baseball with, and took camping, and did all the things that fathers do with their boys?

The things that Josh had never done with his father at all, since he couldn't even remember his dad all that well.

A thought flitted through his mind, but he quickly discarded it, putting the knife down and continuing with the task of storing his things away.

But as he worked, the thought kept cropping up in his mind. When he had put the last of his dirty clothes in the hamper, and hung the last of the not-dirty-enough-to-need-washing shirts in the closet, he sat down on the bed and looked around the room.

Now that it was straightened up, it was surprising how little there was in it.

Even the bookshelves seemed to have a lot more of Melinda's stuff on them than his own.

And in a little while, when she got too big for her crib, she would need a bed.

The room wasn't really big enough for two beds.

And the closet, and the dresser, were already full.

His eyes went once more to the hunting knife that still lay on the table next to his bed.

He picked it up, turning it so that the blade glinted in the sunlight that poured in through the window.

His finger touched the edge. He'd spent hours honing the steel to the point where it would shave the fine hair right off his arm without leaving so much as a scratch.

He moved the blade over the skin of his wrist now, watching the hair fall away. If he twisted the knife just a little, then jerked hard on it—

An image of blood filled his mind, blood spurting from his opened arteries.

Why not?

He asked himself the question silently, letting his thoughts drift over the answer.

Who would care if he was gone?

Not Melinda—she hardly knew him.

And his father sure wouldn't—his father had forgotten about him a long time ago.

Nor were there any friends who would miss him.

His mother?

He thought about his mother for a long time. Finally he decided that she might miss him at first, but the more he considered it, the more certain he was that if he weren't there, her life would be a lot easier. She wouldn't have to worry about him screwing up anymore, and not "living up to his potential," whatever that was supposed to mean.

It was a phrase he'd heard all his life, from the first time he got a report card in first grade, and read the teacher's comments on the back. Even now the words were still burned into his memory: "Josh doesn't seem motivated to work up to his potential."

He hadn't known exactly what it meant until he'd looked up the word when he got home that day. When he'd finally puzzled it out, he wondered what the teacher had meant. He could read and write better than anyone else in the class! In fact, when they'd started, he'd been the only one who could read and write at all. He'd already known his multiplication tables, when all the rest of them were just learning to add and subtract. Why hadn't his perfect grades been good enough?

His mother had told him it was all right; the teacher had only meant that Josh was a lot smarter than the rest of the kids. From then on he'd always had the feeling that no matter what he did, it wasn't going to be quite good enough. Not for the teachers, not for his mom. Not even for himself. Anger burned inside him. What was he supposed to do? Was it his fault he liked to read and already knew all the stuff they were teaching in school? And every year it was the same.

"Josh isn't working up to his potential."

And he was always in trouble, too, and his mom was always getting called into Mr. Hodgkins's office to talk about him.

When that happened, it meant she couldn't be at work, and Max wouldn't pay her.

The blade of the knife shimmered in the sunlight. The thought grew in Josh's mind.

If he were dead—

If he were dead, he wouldn't have to worry about anything anymore. Not about his mom, or about getting in trouble, or the other kids picking on him.

He wouldn't have to worry about not living up to what everyone expected of him.

And his mom wouldn't have to worry about him, either.

She could just go to work, and come home and take care of Melinda, and stop worrying about him. And when Melinda got bigger, she could have this room all to herself.

He held the knife in his right hand, his eyes fixing on the shining blade. He wondered if it would hurt.

But even if it did, it wouldn't hurt for very long.

And it wouldn't hurt nearly as bad as he'd been hurting most of his life.

His hand tightening on the knife's handle, his eyes wide open, he slashed the blade across his left wrist.

Instantly, a geyser of blood spurted from his wrist, and he quickly transferred the knife to his left hand.

A second later another red geyser spouted from the artery of his right wrist.

Oddly, it didn't hurt at all.

But there was a lot more blood than he'd thought there'd be.

Brenda's eyes came back into focus as the soap opera ended and the commercials began. She glanced up at the clock over the television set, realizing that she must have dozed off. The half hour she'd allotted for herself after Mabel Hardwick had finally left was almost gone.

Melinda was sleeping peacefully in her arms. Brenda slowly got to her feet. If she was careful, she could get the baby into her crib without waking her up, and by now Josh should be calmed down enough so she could apologize to him.

She moved silently to the kids' bedroom door, quietly opened it, then froze in shock at what she saw.

Josh, his face pale, was standing in the middle of the room.

There was blood everywhere—his clothes were covered with it, as was the bed, and the carpet on which he stood was no longer avocado green, but a dark, muddy maroon.

The moment in which her eyes took in the scene seemed to stretch on forever as a series of snapshots were etched into her memory forever.

The hunting knife, its blade covered with blood, lying on Josh's pillow.

The sunlight, glowing redly through a smear of blood that had somehow gotten onto the window.

The look of puzzlement in Josh's eyes; the dazed expression on his face.

For a long moment mother and son stared at each other in silent horror. It was Josh who finally spoke, his voice quavering.

"Mom? I—I'm scared."

The words galvanized Brenda. She rushed to the crib, snatching up the blankets with one hand as she laid the startled Melinda, now wide awake again and screaming with outrage, on the mattress. Ignoring the cries of the baby, Brenda flung herself on Josh, grabbing first one wrist, then the other, and wrapping them tightly in the blanket.

"Help!" she screamed. "Someone help me!"

Josh flinched away from her shout, but she hung onto him, fumbling with the blanket. His right wrist slipped free, and a shower of blood sprayed across her pink uniform. Ignoring it, she half carried, half dragged Josh into the bathroom, threw the blanket aside and began wrapping his wrists with the small hand towels that hung next to the sink. Even as she worked, she heard the front door open and Mabel Hardwick's voice calling out.

"Brenda? What's wrong? Was that you yelling?"

"Call 911, Mabel," Brenda shouted. "It's Josh! He's cut himself."

A split second later Mabel had appeared in the doorway and elbowed Brenda aside. "From the blood, it looks like arteries," she said. "You call the ambulance. Let me take care of this." Before Brenda could protest, Mabel had pushed her out of the bathroom and shut the door. Alone with Josh, she unwrapped the towel from his right wrist, twisted it into a thick rope, then placed a bar of soap on the inner side of his right forearm. Looping the towel rope around the arm to cover the bar, she twisted it tight. As the makeshift tourniquet pressed down on the artery, the blood suddenly stopped flowing.

"Hold that," she commanded Josh, her tone leaving no room for argument. As he grasped the towel with his still-bleeding left hand, she grabbed the belt from a robe that was hanging inside the bathroom door and made a second tourniquet to stem the flow of blood from the boy's left wrist. "There," she said as she finished. "Now you just hold still a minute while I take a look at this."

Turning on the water, she rinsed the blood away from the wounds on Josh's right wrist, and felt a wave of relief. At least he'd cut across, and the bones of his forearm had prevented him from cutting too deeply. Just a nick, really. "Where's the adhesive tape?" she demanded, and Josh mutely nodded toward the medicine cabinet.

As she began taping up the wound on his right wrist, the door opened and Brenda, her face almost as pale as Josh's, wriggled into the cramped space. "They'll be here in five minutes. Is—Is it bad?"

Mabel Hardwick kept working as she talked. "Not so bad as it could be. Looks a lot worse than it is. When they get here, you go with him in the ambulance, and I'll stay with the baby and start cleaning up." Looking up for the first time, she saw the shock and panic that seemed about to overcome Brenda. "Don't you even think of falling apart, Brenda MacCallum. Lots worse than this has happened to me, and nobody ever saw me getting ready to faint. Now you go throw some water on your face, and get your purse!"

The sharp words cut through the fear that had gripped Brenda. They set her in motion, automatically doing precisely as Mabel Hardwick had commanded. By the time the ambulance arrived a few minutes later, Brenda was ready, her wits gathered around her once more. The medics insisted that Josh lie on a gurney, despite his objections. As Brenda followed them down the stairs to the waiting ambulance, she called back to Mabel.

"Call the café, will you, Mabel? Tell Max I won't be back today." Not waiting for a reply, she ducked into the ambulance and crouched by the stretcher as one of the medics slammed the door. As the ambulance screeched out of the parking lot, its siren wailing, she gazed down into Josh's pale face.

"What happened, honey? What on earth were you doing?"

Josh looked back at her for a moment, then his eyes shifted away. "I just wanted to get out of the way, that's all," he said, his voice barely audible.

For the first time since she'd seen Josh standing in his room, his wrists spurting blood, she realized that his cuts had not been some kind of terrible accident.

Her son, her wonderful, brilliant, ten-year-old son, had tried to kill himself.

The half hour Brenda spent in the small waiting area at the front of the emergency room of the county clinic seemed like an eternity. She'd called the café herself, and been relieved when Annette had answered the phone rather than Max. Annette had assured her that Mabel Hardwick had already called, and told her she wasn't to worry about anything. Max had even said she shouldn't come in tomorrow if she didn't want to. He was planning to send a pie down to Josh. He was working on it right now, and putting in twice as many pecans as usual. " 'Course he had to say something about having to 'bribe the little shit,' just so he can keep some decent help around the place, but that's just Max," Annette finished. "Now don't you worry about a thing. Soon's I get off, I'm coming over to your place and fix dinner. And no arguments, okay?" Then, even precluding Brenda's thank-you, she hung up.

Briefly, Brenda considered trying to contact Buck MacCallum, but quickly gave up the idea. She'd long ago decided that trying to collect child support from him was a fruitless endeavor. In truth, for the last couple of years she hadn't even been sure where he was living. Feeling desperate, she found herself dialing her parents, waiting apprehensively at the empty sound of ringing at the other end. They had moved away from Eden five years ago, when her father had decided it was time to go into business for himself and sold his house, over her mother's objections, to buy a bait shop on the Gulf coast in Texas. Finally, her mother answered. She listened to Brenda's fragmented story in silence, then said that she'd always known there was something wrong with Josh; this wasn't anything Brenda shouldn't have been expecting.

"Thanks, Mom," Brenda said coldly. "Sorry I bothered you." Hanging up the phone, she shook her head. She shouldn't have been surprised, really. One of the reasons she'd married Buck in the first place was simply to get away from her parents. It was, she reflected, as if the heat of the desert had baked the humanity right out of them.

And then, as she paced nervously around the waiting room, she began turning her own thought over in her mind. Was that why Josh had done it? Did he think she didn't care? She'd been so careful always to make sure Josh knew how much she loved him, how proud she was of him.

But what else could it have been?

Children his age didn't try to kill themselves, did they?

Of course not! They didn't even think about such things.

But Josh had.

She was startled from her thoughts by a woman's voice. A nurse was telling her she could see her son now.

He was sitting up in bed, his face still deathly white, and he looked even younger than his ten years. A doctor stood by the bed. As Brenda came into the room, he gave her an encouraging smile.

"This little guy may have made a terrible mess, but if he was really trying to hurt himself, he didn't do a very good job of it. Three stitches in each wrist, and the bandages are mostly for show. I could easily have made do with Band-Aids." He grinned down at Josh and tousled his hair. "Next time you want to come to the hospital, just walk in the door, okay?"

He started toward the door, pausing only to ask Brenda to drop by his office after she'd visited with Josh. Then he was gone, and Brenda was alone with her son. Suddenly she realized she didn't have the slightest idea what to say to him. She simply stood still, heart pounding, looking at him. At last his eyes met hers.

"A Are you really mad at me, Mom?" he asked, his frightened whisper bringing tears to her eyes. Immediately she knew what to do. She went to him, put her arms around him and held him close.

"Mad at you? How could I be mad at you? You're the best son anyone could ever have. I'm just sorry I was so hard on you today. It's just . . . Oh, honey, I guess it's just that sometimes I'm not a very good mother."

Josh sniffled, and his arms went around her neck, holding on as if he was afraid to let her go. "I'm sorry, Mommy," he said. "I just—I just thought maybe if I wasn't around anymore, it would be easier for you. I don't have any friends, and I don't do good enough in school, and it seems like all I ever do is let people down."

His words tore at Brenda's heart. Her eyes flooded with tears, and she held him even closer. "No, darling," she murmured. "It's not like that at all. I love you, and I'm proud of you, and I don't think I could stand it if anything ever happened to you. So we'll just have to make things right for you, okay?"

For a long time mother and son clung together. At last Brenda eased Josh back onto his pillows. "I'll be back," she promised. "I just have to go talk to the doctor for a minute, but then I'll be right back. All right?"

Josh nodded and managed a weak smile, then closed his eyes. Brenda lingered for a moment, watching him, feasting her eyes on his now peaceful face. But as she slipped out of the room, all her worries and fears closed in on her again.

How would she make good on her promise?

How could she make things right for Josh, when she could barely even feed and clothe him?

But there had to be a way. There had to be.

4

"I hope you didn't misunderstand me a few minutes ago," Richard Hasborough said. Josh MacCallum's medical records were spread out on the doctor's desk. "Please sit down, Mrs. MacCallum." With a nod, he indicated a chair on the other side of his desk, then turned to scan the folder before him. When he looked up, the blue eyes that had reassured Brenda in Josh's room had taken on a much more somber cast. "In cases like Josh's, I think it's important to make the whole experience as nonthreatening as possible. But I don't want you to think for a moment that I was making light of what happened."

Brenda lowered herself into the chair, finally allowing herself to release the tension that had been building in her from the minute she'd discovered Josh in his room. Until this moment, she realized, she had been dealing with the situation more on pure instinct than on any sort of rational thought. Now, as the sheer terror drained away, she found herself trembling. "I—I just can't believe it happened," she said, her voice a murmur, as if she was speaking more to herself than to the doctor. "I knew he was unhappy—I mean, he didn't even want to go to school this morning—but I thought it was just first-day jitters—you know, what with being in a new class and all." As Hasborough's brows knitted in puzzlement, Brenda rushed to explain how Josh had been skipped a grade for the second time, how difficult it was for him to be so much younger and smaller than his classmates, how cruel the bigger kids could sometimes be.

How much she worried about him.

Then, a terrible thought struck her. "Am I going to have to send him away, Dr. Hasborough?" she whispered. "I mean, to a hospital or something?"

The doctor frowned and held up a cautionary hand. "Now, let's not get ahead of ourselves, all right? For now, I think I'd like to keep him here overnight, just to keep an eye on him and try to get some idea of how he's feeling. It would help if I knew exactly what's been going on the last few days."

For the next fifteen minutes Brenda slowly pieced together the story of what had happened that day, nervously answering Hasborough's probing questions about Josh's behavior during the last few weeks of summer vacation, and concluding with a sigh, "All I can tell you is he didn't want to go back to school. But most kids his age don't, do they?" Her question held a plaintive note, as if she was pleading with the doctor to offer her at least a scrap of evidence that Josh wasn't crazy.

"Well, I sure never wanted to go back to school when I was ten," Hasborough agreed, his reassuring smile returning. "And from what you've told me, it doesn't sound as though Josh's stunt with the knife was premeditated. It sounds as though he was just really upset about everything, and mad at you, and he found a way of getting your attention."

Brenda took a deep breath, but her relief lasted only an instant. "But what does it mean?" she asked as a horrifying new thought assaulted her. "Will he . . . could he try it again?"

For a long time the doctor remained silent, as if reluctant to tell her the truth. "I don't know," he said finally. "But it seems to me we've got to find some answers for him." He'd deliberately used the word "we" when he spoke, and he was relieved to see her relax slightly, as if the fact of no longer feeling totally alone with her problems made them seem more manageable. He had already ascertained that Brenda MacCallum had no one to whom she could turn—not her parents, certainly not her ex-husband. And it seemed clear that Eden School could provide no real help. His suspicion on that score was confirmed when he asked Brenda what the school had advised.

"Score one for Mr. Hodgkins," Brenda remarked, rummaging in her purse for the pamphlet the school's principal had given her that afternoon. "This was his big idea." She placed the pamphlet on the desk. "Can you believe it? How am I supposed to send Josh to someplace like that?" She clasped her hands tightly together to control their shaking—whether with anger or fear, she did not know—and watched the doctor nervously as he studied the brochure.

Richard Hasborough made no reply, merely shaking his head, a gesture that Brenda instantly took for agreement with her own judgment of Hodgkins's suggestion. "Dumb, huh?"

Hasborough looked up. "Dumb? No, not at all."

Brenda felt her jaw slackening. "You mean you know about this place?"

"I sure do. It's attached to the university where my wife went to school. She used to work with some of their kids once in a while. Even taught a few art classes there."

"And how much does it cost?" Brenda asked. "Do you know?" Whatever sum he named was going to be totally out of the question.

"If Josh can get in, it probably won't cost a dime," Hasborough replied. "The Academy was never set up to make money in the first place. It operates in conjunction with the university, which studies the children while they're in school there."

Brenda's expression set into a mask of skepticism. "You mean it's like a lab, and they use the kids as guinea pigs?"

Now Hasborough looked surprised. "Nowhere near," he said quickly. "In fact, it's run as much like a family as possible. Though the children are being observed, they're not aware of it." As Brenda opened her mouth to ask another question, he held up his hand to restrain her. "Look, before we get any further into this, let me make a couple of calls. I still know a few people there. Let's just see what the situation is. They might be full, or they might not even be prepared to look at Josh. But it's worth a try."

Brenda found herself sitting perfectly still, even her lungs frozen in mid-breath. Images swirled in her mind: imagined pictures of her son, locked in a room in a mental hospital somewhere; or being bullied on the playground at Eden School. Whatever happened at this new place—a place she'd never even heard of until today—couldn't be worse than the alternatives.

Slowly, she released the breath she'd been unconsciously holding. "All right," she agreed. "I guess I'd better talk to them."

Hildie Kramer sat at her desk in what had originally been one of the smaller reception rooms of the mansion that housed Barrington Academy. A cup of coffee, stone cold now, sat near the telephone, and she raised it to her lips, making a face as the stale brew touched her lips. Replacing the cup, she gazed out the window for a moment, enjoying, as always, the view of the broad lawn, dotted with redwoods and eucalyptus, that fronted the house. Then remembering her tight schedule, she returned to the task of reviewing for the final time the paperwork on Joshua MacCallum, which had come flooding in by fax yesterday afternoon and this morning.

All his school records were there, from kindergarten on, along with the results of the various standardized tests to which he had been subjected over the years.

In Hildie's experience, "subjected" was precisely the word that applied to those tests. Since she'd become part of the team forming the Academy five years earlier, she'd discovered that the various tests meant to measure IQ and achievement gave only the most cursory evaluation of a child's true gifts. They took little account of a child's background—its sex, race, socioeconomic circumstances, home situation—all the variables that tended to skew results one way or another.

As for specialized talents beyond verbal, math, or science skills, they produced nothing, for there was no such thing as a standardized test to calibrate talent in music, or painting, or sculpture. Interest, yes. Aptitude, slightly.

The true gift of talent and genius, practically never.

Still, Josh MacCallum was obviously a highly gifted student, and, judging by the records in front of her—which went far beyond the original IQ score that had, indeed, prompted her to send one of their brochures to Eden Consolidated School—he was exhibiting all the problems concomitant with his intelligence combined with his situation in a tiny desert town in the middle of nowhere.

Without even meeting him, she was certain he was both inquisitive and bored silly.

And now, out of some form of still unidentified desperation, Josh MacCallum had tried to kill himself.

In short, he was precisely the sort of child that the Academy had been designed for. She glanced at the clock embedded in the walnut trim of her desk blotter. Another prospective student, a ten-year-old named Amy Carlson, was due to arrive with her parents shortly for a final interview. Deciding she had just enough time to reach Richard Hasborough, she dialed quickly, then waited, her fingers unconsciously drumming on the desk as her call was put through to the doctor.

"It's Hildie Kramer, Dr. Hasborough," she began, not bothering with a greeting. "I have a couple of questions about Joshua MacCallum. First, has he talked to a psychologist since the incident yesterday? And second, how long will he be required to stay in the hospital?"

While the doctor in Eden made his replies, and Hildie scribbled a few notes in the margins of Josh's records, the door to her office opened and Frank and Margaret Carlson appeared. Seeing her on the phone, they began to back away. Hildie beckoned them in, motioning toward the couch against the wall. A moment later all three Carlsons were lined up on the sofa, Amy between her parents. A thin red-haired child, Hildie noted, with thick, round glasses perched on a snub nose, who looked not only frightened, but angry. Hildie offered the little girl an encouraging smile, but the child's face remained frozen.

"He really can go home anytime?" she asked into the phone. Apparently, the boy's suicide attempt hadn't been terribly serious, or at least didn't appear so to the doctors in Eden. "Do you think his mother could bring him up here on Saturday? Both Dr. Enger-sol and I think he's a prime candidate for the Academy, but of course we never reach a final decision until after we've talked to the children and made our own evaluation." She listened for a moment, then spoke once more. "No, there's no real rush. We've got a couple of spaces still open for this year. As long as we know they're coming by Friday, we can make all the arrangements." Saying a brief good-bye, she hung up the phone, then gathered Josh's records together as she greeted the Carlsons.

Or, rather, Amy Carlson, since her words were directed only at the little girl, who had now drawn her knees up defensively and wrapped her arms around her legs. "Why do I get the idea you're not nearly as glad to see me as I am to see you?" Hildie asked, rising from her chair and circling the desk to drop to her knees and face Amy directly.

"Because I'm not glad to see you at all!" Amy said defiantly, her face screwing up in an expression that clearly reflected the fear that threatened to overwhelm her. Amy had been scared ever since she'd first awakened that morning. "I don't want to come here. I want to go home." She did her best to glare at the woman, but failed as tears welled in her eyes. She clamped them shut, unwilling to let Hildie Kramer see her cry.

"Well, I don't blame you," Hildie agreed. "If anybody had tried to send me away to school when I was ten, I just would have flat out refused to go. I'd have thrown a tantrum so bad my parents never would have suggested such a thing again."

The words startled Amy. Involuntarily, she opened her eyes again. "You would?" she asked, her expression guarded, as if she suspected a trap.

"Of course I would," Hildie went on, rising to her feet, and reminding herself once more that she really ought to take about twenty pounds off her too-ample body. "And I wasn't nearly as smart as you are. If you've changed your mind, how come you didn't figure out a way to make your parents let you stay home? If I could have done it, I can't believe you couldn't!"

"Well, I tried," Amy told her before thinking about her words. "I even locked myself in the closet, but Mom had a key."

"Not smart," Hildie observed. "If you're going to lock yourself in a closet, always make sure you have all the keys with you."

Amy's arms dropped away from her legs, and then her feet edged off the sofa and fell to the floor. The beginnings of a smile played around the corners of her mouth, and she ran her fingers through her shock of red curls. "I already thought of that," she admitted. "But Daddy said he'd have taken the door off the hinges."

"Oh, did he? Well, come and take a look at this." Hildie moved to the closed door of the closet in the opposite wall. After only a moment's hesitation, Amy got up and followed her. "Is this pretty much like the closet in your room?"

Amy studied the paneled door and its richly carved walnut frame, and then nodded. "It's not as nice as this, but it's sort of the same."

"Then look at the hinges, and tell me what happens if you pry the pins out."

Frowning, Amy moved closer and studied the hinges for a second, then examined the crack on the other side of the door. "You can't get it off," she finally announced. "Even if you take the pins out, the door won't come off unless it's open."

"Very good," Hildie told her. "Which is why we don't have any locks on the closet doors around here. Can't have kids like you locking themselves inside and making us rip out the door frames, can we? Now, what do you say we go take a look at your room?"

Taking Amy's hand in her own, Hildie led the little girl out of the office, beckoning the Carlsons to follow. Ignoring the old-fashioned elevator whose ornate brass cage fascinated all the boys of the Academy, she crossed the broad hall to the foot of the stairs that swept up to the second floor in a graceful, oddly romantic, curve. Just by the look on the little girl's face, Hildie knew she was correct in her guess that Amy would find the stairs far more appealing than the rattling old elevator. With Amy's parents behind them, Hildie ushered their daughter up the stairs, then up a second flight to the third floor, where there were ten rooms, five on each side of a narrow hallway that ran the length of the house. Halfway down the hall, Hildie opened a door and stepped aside to let Amy enter first.

Amy paused at the threshold and peered suspiciously inside, as if sensing that by going into the room, she would be agreeing to accept it.

Inside, directly opposite the door, Amy peered at a dormer window with a cushion-covered seat in it and brightly flowered curtains pulled back to let the sunlight flood into the room. The room was papered in a rosebud pattern that matched the curtains. Against one wall stood a daybed, heaped with pillows. Opposite it was a chest of drawers, a small desk, and a set of bookshelves. In one corner, its door standing ajar, was a closet.

Without thinking, Amy headed to the closet and examined its latch. "It really doesn't have a lock," she said, almost to herself.

"Would I lie to you?" Hildie asked.

"But what if I have something I want to lock up?" Amy asked, then realized the implication of her own question. "I mean, if I decide to stay," she added.

"Why don't we figure that out when, and if, it happens?" Hildie paused, then asked gently, "So, what do you think, Amy? Will this be all right?"

"It—It's pretty," Amy admitted. "But—" She turned to her mother, her eyes flooding once more with tears. "Do I really have to stay here, Mom?" she pleaded, running to fling her arms around her mother's waist. "Why can't I go home?"

Margaret Carlson patted her daughter gently, while her worried gaze met Hildie Kramer's encouraging smile. "But, honey, just yesterday you were excited about coming here. Don't you remember?"

Amy did remember. When they'd visited the week before, the big old house had seemed really neat and Mrs. Kramer had appeared to be nice. Now, however, the thought of being left all alone here made her tremble. "I changed my mind," Amy wailed. "I want to stay with you and Daddy, and Kitty-Cat!"

"Kitty-Cat?" Hildie Kramer asked. "You didn't tell me you had a cat."

"He's all black, with white feet, and he sleeps with me," Amy sniffled.

"Well, for heaven's sake, we have a cat here. His name's Tabby,
and he was wandering around all day yesterday, looking for a place
to sleep. But nobody seemed to want him. Maybe he could sleep
with you."

"But—" Even as Amy started to protest, a yellowish cat appeared at the door, almost as if by some prearranged signal. It
looked around for a second, then went directly to Amy, rubbing up
against her leg and mewing plaintively. Amy hesitated, then squatted down and put her hands on the cat's head. "Is what she said
true?" she asked the cat. "Don't you have anyplace to sleep?"

As Amy gathered the cat into her arms and sat down on the bed
to begin making friends with it, Hildie nodded to Frank Carlson.

Amy's father, understanding the unspoken signal, went downstairs to bring his daughter's luggage up.

━━━

Josh was propped up in bed, a new copy of *Les Miserables* that
Dr. Hasborough had brought him that morning open in his lap, a
piece of Max's pecan pie sitting half eaten on the bedside table.
Outside, a vulture was circling, descending lower and lower, and
Josh was waiting for it to land, and wondering what it might have
found.

A coyote?

Probably just a rabbit.

Maybe he should get dressed and go see.

After all, hadn't Dr. Hasborough agreed that he could go home
that afternoon? It wasn't like he was sick or anything. In fact, his
wrists didn't even hurt anymore. So why did he have to wait until
his mother was done with work and could come and talk to the
doctor? Why didn't they just let him go? He wasn't more than a
mile from where he lived—what was the big deal if he walked
home?

He glanced at the clock, frowning. Where *was* his mother? It
was almost five, and she was supposed to be here at four-thirty.

What had gone wrong?

Had they decided not to let him go home after all?

Putting the book aside, he got out of bed and went to the door, peering out into the hallway. Except for the nurse sitting behind the desk, there was nobody in sight.

Maybe he should just get dressed and walk out.

Or, even better, climb out the window?

Except if his mother showed up, she'd be worried about him, and maybe be afraid he'd tried to kill himself again.

He moved back to the bed and decided to wait a little while longer. He pulled the sheet up, then picked up the book again, but instead of starting to read, found himself thinking about yesterday.

Had he really tried to kill himself? He thought about it, remembering what he'd told the psychologist who'd come to see him that morning. "I guess I must have," he'd said. "I mean, I cut my wrists, didn't I?"

But now, as he thought about it some more, he began to wonder. Maybe he'd just been mad at his mother—and everyone else, too—and was just trying to get even with them.

And what if he'd bled to death?

He tried to imagine himself dead. He pictured himself in a coffin, lying in front of the altar at church while his funeral was going on. Except, he quickly realized, he wasn't imagining himself dead at all. He was imagining himself alive, and watching his own funeral.

Images flicked through his mind: his mother, dressed in black, sobbing with grief. All the kids from school looking really sad, sorry now, when it was too late, that they'd picked on him.

Except that if he'd actually died, he wouldn't have been there to see them, and what good would it have been to make them sorry if he wasn't even around for them to apologize to?

He started over again, shutting his eyes and trying to block out all the sounds around him. That was it—if he were dead, everything would be black, and there wouldn't be any noise.

Except the harder he tried not to hear things, the louder everything seemed to get. All of a sudden the soft ticking of the clock by the bed appeared to be banging in his ear, and the sound of cars going by on the street was a steady roar.

Dead.

What would it really be like? Not that he really wanted to know, he decided, at least not yet. He could still remember how scared he'd been yesterday, when he'd started bleeding. He'd stood up right away, intending to run out to the living room, but then realized how much blood there was, and how mad his mother would be when she saw the mess he'd made. So he'd just stood there like a dummy, not doing anything.

What if he'd actually bled to death?

He shuddered at the thought, and decided that whatever he'd been thinking yesterday, it had been pretty dumb. All he'd done was make a mess and cause more trouble.

But at least his mother had forgiven him. That, he decided, was one of the neatest things about his mother. No matter what he did, or how mad she got at him, in the end she always forgave him. From now on, he decided, he'd try to do better.

He glanced up at the clock again and was about to start dressing when the door opened and his mother came in, smiling at him.

"Hey, you," she said. "You look pretty good. Feel like going home?"

Josh's eyes widened hopefully. "It's okay? They're really going to let me go home?"

Brenda nodded. "And I've got a surprise for you, too."

"A surprise?" the boy demanded. "What?"

"Well, I'm not sure I should tell you right now," Brenda teased. "Maybe I ought to wait till we get home, or maybe tomorrow morning."

"No!" Josh protested. "Now. Please?" He'd scrambled out of bed and was already half dressed.

"Well, all right," Brenda said, acting as if she'd just made up her mind to tell him. "How would you like not to have to go back to Eden School?"

In the middle of pulling up his jeans, Josh froze, staring at his mother as if he couldn't believe what he was hearing. "Not go back?" he echoed. "What do you mean?"

"What if you could go to another school, one that was set up especially for kids like you?"

Josh's mind raced. What was she talking about? And then he thought he knew.

She was talking about a school for crazy kids.

Kids who had tried to kill themselves.

But he wasn't crazy—he'd already told her that, last night, and then again this morning. He'd just been feeling bad, that's all.

"Wh-What school?" he breathed, suddenly terrified.

"The one Mr. Hodgkins told us about yesterday. Barrington Academy, up north."

"B-But you told him it was too expensive—" Josh began.

Brenda didn't let him finish. "Well, it seems that maybe it might not be," she told him. "Dr. Hasborough knows them, and called them up. We sent them all your records, and they want to talk to you."

Josh's uncertainty deepened. "You mean they want to take me, without even meeting me? How come? Is it a place for crazy kids?"

Brenda's jaw dropped. "Of course not!" she cried. "It's not that at all! It's a place for gifted kids, kids like you!"

But Josh was shaking his head. "You're sending me away because of what I did, aren't you? Before I cut myself, you said there was no way I was going there. But now—" His eyes dampened, and he ran to his mother and threw his arms around her. "I'm sorry," he said. "I didn't really want to die. I was just mad. Don't send me away. Please?"

Brenda was silent, holding her son while she tried to sort it all out. Clearly, he didn't understand that she wasn't trying to punish him, that she just wanted the best for him. "Honey, it's all right," she whispered. "I'd never send you away, don't you know that? This doesn't have anything to do with that stupid knife. All it's about is getting you into a school where you can be happy, and have friends who understand you."

Josh's sobs stilled, and he recalled his vow of only a few minutes ago to try not to cause his mother any more trouble. Finally, when he trusted his voice not to crack, he pulled away from her. "Wh-What if I don't want to go?" he asked.

"Then you won't have to," Brenda replied. "Besides, they haven't said they want you yet. They just want us to come up on Saturday, so they can talk to you and give you some tests. Now that won't be so bad, will it?''

Josh considered it. Maybe it really *wasn't* a place for crazy kids. After all, Mr. Hodgkins had started talking about it before he'd held the knife in his hand. . . . And his mother had said he didn't have to go if he didn't want to.

He made up his mind.

"I guess we could go see it," he said. "I mean, just to take a look, okay?"

"Okay," Brenda breathed. "Double okay! Now finish dressing so we can get out of here."

As they emerged from the hospital a few minutes later, Brenda breathed deeply of the desert air. Things, finally, were working out.

Unless the Academy decided not to take Josh.

But she couldn't worry about that until it happened; she'd learned long ago not to try to cross any bridges until she came to them. Besides, she'd already made up her mind: One way or another, the Academy would take her son.

His mind was far too good to waste in the Eden school.

He'd get into the Academy—she just knew it!

He'd get in, and he'd be the most brilliant student they'd ever had.

And then she stopped herself before she tried to run across a bridge that had barely come into view yet.

Saturday, she decided as they started home.

Saturday would tell the tale.

5

It wasn't until she'd turned off Highway 101 and started up into
the hills between San Jose and the coast that Brenda finally relaxed and began to believe that the old Chevy was going to survive
the four-hundred-mile trip from Eden. They'd left at four o'clock
that morning, with Josh complaining that it was too early to get up,
but Brenda insisting that if the car were to get them to the Academy
at all, they'd better get out of the desert before the heat of the day
set in. So they'd set out in darkness, crossing the desert and into
the San Joaquin Valley, then heading west just to the north of Ba-
kersfield, picking up the freeway at Paso Robles.

Beside her, Josh stirred, awakening from the light sleep he'd
fallen into an hour before. Rubbing his eyes, he blinked, then spotted one of the big green signs that hung above the road to Santa
Cruz: Barrington—25 miles.

"We're almost there," he said, gazing around at the unfamiliar
landscape. Grassy hills were dotted with clumps of eucalyptus trees
and an occasional stand of coast redwoods. "It sure doesn't look
like Eden, does it?"

"It sure doesn't," Brenda agreed, smiling wryly. Indeed, before
Josh had awakened, she'd been gazing with fascination at the area
outside of San Jose. The last time she'd been here, when she was a

51

little girl, most of it had still been farmland, and San Jose had been a fairly small town. Now, it had spread out, serving as the center for the booming computer industry, the farms replaced by an endless parade of housing developments and industrial parks. Finally, they'd left all that behind, climbing into the hills where, except for a few large houses that appeared to have sprung from nowhere, the landscape was still largely undisturbed.

Half an hour later they came to the outskirts of Barrington. It was a small town, but still larger than Eden. Situated on the coast and nestled comfortably between the beach and the hills rising behind it, it had none of the look of self-conscious newness that clung to all the burgeoning towns around San Jose. There was a neat town center, with stores whose facades varied between mission architecture and the old arts-and-crafts shingle-covered style of the twenties and thirties. The downtown area was surrounded by a residential district of neatly laid out streets filled with small, shingled houses, and trees that had reached full maturity decades earlier. Even now, in September, fuchsias were blooming everywhere, and flowering vines crept up the walls of many of the homes.

Following a series of discreet signs, Brenda finally came to the university. The campus instantly struck her as looking exactly the way a college should look. The buildings were old brick structures, arranged around a broad green lawn dotted with towering redwoods and clumps of flowering bushes she'd never seen before. Behind the older buildings, creeping up the hills, were a series of newer structures, which almost disappeared into the surrounding landscape, adding modern space to the campus while not detracting from its charm.

"But where's the Academy?" Brenda wondered out loud. "It's supposed to be part of the campus."

"There," Josh said, pointing to another of the small signs that had guided them this far. "Turn right and go up the hill."

Though she hadn't seen the sign herself, Brenda followed Josh's directions. A few minutes later they came to a wide wrought-iron double gate that stood open at the foot of a long driveway. Awed by what she saw, Brenda brought the car to a halt.

At the head of the redwood-lined driveway, nearly a quarter of a mile away, stood the largest house Brenda could remember ever having seen. Three stories high, it had two wings that stretched away from the center of the house, which itself was surmounted by yet a fourth floor—apparently a private apartment of some kind, with large windows that would give it a panoramic view in every direction. Though the enormous house was now flanked by two other buildings, one at each end of it, Brenda understood instantly that it had originally been built as a private residence. "My Lord," she breathed. "Can you imagine living in a place like that?"

"It was Mr. Barrington's house," Josh told her. "You know—he built Barrington Western Railroad."

Brenda gazed blankly at her son. "No," she replied, "I didn't know. But obviously you do."

Josh grinned, his face taking on an impish look. "I went to the library yesterday and looked it up. The man who built that was named Eustace Barrington, and he used to own practically all the land from here to San Francisco. This was his summer house, and the town started because it took so many people to run the ranch."

"Ranch?" Brenda echoed blankly. "I thought you said he started a railroad."

"He *did*," Josh insisted, his tone indicating that he thought his mother was being deliberately dense. "But he made a deal with the government, and got most of the land next to the railroad tracks. That's when he started the ranch, and just kept buying more and more land. And he got most of it practically free, too, because the only way to get to it was the railroad, and he wouldn't let the trains stop at anyone else's land."

"And now they think he was some kind of hero, right?" Brenda replied, shaking her head in wonder at the sheer gall of Barrington's scheme. To her, it sounded like nothing short of blackmail. She put the car back in gear and started up the long drive toward the house. As they passed between the twin rows of redwoods, they could glimpse children here and there, some of them in groups of two or three, but several of them by themselves, sprawled out on the lawn, reading or working over sketch pads. And yet, though the scene looked perfectly peaceful—idyllic, even—Brenda felt an uncanny chill of foreboding creep down her spine.

It was *too* peaceful. *Too* quiet.

There was something wrong, something she couldn't quite put her finger on.

But that's ridiculous, she told herself. *There's nothing wrong! You just have cold feet about Josh leaving home!*

Of course, she decided. That was it. There wasn't anything wrong with the scene. It was just different from Eden, that was all.

In Eden, if a group of kids this size—and there must have been nearly twenty of them—had been thrown together, raucous games would already have sprung up, and they would be milling around, shouting and arguing with each other.

The children of the Academy, however, were subdued, absorbed in quiet activities. Even the groups of two or three were quiet, the kids talking softly among themselves.

Firmly, she put aside her first reaction of instinctive apprehension and drew the car up to the immense Mediterranean-style villa. Two boys, no more than twelve years old, were hunched over a chessboard that was set up between them on the tiled loggia that ran the full length of the front of the mansion and curved around it at either side. The boys glanced up at her, then their gaze shifted to Josh, who was just coming around the front of the car.

"You the new guy?" one of them asked.

Before Josh could reply, the front door opened and a somewhat overweight woman of about forty-five appeared. She was dressed in a pair of loose-fitting white cotton slacks and a brightly colored tunic that made her look somewhat thinner than she really was. Her feet were clad in sandals, and around her neck was draped an elegantly patterned silk scarf. Suddenly Brenda felt embarrassed by her own lime-green polyester pants and jacket. Back in Eden, the outfit had seemed like the right thing to wear today. Now it felt like exactly the wrong thing.

But the woman on the porch didn't seem to notice her clothes at all. She had started down the steps, her hand outstretched. "Mrs. MacCallum? I'm Hildie Kramer. I was beginning to get a little worried about you."

"I—We weren't really sure how long it would take," Brenda stammered. "We're not too late, are we?"

Hildie laughed, a warm, bubbling sound that welled up from deep within her and immediately made Brenda feel better. "Oh my, no. Any time would have been fine." She turned to Josh and offered him her hand just as she had to his mother. "And you're Josh, right? Or is it Joshua?"

"Josh," the boy replied, uncertainly taking the woman's hand.

"Good," Hildie declared. "I like that name. It's nice and strong-sounding. Have you met Jeff Aldrich and Brad Hinshaw?" she asked, turning to the two boys who were once again hunched over the chessboard. Hearing their names, they glanced up, then scrambled to their feet. Hildie introduced them to Josh. "Do you know how to play chess?" she added.

Josh hesitated, then shook his head.

"Then they'll teach you, while I have a talk with your mother. Okay?"

Josh paled slightly, his eyes darting to the two other boys. They looked like they were a couple of years older than he was. He was sure they'd groan and start rolling their eyes, like the boys in Eden had last summer when his mother had made him go to the summer sports program at the school, and the coach had put him on the softball team. He'd played one inning, then gone home, the taunts of the other guys still ringing in his ears after he'd been unable to catch a single ball in right field, and had struck out on three pitches when he'd come up to bat.

Now, to Josh's surprise, the boy named Jeff motioned him to come over to the board. As Josh hunkered down between the two of them, Brad said, "That's the king," and pointed to the largest of the pieces. "I'm playing white, and Jeff's playing black, and all you have to do is capture the other guy's king." He pointed quickly to the various other pieces, naming each of them. "Just watch for a while, and you'll see how it works."

"And make them tell you *all* the possible moves," Hildie warned. "They like to hold a few things back, then spring them on you. Like castling. Make sure they tell you how to do it."

"Aw, come on, Hildie," Jeff Aldrich complained. "It's more fun if we cheat."

"Sure it is," Hildie agreed. "And if what I know about Josh is right, cheating's going to be about the only way you'll beat him, once he catches on."

Jeff grinned slyly up at her. "Wanta bet?"

Hildie's brows rose. "Sure," she agreed. "I've got a dollar that says Josh beats you first time out. But you have to promise to show him all the moves, and not get creative when you play. Deal?"

"Deal," Jeff agreed.

"I'll make sure he doesn't cheat," Brad Hinshaw said. Instantly, he shifted from playing against Jeff to demonstrating to Josh how all the moves worked and why he was making them. Though he talked so quickly that Brenda was immediately confused, Josh seemed to be following every word he said. After watching for only a few seconds, Brenda let herself be guided into the house.

Thirty minutes later, after she'd had a full tour of the house—save for the cupola on the fourth floor, which Hildie had explained was Dr. Engersol's private apartment—Brenda sank down into the depths of the leather-covered sofa in Hildie Kramer's office, grateful for a moment in which to collect her thoughts in such a comfortable setting. Hildie's big desk was cluttered with papers and framed photos, and a well-used ceramic mug sat next to a plate on which a doughnut—clearly part of Hildie's morning snack—remained. Brenda felt overwhelmed by everything she'd seen. Nothing about the place was anything like what she'd been expecting. From what she'd seen so far, the Academy didn't resemble a school at all. Instead it appeared to be just what it looked like from the outside: a huge home where people lived.

She'd seen the immense dining room. Like most of the house, it appeared very much as it had been when old Eustace Barrington had died back in 1942, at the age of 103. The walls were still covered with red silk, and the original sideboards, filled with china, stood against them as they had for more than a century. An immense crystal chandelier hung in the center of the room, its pendants brightly polished. The only change, Hildie explained, was that the original dining table at which Eustace Barrington had often entertained fifty people at formal dinners, was gone, replaced by much smaller tables for four or six.

In each of the more than twenty rooms Brenda had been shown, mahogany paneling gleamed on the wainscoting, and ornate plaster moldings adorned the ceilings.

A music room at the back of the ground floor overlooked a broad terrace and the hills rising up behind the school. "According to Mr. Barrington's will," Hildie had explained as they'd entered, "the house was to be preserved in its original condition, right down to the furniture. He left a huge endowment, and directed that the place be kept as a museum. But he did realize that a time might come when even the endowment wouldn't be enough to maintain the mansion, and he put in a clause to the effect that in the event the endowment wasn't sufficient for upkeep, the university could put the house to use, provided that—and I quote—'it be maintained as a residence in as close as is practically possible to its original condition, which was as a home for the children to use and enjoy.' "

She'd gone on to note that the word "children" had proved to be the key. The lawyers were able to argue that since he hadn't specified *his* children, the clause could be interpreted to mean that *any* children could enjoy the house, and that as long as the building was used for the benefit of children, the will would be satisfied. "Actually, it was Dr. Engersol who first came up with the idea," Hildie told her now.

"Dr. Engersol?" Brenda asked.

"The director of the school," Hildie explained. "The Academy was his idea. He's always been interested in gifted children, and when it became obvious that the house was turning into a massive white elephant, he went to work." She smiled as she recounted the manner in which George Engersol had gone about building his school. "I assume you're familiar with the term 'nerd'?"

Brenda nodded. "Some of the kids call Josh that all the time."

"I'll bet they do," Hildie agreed. "Anyway, this whole area is filled with people who were nerds when they were kids. Except they're not nerds anymore. Now they're computer millionaires, and they have more money than they know what to do with. Dr. Engersol went to every one of them and explained what he wanted to do.

It was very simple, really. He just told them he wanted to set up a school for kids who were like they'd once been—a school totally geared to meet those needs. Not just academic needs, but social and psychological needs as well. Needless to say, the response was incredible. Within a year the Academy was totally funded. The money still pours in."

Brenda spotted an opportunity to voice the worry that had been growing within her from the moment she'd heard about the school. "But it has to be expensive," she ventured.

Hildie nodded. "It costs a fortune to run," she agreed. "But Dr. Engersol covered that, too. Since brilliance isn't a function of wealth, he insisted that no financial demands be put on any of our kids' families. So we operate on a sliding scale. The higher a family's income, the higher our fees. But they never exceed what the family can comfortably afford."

Brenda swallowed nervously, and hoped her voice didn't betray the extreme embarrassment she was feeling. "I—I don't know if I can afford anything at all," she began.

Hildie stopped her with a gesture. "We already know that," she said gently. "You must understand that money isn't a problem here. We were set up with the purpose of dealing with children like Josh, no matter what they can afford to pay. Dr. Engersol's interest is in providing them with an environment in which they can flourish. We're not here to take your money, Brenda. We're here to help kids like Josh, who have brilliant minds and all the problems that usually go along with that brilliance."

"Lord knows, he's got problems." Brenda sighed. "Sometimes it seems like he's got nothing but problems."

"A lot of the kids are like that here," Hildie said ruefully. "At least they are when they come. And a lot of those problems run far deeper than their families know. Or at least," she added carefully, "they don't know about them until their kids try to kill themselves."

The words struck Brenda sharply. "You know about what Josh did?" she asked.

"Of course." Hildie looked deep into Brenda's eyes as she spoke, her voice warm. "That's one of the reasons we wanted to meet him as quickly as possible." She moved out from behind her desk and joined Brenda on the sofa. "I know what Josh did must have struck you as bizarre," she went on. "But with children like him, suicide is much more common than it is among children whose intelligence falls within the normal range. When you think about it, it makes sense. They're bored in school, they have little in common with their peers, and when they start getting into trouble—which they often do, simply as a way of entertaining themselves—they begin to feel like failures. The whole thing can turn into a downward spiral in which the child feels more and more isolated, more and more out of touch with everything around him, and finally death seems like the only way out of what, to them, is a miserable life. Children, no matter how gifted, can't see far into the future, you know. To them, a year is almost a lifetime, and telling them that things will be fine when they grow up does no good at all. So here we try to put them in an environment where they are with their intellectual and emotional peers, rather than simply their chronological peers. I'm sorry to have to say it, but what they told you in Eden was true—there's nothing they can do for Josh there, nothing they have to offer him. If he stays there, his isolation will only get worse."

Brenda took a deep breath, knowing that Hildie Kramer's words had the ring of truth. "Are you saying you'll take him, then?" she asked, uncomfortably aware that her hands had begun sweating.

"I'm almost certain we will," Hildie replied. "This afternoon, after lunch, Dr. Engersol will give Josh some tests and have a talk with him. From his records, I doubt very much that there will be any reason for us to turn him down. But there's another question, of course," she added.

Brenda's brow furrowed with uncertainty. "Another question?" she repeated.

Hildie smiled thinly. "The question of Josh himself. Does he want to come here?"

Brenda felt the hope that had been building inside her begin to crumble. Should she lie to this woman? But there was something about Hildie Kramer that she found reassuring. Even though she hadn't met Hildie until less than an hour ago, she felt she could trust her. "I—I'm not sure," Brenda said. "When I first suggested it to him, he thought—well, he thought it was a place for crazy kids, and that I was trying to punish him for—for what he'd done."

Hildie nodded thoughtfully. "That's only to be expected. But you said that's what he thought at first. Has he changed his mind?"

Brenda thought about it, remembering Josh's quietness over the last few days, when he'd stayed at home with his sister and Mabel Hardwick while she'd gone to work. As she thought about it, she realized that he'd seemed to be on good behavior since she'd brought him home from the hospital.

As if he was hoping that if he were good enough, she wouldn't send him to the Academy?

But he'd gone to the library, and apparently read everything he could about not only the Academy, but the man for whom it was named, as well. "I don't know," she finally admitted. "He's been awfully quiet, and I haven't sent him back to school yet. He really hasn't said much one way or another. Except he's always hated school. I don't have any idea what he might say if we asked him."

Hildie smiled almost conspiratorially. "In that case, let's not ask him. Let's just let him get a feel of the place, and get to know some of the kids. If he's like most of them, he'll have slid right into things before he even stops to think about whether he wants to or not."

Brenda cocked her head, regarding the older woman. "Is that why you left him outside, instead of bringing him in to show him around?"

"Of course," Hildie said. "The sooner he starts making friends, the more he's going to want to be here." She glanced out the window, sizing up the chess game that was still in progress only a few yards away. "From what I can see, it looks like we're stuck here for about another thirty minutes. Would you like a cup of coffee?"

Brenda eyed the single doughnut that remained on the plate on Hildie's desk. "Would you mind if I ate that?" she asked timidly. "I'm afraid I didn't take time for us to stop for breakfast." She didn't add that she also hadn't wanted to spend the money breakfast would have cost. While Hildie passed her the plate with the doughnut, then picked up a phone and asked someone for a pot of coffee and two cups, Brenda looked out the window, trying to follow the chess game in which her son appeared to be totally engrossed. As she watched, Jeff Aldrich moved a piece, capturing one of Josh's.

"I guess he's not doing too good," she observed, hearing her own defensiveness. "But it's only his first game. I don't think he ever even saw a chess set before, except on television."

Hildie stole another peek out the window, then smiled. "Looks to me like he's doing just fine. Right now, I'd say the odds are about two-to-one that Jeff's going to have to pay me off." She chuckled mischievously. "And, oh, how that boy hates it when he loses bets with me!"

Brenda took a bite of the doughnut, then smiled at Hildie. "You really love these kids, don't you?" she asked.

"Every one of them," Hildie replied. "There's nothing as satisfying as watching these children grow up and become everything it's possible for them to become."

They'll take him, Brenda said silently to herself, forming the words more as a prayer than anything else. *They've just got to take him. He belongs here.*

═══

As Brenda MacCallum and Hildie Kramer stepped out onto the loggia half an hour later, Josh glanced up for a split second, then quickly returned his attention to the board. In his mind, he reviewed once more all the various moves the pieces he still controlled could make, then shifted his point of view to the other side, calculating all the possible countermoves Jeff could make to whatever he might do.

Unless there was something he hadn't noticed, he could move his castle four spaces ahead, and no matter what Jeff did, he would be able to capture Jeff's king on his next move.

And then what would happen?

Jeff was the same age as the boys in Josh's class at Eden School, and he remembered the looks in their eyes on Monday, when he'd been able to answer the questions they had not.

Angry looks, looks that had hurt him almost as much as if they'd hit him.

Would Jeff look at him the same way?

Or had Jeff deliberately lost, making mistakes on purpose?

In his mind he reviewed the whole game, move by move. The image of the board was clear, and as he mentally replayed the long match, he very carefully studied everything Jeff had done.

None of his moves had been stupid, and none of his mistakes— if there had been any—had been obvious.

And the situation now was obvious, too.

So if he didn't make the move with the castle, Jeff would know that he himself was throwing the game.

Still he hesitated.

And then, next to him, he heard Brad's voice. "Come on, Josh, do it. He knows you're going to. Why don't you just finish him off?"

Josh glanced up to see both boys watching him. Brad looked eager to see the last move, but Jeff looked . . .

What?

Not mad. In fact, he looked as if he knew what was coming, and was just waiting for it to happen.

Tentatively Josh reached out and shifted the castle.

"Checkmate!" Brad crowed. "He got you! On his very first game, he got you!"

Josh didn't move, waiting.

A smile—slightly twisted, but nevertheless a smile—appeared on Jeff's lips. If he was angry, his eyes didn't show it. Indeed, they barely showed anything. "Pretty good," Jeff admitted. "Maybe we ought to enter you in the tournament this year."

"And maybe you ought to pay me my dollar," Hildie Kramer, appearing at the door, reminded him.

Jeff shrugged. "All my money's up in my room. How 'bout if I pay you later on?"

"How 'bout if you get my dollar before I forget about it?" Hildie countered.

"Aw, come on, Hildie, gimme a break—"

"A bet's a bet. If you can't stand to lose, don't play the game. Now go on."

"Aw, Jeez," Jeff groaned, but got to his feet and signaled to Josh to come with him. "Come on, you might as well see how terrible the rooms are here. Maybe you can talk your mom out of putting you in this jail." He ducked out of the way as Hildie took a playful swipe at him, and a moment later darted into the house, with Josh following.

As they entered the huge foyer, Josh stopped, gazing around him in wonder. At the foot of the stairs, Jeff grinned at him.

"Cool, huh?" he said.

Josh nodded, his eyes fixed on the brass cage of the elevator. "Does that work?" he breathed.

Jeff's grin broadened. "Sure. Wanta ride it?"

Josh nodded mutely, already moving toward the ancient contraption. He pulled the door open, watching as the polished brass slats of the barrier folded in on themselves. Stepping inside, he waited for Jeff, then closed the door with a resounding clang. He pressed a worn black button with a faintly visible arrow pointed upward still etched into its surface, and the machine came to life. From somewhere below, gears meshed, and the car jerked into motion, rattling satisfyingly as it rose slowly to the second floor, guided only by its skeletal frame.

"*Really* cool," Josh breathed as he followed Jeff out onto the second floor landing.

"Wait'll you see my room," Jeff replied. "It's the coolest one in school."

Josh frowned, remembering Jeff's words of only a few moments ago. "But you said it was like a jail—"

"I was just giving Hildie a hard time. Come on."

He led Josh to a room at the end of the hall. Opening the door, he stepped aside to let Josh go in first. "Ta-da!" he sang, flinging out an arm as if he were a magician who'd just amazed his audience. "The most excellent room in school, awarded to me because I'm a truly awesome person!"

Josh gazed around the large room. It was at least four times the size of the one he shared with his baby sister at home, and had windows on two sides. There was a desk covered with a scattering of books and papers, and an unmade bed with a jumble of dirty clothes at its end. But what grabbed Josh's attention was an enormous aquarium that sat against the wall next to one of the windows. It wasn't like anything he'd ever seen before, and it was filled with fish he instantly recognized from pictures he'd seen in the Eden library's collection of *National Geographic*s.

"Jeez," he whispered. "That's saltwater, isn't it?"

"Uh-huh," Jeff grunted. As Josh went over to look more closely at the aquarium, Jeff began rooting around in his desk in search of the money he kept hidden there.

"How do you keep it so clean?" Josh asked. "In school, we couldn't even keep a little freshwater one balanced."

"It's computerized," Jeff told him. "See?" He began showing Josh all the sensors in the tank, sensors that were attached to the computer that sat on his desk. "The computer's always monitoring it, keeping the water aerated and checking all the filters. It even keeps track of the salinity, and tells me what I need to add."

"Wow," Josh breathed. "How long have you had it?"

Jeff shrugged. "A while. Since last year. But I'm getting kind of tired of it. I mean, fish don't *do* anything, you know?"

"But it's neat," Josh protested. "If I had something like this—"

But Jeff wasn't listening to him. "If you want to see something neat," he interrupted, "you should see what my brother's got."

"Your brother?" Josh asked. "Where is he?"

"Next door," Jeff replied. "Come on."

He led Josh to the room adjoining his own. Without bothering to knock, he pushed the door open and walked in. In contrast to the chaos in his own room, this room was neat and tidy, the bed made, all the clothes put away in the closet and dresser. The desktop was bare save for a computer, and all the books were neatly arranged on the shelves.

A boy sat at the computer terminal, his fingers flying over the keyboard, his eyes glued to the monitor. If he was aware he was no longer alone in the room, he gave no sign. Jeff nudged Josh, held his finger to his lips, then crept up behind the other boy. Abruptly, he grabbed his brother's chair and spun him around. "My brother, the computer nerd," he announced.

Josh's eyes widened.

Sitting in the chair was a carbon copy of Jeff. He glanced from one face to the other, searching for differences.

There seemed to be none.

Each of the boys had the same black, curly hair, the same dark brown eyes, the same square jaw.

"This is Adam," Jeff announced. "He's my kid brother by ten whole minutes."

Adam's face flushed and he tried to push Jeff away, but Jeff held onto the chair and began pushing it toward Josh. "This is Josh MacCallum," he told his twin. "He wants to see your virtual reality setup."

"Can't you knock?" Adam complained. "You're not supposed to come into people's rooms when their doors are closed. And I'm right in the middle of something."

"You're always in the middle of something," Jeff told him. "And don't be a creep—lighten up and have some fun. Get the helmet and glove, and show Josh how it works."

For a moment Josh thought Adam was going to argue with Jeff. He watched in silence as the twin brothers stared at each other. In a few seconds, almost as if Jeff held some sort of power over him, the defiance drained out of Adam's eyes. Though neither of the boys had spoken, Josh had the eerie feeling that they had nonetheless had some kind of argument, and that Jeff had clearly won it. Silently, Adam left his chair and went to the dresser.

Jeff grinned mischievously at Josh. "He's a nerd, but he does what I tell him to. Wait'll you try this. It's really cool."

A moment later Jeff was fitting a strange kind of helmet onto Josh's head, along with a heavy glove that went on his right hand.

"I can't see anything," Josh protested as the front of the helmet dropped in front of his eyes.

"You're not supposed to," Jeff told him. "Just sit in the chair and wait a minute while Adam gets it hooked up."

"We're not supposed to—" Adam began, but Jeff cut him off.

"Just do it, Adam, okay? It's not like this is some kind of big secret. Josh'll probably have one himself by next week!"

Adam made no reply, and Josh let himself be guided into the chair, and waited to see what was going to happen.

A moment later the front of the helmet came to life. A picture appeared before his eyes, an image of the room he was in. It was so perfect in every detail that he would have sworn the helmet had somehow turned transparent.

"Turn your head," Jeff instructed, the sound of his voice coming through speakers within the helmet itself.

Josh did, and the image of the room shifted.

"Get up and move around," Jeff told him.

Josh hesitated, but finally stood up and took a tentative step forward. Again the image shifted, exactly matching the perspective he'd have had without the helmet.

"It's all digitized," Jeff explained. "If the cable was long enough, you could wander all over the house, and everything would show up in the helmet."

"Wow," Josh breathed. "Awesome!"

"You ever want to fly?" Jeff asked.

"Huh?"

"Watch."

Within seconds the image changed, and Josh found himself in the cockpit of some kind of airplane, peering out the window at the scenery below. But he could also see the controls of the plane.

"See the joystick?" he heard Jeff ask. "Use your right hand to control it."

"But—But it's not real," Josh objected.

"Just try it," Jeff told him. "Use your right hand, and pretend you're reaching for the stick."

As he mimed the action with his right hand, which was still inserted into the bulky glove, he saw his hand on the screen of the helmet, moving toward the joystick.

As he "touched" it, something in the glove stimulated his hand, so that he imagined he could feel the object he appeared to be clutching.

"Now, fly," Jeff told him.

Josh, entranced by what was happening, moved the joystick to the right, and the "plane" appeared to bank over, the horizon tipping, the view of the landscape below veering sharply. Almost instinctively he straightened the "plane" out.

"Wh-What happens if I crash?" he asked.

He heard Jeff laugh. "Maybe you die," the other boy said. "Why don't you try it?"

There was a mocking note to Jeff's voice, a note that Josh had heard before, from the kids in Eden.

Certain that Jeff was laughing at him, he defiantly pushed forward on the joystick.

The "plane" plunged downward, and Josh felt dizzy as the image on the screen—a landscape of the coastline, with cliffs dropping away to the beach and the sea—raced up at him.

"Better pull it up," Jeff teased.

Josh waited, certain that nothing was going to happen. But as the "plane" dove lower, and the sea itself came rushing up at him, he finally lost his nerve. He jerked his hand backward, and the phantom joystick reacted instantly. The "plane" pulled up, and for an instant Josh could almost feel the forces of gravity pulling at him.

And then the screen filled with the face of a cliff, and it was too late. The "plane" smashed into the cliff, the window shattering as the roar of the crash exploded in his ears.

Screaming in spite of himself, Josh jerked the glove off his hand and ripped the helmet from his head. Pale and shaking, he stared at Jeff, who was laughing out loud now.

"Is that cool?" Jeff demanded. "Is that cool, or what? Jeez, you look like you're gonna puke!"

For a second Josh truly thought he *was* going to throw up. The whole experience had been so real, so frightening.

And Jeff had done it to him on purpose—

No!

Jeff had warned him what would happen if he crashed, warned him to pull up on the stick.

And nothing, really, had happened to him. He was all right. He was still in the room, and he wasn't hurt at all.

And Jeff *had* warned him. He wasn't like the kids at home, who always seemed to be waiting for something to happen to him, setting traps for him to fall into.

Jeff had just been showing him how it worked.

As his feeling of nausea passed, he managed a weak smile. "It's neat," he agreed. "But how does it work?"

Jeff's grin broadened. "You really want to know?"

Josh nodded.

Jeff leaned forward to whisper in Josh's ear.

"Magic," he said. "It works by magic."

For just a moment, Josh almost believed him.

6

"Another twenty minutes," George Engersol said. Brenda MacCallum automatically glanced up at the clock. Even as she watched, the hand ticked forward another minute, pausing at nineteen minutes before five. She'd been sitting here, waiting, for nearly three hours.

Since two o'clock Josh had been alone in a room adjoining Engersol's office in one of the two new buildings that stood on the grounds between the Academy and the main campus of the university, working on the battery of tests that would finally determine his eligibility for the school.

For the first hour, Brenda had tried to pretend that she wasn't worried, that whatever the tests contained, Josh would pass them with flying colors. She'd listened in rapt fascination as Engersol, a man of about forty-five, with iron-gray hair and horn-rimmed glasses that, though they had gone out of style at least twenty years ago, still looked perfect on his craggy face, explained to her more of the details about how the Academy had been structured and what they were trying to accomplish. And not only for their students, but for gifted children everywhere. The more she heard, the more Engersol had impressed Brenda—with his ideas and the simplicity with which he was able to explain them. It was clear to her that Engersol regarded his students not merely as gifted children to be taught, but almost as if they were his own children. His paternalism toward them permeated every phrase he uttered, and it was only reluctantly that she had finally shifted her attention to Josh's image on the closed circuit television screen mounted on the wall of the director's office.

"Does he know we're watching him?" she asked now.

"Not unless the camera isn't hidden as well as it should be," Engersol replied. "Knowing he was being watched would be too distracting, and would skew the results of the test."

"But it seems—I don't know, it seems sort of wrong to be watching him without him knowing it."

Engersol shook his head. "Not really. Part of what I need to know is how he goes about the testing procedure. If he knows he's being watched, he'll unconsciously do whatever he thinks I might expect of him. For instance, look what he's doing now. And keep in mind I told him he was free to go about the tests any way he wants."

As Brenda watched, Josh flipped quickly through the thick booklet that contained the test, then frowned and started over again. But on the second run-through he paused here and there, then quickly marked a spot on the answer sheet.

"What's he doing?" Brenda asked.

"What I've done is structured the test differently from most such things. There are no separate sections to it—everything's mixed up together. There might be a problem in algebra, immediately followed by an analogy, or one of the aptitude identifiers."

"I'm afraid I don't understand." Brenda sighed, wondering, not for the first time, where Josh's brilliance had come from. Certainly not from herself, she reflected ruefully. Despite Engersol's efforts to make everything he'd said clearly understandable, she'd still had to struggle to keep from getting lost every now and then.

"I'm not only interested in how well he does on the test, but how he goes about working on it," Engersol went on. "The whole concept of the function of intelligence fascinates me. Some of the children, for instance, seem to concentrate only on certain areas of the test, mathematics, of course, being the most popular. In fact, I suspect what Josh is doing right now is going through the math problems, solving them as fast as he can, getting the easy part out of the way first. Often, however, the brightest of the children start with the hardest problems, getting the worst of the work out of the way while they're still fresh. You never know until you score it, but I can tell a lot simply by watching them work." He nodded toward the monitor, where Josh had abruptly stopped, frowned uncertainly, then flipped back to the third page. A moment later he went all the way to the back of the book and began paging quickly toward the front, his eyes scanning the problems so fast, Brenda could hardly believe he was actually reading them.

"He's not," Engersol replied when she voiced her question. "He's discovered one of the tricks, and I think he's checking himself out."

"Tricks?" Brenda asked.

"There are a lot of duplicate problems. Let's see what he does next."

In the room where he was working, Josh's mind was racing. So far, the test had been pretty easy. He'd glanced through the whole thing, and immediately realized that if he were going to get through it in the required time, he'd have to work fast.

He'd started with the math, where he didn't really have to think. All he had to do was look at the numbers, and the answers were pretty clear, especially since all he really needed was a pretty good guess. After all, who would really think the cube root of 27 could be 9? On a lot of the problems he'd simply been able to eliminate the wrong answers and mark the right one.

But there were so many of them . . .

And then an idea came to him. He was going at it the wrong way. He didn't *have* to solve all the problems. If he got the hardest ones right, it would be obvious he knew the answers to the easiest ones.

He flipped through the booklet once again, searching for something he couldn't solve at all.

He gazed at an advanced calculus equation, and his heart sank. He didn't know anything about calculus at all.

Feeling the first twinge of doubt since he'd begun the test, he

kept going through the book, searching for questions that challenged his math, but that he at least knew how to work out.

And then he noticed that he was repeating a problem he'd already solved. He flipped forward, finding the same problem on the
next to the last page. Frowning, he leafed through the book once
again, quickly spotting more duplicate problems. He thought for a
moment. Should he find *all* the duplicates, and make sure he put
down the same answers on each of them?

But that was stupid. Once he'd gotten a right answer, why even
bother to repeat it? He decided to ignore the duplicates, just leaving
them blank.

He went back to work, solving one problem after another until
he'd gotten down to the point where he didn't have to think about
them at all, then abandoned the math questions, skipping over
them as if he didn't even see them.

He went to work on the analogies, searching immediately for
the most obscure problems and the words he couldn't define.

While he puzzled out the analogies with part of his mind, he
simultaneously leafed through the test book, picking out his purely
subjective choices in the aptitude questions, which were mixed in
with the objective questions that dealt with his knowledge and abil-
ity to reason. Soon a rhythm developed and he was flying through
the book, part of his mind processing the more difficult problems
while the rest of his concentration focused on the questions that
had no right answers, but were designed to build a profile of his
talents and interests.

His confidence grew as his involvement in the test deepened.

He was going to ace the test, like he'd aced all the other tests
he'd ever taken.

In Engersol's office Brenda stared at the screen in puzzlement.
"I don't get it," she murmured. "What's he doing?"

George Engersol made no answer, for he, too, was staring at
the monitor, his gaze seeming almost to bore right into the image
on the screen. Josh MacCallum was working in a way he'd never
seen before—he appeared to be flipping the pages almost randomly, as if he weren't even bothering to read the questions any-

more, but simply picking an answer at random from the multiple choices.

Had he given up?

But if he had, and was just marking answers at random, why was he even using the test book anymore? Why wasn't he simply going through the answer sheets, marking numbers?

A bell sounded in both Engersol's office and the adjoining room.

Josh, his thoughts interrupted by the sudden noise, looked up at the clock and was surprised to see that the allotted three hours had passed.

His eyes shifted to the sheets on which he'd marked his answers, and he felt a vague queasiness in his stomach.

At least a quarter of the questions weren't marked at all. And how many of the ones he'd answered were wrong?

But it wasn't possible—he'd never failed to complete a test before, not even the ones they'd said no one was *supposed* to finish. He'd always done them all, finishing with plenty of time left over.

And now he'd failed.

He wasn't going to get into the Academy at all!

A wave of frustration crashed in on him, and he picked up the pencils that were arranged neatly on the table in front of him and hurled them across the room. Then, snatching up the test booklet, he burst through the door to Dr. Engersol's office.

"There wasn't enough time!" he yelled, his face red, his eyes screwed into tiny slits. "Nobody could finish your stupid test!" Flinging the book at Dr. Engersol, he stormed out of the office, slamming the door behind him. Feeling her own face turning crimson with embarrassment, Brenda leapt to her feet and started after him.

"I'm sorry," she said over her shoulder. "I don't know what got into him. I'll make him apologize."

Before she could leave the room, George Engersol stopped her. "It's all right, Mrs. MacCallum," he said, grasping her arm and leading her back toward the chair. "Believe me, no matter where he's gone or what he's doing, someone is keeping an eye on him."

Brenda froze. What was he saying? Did they watch all the kids here, all the time? But why?

And then she thought she knew the answer. They would do whatever they had to do to prevent exactly the sort of thing Josh had done on Monday. The last thing this school would want was for their students to do themselves any harm.

"But he still can't act that way!" she grumbled. "He hasn't any right to be rude to you, no matter what he thinks!"

Engersol smiled thinly. "Well, at least I know where he gets his temper, anyway," he observed. "I'm not sure he's any angrier than you are right now."

"But he—"

"He just experienced the hardest test he's ever taken," Engersol said. "He didn't finish it—*couldn't* finish it—and he's feeling totally frustrated. But he's right about one thing," he went on, his smile broadening. "No one can finish that test in the allotted time. That's part of the point of it—I need to know how the kids react to being stymied. And Josh reacted very, very well."

Brenda gaped. "Well? You call that fit reacting well?"

Engersol chuckled. "In terms of Josh, yes. It tells me he's not lazy, and that he likes to get things done. All he wanted to do was finish the test, Mrs. MacCallum, and I frustrated him, which was part of the test. And frankly, I'd rather see him get mad than just accept the limitations of even an intellect as good as his. So let's let him cool off, and find out how he did, all right?" Going to the next room, he picked up the sheets that were covered with Josh's answers to the hundreds of questions that had been posed, and frowned.

Until now, none of the students had ever filled in so much as half the answer sheets. It looked as though Josh had come close to completing nearly seventy-five percent of it.

Unless, at the end, he'd simply been taking blind guesses. Well, Engersol thought, he'd soon know. Taking the sheets back to his office, he began scanning them into his computer.

In less than a minute he'd have Josh's results.

"Hildie?"

Hildie Kramer looked up from her desk to see Tina Craig standing in the doorway to her office. At thirteen, Tina was already blossoming rapidly into womanhood, and by next year, when she would begin taking all her courses at the university, she would undoubtedly look several years older than she actually was. Which meant that once more there would be boys between eighteen and twenty-one arriving at the house, trying to figure out why the girl they'd made a date with was living with "the kids." First, of course, they'd assume she worked there—they always did. And then Hildie would have to explain Tina's true age, and that she lived there because she was part of the Academy. The boys would flush with embarrassment, unless they were a lot more mature than they normally were, and then flee, leaving Hildie to explain to Tina that she'd been stood up. Hildie sighed. Tina was going to be a problem. "What is it, Tina?" she asked, beckoning the girl into her office. "Is something wrong?"

"Not with me," Tina replied. "It's Amy Carlson. I've been trying to talk her into coming to the picnic, but she won't leave her room. She's even more homesick than I was when I first came, and I didn't think anyone could get it worse than I did. All Amy says is that she wants to go home, and she's not leaving her room until her parents come and get her."

"All right." Hildie sighed, putting aside the report she was working on and lifting herself out of her chair. "I'll see what I can do."

Sometimes, she reflected as she started the long climb to the third floor, trying to act both as administrator of the Academy and chief housemother as well seemed like too much. And yet everything was going so well, and George had accomplished so much in the few years since the Academy had been established, that it made the long days all worthwhile. Amy was just the kind of child the Academy had been created for. To lose her now, before they'd even had a chance to get started with her, would be a shame.

She tapped softly at the little girl's door. When there was no answer, she twisted the knob and let herself into the room.

Amy was lying on her bed, her eyes red from crying. Next to

her, rubbing against her legs and mewing to be petted, was Tabby, obviously aware that something was wrong with his new friend, and worried about it.

"Didn't you hear me knocking?" Hildie asked, sitting down on the chair in front of Amy's desk.

Amy, her face stormy, made no reply, and when Tabby tried to work his head under her hand, she jerked the cat petulantly away.

"That's not very nice," Hildie commented. "All he wants is to be petted."

Amy's little chin jutted out. "I'm not feeling very nice," she said. "I wish Tabby would go away and leave me alone. And I wish you would, too."

"Well, I'm not going to," Hildie replied. "At least not until you tell me why you won't go to the picnic. It's a beautiful day, and I know you like to go swimming."

"I don't want to go swimming," Amy shot back. "I just want to call my mother and have her come and get me."

"I thought we had an agreement," Hildie said reasonably, choosing to ignore Amy's angry tone. "You talked to your mother twice on Thursday, and again yesterday. And we agreed that you'd talk to her again tomorrow, but not today."

Amy's chin began to tremble, and her eyes glistened with tears. "I don't care! I miss my room, and Kitty-Cat, and everything else. I hate it here, and I want to go home!"

"But we all agreed that you'd try it for a week. That's only a few more days, and—"

"I want to go home *now*!" Amy demanded. "Nobody here likes me, and I don't have any friends."

"Well, that's just not true," Hildie argued patiently. "Tabby likes you, and I like you, and Tina likes you—"

"She does not! She's just being nice to me because you told her to!"

"Actually, she's worried about you. She didn't think anyone could be more homesick than she was, but she thinks you are."

For a split second Hildie thought she saw a flicker of uncertainty in the little girl's eyes, but then her face settled once more into a stubborn mask.

"If I have to stay here, I'll die," she said.

"Now, that's just silly, Amy. Nobody dies of homesickness. I know how much it hurts, but you'll get over it—"

"I will not!" Amy shouted. "Why don't you just leave me alone? I didn't ask you to come up here. All I want is to be left alone!"

Ever since Wednesday, Amy had spent as much time as she could alone in her room, and yesterday hadn't even gone to her classes. If it went on much longer, Hildie would have no choice but to call the Carlsons and tell them that it wasn't working out. But she wasn't ready to give up. Not yet.

"I'll tell you what I'm going to do," she said. "I'm just going to stay right here with you, and not leave you alone for a minute. I can have a bed brought up here, and then I can even sleep with you. After all, homesickness is mostly loneliness, and if we're together all the time, how can you be lonely? We can even have our meals brought up here. I'll just take a few days off—"

Amy was staring at her now, her eyes wide. "No," she wailed. "I don't want you staying with me. I want you to go away!"

"Well, that may be what you think you want, but it's not what you're going to get," Hildie said placidly. "After all, I'm a lot older than you, and I think I know a lot more about it than you do." She would have gone on talking, but Amy leaped off the bed, sending Tabby sprawling to the floor, and stormed out of the room. By the time Hildie had gotten to the hall, Amy was pounding down the stairs. Smiling, the housemother followed. When she reached the loggia, she found Tina standing there, looking even more worried than before.

"Amy just went tearing outside," the girl told her. "She was crying like crazy, and when I tried to stop her, she just jerked away from me and kept going."

"Which way did she go?" Hildie asked.

"Out there," Tina said, pointing to a clump of redwoods planted in a circle near the middle of the front lawn, their massive roots completely hidden by thick shrubbery.

Hildie nodded in satisfaction. "She'll be fine," she told Tina. Amy hadn't taken off for the front gate after all, but only for the hiding place the children had named the Gazebo. Yes, little Amy would be just fine.

Tina cocked her head and regarded the housemother, remembering the day five years before when she herself had wanted more than anything to go home. When the house had finally closed around her, and she hadn't thought she could stand it anymore, she had run.

All the way out to the front lawn, where she'd burrowed through the shrubbery beneath the trees that formed the Gazebo. Within the circle of immense trees, hidden from view, she'd slowly begun to feel better. She'd sat down on the thick mat of fallen needles that blanketed the ground within the circle, and decided that it was her own secret place, a place she could retreat to when she just wanted to think, or be by herself. In the five years since, it had never occurred to her that she wasn't the only person at the Academy who used the Gazebo for exactly that purpose. She studied Hildie. "Did you know that's where I went, when I first came here?" Tina asked.

"Of course," Hildie said blithely. "I know everything that goes on here. Now go along down to the beach. I'll be along later, when Amy's ready to come. And don't let them eat all the potato salad before I get there!"

As Tina headed off to the beach a mile away, Hildie returned to her office, determined to finish the report she was working on. Yet even as she worked, she kept half an eye on the Gazebo. It wouldn't do to lose Amy Carlson now.

The little girl had far too good a mind to allow it to go to waste somewhere else.

———

Amy crawled through the dense shrubbery, ignoring the twigs that scratched at her face and caught at her T-shirt. A few seconds later she emerged from the bushes and paused to catch her breath. Sprawling out on her back, she peered at the branches that mingled a hundred feet above her head, casting their deep shade into the clearing within the circle. It was cooler here, and the air smelled of the fallen needles that carpeted the ground and squished softly under her whenever she moved.

Then, from off to the right, she heard a sound.

Startled, she turned her head and saw a boy about her own age, staring at her. For a moment she didn't recognize him, but then realized she'd seen him from her window, arriving with his mother that morning. But what was he doing here? If he was coming to the school, why wasn't he down at the beach?

She thought she heard him sniffle, and saw him wiping his nose on the sleeve of his shirt.

"That's gross," she said. "Don't you have a handkerchief?"

The boy shook his head. "I don't need one. I'm okay."

Amy rolled over and propped her chin on her hands. "You don't look okay."

"You don't, either," the boy replied. "Why don't you blow your nose? It's dripping snot all over your chin."

Reaching into the pocket of her jeans, Amy pulled a wadded-up hankie out and wiped at her face. "Why don't you go away?" she challenged.

"I was here first. Why don't you go away?"

"Maybe I don't want to," Amy shot back.

"Well, maybe I don't, either," Josh replied, his voice turning truculent.

The two children stared at each other for a while, until Amy looked away. "Is your mom making you come here?" she asked, sure she knew why the boy was hiding in the circle of trees.

"She's not *making* me," Josh replied with a show of bravado he didn't feel. "Besides, it doesn't make any difference what she wants. I flunked the test."

Amy cocked her head. "Don't be stupid. Nobody flunks the test. It's not that kind."

"But I couldn't even finish it," Josh said, his voice catching in spite of himself. "I mean, I didn't even come close!"

Amy, her own problems suddenly forgotten for a moment, moved closer to Josh. "How much did you get done?"

Josh shrugged. "I don't know. Maybe three-fourths of it."

"Three-fourths!" Amy squealed. "I didn't even get half of it done! How'd you do so much?"

Josh stared at her. Was she lying to him, just trying to make him feel better? "What are you doing here?" he asked, instead of answering her question. "How come you're not at the beach with everybody else?"

Amy felt herself flush. "I . . . didn't want to go," she said so quietly Josh could barely hear her.

"How come?" Josh asked. "Don't you like the beach?"

"Do you?" Amy countered.

Josh shrugged. "I don't know. I've never been. I live out in the desert."

"Not anymore," Amy said darkly. "If your mom's like my mom, you're gonna have to live here now."

Josh's brows knit into a frown. "But everyone likes it here, don't they?"

Amy shrugged. "I don't. I hate it. I don't have any friends, and nobody likes me. I just want to go home."

Josh was silent for a moment, then he giggled.

"It's not funny!" Amy exclaimed.

"Sure it is," Josh told her. "I'm hiding out 'cause I flunked the test and I'm not gonna get in, and you're hiding out 'cause you want to get out. That's kind of weird, isn't it?"

Amy thought about it, then nodded. "I guess so," she conceded. "What's your name?"

"Josh MacCallum. What's yours?"

"Amy Carlson. And you didn't flunk the test. I already told you, it's not that kind of test. It's just to find out how smart you are, and how much you already know. And it finds out a bunch of stuff about what you're good at, too."

Josh eyed her suspiciously. "You really only finished half of it?"

Amy nodded. "It's the only hard test I ever took. How come they made it so hard?"

"I don't know," Josh said. Then: "So what's the beach like?"

Amy shrugged. "I haven't been to the one here yet. But in L.A. it's really neat. We always go to Huntington Beach, and it's real wide. And when the surf's high, it's scary. But my dad taught me to body surf this summer, and it's really fun."

Josh was silent, wondering what it would be like to have a father who took you to the beach and taught you things. He guessed he'd never know. "D-Did your friends go to the beach with you?" he asked, his voice suddenly shy. "I mean, in L.A.?"

Amy glanced at him quickly, wondering if he knew she didn't have any friends back home, either. But there was something about Josh's voice that made her hesitate, and when she spoke, she found herself telling him the truth. "I didn't have any friends there, either," she admitted. "They kept skipping me in school, and I was always the youngest one in my class."

Josh nodded. "Yeah. That's what happened to me, too. That's why my mom wants me to come here." He looked away then, and when he spoke again, he couldn't bring himself to look at Amy. "I—I was just thinking that if I get in, and you don't go home, maybe—well, maybe we could be friends."

Amy, feeling flustered, didn't say anything at all for a long time, and Josh wished he'd kept his mouth shut. She was just going to laugh at him, like all the rest of the kids. Just as he was turning away from her to start crawling back through the bushes, he heard her speak.

"That'd be nice," Amy said softly. "Maybe we could just talk to each other sometimes."

A couple of minutes later they emerged from the Gazebo and brushed the twigs and needles off their clothes before starting back toward the building in which Dr. Engersol's office was located.

Hildie, leaning back in her chair and watching them through her window, smiled.

Amy Carlson, she was sure, had just gotten over her homesickness. And Josh MacCallum, she suspected, was never going to have much of a problem with it at all.

George Engersol went over the results of Josh's tests once more, looking for some possibility that a mistake had been made.

Yet there was none.

The computer had scored the test in an instant, charting Josh's scores on the various scales: Intelligence, Mathematical Skills, Logical Abilities, Vocabulary, Science, Aptitudes.

What Engersol couldn't get over was the proportion of the test the boy had succeeded in completing. From the speed with which he'd been working, Engersol had been certain that toward the end he'd simply been making guesses.

And yet, in the sections of the test that required answers that were either right or wrong, the boy had made no mistakes at all.

Not one.

Though he hadn't been able to finish all the problems, he'd solved the ones he had attempted.

Finally, as he'd reviewed the tape made by the camera that had been placed just above the table at which Josh was working, the answer to the puzzle became clear.

Clear, but almost unbelievable.

In the last half hour, when Josh had realized he was running out of time, he had changed his working method.

The tape bore witness to the transformation. At four forty-one, Josh had spent precisely eight seconds staring at a complicated algebraic equation.

Only eight seconds.

Then he had begun turning the pages, marking answers to the aptitude questions, which required little thought, only reactions to statements of choice. He'd worked quickly, picking the questions out and marking his answers, until he'd abruptly stopped and flipped back to the page containing the complicated equation. Selecting the correct answer from among the five choices, he'd marked its space on the answer sheet, then found the next problem, one having to do with physics, a subject about which he should have known very little.

Again he'd simply looked at the question, his finger touching it briefly before going back to the subjective questions.

What he'd been doing, George Engersol realized, was solving the difficult mathematical problems in his head, while at the same time working on other questions. Only when he had the answer in his mind did he go back to the question, identify the code for the answer he'd come up with, and mark the sheet.

In all his experience with gifted children, he'd never seen anything like Josh MacCallum.

At last he leaned back in his chair and faced the boy's mother, who was perched nervously on the edge of her chair.

"Well?" Brenda asked. "How did he do? Did he pass?"

Engersol spread his hands helplessly. "As I told you, there isn't any passing or failing. But I have to tell you, Mrs. MacCallum, that I've never seen anything quite like this before. Josh—Well, he seems to be unique, at least in my experience." Slowly, choosing his words carefully, he explained to Brenda what her son had done.

"The thing that amazes me," he finished, "is that he was able to work these problems out in his head while he was thinking about other things."

"But what does it *mean*?" Brenda pressed. "Are you going to take him?"

Engersol arched an eyebrow. "Oh, yes. We'll take him, with pleasure. In fact, I suspect he'll be the biggest challenge we've ever faced. I have to tell you, Mrs. MacCallum, Josh is probably the brightest child I've ever come across. After looking at these"—he held up the test results—"it's easy to imagine the problems he must have had."

Brenda sighed. "It's been terrible," she agreed. "I just wish you could take him right now. I know he belongs here, and I just don't know how much longer I can cope with him at home—" She was about to say more when the door, which had been only partly ajar, was pushed open. Josh was standing there, his face stormy.

"I knew it," he shouted. "You *are* mad at me for what I did, and you're just sorry you can't get rid of me! I'm glad I flunked the stupid test. Do you hear me? I'm glad!"

Turning, he raced away again, and this time Brenda followed him, almost stumbling over the little girl who was also standing in the hall, staring after Josh. Only when Brenda was gone did Amy step shyly into Dr. Engersol's office.

"Is it true?" she asked. "Did Josh flunk? Isn't he coming here?"

Engersol shook his head. "Of course he didn't flunk, Amy," he told the obviously worried little girl. "If he wants to, he's certainly coming here. And I very much hope he does."

"I do, too," Amy agreed, then left the director's office, intent on going to find Josh. If she couldn't talk him into staying, she decided, she was definitely going home, too.

Even if she had to run away.

———

Brenda found Josh by the car, sobbing. "Honey, what is it?" she asked. "What's wrong?"

"I heard what you said. You don't even want to take me home!"

"Honey, that's not true—" Brenda protested, then stopped, hearing her own words ringing in her ears, words she'd never intended for Josh to hear—words that certainly hadn't been meant in the way he'd interpreted them. But if all he'd heard were the last few words she'd said to Dr. Engersol . . .

"Oh, darling, I'm sorry," she told him, kneeling down and hugging him close. "Of course I want to take you home. But this is where you belong. You didn't flunk the test. You did better on it than anyone ever has before! All I was saying was that I'm sorry you can't start right away!"

Josh was staring at her, his eyes widening as what she was saying sank in. "I passed?" he asked. "I got in?"

"Of course you did," Brenda told him.

"B-But what if I don't want to stay?" he asked, his voice quavering with uncertainty. "What if I don't like it here? What if I want to go home?"

Before Brenda could answer, the little girl she'd seen outside George Engersol's office a few moments ago tentatively approached the car.

"Josh?" Amy asked. "What's wrong?"

"N-Nothing," Josh stammered, unwilling to tell Amy how frightened he suddenly was. "Maybe I just don't want to come here."

Amy looked hurt, but then reached out and took Josh's arm.

"But you have to," she argued. "You promised, remember? If you got in, I'd stay, and we'd be friends."

"That was before," Josh mumbled.

Amy's eyes welled up, but she stood firm. "You mean you don't want to be my friend?"

"N-No," Josh said. "I mean, that's not what I mean. It's—"

"But you can't be my friend if I never see you again," Amy told him.

"So what?" Josh objected. "You don't even know me."

Amy hesitated, then made up her mind. "Yes, I do," she said, her own face setting as stubbornly as Josh's. "You're just like me. You're scared, that's all. And you said you don't have any friends back in the desert anyway. So you might as well stay. Okay?"

Josh blinked at the little girl. Was it possible she really meant it? That she really wanted him to be her friend? But he'd already made up his mind. How could he change it now?

And then his mother spoke. "Look," she said. "I didn't mean what you thought I meant, and I'm not going to make you do anything you don't want to do. So why don't we go to the picnic on the beach, like Mrs. Kramer asked us to, and you can make up your mind later on. Afterward, if you still don't want to stay here, I promise I'll take you home, and never even suggest a place like this again. Okay?"

Josh gazed suspiciously up at her. "Cross your heart?"

"Cross my heart," Brenda replied, somberly making the required gesture.

Josh hesitated, then nodded. "All right," he said. "But remember, you promised."

Breathing a sigh of relief, Brenda followed the two children as they headed back toward the mansion so Amy could get a beach towel.

It was nearly six o'clock by the time Josh and Amy, accompanied by Brenda, reached the top of the cliff that overlooked Crescent Cove, a narrow strip of sand caught between two rugged points that jutted out into the sea. The points, rocky crags that bore the brunt of the winds off the Pacific, were studded with twisted cyprus trees. Brenda paused for a moment to gaze at the panorama spread before her. "Isn't it gorgeous?" she asked. "Maybe I ought to quit my job and move here." But even as she spoke the words, she knew it was impossible. Every one of the restaurants they had passed as they walked through the town seemed to have an ample supply of college girls working as waitresses. Even if she could find a job, she'd never be able to afford to rent an apartment here. "Or maybe I ought to be thankful for what I've got, huh?" she added.

When Josh made no response, she tore her eyes away from the view and glanced down at him. But he wasn't paying any attention to her, or to the view of the ocean. Instead, he was staring at Amy, who, in turn, had turned pale, her eyes wide as she stared down at the beach below.

"Amy?" Brenda asked. "Are you all right?"

The little girl shook her head. "I—I feel dizzy," she said. She took a step backward and turned away from the precipice. "I felt like I was going to fall off," she whispered.

"It's called acrophobia," Josh announced. "It's when you're afraid of heights."

"I *know* that," Amy retorted. She moved farther away from the edge, then turned back, her eyes fixing fearfully on the rickety-looking landing from which wooden stairs zigzagged down the face of the cliff to the beach below. "M-Maybe I'll go back to the school," she said, her stomach tightening with just the thought of going down those stairs.

"What about the picnic?" Josh protested.

"I—I don't really like picnics," Amy lied, her eyes still fastened on the stairs.

"You're scared of the stairs, aren't you?" Brenda asked, crouching down next to the little girl. Amy said nothing, but her head bobbed emphatically. "I'm sure they're perfectly safe," Brenda assured her. "Look at all the people down there. They all went down the stairs." She took Amy's left hand and tried to lead her closer to the edge so she could see the rest of the kids playing on the beach, but Amy hung back.

"Wh-What if I fall?" she asked, her voice quavering.

Josh moved over to her and took her other hand, so she was between him and his mother. "I won't let you fall."

Uncertainly, Amy let herself be drawn closer to the edge, but once more the dizziness seemed to overwhelm her, and she almost felt like she was being pulled over the cliff.

"It's okay," Josh told her, squeezing her hand. "You're not gonna fall."

A moment later they came to the landing at the top of the stairs. Amy froze, refusing to put even her toe on the weathered, splintery wood.

"You go first, Mom," Josh said. "Then she'll see that it's not going to collapse."

Brenda, feeling a touch of vertigo herself, hesitated a second, praying that her son was right, but then stepped onto the landing and started down, her hand grasping the rail with every step.

"See?" she said with more brightness than she felt. "It's perfectly safe."

Amy watched her warily, then looked fearfully at Josh. "Promise you'll hold my hand all the way down?" she asked.

"I promise," Josh replied. "If you stay on the inside and don't look down, you'll be okay. Come on."

He moved out onto the landing. Clutching his hand tightly, Amy took a deep breath and put her foot on the wooden planks.

Was it her imagination, or could she feel them shaking beneath her foot?

Holding on to Josh with one hand, her other steadying herself against the face of the cliff, she started down.

With each step, she imagined herself pitching forward, tumbling off the stairs, plummeting to the rocky beach below.

"It's gonna be okay," Josh assured her, sensing her fear. "You'll see. Just keep going."

A few minutes later they came to the last turn. Only fifteen more steps separated them from the beach. Amy, her panic finally releasing her from its grip, let go of Josh's hand. "I did it," she breathed. "I made it." Breaking into laughter, she skipped down the last of the steps, picked her way over the rocks and ran down the beach to the water, kicking off the rubber sandals she was wearing as she went.

Brenda, already on the beach, watched Amy go, then shifted her attention back to George Engersol.

Halfway down the steps she'd noticed him, already on the beach, watching Amy's progress as she crept down the stairs. Indeed, she'd paused for a moment, watching him as he observed the little girl. When he finally felt her eyes on him, and looked directly at Brenda, she ducked her head and hurried on down. But as she waited on the sand, she noticed that he was still watching Amy. And his expression had struck her as odd.

An expression of such intense concentration—lips compressed in a grim line, eyes narrowed into a stare sharp enough to cut bone—that Brenda felt a shudder course through her, as though a chill wind had come off the ocean. By the time she shook off the feeling Amy had finally come to the bottom and dashed off toward the water. Still, Engersol remained motionless. He didn't turn to speak to Brenda, although she was standing only a few feet away from him. Instead, his head down and his hands clasped behind his back, he had finally moved away.

She watched him go, uneasiness stirring again inside her. His reaction to the little girl's conquering of her fear, she thought, was strange.

But before she could analyze it any further, Hildie Kramer approached her, holding out a welcoming hand. "Come on," the matronly woman said, her warm smile wreathing her face. "There's a couple of people I want you to meet."

While Josh headed off after Amy Carlson, Brenda was drawn into a group that included a few of the teachers at the Academy, as well as the parents of two of its students. Within a few moments she was deep in conversation with Chet and Jeanette Aldrich, one of whose sons, Jeff, she'd already met.

"That's the other one," Jeanette told her, pointing to Adam, who, with his brother, was bobbing in the water a few yards from the shore.

Brenda stared at the twin faces with undisguised surprise. "Two of them?" she breathed. "My God, when I think of the problems I've had with just Josh—" She broke off in sudden embarrassment. To her relief, Jeanette Aldrich only chuckled ruefully.

"Tell me about it," Jeanette said. "Only double it. Two kids with enough brains for four." A look Brenda could not quite read shadowed the woman's face for an instant before she brightened and said, "Believe me, without this place, I'd have been in a mental hospital by now."

Chet Aldrich handed Brenda an already opened can of beer. Then the questions in Brenda's mind began bubbling out of her. The Aldriches, apparently having been through all this before, listened patiently. For the first time, Brenda realized she was talking to people who understood exactly what raising Josh had been like.

Even if, in the end, Josh refused to come to the Academy, just spending a few hours talking to the Aldriches was going to make the whole trip worthwhile.

Josh and Amy were wading slowly along the shoreline, the gentle waves in the cove breaking over their feet. They'd been on the beach for almost half an hour, but neither of them had made any move to join the rest of the kids, preferring to remain by themselves, poking around among the tide pools at the northern end of the cove, Amy showing Josh the various creatures that lived among the crevices and crannies of the rocks. As the tide had begun coming in, and the pools had flooded with water, they started reluctantly back toward the other kids, who were gathered around a man Josh hadn't seen before.

"Who's that?" he asked Amy, nodding toward the tall man with blond hair and a beard.

"Mr. Conners," Amy told him. "He's the English teacher."

"What's he like?"

Before Amy could answer, Jeff Aldrich dashed over to them. "Come on," he urged. "We're gonna play volleyball!"

Josh felt his heart sink. He glanced at Amy, who didn't seem any happier about the idea than he was. He already knew what was going to happen. The teacher would choose the two biggest guys as captains, and then they'd start choosing up sides. And if it happened like it always did in Eden, he'd be chosen last, even after all the girls.

"I don't want to," he told Jeff. "I hate volleyball."

"I hate it, too," Amy agreed, and suddenly Josh was certain she was thinking the same thing he was. "We'll just watch."

The two of them started toward the area of the beach where the blankets were spread out on the sand, but before they'd gotten past the crowd of kids, Steve Conners called out to them.

"Hey, you two, come on! Nobody gets out of this!"

Josh and Amy froze, glancing at each other. What would happen if they said no?

Neither of them was sure.

They both hesitated, as if each was waiting for the other to decide what they both should do. "M-Maybe we better do it," Josh finally said. "I don't want to get in trouble."

"But I *hate* it," Amy blurted out. "Nobody ever chooses me, and they all make faces when they get stuck with me!"

"That's what happens to me, too," Josh admitted.

"Will you two come on?" Conners shouted once more. "Amy, you stay on this side, and Josh can go over there."

Suddenly, without anyone choosing up sides, the group split up, some of them going to the other side of the net to join Josh, the rest staying with Amy. "Too many people on that side," Steve Conners called out after taking a quick count. "Somebody else come over here." Adam Aldrich, who happened to be standing closest to the net, ducked under, switching teams. "Okay, who wants to serve first?" Conners called. To Josh's surprise, nobody demanded the ball.

Finally, Brad Hinshaw pointed to Josh. "Let him serve," he crowed. "If he's as good at this as he is at chess, maybe we can score some points!"

Before Josh could say anything, Steve Conners tossed him the ball, which hit him in the chest, then fell to the ground. He froze, waiting for the other kids to laugh, but no one did.

He picked up the ball and took it to the end of the court, or at least what he thought might be the end of the court, since there weren't any lines marking the boundaries. "H-Here?" he asked Steve Conners uncertainly.

The teacher shrugged. "Looks as good as anyplace else."

Josh felt the eyes of all his teammates watching him.

In a minute, when they found out he wasn't any good, they'd start razzing him.

Maybe he should trip accidentally-on-purpose and pretend he'd twisted his ankle. Then at least he wouldn't have to play.

But he'd have to remember to limp around for the rest of the night, and they might even make him go see the nurse or something.

Resigned to what was about to happen, he held the ball in his left hand, then dropped it as he swung up at it with his right.

Just as he knew it would, the ball shot off the wrong way, dropping into the sand way out of bounds. He felt his face turn crimson as he waited for the laughter he expected.

"Doesn't count!" Brad Hinshaw yelled.

Josh, baffled, stared at Brad, who only shrugged. "It went out of bounds. It only counts if it goes over the net."

"That's not how they play it at home—"

"Well, it's how we play it here," someone else yelled. "Try it again, but get closer to the net. And hit it overhand!"

Josh picked up the ball, then moved a little closer to the net. Aware of everyone watching him again, he held his breath, clenched his right fist, and tossed the ball into the air. He swung at it hard—and missed. Losing his balance, he tumbled into the sand and felt the ball hit him on the back as it dropped.

And now he heard them laughing.

Tears coming to his eyes as he realized he'd made an idiot of himself, he scrambled to his feet and ran down the beach, putting as much distance between himself and the rest of the kids as possible.

Brenda, seeing Josh race off, started to stand up, but Jeanette Aldrich, sitting next to her on the blanket, held her back. "Don't," she said. "Let Steve Conners handle it."

"But Josh hates sports," Brenda protested. "And wasn't it Mr. Conners who made him play?"

"It'll be all right," Jeanette assured her. "Steve knows what to do."

All Brenda's instincts told her to ignore the other woman's words, to go to her son and try to soothe his bruised ego, but then she stopped herself. If Josh was going to stay here, he'd have to get used to not having her around to help him out.

And if she went to him now, given what had just happened, she was sure she knew what he'd say: "See? They're laughing at me! I'm not going to stay here! I want to go home!"

Checking her urge to mother him, she forced herself to remain where she was.

━━━

A hundred yards down the beach, crouched by himself, Josh wondered why he'd ever let his mother bring him here in the first place. It was going to turn out just like the school at home, with everyone laughing at him. The humiliation of what had just happened wiped out the memory of the chess game with Jeff Aldrich, and the friendliness of Brad Hinshaw.

And now, after he'd acted like a jerk, even Amy probably wouldn't like him anymore.

He sensed a presence behind him and stiffened. Oh, Jeez—his mother hadn't come after him, had she? Now they'd all think he was a baby. But the voice that spoke to him wasn't his mother's at all.

It was Mr. Conners, and Josh was sure he knew why he was there: to give him a lecture on being a good sport. He hunched further into himself, wrapping his arms around his legs.

"Want to tell me what went wrong?" Steve Conners asked, hunkering down next to Josh.

Josh shook his head, not even looking up.

For a moment Conners didn't say anything, but finally reached out and ran his hand through Josh's hair. "Hey, come on, everybody misses serves. Happens all the time."

"But it *always* happens to me, and everybody was laughing at me!" Josh's voice trembled, and he tried to duck away from the teacher's hand.

"Well, I'm not sure they were actually laughing *at* you," Conners told him. "I think it was more what happened to you. You just looked funny when you missed the ball, that's all. You should have seen the look on your face. You'd have been laughing, too. It was as if the last thing you expected to happen was that you'd miss it completely."

"How come that guy told me to hit it overhand?" Josh demanded. "He knew what was gonna happen, and he just wanted to make me look like a jerk."

"Now, how was Philip Meredith going to know that?" Conners asked. "He never saw you play volleyball before, did he? Maybe he was just trying to help."

"No, he wasn't. Everybody always laughs at me when I try to play some stupid game. And if they don't laugh at me, they yell at me. Just because I'm no good at it."

"Who said you were no good?" Conners countered. "Besides, being good at things like volleyball doesn't count for much around here. As you said, it's only a game."

Josh scowled deeply. "I said it was a *stupid* game, and it is!"

"Well, it is if you get upset about it," Steve Conners agreed. "In fact, if you get upset about it, it sort of stops being a game at all, doesn't it? I mean, games are supposed to be fun. It doesn't really matter who wins."

"But everybody cares who wins," Josh replied.

"Do you?"

Josh cocked his head, looking up at the teacher. "I—I don't know."

Steve Conners's eyes widened in mock surprise. "What? There's something you don't know? Maybe they made a mistake after all. You sure you're in the right place? All you kids are supposed to know practically everything." The bantering tone left Conners's voice. "Look, Josh, I know things haven't been going too well for you lately. And I'm really sorry everyone laughed at you. Maybe they shouldn't have. But give them a chance, okay? Don't forget, they've all had exactly the same kinds of problems you've had. And believe me, they don't care any more about volleyball than you do."

Josh stared up at the teacher. "But at home—" he began, doggedly refusing to understand Conners's point.

"At home things are different. Which is why you're here, not there. Now what do you say you just come and watch the game? If you want to play some more, fine. If you don't, that's fine, too."

Without waiting for Josh to answer, Steve gently drew the boy to his feet and started back down the beach, his hand draped over Josh's shoulder.

As they drew closer to the game, Josh saw that what Steve had told him was true—though the kids were playing hard, doing their best to get the ball over the net, only two or three of them were any good at it. Most of them, like him, missed at least half their shots entirely, and most of the shots that connected went wild.

Catching sight of him, Amy waved wildly. "You should have

seen it, Josh!" she yelled. "1 did it! I got the ball over the net! And it was only my third try!"

Before he realized what had happened, Josh found himself back in the game. The next time his turn to serve came up, he, too, managed to get the ball over the net.

Of course, it didn't go over until the fourth try, which wasn't as good as Amy had done, but on the third try, when he'd fallen over backward trying to hit the ball after a bad toss, he'd laughed as hard as everyone else.

Maybe, he decided, volleyball wasn't such a bad game after all. At least not the way they played it at the Academy.

———

By ten o'clock, when the picnic was breaking up, and Josh was helping the other kids throw sand on the dying fire, Brenda was sure he'd made up his mind. She watched him all evening, as he'd sat next to Amy, munching on hot dogs, then joined the circle of kids around the fire to listen to Jeff Aldrich tell the Academy's favorite ghost story—a terrifying tale about old Mr. Barrington, whose specter still roamed the darkened house at night, seeking vengeance for the death of a child who may or may not have ever actually existed.

"No one knows how old Mr. Barrington's son was when he died," Jeff told the circle of entranced children. "But they say something was wrong with the boy, and Mr. Barrington kept him hidden somewhere in the house. But no one knows where, and no one knows what was wrong with the boy. But when Mr. Barrington got really old, he got really strange, too." Jeff's voice dropped slightly, taking on a mysterious tone as he retold the old legend of the Academy's mansion. . . .

Eustace Barrington stepped off the elevator, blinking in the bright sunlight that flooded through the large windows in the cupola. He closed the mahogany bookcase that concealed the elevator's doors, then went to the window and gazed out.

He'd been right to build the house here, right to perch it high on the hillside, so that from this small apartment on the roof he could see not only the mountains behind the house, but the sea as well, sparkling in the distance.

See all the things his son could no longer see.

Or did not choose to see.

When he'd begun building the house, Eustace Barrington had already known there was something wrong with the boy, something that made him different from any other child Barrington had ever known.

His son didn't talk like other children, didn't act like them. Instead, he kept to himself, seeming more interested in what was going on within his own mind than in the outside world.

Finally, when the boy had stopped talking altogether, Eustace Barrington had taken his son to the family doctor, then to every other doctor he could find.

All of them had shaken their heads.

"Just slow," one of them had said.

"He'll grow out of it," another had assured him.

"Perhaps you should put him somewhere," someone else had suggested, and given him the name of a place on the other side of the country, where he'd never have to see his son again.

Instead, Eustace Barrington had built this house, and constructed a special place for his son deep beneath the basement, accessible only by the elevator from his private suite, a suite that jutted up above the roof-line of the rest of the house, allowing all the light that could never reach the chambers below the basement to fill these rooms, as if by compensating for his son's lack of sunlight, he could ease the pain he felt for all these years.

Still, Eustace Barrington was certain he'd done the right thing, for when his son had finally withdrawn so deeply into himself that he no longer responded to the outside world, and when the Barringtons' friends had begun to talk about the boy as if he were some kind of inanimate object to be disposed of unless a reason for keeping him could be found, Eustace had brought him here.

He'd moved the boy into the subterranean chambers, which he'd furnished with far more care than he'd given to the rest of the house, making sure his son would be comfortable, and have everything he could possibly need, and couldn't accidentally hurt himself.

The main room contained the boy's bed, and enough furniture so the two of them could be comfortable while the man sat with the boy, and talked to him, disregarding the near certainty that his son no longer heard him.

In another room was a dining table and two chairs, where he took his son's meals every day, and ate with him.

He took them himself. Never a servant, because he did not trust servants.

No one but Eustace Barrington knew the boy was there at all, for he had decided long ago that it would be better for this child to be kept at home, where he would be loved and left to whatever mystic thoughts he may have, than to be turned over to the care of strangers who would neither love, nor understand him.

His son, Eustace Barrington was convinced, was a genius.

Though the boy never spoke except to mutter numbers, and seemed to be both blind and deaf, Barrington was still certain that his son's mind was special, not insane.

Sometimes, when he could make out the numbers his son spoke, he wrote them down, and spent hours alone at his desk, working out the relationships of the numbers to each other.

What his son was apparently calculating in his head in seconds, it took Eustace Barrington hours to work out on paper.

Today, though, he was worried.

He, after all, would be ninety-six on his next birthday.

His son was only fifty-five.

And it had been fifty years since his son had been taken to live in the suite of rooms beneath the basement.

Eustace Barrington, after all his years, had only one wish left.

That he would outlive his son, so the boy would never have to be delivered into the hands of strangers.

But if he died before his son, there was something else he would do.

He would find a way to destroy anyone who might threaten the boy beneath the basement.

The boy who lived in shadows.

If the boy were harmed, so also would others be harmed. . . .

"Has he ever come back?" Josh MacCallum breathed when the story was over. "Has he actually done anything?"

Jeff Aldrich smiled mysteriously. "Maybe he has," he whispered. "Maybe sometimes he comes back in the night, and creeps around the house, looking for his son. And they say," he went on, his voice dropping so it was barely audible, and his gaze fixing on Josh, "that when he finds the right boy, he'll take him away with him. In fact, last year—"

"That's enough, Jeff," Hildie Kramer cut in, breaking the ghostly mood with a laugh. "You don't want to scare poor Josh away on his very first night with us, do you?"

"It's okay," Josh protested. "I *like* ghost stories!" As Jeff Aldrich gazed appraisingly at him, he decided to add just the tiniest little fib. "They don't scare me at all!"

Jeff's eyes held his own for a moment, then shifted away, leaving Josh wondering if his new friend had believed him or not.

———

Brenda MacCallum watched her son slowly being absorbed into the group. She had seen his guard drop lower and lower as these kids—bright kids so much like Josh himself—took him into their circle, making a place for him when he approached, listening to him when he talked, accepting him.

Brenda herself, torn between her unease at leaving her little boy among strangers, four hundred miles from home, and her desire to give him a better opportunity than she could provide, spent the evening talking quietly with the Aldriches and learning that her problems were not unique. She listened in silence as Chet Aldrich, speaking softly, related the story about the night almost a year before when they'd found Adam in the bathroom, unconscious, an empty bottle of Jeanette's sleeping pills next to him on the floor. After the shock and horror of that event, the two of them had finally faced up to the fact that both their boys needed special programs, and had brought them to the Academy. "Kind of makes you wonder about our own intelligence," Chet remarked wryly, adding that the transformation in the twins had been nothing short of miraculous since they'd been at the school.

And this is my miracle, too, Brenda thought. The miracle I've been waiting for.

With that, the last of her ambivalence crumbled.

Tomorrow morning she would sit down with Hildie Kramer and go through the formalities of enrolling Josh in Barrington Academy.

The strange uneasiness she'd felt earlier, when George Engersol, watching Amy trying to conquer her fear, had stood by with that odd detachment, observing her as if she were some kind of scientific specimen beneath a microscope, had been completely forgotten.

Indeed, all the misgivings she'd felt in the last few hours, from her first sense of foreboding as she'd seen the immense old house and the almost abnormally quiet children spread around it, to her dislike of George Engersol, were forgotten, for Josh, she could see, was going to be happy here.

In the end, that was all that really counted.

That first morning, when he awoke to the sound of classical music, Josh had felt a momentary disorientation. Blinking in the strong sunlight that flooded through his east-facing dormer, he had one of those awful seconds of panic when he didn't know where he was. And when he finally remembered, the panic only swelled, for he also remembered that last night, Sunday, his mother had kissed him good-bye after getting him settled into his new room, assuring him that she'd come back to visit him the next weekend, bringing the rest of his clothes with her. Josh, putting on a braveness he didn't feel, told her just to send his stuff. He didn't need her coming back to see him, he'd insisted. But that first morning he wasn't so sure. He'd stayed in bed for a few minutes, paralyzed with a sudden fear.

What was he supposed to do?

Was he supposed to take a shower this morning, like he had every morning at home?

Deciding it couldn't hurt, he pulled on the worn flannel bathrobe that had been his Christmas present last year, but was already too small for him, and padded down the narrow hall to the boys' room at the end. Someone was already in one of the shower stalls, but the other one was vacant. Feeling self-conscious as he took off his bathrobe and stood naked in the rest room, Josh reached into the empty shower and turned on the hot water.

"Jeez!" The boy in the other stall screeched as the temperature of his own shower instantly dropped ten degrees. "Will you get out of here and leave me alone, jerkface?"

"I—I'm sorry," Josh stammered, stung by the boy's words, and all the memories of the torment he'd received from the kids in Eden rising with the force of a gale off the ocean. He was about to slink out of the bathroom when the door opened, and Jeff Aldrich came in. Seeing the other boy in the shower, and holding his finger to his lips to prevent Josh from protesting, Jeff reached into the vacant stall and twisted the hot water off while turning the cold on.

A scream, this time of pain, erupted from the occupied stall, and instantly Brad Hinshaw burst out, his face red with fury. "What the hell are you—" he demanded, his outcry cut off as he saw Jeff Aldrich grinning wickedly at him.

"Gotcha!" Jeff cried, bursting into laughter at Brad's fury.

"Jeez," Brad groaned. "Why can't you leave me alone?" Grabbing his towel, and pulling on his bathrobe, he stomped out, still dripping with water.

"That's five mornings in a row," Jeff told Josh. "When I couldn't find him in the boys' room downstairs, I figured he'd sneaked up here."

Josh found himself laughing, too. "I got him just before you came in. It was just an accident, but he must have thought I was you. He was really pissed off at me."

Jeff Aldrich, satisfied with the success of his prank, started out of the bathroom, but then turned back. "Hey," he said. "Which room did they give you?"

"One in front. The second one from the stairs."

Jeff Aldrich's lips twisted into a strange grin. "Boy, I wouldn't want to be in that room. That was Timmy Evans's room."

"Who?" Josh asked.

"Timmy Evans," Jeff repeated. "He was here last year."

Josh frowned. "How come he's not here this year?"

Jeff Aldrich's grin widened. "He died," he said.

"D—Died?" Josh stammered, feeling a chill run down his spine. "What happened?"

Jeff shrugged. "They said he killed himself," he replied. "But maybe he didn't at all." He paused, appraising the look on Josh's face. "Maybe old Eustace Barrington came for him. Maybe the old man thought Timmy was his son, and took him away. Anyway, I sure wouldn't want to sleep in that room." Shooting Josh one last look, as if to say, "Watch out!" Jeff Aldrich sauntered out of the bathroom, leaving the door swinging slowly behind him.

A few minutes later, his shower forgotten after what Jeff had told him, Josh had gone down to the dining room, where most of the other kids were already eating. He'd chosen his breakfast from the table where the food was set out, and automatically headed toward an empty table, but before he'd gone more than a few steps, Jeff had waved to him. He hesitated for a second, the story of Timmy Evans still fresh in his mind, but then, when Jeff beckoned to him a second time, he'd joined the twin brothers.

When Amy appeared in the dining room, Jeff had waved her over, too. For the rest of the week, the four of them would sit together at every meal. To Josh's relief, Jeff hadn't mentioned Timmy Evans again.

The days passed quickly. Both Josh and Amy discovered that the Academy was nothing like the schools they had come from. While there was still a lot of teasing among the kids, for the first time in their lives both of them felt that they were part of the group, not outside it, and both of them had begun to join in the good-natured banter, and even to share in the laughter when the jokes were at their own expense.

Josh was finally beginning to think that maybe he wasn't the kind of freak all the kids in Eden had made him feel he was.

Now, on Friday, he sat in Steve Conners's English class, a copy of *Hamlet* open on his desk. They'd started reading the play at the beginning of the hour, with himself as Hamlet and Amy as Ophelia. At first it had been kind of boring, but then Mr. Conners—Josh still hadn't gotten up the nerve to call him Steve, as the rest of the class did—had stopped the reading and stared at them in mock exasperation.

"What's going on with you guys?" he'd demanded. "This is a *play*! It was written as entertainment. Who do you think would have paid good money to see it if the actors had read it the way you do? Come on, gang, a little ham, okay?"

They started over again from the beginning, and suddenly the play that had seemed to Josh to be incredibly dull when he'd read through it the night before, marking Hamlet's lines in yellow so he wouldn't lose his place during the reading this morning, came alive. As his classmates got into the spirit of it, becoming caught up in the drama of the piece, Josh began to imagine himself in the vast, cold chambers of Elsinore Castle.

But in the midst of one of his speeches, the door opened, and Josh looked up to see Adam Aldrich coming in. He faltered, then stopped, for the one thing that Steve Conners was absolutely strict about was promptness.

"I only have an hour a day with you, and I don't intend to waste it," he'd explained on Monday, when Josh himself had been late because he hadn't been able to find the room. "So if you're not going to show up on time, don't bother to come at all. Clear?"

Josh, his eyes wide at the rebuke, had nodded mutely and slid into his seat. Now he waited to see what would happen to Adam.

Steve Conners gazed steadily at Adam, who seemed totally unconcerned about his tardiness. "Didn't you understand what I said Monday?" the teacher asked.

Adam shrugged. "I've got a note from Dr. Engersol," he said.

He handed the note to the teacher, and Conners glanced at it briefly before nodding Adam into his chair, making a mental note to talk to the director that afternoon. "Okay, let's pick it up where we left off. Adam, you take over the part of Polonius. We're on page twenty-seven."

The reading began again, but when Polonius's next line came up, there was only silence from Adam Aldrich.

Conners frowned at the boy. "Adam?"

"I lost my place," Adam replied. He read the line, but with absolutely no expression to his voice, stumbling over the rhythm of the speech. When his next line came, he missed it again.

"What's going on, Adam?" Conners asked. "Didn't you read the play last night?"

Adam slouched low in his chair. "I didn't have time," he muttered, so softly that Conners could barely hear him.

Conners eyed the boy. Every day, it seemed, Adam was showing less and less interest in the class. Yesterday, in fact, he'd spent the entire hour staring out the window, taking no part at all in the discussion of Shakespeare and the theater of the Elizabethan era. Yet last year, he knew, Adam had been involved in both plays the Academy had staged, and even tried out for one of the productions the university drama department had put on.

"What were you doing that was more important than your homework?" Conners asked, keeping his voice mild.

"I was just doing something else, that's all," Adam replied, his normally placid expression turning sullen. "It's none of your business."

Conners frowned. "Come on, Adam. If it affects what's happening to you in my class, I think it is my business."

"Then maybe I won't be in your class anymore," Adam said. As the rest of the students watched in astonished silence, Adam Aldrich picked up his book bag, pulled his English text out of it, and stood up. "I hate this class," he announced. "It can get stuffed, for all I care."

He walked out.

As a tense silence hung over the class, Josh gazed at the door through which his friend had disappeared, wondering what was going to happen. Would Mr. Conners go after him and bring him back? And the way Adam had talked to the teacher . . .

"All right, gang," he heard Mr. Conners saying. "Just go on with the reading. Brad, you pick up Polonius's lines, okay?"

Brad nodded silently as Steve Conners hurried from the room. At the end of the hall he could see Adam Aldrich just starting out of the building. Breaking into a run, Conners caught up with the boy as he was reaching the last step down from the building's porch and heading across the lawn toward the mansion.

"Adam?" Steve said as he came abreast of the boy. "Hey, come on, you can't just walk out like that."

Adam kept going, his hands stuffed in his pockets, his book bag hanging from his right wrist, barely clearing the ground. Conners put his right hand on the boy's shoulder, stopping him and turning him around so they faced each other. "You want to tell me what's going on, Adam? I'm on your side, you know."

Adam's eyes shifted away from the teacher's. "Nothin's going on. I just don't like your class, and I'm not going to it anymore."

"Oh, you're not, huh?" Steve said, trying to keep his voice light, though the fleeting worries he'd felt about Adam all week were suddenly coalescing. "How do you figure you're going to get out of it? English isn't an elective, you know."

"I'll get out," Adam announced, his eyes shifting away from Steve Conners and fixing on the large cupola that formed the fourth floor of the mansion. "Dr. Engersol will get me out."

Conners frowned, his own gaze following Adam's. Was that where Adam had been that morning? Up in Engersol's private aerie atop the mansion? "What's going on, Adam? How did you get that note from Dr. Engersol? He knows how I feel about people coming in late."

"We were working on something," Adam told him, in a voice that informed Conners that exactly what they had been doing was none of his business.

"Look, Adam," Conners said, deciding to start all over again. "I don't know what's going on with you, but I think maybe you ought to tell me about it. I can't help you—"

Adam twisted away from him. "I don't need any help!" he said. "And nothing's going on with me. Can't you just leave me alone?" He backed a couple of paces away from the teacher, then turned and sprinted across the lawn toward the main house.

Conners was tempted to follow him, but then remembered the rest of his class, still inside, theoretically reading the play he'd assigned them. Still, he waited until he saw the massive wooden door close behind Adam before starting back to his classroom. Hildie Kramer, he was certain, would have seen Adam from her office and immediately dropped whatever she might have been doing to find out what had upset the boy. Hildie's instincts with the kids, Steve had discovered in the short time he'd been with the school, were rarely far off the mark. She often seemed to know when one of them was heading for trouble even before the child himself knew.

Nevertheless, he added another mental note to his list of things to attend to later on.

Check with Hildie, and find out what's going on with Adam.

===

"What's going on with Adam?" Josh asked that night. It was an hour after dinner, and he was in Jeff Aldrich's room, working out a problem in trigonometry that had stumped him. Amy Carlson, who had come with him, was flopped on Jeff's bed, a history book open in her lap. As Josh asked the question, she looked up from her reading to hear Jeff's reply.

Jeff, who had been concentrating on the computer monitor on his desk, turned to peer at Josh. "Maybe," he began, his voice dropping into the same mysterious tone he'd used when he was telling ghost stories at the picnic the previous weekend, "he's seen Mr. Barrington."

Josh groaned. "Come on, man. That's such a lie! There's no such thing as ghosts."

"Really?" Jeff drawled. "You mean you haven't heard him at all?"

Josh frowned suspiciously, remembering once again what Jeff had told him about Timmy Evans. "Heard what?"

"The elevator," Jeff intoned, making the word itself sound ominous. "Sometimes, late at night, you can hear it running, but if you go to look, it's not moving, and there's no one in it."

Amy, her eyes wide, gazed raptly at Jeff. "Then if it's not the elevator, what is it?" she asked.

Jeff's eyes shifted from Josh to Amy, and bored into her. "It's like I told you at the picnic," he whispered. "It's old Eustace Barrington, creeping around the house at night, looking for the people who killed his son. Or maybe," he added, deliberately edging his voice with menace, "he's really looking for his son!"

Josh swallowed the lump that had risen in his throat. "Wh-

What son?" he asked, his voice catching despite his efforts to control it. "You said the boy might not even have existed!"

"But he *did*," Jeff declared, returning his gaze to Josh. "He disappeared when he was five years old, and nobody ever saw him again or found his body. No one knows what happened to him. But they say he died in this house, and the old man's still here, looking for the people who killed him. And maybe that's why Adam's acting so weird. Maybe he's seen Mr. Barrington! Maybe," he added, "just maybe, Timmy Evans saw him, too!"

"Come on," Josh protested, trying to shake off the chill that had gripped him. "Don't tell Amy stories like that! You'll scare her!"

"Her?" Jeff echoed. "What about you? You look pretty scared. And maybe the story's true."

"Who's Timmy Evans?" Amy demanded, then listened, entranced, as Jeff repeated what he'd told Josh a few days earlier. "What if it's true?" Amy whispered when Jeff was finished. "Adam was acting really strange today. Could he really be afraid of a ghost?"

Jeff shrugged. "Don't ask me. Nobody ever knows what goes on with Adam. Sometimes he just gets real quiet."

"He wasn't quiet today," Josh told him. "He talked back to Mr. Conners."

Now Jeff turned to look at Josh. "Aw, come on," he said. "Adam? He wouldn't talk back to anyone."

"Well, he did this morning," Josh shot back. He told Jeff what had happened in the English class that morning. "What's he doing with Dr. Engersol?" he asked when he was finished.

When Jeff hesitated, Amy glared at him. "What is it? Some kind of big secret?" she demanded.

"It's a special seminar," Jeff replied. "It's about artificial intelligence."

"There isn't any such thing as artificial intelligence," Amy announced with the absolute certainty of her ten years. "There can't ever be, until someone figures out how people think. And so far, nobody has."

"Yeah?" Jeff teased. "What makes you so sure?"

"I read about it," Amy replied. "In *Scientific American*. It was all about what they're trying to do at Stanford and M.I.T. and all those places. So far, they can't even make a computer think of putting on a raincoat if it's raining outside."

Josh giggled. "So what? Computers don't go outside."

Amy rolled her eyes. "I mean if they did. Besides, it wasn't like it was anything real. It's just one of the things they were trying to do to get the computer to think. And it couldn't."

"But it's what we're working on," Jeff retorted. "Dr. Engersol's trying to figure out how people think, and if he does, it's going to change everything."

Amy frowned curiously. "So what was Adam doing this morning?"

Jeff's brows lifted and his air of mystery returned. "It's a secret," he said. "Nobody in the class tells anyone what we're doing. I shouldn't have told you as much as I did."

Amy rolled over. "That is so stupid. I don't believe you. I bet if I asked Adam, he'd tell me."

Jeff's lips twisted into a knowing sneer. "Bet he wouldn't."

The three kids immediately trooped over to the room next door, where Adam was sitting at his computer, the helmet of his virtual reality setup on his head, the glove on his right hand.

Jeff, signaling Josh and Amy not to say anything, moved to the computer and glanced at the screen. Then he picked up the microphone that sat on his brother's desk, pressed the button on its side and whispered into it.

"I'm here, Adam. I'm here, and I'm watching you."

Adam froze, then jerked off the helmet, glaring at his brother. "What the hell do you want?" he demanded.

"Hey," Jeff told him. "Chill out, huh? We just wanted to talk to you for a minute."

Adam noticed Josh and Amy standing uncertainly near the door. "I'm busy," he said. "Couldn't you see my door was closed?"

"We just wanted to ask you what your class with Dr. Engersol is about," Josh told him, already edging toward the door. "What's wrong with you, anyway? How come you're acting so weird?"

A guarded look crossed Adam's face, then disappeared as

quickly as it had come. "I—I'm okay," he stammered. "I'm just busy with something, all right?"

"But what?" Amy asked. "What's that helmet thing?"

Adam licked his lips nervously, his eyes flicking toward his brother. "It's something Dr. Engersol gave me," he said.

"Why don't you tell her?" Josh asked. "You showed it to me the other day." He turned to Amy. "It's called a virtual reality helmet. When you put it on, it shows you things on a screen, but it looks just like you're really seeing them."

"Really?" Amy asked. "Can I try it?"

"No!" Adam shouted.

Amy, smarting from the rebuff, glared at him. "Well, who wants to see your stupid helmet? I'm leaving!"

Turning on her heel, she stamped out of the room, while Josh eyed Adam curiously. He'd never acted like this before. Until today, he'd always been quiet, letting Jeff speak for him most of the time, and he'd always been nice. "You didn't have to be mean to her," he began, but Adam cut him off.

"And I didn't invite her in here, either, did I? Or you. So why don't you just go with your girlfriend and leave me alone?"

Josh felt himself turning red. "All right, I will," he said, wheeling and stomping out of the room, slamming the door behind him.

When Josh was gone, Jeff gazed steadily at his brother. "Is it going to be tonight?" he asked.

Adam shrugged uncertainly. "I don't know. It might be. I haven't decided yet."

Jeff's eyes hardened. "Well, when *are* you going to decide?"

Adam dropped down in the chair in front of his desk, avoiding his brother's gaze. "I don't know," he said. "I—I don't even know if I want to go yet."

Standing behind his brother, Jeff frowned. Adam wasn't going to chicken out, was he? He couldn't! Not now, not after everything they'd planned. "Come on," he said. "I thought we'd already decided. You hate it here. You hate it everywhere. So what's the big deal? If you want to get out, you get out. Isn't that what we decided?"

Adam shrugged, but then went to the window. "What—What if I changed my mind? I mean, afterward?"

Jeff chuckled hollowly. "It'd be sort of too late, wouldn't it? I mean, you'd already be gone."

"I know," Adam agreed, his voice barely audible. "That's what I keep thinking about."

He turned around to see his brother regarding him angrily.

"You *are* chickening out, aren't you?" Jeff accused.

"I didn't say that," Adam argued, his voice taking on a plaintive note.

"Yeah, but it's what you meant. Jeez, Adam, you really are a wimp, aren't you? All you ever do is whine about everything, but when you have a chance to do something, you chicken out. Well, if you don't go tonight, you might as well forget it. I'll tell Mom and Dad about what you're planning, and they'll stop you. This time, they'll probably send you to Atascadero, or something."

Adam's eyes widened with fear at the thought of being locked up in the state mental hospital. "You wouldn't do that, would you?"

"I might. Anyway, even if they don't lock you up, I bet they'll take you out of school and keep you at home. Then you'll never have another chance to do it, will you?"

Adam swallowed. "I—"

Jeff could feel his brother wavering. "Come on, Adam. Tonight. You've got to do it tonight."

Adam's temper, usually held perfectly in check, suddenly flared. "If you're so hot for it to happen, why don't you do it yourself?" he demanded.

Jeff said nothing, his mind racing. They'd already talked it out, spent hours arguing about it. And Adam had agreed that he was the one who should go. Now he was trying to back out, losing his nerve at the last minute.

Well, it wasn't going to happen. It had all been planned, all been decided, and this time Adam wasn't going to chicken out at the last minute. "You're going to do it," Jeff finally said, his voice dropping to a furious whisper that sent a chill through Adam. "If you don't do it, I'll kill you myself, Adam. I'll figure out a way so no one will know it was me. And I'll make sure it hurts. Is that what you want me to do? Do you want me to hurt you?"

Adam shrank back in his chair. "No," he breathed. "And I'm not saying I'm not going to do it. I just—"

Jeff didn't let him finish. Instead, he kept talking to his brother, browbeating him, convincing him, putting his own thoughts into Adam's mind, just as he had since they were old enough to talk.

At last, as always, Adam nodded.

"Okay," he said, his face pale. "I'll do it tonight. So just leave me alone, and let me get ready, all right?"

"You swear you're going to do it?" Jeff demanded.

Adam held up both his hands, intertwining his fingers with his brother's, in the way they had ever since they were little more than toddlers. It was a gesture that meant one of them had made an unbreakable promise to the other. "Swear," he said.

Jeff finally smiled, but there was no kindness in it. "Okay." He started out of the room, then paused at the door.

He looked back at his brother, his eyes devoid of emotion. "Afterward, I'm going to take your leather jacket. Okay?"

Adam shrugged. "If I don't wear it when I go," he said. "Anyway, tomorrow you can take anything you want. It'll probably be here."

Jeff paused for another moment, then spoke once more. "Just make sure you leave it. See ya." Then he was gone, and Adam was alone in his room.

"Yeah," Adam replied. "See ya."

But he wondered: Would he really ever see his brother again?

Probably not.

But what did it matter?

What, really, did anything matter?

After all, he couldn't ever remember having been really happy, not on a single day of his life. For every day of his life, Jeff had always been there, thinking for him, making up his mind for him, telling him what to do.

And he had always given in.

So wherever he was going tonight, it couldn't be any worse than it was here.

After all, wherever he was going, Jeff wouldn't be there. At least not for a while.

Picking up his virtual reality helmet, he placed it on his head once more.

A second later he was lost in the world conjured up by the computer, a world that was nothing more, or less, than a projection of what it would be like to be inside the computer itself, to be an electron whizzing through the minute circuitry, exploring the endlessly complex world contained on the surface of the microchip.

That's what I should have been, Adam told himself.

I never should have been born at all.

I should have been something else, something that doesn't feel any pain.

Tonight, he reflected with a cold shiver of anticipation, he would run away from the pain. And never come back.

Adam Aldrich waited until thirty minutes after the Academy's ten-thirty lights-out before he rose from his bed and, without turning on the light, quickly pulled on his clothes, choosing a pair of jeans that were all but worn-out, and a bright red shirt that he'd never liked. Unlike Jeff, Adam had never much cared about clothes. Clothing was just stuff, and *stuff* had never mattered to him at all. The only thing that really mattered to Adam was the world inside his own brain, and, once he'd discovered it, the world inside his computer. And the only person who mattered at all to Adam was Jeff.

Jeff.

The one person who knew him almost better than he knew himself.

The person who could talk him into absolutely anything.

The person with whom he had been closest all his life.

And who, tonight, was sending him away.

But maybe, somehow, they'd be together again. At least they would be if it was anything like Adam thought it was going to be.

It.

That was how he always thought about what he'd decided to do.

Even tonight, when the time had finally come, he still put no other name to it.

Dressed, he moved to his computer and turned on the screen. It glowed softly in the dark, and Adam sat down at the keyboard. When the menu came into focus, a menu Adam had designed himself, he stared at it for a few seconds, then chose one of his utilities programs from the list.

Slowly, almost regretfully, he began deleting all the files from the eighty-megabyte hard drive in the computer. Finishing the task, deleting the directories and subdirectories one by one, he stared silently at the new directory tree, which now showed nothing more than the utility program he was using.

He could still change his mind. After all, the files weren't really gone yet—all he'd done was erase the first letter of the file names. The data itself was still there on the hard drive. If he wanted to, he could recover it all in just a few more minutes.

He hesitated, then made up his mind.

His fingers working quickly, he typed in the commands that would begin washing the disk, going through the whole drive, recording a series of randomly selected digits over all the existing data.

The computer would go through the process three times. When it was done, nothing at all would remain except the single utility program.

It would be gone, all of it. All the programs he'd learned to use in the five years since he'd gotten his first computer, all the data he'd compiled, all the games he'd not only loved, but reconstructed to suit himself, reworking the codes so that no one but he could play them.

In a way, it was as if he was wiping his life out, obliterating it, so that no one would be able to search for clues as to why he'd done what he'd decided to do.

After all, it wasn't anybody else's business—it was his life, and he could do anything he wanted to with it.

The computer beeped softly, indicating that its task was completed.

Adam dropped the utility program out of memory, and when the "C:" prompt appeared, typed a single line:

C: ERASE*.*

He pressed the enter button, and a question appeared:

ARE YOU SURE? ALL FILES WILL BE ERASED. N (Y)

For a fleeting moment he was once again tempted to change his mind. Then, taking a deep breath, he hit the Y key. When the final question reappeared, giving him one last chance to reverse his course, he pressed it again.

A second flicked by, and then the "C:" prompt reappeared. Though the computer was still functioning, there was nothing it could do, for Adam had stripped away everything that made it useful. Now it was nothing more than a blank memory, waiting for data to fill it up.

Adam typed for a few seconds, then turned off the monitor, plunging the room again into total darkness. Moving silently to the door, he opened it a crack and peered out into the dimly lit hallway that ran the length of the second floor.

The hall was empty, and he could hear nothing.

He stepped into the corridor, pulling the door closed behind him, its soft click resounding in his ears with an unnatural loudness. He froze, half expecting the doors along the hall to open as the other kids peered accusingly out at him.

Nothing happened.

The silence of the building closed around him like a shroud.

He crept to Jeff's door, pausing for a moment. Should he go in and say good-bye to his brother?

No.

Better just to disappear into the darkness of the night.

Moving silently down the hall, he came to the top of the broad staircase that curved down to the floor below and listened once more.

Silence.

The chandelier hanging in the entry hall had been dimmed for the night, casting only a soft glow through the spacious room. For a moment Adam gazed at the crack under Hildie Kramer's office door.

Was there a light on inside?

He wasn't sure.

He crept down the stairs, clinging to the wall as if its mass could somehow shelter him from any eyes that might be watching, waiting for him.

At last he came to the front door. He twisted the knob slowly, as if even the faint sound of its sliding bolt might betray him. Pulling the door only wide enough to slip through the narrow opening, he moved out onto the porch, waiting in the deep shadows of the loggia until he was certain no one was on the grounds in front of the house. Then, at last, he made his move, darting across the lawn, scuttling from tree to tree like a small animal exposed to predators. Only when he was through the gate did he allow himself to breathe easily.

When his pulse, racing from the tension of his clandestine departure from the Academy, finally settled into a normal rhythm, he moved off into the night. Though the air was unseasonably warm, even for mid-September, he felt a chill run through him.

But his mind was made up.

Twenty minutes later he stood in front of the house he'd grown up in, the old shingled two-story house his parents had bought when he was only two years old. Three blocks from the beach, it was surrounded by a neat lawn that was his father's pride, with enormous camellia bushes growing on either side of the front porch. Adam's eyes drifted over the house, pausing briefly at the second floor, on the room that had once been his. A lot of his stuff, he knew, was still in that room, waiting for him when he came home.

Now it would wait forever. He would never come back to this house again.

Another tiny doubt assailed his mind. For just a second he had an urge to go into the house and wake up his mother. Maybe he should talk to her about what he was going to do—

No!

Joff's threats rang in his mind, and Adam knew what she'd do.
Call the doctor and have him taken away.

Away, where he'd never be able to do what he wanted again.

He turned away from the house and moved on to the town's
small business area, pausing in front of the stores to look at the
displays in their windows. There was nothing in any of them he
wanted, nothing he would miss.

He walked on, glancing warily around every few seconds, ducking into deep shadows whenever a car approached. He couldn't get
caught now, not when he was so close.

He started back toward the Academy, moving quickly now, feeling every minute passing. He came to the gate, edging through it,
then skirting around the lawn, staying near the fence. Finally he
moved toward the mansion itself.

He gazed at the darkened windows of the enormous house, and
then his eyes moved up to the fourth floor, to the odd cupola
perched atop the structure almost like a bird hunching above its
prey.

He could see lights glowing in Dr. Engersol's windows.

He stared at those lights, shining brilliantly while the rest of the
Academy slept.

The rest of it, except for him.

Ducking his head and hunching his shoulders, he shoved his
hands into his pockets.

It was time to get on with it.

———

The train moved fast down the track, for it was barely a train at
all. Nothing more than an engine, a couple of empty cars, and a
caboose. There would be no stops on the trip—there never were—
for this was no more than one of the weekly runs the train made
up the spur from Salinas, moving through Santa Cruz, then running up to the end of the track. It was a pointless run, except for
one thing.

It kept the right of way open, protected the Barrington Western Railroad's right to use it.

It was a boring run, the only interesting part of it being the northern leg, when the train ran steadily backward, creeping slowly along while a member of the crew stood in the caboose, watching the track and giving an unbroken stream of all-clear signals to the engineer. But once it reached the dead end forty miles north of Barrington and started back, the crew was tired, more inclined to watch the moonlight playing on the sea than the track ahead.

After all, in the twenty-five years the engineer had been making the run, there had never been an event worth reporting to his supervisor. So tonight, as the train hit sixty along the straightaway north of Barrington, and the engineer prepared to begin his slow deceleration to the fifteen mile speed limit through the town itself, he wasn't really paying too much attention to the track ahead.

Not that it would have made any difference, for by the time he saw the object on the track as he came around a curve, it was far too late to stop the train anyway.

Still, he slammed on the brakes and shouted to the fireman. "Jesus Christ! Looks like some idiot dumped a bag of garbage on the track!"

The train began to slow, the brakes screaming as the engineer pulled hard on the lever.

Then, as the brilliance of the headlight caught the object in the full glare of its beam, he realized that the object wasn't a bag of garbage at all.

It was a person, crouched down between the tracks, hunched over, his back to the train.

The engineer hit the horn, and a blast of noise tore the night, rousing a flock of sparrows from their roosts in the trees along the track. They burst into flight, disappearing instantly into the night.

The person on the railroad tracks didn't move.

The engineer felt a sheen of sweat break out over his whole body as he realized what was about to happen, and that there was no way on earth he could avoid it. The inertia of the big diesel engine was enough that even if he managed to lock the brakes completely, the machine would lunge on, steel skidding against steel, sparks flying.

But it would not be enough.

The train bore down on the object, losing speed with every second. For just a split second the engineer prayed for a miracle.

It didn't come.

The engine struck the person on the tracks, and as the body flew into the air, the engineer realized it was a boy.

A young boy, dressed only in worn jeans and a red shirt.

Oddly, he found himself wondering if the boy had worn the red shirt on purpose, so the blood wouldn't show as much when the train struck him.

Not that it mattered, the engineer reflected as the train finally ground to a stop two hundred yards farther on. Red shirt or not, the force of the blow when the train hit him would have turned the boy into little more than an unrecognizable mass of torn flesh and broken bones.

Instinctively, the engineer looked at his watch. It was almost half past four in the morning.

A miserable time to die.

Though the room was dark, so dark he couldn't see anything at all, Jeff Aldrich knew he wasn't alone. And the room was big, too. So big he couldn't sense either the walls or the ceiling, though he was certain they were there.

He could, however, sense the other person in the room with him.

Adam.

It was Adam who was there, lost in the dark somewhere, looking for him.

Jeff called out to his brother, but there was no answer.

He took a tentative step forward, feeling his way in the dark, but touched nothing, felt nothing.

He called out again. "Adam? Hey, Adam, where are you?"

Though he'd shouted at the top of his lungs, his voice seemed tiny, constricting in his throat, the words barely audible, even to himself.

Now the fear began to close around him, reaching out of the darkness, touching him, its slender tentacles wrapping around him, seeming to draw him into the darkness itself.

"No," he moaned. "I'll find him. I've got to find him."

He struggled against the fear, tried to run away from it, but now his feet seemed mired, as if he were caught in a thick, wet mud, or quicksand.

He struggled harder, screaming out again. "Adam? Adam, I didn't mean it. I'm sorry, Adam!"

He began pulling himself free from the mud, and then he was running, running through the darkness as fast as he could. And around him the darkness changed.

He wasn't in the room anymore. He was outside now, and though everything looked the same as it had before, it was still different.

And he was getting closer to Adam—he could feel it!

Finally, ahead, he saw a point of light.

The last of the fear drained out of him as he ran toward the light, his heart pounding, his legs aching from the effort. But he couldn't slow down, for the light was Adam. If he could get to it—

It began to take shape then. No longer a point, it was a beam now, and it was shining down from overhead, though when he looked up, he couldn't see the light's source.

But in the beam, seeming almost to be suspended in midair, he could finally see Adam.

Adam was looking at him, his eyes accusing him.

Jeff stopped. "Adam?" He uttered the word uncertainly, for there was something different about his brother, something he didn't understand.

He reached out, thrusting his hand into the beam of light, trying to touch his brother. But as his hand entered the beam, it disappeared, and Adam, still staring at him, began to laugh.

"You thought I wouldn't do it, didn't you?" Adam asked. "You thought I'd chicken out. You *always* thought I'd chicken out."

Jeff felt a terrible wave of remorse wash over him. "N-No," he stammered. "I didn't think that. I—"

But it was too late. Even as he spoke, the beam of light began to fade away and his brother's image began to shimmer, then slowly disappear. As the last of the light died away, Jeff screamed out his brother's name once more.

"Adam!"

In his room on the third floor Josh MacCallum lay wide awake. He'd been lying there for what seemed like an eternity, listening in the darkness.

Sometime earlier—he didn't know how much earlier—he'd awakened, hearing a sound.

It hadn't taken him more than a moment to realize what it was.

The elevator, its gears grinding, its cage rattling in its frame.

Instantly, Jeff Aldrich's tale of the ghost of Eustace Barrington had popped back into his mind, and his first instinct had been to hide his head under the covers and try to blot the sound out of his ears. But then he'd realized what was happening.

It was Jeff himself, riding the elevator in the darkened house, and no doubt laughing silently at the scare he was giving him.

So Josh had gotten up, pulled on his bathrobe, then gone out into the hall, creeping down the dark corridor until he came to the elevator shaft.

He could still hear the sound of the machinery.

But the elevator wasn't moving. In fact, when he peered down the shaft, he could just make out the top of the cage barely illuminated by the chandelier in the foyer.

The sound had suddenly stopped. Josh had held his breath, afraid even to move.

Nothing had happened.

He'd waited for several seemingly endless minutes, half expecting the ghost of Eustace Barrington to appear on the stairs, floating toward him in the darkness. But at last, when nothing more occurred, he went back to bed.

And lay awake, listening.

Once more he heard the sound of the elevator, and once more he went to look.

The cage remained at the bottom of the shaft, exactly where it had been earlier.

Now, though, there was a new noise. Josh jerked upright, bolting into a sitting position. What had it been?

Then, coming in through his open window, he heard an anguished voice calling out.

"Adam, come back!"

Jeff! It was Jeff's voice.

Jumping out of bed, clad in his pajamas, Josh ran out of his room and raced down the hall to the stairs. Taking them three at a time, he arrived at the second floor in time to see sleepy faces peering out at him.

"What's wrong?" someone asked. "What's going on?"

Josh didn't reply. He continued racing down the hall to Jeff's room, where he pushed the door open and flipped on the light in one motion. And then he stopped, staring.

Sitting up in bed, his face pale, his whole body trembling, was Jeff.

Except for the curtains fluttering gently at the open window, the room was still and quiet.

"Jeff?" Josh breathed. "What's wrong? You okay?"

Jeff Aldrich said nothing for a second, then managed to nod. "I—I had a nightmare. It was about Adam. He—He was gone. It was like he was dead or something, and it was my fault."

"Jeez," Josh breathed.

Jeff shuddered. "It was so real." He was awake now, his whole body covered with an icy sweat, the terrible feeling that had come over him as he'd called out to his brother one last time still gripping him.

"What's going on?" Brad Hinshaw asked, coming into the room. Then he saw Jeff. "Jeez, man, you look like you saw a ghost or something."

"H—He did," Josh stammered. "He dreamed that Adam was dead, and that it was his fault."

"Shit," Brad breathed. But before he could say anything else, someone else came into the room.

"Is Adam in here?"

A deathly silence fell over the room as the three boys stared at one another. Then Jeff got slowly out of bed and made his way toward the door, Josh and Brad instinctively backing away to let him pass. He walked to the room next to his own, hesitated a moment, then went inside.

The bed was empty, though it looked as if it had been slept in.

All Adam's things were in their usual places.

"M—Maybe he just went to the can," Brad Hinshaw suggested, but then a new voice spoke.

"I just looked. It's empty."

Jeff stared at the empty bed for another moment, and then his eyes shifted to the computer on Adam's desk. Moving slowly, almost as if he were being drawn to it against his will, Jeff approached the desk and pressed the power button on the bottom of the monitor. A green light flashed on, and then the monitor began to glow. A second or two after that, the last words that Adam had typed appeared next to the prompt. Jeff, along with Josh and Brad, stared silently at the words:

C: NO ONE UNDERSTANDS ME, SO IT IS TIME
THAT I MOVE ON. I AM GOING TO
A BETTER, HIGHER PLACE.

Josh, gazing at the message, felt his stomach tighten as he realized what it meant. In his mind he was suddenly back at the beginning of last week, when he'd sat on the bed in his own room back home in Eden, the hunting knife in his hands.

Unconsciously, the fingers of his left hand touched the scabs on his right wrist, all that was left to remind him of what he'd done.

Suddenly he understood why Adam had been acting weird the last few days. Josh knew he'd thought about dying for only a few minutes when he was angry. Unlike him, Adam must have been thinking about it for days.

Thinking about it, and making up his mind.

But what had he done? Where was he?

"Wh—Whatcha going to do?" he asked, his voice barely audible.

But Jeff merely turned and walked away.

Just as Jeff Aldrich emerged from his brother's room, Hildie Kramer appeared at the top of the stairs.

She seemed puzzled when she saw him, but spoke to him in a soft, steady voice. "Jeff? Could you come downstairs with me, please? There's something I have to talk to you about."

A minute later, sitting in his pajamas on the sofa next to Hildie, Jeff listened in silence as she told him that Adam's body had just been found.

"It was on the railroad tracks," she said. "I—I suppose it might have been an accident . . ." Her voice trailed off, and she slipped an arm around Jeff.

The boy stiffened in her embrace.

"No," he said. "It wasn't an accident. He left a note on his computer."

For a long moment Hildie said nothing. Then, after discharging a deep breath from her lungs, she said, "I think I'd better get you to your parents."

Jeff said nothing, letting her lead him back to his room so he could dress. But even as he began pulling his clothes on, the dream kept coming back to him.

So what Adam had said in the dream was right: he hadn't chickened out at all.

Oddly, Jeff Aldrich felt proud of his brother.

And even as he felt that wave of pride, he knew it was something he would never tell anyone about.

Not ever.

10

Chet Aldrich awakened slowly, his eyes automatically seeking out the blue digits of the clock radio on his nightstand: 5:47. The alarm wasn't due to go off until six-thirty.

Chet scowled in annoyance. He never wakened so long before the alarm went off; indeed, he invariably woke up a minute before the alarm sounded, squelching it before its irritating beep even had a chance to begin.

But something had disturbed his sleep. He glanced out the window to see the sky, already brightening. Thunder? He dismissed that idea from his mind when he noticed the moon still hanging above the horizon. Then, as he was about to roll over and bury his head in the pillows once more, he heard the ringing of the doorbell, the sound muffled through the closed bedroom door.

Instantly, the last vestiges of sleep left him. He slid out of bed, reaching for the robe he always left draped over the back of the chair in the corner. Pulling it on, he glanced at Jeanette, who was still sound asleep, lying on her left side, her hair spread out on the pillow around her head.

As the doorbell sounded again, Chet hurried downstairs, a growing sense of foreboding looming within him. Someone at the door this early could only mean bad news.

Very bad, his mind corrected, fully awake now. As he reached for the doorknob, and the bell rang yet again, an idea of what must have happened took shape in his head. His heart had begun to race even before he opened the door and saw Jeff, pale and wide-eyed, trembling on the front porch. Behind him stood Hildie Kramer, flanked by two police officers.

For a moment he had a fleeting feeling of hope—he'd been wrong, and all that had happened was that Jeff had sneaked out in the middle of the night and gotten himself into some kind of trouble. But even as the idea formed, he dismissed it, for he could read Hildie Kramer's eyes clearly. They weren't reflecting anger, or even disappointment.

What he saw in them was grief.

Grief, and sympathy.

"What is it?" he asked, opening the door wide so the four people on the porch could come inside the house. When no one said anything, as if each of them was waiting for someone else to pronounce the news they had come to tell him, he knew.

"It's Adam, isn't it?" he breathed. "Something's happened to him."

It was Hildie Kramer who finally broke the silence of the group. Stepping forward, she gripped his arm, almost as if to steady him. "I'm sorry, Chet," she told him. "He's—I'm afraid he's dead."

"Dear God," Chet muttered, the words catching in his throat as he felt himself begin to sink down onto his knees. Only Hildie's strong hold kept him upright. "No. There's a mistake. . . . There has to be—"

"I'm sorry, Mr. Aldrich," one of the policemen said. "It happened about an hour ago, maybe a little more. He was on the tracks when—"

His words were cut off by Jeanette, who was now standing at the top of the stairs, her robe clutched protectively around her body, her face still puffy with sleep.

"Tracks?" she asked. "What are you talking about?"

Chet, struggling once more to remain on his feet, gazed bleakly up at his wife. "It's Adam," he told her. "He's—Hildie says he's dead."

Hildie says . . .

As if to leave open the possibility that Hildie was wrong, that it was all some kind of terrible mistake, that Adam was still alive somewhere. And yet the words had their effect, whether Chet had intended it or not, for Jeanette's eyes, wide and disbelieving, shifted immediately to the housemother and chief administrator of the Academy.

"Adam?" Jeanette breathed. "But that's not possible. You said he was doing fine." Her voice rose as she rejected the idea of her son's death. "He *was* doing fine! Last weekend, at the picnic—"

Hildie moved up the stairs, brushing past Chet, who was still frozen in place, as if the news had drained the strength from his muscles. "We don't know exactly what happened, Jeanette," she said, casting about in her mind for some possible straw for the shocked woman to grasp at. "Perhaps it was some kind of an accident—"

"Accident?" Jeanette echoed. "Wh-What happened?"

Half supported by Hildie Kramer, Jeanette came slowly down the stairs as one of the policemen recounted the engineer's story.

"He said there was nothing he could do," the cop finished. "He hit the brakes and the horn as soon as he saw your son, but it was too late. The boy didn't move at all, and the train was going too fast to stop."

"D-Didn't move?" Jeanette repeated. "H-He just sat there?"

"I'm sorry," the policeman said. "The engineer said it was as if he was just waiting for the train to hit him."

Jeanette slumped against her husband. As Chet's arms went around her, she began sobbing softly. It was impossible—the whole thing. She wouldn't—couldn't—accept it. That was why they'd sent Adam to the Academy, just to prevent something like this. "No," she whispered. "I don't believe it. It's not Adam. It—It's someone else. It has to be."

"I'm so sorry, Jeanette," Hildie Kramer told the distraught woman. "I wish it *were* somebody else. But there isn't any mistake."

Jeanette only shook her head, her body suddenly filling with an unnatural strength. "I want to see him," she said. "I want to see him for myself."

Jeff had been standing silently just inside the door, his face pale as he listened to his parents being informed of his brother's death. Now he darted across to his mother and pressed himself wordlessly against her. Almost unconsciously, Jeanette's hand smoothed her remaining son's hair, but her eyes remained fixed on the policeman who had just told her what had happened. "I want to see where it happened," she said almost tonelessly. "And I want to see my son. I think I have the right, don't I?"

The young officer shifted uneasily. "It's not really necessary, ma'am," he replied. "I mean, there isn't any doubt about what happened—"

"No!" Jeanette said sharply. "*I* have doubts. I want to *see* him! Can't you understand? He's my son, and I want to see him!"

As her voice rose again, taking on a note of hysteria, Jeff pressed closer to her, and Hildie Kramer exchanged a glance with the policeman. "I can stay here with Jeff," she said. "Can you take Mr. and Mrs. Aldrich?"

Now Chet spoke, his voice strangling on his words. "Jeanette, we don't have to do this. We—"

But Jeanette only shook her head once more. "No, Chet. *I* have to do it. I won't believe it unless I see it for myself." Gently, she disentangled herself from Jeff's arms.

"Can I go, too?" the boy asked.

Though Jeanette seemed not to hear the question, Chet shook his head. "You don't want to, son," he said, his voice breaking. "Just stay here with Hildie, and we'll be back as soon as we can. All right?"

"But I want to go," Jeff protested, his face setting stubbornly. "I want to see what happened, too." Though he'd said nothing about his dream either to Hildie Kramer or anyone except Josh Mac-Callum and Brad Hinshaw, it was still fresh in his mind.

And in his dream—

No! What had happened in his dream wasn't real. The only thing real was that Adam was dead. But he couldn't be dead! He couldn't be! He'd said he was going away—

"Come on, Jeff," Hildie said quietly, gently steering the boy toward the kitchen at the back of the house. "Let's leave your parents alone for a little while, all right?"

Jeff, still trying to piece it all together in his mind, to reconcile the dream of his brother's death with the reality of it, allowed himself to be guided down the hall as Jeanette and Chet, escorted by the two policemen, left the house.

═══

The police car pulled over to the side of the road. They were some four miles north of Barrington. A hundred yards ahead the road, and the railroad track next to it, curved away out of sight, following the contour of the coast. Beyond the track a concrete retaining wall held the cutaway hillside in place, and as Jeanette emerged from the car into the steadily brightening morning sunlight, she felt a chill as she saw the blood that was smeared along the retaining wall.

People swarmed over the site, taking pictures, making sketches, and taking various measurements that would eventually determine the precise speed at which the engine had been traveling when it struck Adam Aldrich. Two members of the train's crew hovered nervously near the caboose, but the engineer himself was nowhere in sight.

"They took him down to the station to check his blood for alcohol or drugs," one of the detectives told Chet when he asked where the engineer was. "Not that we expect to find anything," he went on. "The rest of the crew says Lawrence—that's the engineer, Gary Lawrence—is a real teetotaler. His wife was an alkie, and he won't touch the stuff. No one's ever seen him with anything stronger than coffee."

While Jeanette gazed silently at the spot where the train had struck her son, Chet's eyes reluctantly searched for any sign of the body's presence. The detective, sensing what Chet was looking for, lowered his voice so Jeanette wouldn't hear his words. "They've already taken your boy away, Mr. Aldrich. It's—Well, it's pretty messy, and I'm not sure you'll want to see him."

Chet nodded, feeling a sense of relief that for the moment, at least, both he and Jeanette would be spared the stark reality of what had happened to their son.

"Where did they take him?" Jeanette asked, emerging from her reverie. "Where is he?"

In unconscious imitation of the cop whose job it had been to inform the Aldriches of the death of their child, the detective shifted uneasily. "They'll have taken him to the hospital in Santa Cruz," he said. "Once he's been pronounced, they'll keep him until you give them instructions."

"I want to go to the hospital," Jeanette announced. "Now, please."

Chet felt his stomach tighten as he helped his wife back into the car. She insisted on being taken to see her child and would not be dissuaded.

Straws, Chet thought. She's grasping at straws. But he knew that for now there was nothing he could say to her, that all he could do was stay with her, offering her whatever support she needed while she came to grips in her own way with what had happened.

And yet, he reflected, what about him? To whom was he supposed to turn? The knot of grief that had begun forming inside him from the second he'd opened the door and seen the look on Hildie Kramer's face now threatened to strangle him. How long had it been? Half an hour? He glanced at his watch, wondering if it was possible that only thirty minutes had passed since he'd heard of his son's death.

And in those thirty minutes, he'd felt himself turning numb, dealing with the cold reality of Adam's death by turning cold himself, going through the motions of dealing with the situation even while he, in his own way, rejected the reality of it no less than Jeanette.

Was it really possible that Adam was dead? That he was never going to see his son's face, so different from Jeff's, yet so much the same, again?

An image of Adam came into his mind, a quiet image, of Adam as he so often was, alone, exploring some world within his own mind that was totally unknown to anyone else, even his twin brother. For it had always been Jeff who was the extroverted one, Jeff who made friends with other kids, and dragged Adam, often protesting, into his games.

Was what had happened this morning Adam's final protest, his final rejection of a world he'd never really been a part of? Or had it been just a momentary whim that he would have gotten over, given enough time?

Chet realized that he would now never know. Adam was, irretrievably, gone.

They arrived finally at the hospital's emergency entrance. Together, the Aldriches went inside, where they were met by a pale, lanky man in a rumpled white coat, a resident whose young face reflected the ravages of the long hours he'd put in during the night. He came toward them almost reluctantly, and Chet caught himself abstractly wondering if this was the first time this doctor had ever had to deal with parents who had just lost a child.

"Mr. Aldrich? Mrs. Aldrich?" he heard the doctor saying. "I'm Joel Berman. I was on duty when they brought your son in." He gestured toward a sofa and two chairs arranged around a messy coffee table in the reception area. "If you'd like to sit down . . . ?"

Jeanette shook her head. "I want to see Adam," she said, but her nerves were beginning to betray her, and her voice was unsteady as she uttered the words. "Please, I have to see my son."

Joel Berman's face tightened. "I—Mrs. Aldrich, I'm not sure you want to see him."

"I do," Jeanette said simply. "I have to."

Berman seemed about to object further, then apparently changed his mind. "This way," he said softly. He led them down a short corridor and then into an examining room. On a gurney, covered by a sheet, was the form of a body. Jeanette paused at the door, but then steeled herself. Moving across to the gurney, she hesitantly touched the cover, then gently pulled it back.

She stared into Adam's face.

Smeared with blood, and battered by the impact of the locomotive, it was barely recognizable, and yet she knew instantly that it was her son. At last the wall she'd built inside her broke and she began sobbing. "Oh, Adam," she whispered, the words choking in her constricted throat. "I'm so sorry, baby. I'm so sorry. Why didn't you just come home? I would have made it right, honey. I would have taken care of you." Her tears flowing freely, she bent down and, oblivious of the blood that still stained her son's cheeks, gently kissed him.

Only then did she allow the doctor to cover her son's face once again, and her husband to lead her out of the room.

A few minutes later, her hands trembling, she tried to force herself to drink a cup of scalding hot coffee while the doctor did his best to reassure her that Adam hadn't suffered.

"He would have died instantly. Apparently he was sitting in the middle of the tracks, his back to the train. The first contact would have killed him. I'm sure he felt nothing at all."

But the terror, Jeanette found herself thinking. How he must have felt, hearing the train thundering toward him. In her mind she heard the blast of the horn, the roar of the locomotive; she even imagined she could feel the tracks vibrating as the train rushed toward her son. She shuddered, and the coffee slopped over, staining the white terry-cloth robe she was still wearing.

Through it all, she'd never once, until that very instant, realized she'd left the house without dressing. Shakily, she put the coffee cup down. "Take me home, Chet."

As her husband led her out of the emergency room and back to the waiting police car, grief at last began closing in on Jeanette Aldrich.

———

At a little after seven o'clock that morning, Steve Conners arrived at the Academy, and knew at once that something was wrong. Two police cars were pulled up in the driveway in front of the main building, and he could see Dr. Engersol's dark blue Oldsmobile as well. Ignoring his usual morning routine of going first to his classroom in the west wing building, he parked next to one of the black-and-whites and mounted the steps to the broad loggia. As he let himself in through the front door, the first person he saw was Hildie Kramer, talking to one of the policemen. Near the foot of the stairs a knot of children whispered among themselves, their eyes wide as they watched the policeman talking to their housemother.

"What's going on?" Steve asked as he joined Hildie.

Hildie's eyes shot briefly toward the group of children by the stairs, but then she decided there was no point in retreating to her office. Certainly, there wasn't a child in the house who didn't already know what had happened. "It's Adam Aldrich," she said. "I'm afraid he killed himself last night."

"Oh, Jesus," Steve groaned. Suddenly he remembered the things he hadn't done yesterday.

He hadn't mentioned either to Hildie or to George Engersol his concerns about the boy. He'd intended to, but then something had come up—he couldn't even remember what it had been right now—and the whole thing had slipped his mind.

Slipped his mind! And now Adam Aldrich was dead.

His horror at the thought must have showed clearly on his face, for Hildie was staring curiously at him. "Steve, what is it?"

Steve shook his head as if to push back the tide of guilt that was washing over him, but the gesture did no good. "I should have done something," he said. "I knew something was wrong. I was going to talk to you about him. And George, too."

Now the policeman's eyes were fixed on him. "You know something about the boy?"

Steve nodded unhappily. "He's in my English class." Briefly, he filled in the policeman—and Hildie Kramer, too—on what had happened in his class the previous morning. "I knew he was upset about something, and I was going to talk to you about it, but it just went out of my mind. And now—"

"And now you feel as though you could have prevented it," Hildie finished for him. Her attention shifted momentarily back to the police officer. "If you're finished with me for now, I think I'd better have a talk with Mr. Conners."

The officer nodded, closing his notebook. "I think I've got all there is to get. It doesn't seem like anyone talked to him or heard him leave. And the note on his computer is pretty clear. If there's anything else, I'll call you."

When he was gone, Hildie took Steve Conners into her office, and gestured him into a chair. "Steve, I'm not going to pretend that your forgetting to speak to me about Adam wouldn't have made any difference. It probably would, at least in the short run. But there's something else you've got to understand, or you'll never be able to deal with this school." She paused, as if waiting for a response from the young teacher. When there was none, she went on. "This isn't the first time we've lost a student this way, and it won't be the last. In fact, it's one of the reasons we exist. Our students almost all have problems of one sort or another, and several of them have tried to kill themselves in the past. Adam was among them. And, of course, had you told me what happened yesterday, I would have talked to him, possibly even put him into counseling immediately. But I probably wouldn't have put him under a twenty-four-hour watch."

Conners frowned. "But why not? If he'd tried something like this before—"

"The last time he tried it, no one thought it was truly serious. Often—in fact most times—when children try to kill themselves, they aren't truly serious. Most children really have no concept of death, you know. They know it exists, but only in the abstract. Most children feel immortal—they have no sense that they're ever going to die. For a child, even growing up is something that's barely comprehensible. So I doubt that I would have hospitalized Adam, given all the circumstances. I would have talked to Dr. E, of course, but there's no guarantee that this wouldn't have happened anyway. And I have to tell you that there's no guarantee that it won't happen to other of our students. In fact, I can almost guarantee that it will. Sad as it is, there's no way, short of isolation of every one of them, that we can stop it entirely." She smiled wanly. "I doubt you'd be any more in favor of locking these kids up than anyone else here is."

Steve Conners listened to her words silently, knowing that no matter what she said, he would still feel the guilt for what had happened, perhaps for the rest of his life. He'd *known* the boy was in trouble, but done nothing about it.

Because it had slipped his mind.

Slipped his mind!

And now there was nothing he could do about it, nothing he could do to put the situation right, nothing he could do to bring Adam back to life.

Except see to it that from now on he kept a better eye on the kids, never again failed to act if he saw that one of them was in trouble.

But even as he made his silent oath, he knew that it still wouldn't be enough.

No matter what he might do, it wouldn't assuage the guilt he felt over the death of Adam Aldrich.

11

"Josh?"

Josh looked up from the book he was reading while he ate his breakfast. At the sight of Amy Carlson's pale face and the wild look in her eyes, he pushed the book aside.

"Have you ever been to a funeral before?" Amy asked.

Josh shook his head. "I never even knew anyone who died before."

"Are they going to make us look at Adam?" Amy's voice was anxious, and even as she uttered the words, her face turned pink.

"What's the matter?" Josh teased. "You scared to look at a corpse?"

Amy's blush deepened. "I—I don't know," she stammered. "It's just—well, I'm not sure I *want* to look at a dead person."

"Well, they probably won't. I mean, if Adam got hit by a train . . ." Josh left the words hanging, picturing in his mind an image of the train barreling down the tracks, striking Adam Aldrich, sending his body flying into the air. Had his arms and legs been severed? Maybe. Even his head could have been torn off, if the train hit him a certain way. The image made Josh shudder, and he decided not to think about it anymore.

Except that all day Saturday, and Sunday, too, all anybody was talking about was Adam, and what had happened to him.

Jeff hadn't been back to school since Hildie had taken him to his parents' house early Saturday morning, and most of the kids didn't think he'd be coming back at all.

Brad Hinshaw, however, hadn't agreed. "I talked to him a little while ago," he'd reported yesterday afternoon. "He says he's coming back, and Jeff always gets what he wants."

"I bet he doesn't," Amy Carlson had argued. "I bet his mom keeps him at home. I mean, wouldn't she be worried that he might do it, too?"

"Not Jeff," Brad had replied. "If he wants to come back, he'll come back."

Josh, though, had stopped listening, his mind lingering on the word Amy had used when she'd talked about what had happened to Adam.

It.

That seemed to be the word everyone was using, as if actually saying out loud that Adam had killed himself was wrong.

But that's what he'd done, wasn't it? Just sat down on the railroad tracks and waited for the train to hit him. Josh shuddered again, just the thought of it sending an icy chill through his body.

"I wonder how messed up he was," he mused out loud. Amy, her mouth full of oatmeal, choked, and spit her cereal into her napkin.

"That's gross, Josh!" she said when she'd recovered enough to speak.

"Well, I was just wondering," Josh replied. "What's wrong with that? Didn't Mr. Conners say it was all right to talk about it?"

Amy's eyes rolled disdainfully. "He said it was all right to talk about what Adam *did*," she told him. "But he didn't say we should talk about how—" She broke off, unable to find the words she wanted. From the next table, Brad Hinshaw, who had been listening to the conversation, smiled darkly.

"How *squashed* he was?" he asked.

Amy, looking slightly ill, glared at Brad, then shoved her chair back from the table. "You guys are so gross! I don't want to talk to you anymore." She turned and started away from the table. A second later Josh went after her.

"Don't be mad," he said, catching up to her in the foyer. "I was just thinking about what happened to him, that's all." He fell in beside her, and though Amy didn't reply to him, she didn't tell him to leave her alone, either. They went out the front door and dropped down onto the steps. Josh glanced around. Seeing no one within earshot, but still lowering his voice, he spoke again. "D-Did you hear anything Friday night?"

Amy frowned, puzzled. "Like what?"

Josh reddened, but was determined to go on, no matter how dumb Amy might think he sounded. "Th-The elevator," he said. "I heard it twice, and after that story Jeff was telling us about old Mr. Barrington, I went to look."

Amy's lips pursed. "So?" she asked, suspicious.

"So it wasn't running," Josh told her. "It was just sitting on the main floor, like it always is. But I could *hear* it!"

Amy glared at him. "Don't you try to scare me, Josh Mac-Callum!"

"I'm not," Josh protested, his voice rising in spite of himself. "I'm just telling you what happened. And what if"—he hesitated, then plunged on—"if Adam didn't kill himself at all? What—Well, what if old Mr. Barrington really got him!"

Amy's eyes widened for a second as the story took hold of her imagination, but then she shook her head violently. "That's just a story Jeff made up!" she insisted. "I bet you didn't even hear anything. Besides, everyone knows Adam killed himself!"

Josh was silent for a moment, pondering Amy's words. What if he *hadn't* really heard those noises? Was it possible? Could he have just imagined it, because Jeff had told him that story?

His mind wrestled with the problem, but then he decided there was no way he could know what had really happened that night. When he finally spoke again, his voice was low, and trembled slightly, and he made no further mention of the strange sounds he'd heard. "Could you have done that?" he asked. "Just sat there on the tracks and waited for the train to hit you?"

Amy shook her head. "I can hardly even stand to think about it."

Josh turned to look at her. "What would you do? I mean, if you were going to kill yourself."

Amy, her eyes staring off into the distance, shrugged. "I don't know. Who even thinks stuff like that?"

"You mean you never have? You never thought about killing yourself?"

Her brows knitted into a frown. "I—I don't know," she said doubtfully. "I mean, last year, when I was in regular school and didn't have any friends, I used to go to sleep sometimes hoping I just wouldn't wake up in the morning." She glanced at Josh. "Did you ever feel like that?"

Josh nodded, picking up a twig that was lying on the top step and twirling it in his fingers. "I used to wish that all the time. I always felt like maybe my mom would be better off if I hadn't been born."

"That's how I felt, too," Amy agreed. "But I don't think I ever thought about killing myself. I mean, that's kind of different from just wishing you wouldn't wake up, isn't it?"

Josh shrugged uncertainly, and the twig fell from his fingers as they went to the scars on his wrist. Amy, seeing him touch the still-fresh scars, hesitated, then asked him the question she'd been thinking about ever since Saturday afternoon, when Mr. Conners had spent an hour talking with all the kids about what had happened. When the teacher had asked if they had any questions, Amy had remained silent. Now, alone with Josh, she said, "Did it hurt? I mean, when you cut yourself?"

Josh hesitated, trying to remember. It was funny—he could remember holding the knife in his hand, and he could remember the blood spurting out after he cut his wrists, but he couldn't remember actually doing it.

Nor could he remember whether or not it hurt.

"I don't remember," he finally replied. "I mean, if it did, I'd remember it, wouldn't I?"

Now it was Amy who shrugged. "I—I wonder if Adam felt anything when the train hit him," she said pensively. "I mean, I guess being dead wouldn't be so bad if you weren't ever happy about anything. But if dying hurts—"

"I know," Josh said. "That's what I keep thinking about. And once you've done it—well, it's not like you can change your mind, is it?"

Amy shook her head. "I don't think I could do it," she decided. "I mean, no matter how bad things were, I think I'd be too scared even to try."

Their conversation was interrupted by a car turning through the gates and starting up the long drive. As he watched it approach, Josh suddenly recognized it.

It was his mother. What was she doing here?

And then his heart sank. She'd heard what had happened to Adam, and she'd changed her mind about him being here. She'd come to take him home.

His first instinct was to go and hide somewhere, but he knew it wouldn't do any good. If she'd come to take him home, they'd find him no matter where he was, and then he'd just be in trouble. So he stood nervously where he was, watching while his mother parked the car and got out, already waving to him. A moment later she ran up the steps and swept him into her arms, hugging him as if she hadn't seen him for a year, instead of just a week.

"Jeez, Mom," Josh complained. "Put me down! What if the kids see? They'll tease me for the rest of the year!"

Despite the reason for her visit to the Academy, Brenda couldn't help laughing at her son's embarrassment. "And what'll they think if your mother doesn't give you a hug when she sees you?"

"You don't have to pick me up," Josh groused. "I'm not a baby anymore!"

"Right," Brenda agreed, setting him back on his feet. "You're all grown up, and ready to go out and start earning a living so you can support your old mother, huh?"

"Mo-om," Josh groaned.

Brenda turned to wink at Amy Carlson. "Does your mom embarrass you as bad as I embarrass Josh?"

Amy shrugged. "I guess," she said. Then, voicing the thought that had been in Josh's head from the moment he saw his mother's car: "Are you going to take Josh home?"

Brenda's smile faded, and she gazed down at Josh. "I don't know," she admitted. She dropped down onto the steps, suddenly feeling the fatigue of the all-night drive. She'd only heard the news about Adam Aldrich yesterday afternoon, when Hildie Kramer had called, and she still wasn't quite over the shock of it. Of course she'd barely known the boy, but after last weekend she'd already come to think of Jeanette and Chet Aldrich as friends. All through her shift at the café she'd thought about whether or not to make the drive up to Barrington, and she'd set out as soon as she'd gotten off work at midnight.

In the end, of course, she realized she had no choice. It wasn't just for the funeral, which was going to be at ten o'clock that morning.

It was Josh.

She had to see for herself how he was doing, make up her own mind how he'd dealt with the suicide of one of his schoolmates.

Most important, she had to see how he was reacting to the school. And she decided if he wasn't happy there, she was prepared to pack him up and drive him home that very afternoon, taking him away from the Academy even more quickly than she'd put him in.

For if Adam Aldrich hadn't responded to the school, and followed up his unsuccessful suicide attempt with a successful one, what was to say that Josh wouldn't do the same thing? Just the thought of it had made her blood run cold. Through the long hours of the night, as she'd driven across the desert and into the San Joaquin Valley, she'd been certain that the school had been a mistake.

But as the sun had risen and she'd driven up Highway 101 toward Salinas, she'd begun having second thoughts.

Josh wasn't like Adam—no two of the kids at the Academy were exactly alike. Even Adam's twin brother was completely different from him.

And hadn't they told her that suicide was a problem among their students?

But they'd failed Adam Aldrich. They hadn't been able to see what was coming, and head it off.

Back and forth she went, arguing every point with herself, her mind finally reeling with exhaustion. As she'd driven into Barrington and started up toward the Academy, she'd made up her mind simply to watch Josh and talk to him, and decide for herself how he was doing.

Now, as the serious little girl with bright red hair and thick glasses stared earnestly at her, she managed a smile. "I guess I'm kind of worried about him," she said.

"Because of Adam?" Amy asked.

Brenda blinked at the stark honesty of the question. "I—I guess so," she stammered.

"We were just talking about it," Amy told her. "We don't think we could ever do anything like that."

"You don't?" Brenda asked. She felt her head spinning. Could she actually be sitting here in the bright morning sun discussing suicide with a ten-year-old girl? And yet Amy, and Josh, too, seemed to think it was the most natural thing in the world.

"We've been talking about it a lot," Amy told her. "And the trouble is, if you do what Adam did, you can't change your mind later. I mean, once you're dead . . ." Her voice trailed off.

"Besides," Brenda said. "Killing yourself is wrong."

"Why?" Josh asked.

Brenda's eyes shifted to her son, who was gazing steadily at her, waiting for an answer.

But did she have one? She realized she didn't know. She'd just always accepted that suicide was wrong. But why? "Well, because God doesn't want you to kill yourself," she said, remembering what the Catholic Church had taught her years ago, before she'd stopped going.

"My father says there isn't any God," Amy told her. "He's an atheist."

"I see," Brenda said, though she didn't really see at all. How could anyone not believe in God? Although she hadn't been to church in more than ten years, she still believed in God. She was still trying to figure out how to respond to Amy's statement when Hildie Kramer appeared at the front door, rescuing her.

"Mrs. MacCallum? I thought that was you."

Hurriedly, Brenda got to her feet. "I just couldn't stay away," she explained. "I decided to drive up for the funeral."

Hildie had spent most of the last two days on the telephone with the parents of nearly all of Barrington's students. Now, she managed a tired smile. "I'm glad you did," she said. "And I'm especially glad for Josh's sake. It'll give you a chance to see how well he's doing." She reached down and ruffled Josh's hair, chuckling as he ducked away from her hand. "Why don't you two go start making yourselves look decent, okay?" she suggested, pointedly looking at her watch. "The service is going to start at ten, and we don't want to be late."

"But it's not even nine yet," Josh protested.

"How long are you going to have to wait for a shower?" Hildie countered. "And don't try to tell me you already took one—I can see the dirt behind your ears even from here. Now go along, both of you," she told the children. To Brenda's surprise, both Amy and Josh obediently trotted up the stairs and disappeared into the house. When they were gone, Hildie turned back to Brenda. "I assume you're here because you're worried about Josh," she said.

Brenda hesitated, then nodded. "After what happened to Adam Aldrich—"

"Of course," Hildie told her. "I can't say I'm surprised to see you. You're not the only parent who's worried, and you have every right to be. I really am glad you've come. Why don't we go get some coffee, and I'll try to fill you in on what's been happening and how we're handling it."

An hour later, Brenda, who had prepared herself for a certain defensiveness on the part of the Academy, found herself impressed by Hildie Kramer's openness in discussing not only Adam Aldrich's suicide, but its possible effects on his classmates. "As for Josh," Hildie told her at last, "all I can tell you is to watch him today, and then make up your own mind about whether you want him to stay with us or not."

In the end, it was Hildie's decision not to pressure her to keep

Josh at the Academy that impressed Brenda the most. By the time Hildie took her into her own small apartment on the ground floor of the mansion so she could freshen up and change her clothes for Adam's funeral, Brenda was already half convinced that despite what had happened, she would not be taking Josh home with her that afternoon.

But still, she would watch Josh carefully through the rest of the morning and into the afternoon.

And only then, if she were satisfied that he truly was as happy as Hildie Kramer claimed he was, would she make up her mind.

12

Jeanette Aldrich sat in front of the mirror on her vanity table, staring at the image reflected in the glass. Could it really be her? Those puffy eyes, red from lack of sleep, and surrounded by dark circles of fatigue?

The gray strands that seemed to have salted her curly mass of chestnut hair virtually overnight? Could they really be hers?

Was it really only three days since she had not only looked, but felt, ten years younger?

It seemed more like a year, for every minute since she had gazed at Adam's distorted face on Saturday morning had dragged by like an hour of pure torture. Always, that image hung in her mind.

Not the Adam she had known, not the beautiful, quiet boy with large dark eyes and thick curly hair that matched her own. That image, the image that smiled enigmatically at her from a framed photograph on the vanity, was gone. Gone forever, to be replaced by the grotesquely smashed face she'd seen on the gurney on Saturday morning.

All his features twisted out of position, his skin torn and smeared with blood, his hair matted, his scalp nearly torn away.

Would she ever forget that image, ever be able to replace it with

145

her memories of the living child? Or would it always be there, superimposing itself on every memory she had of Adam?

She shouldn't have done it—shouldn't have insisted on seeing his body, shouldn't have irrationally refused to accept the truth of his death until she'd seen the corpse for herself.

She shuddered at the word.

Corpse. Such an ugly word to describe what was left of her beautiful child.

But it was too late—too late to go back and choose to remember Adam the way he had been. For the rest of her life that battered visage would haunt her.

Her fingers feeling nearly as numb as her mind, she began putting on her makeup, doing her best to repair the ravages of her grief, but knowing even as she worked that it would do no good. No matter what kind of mask she put on her face, there was no way to cover the bleeding wound inside her, no way to still the pain raging within her soul.

Twelve years old!

He was only twelve! It wasn't fair. Why couldn't he have come home that night and let her take care of him? Why had he turned away from her?

Now she would never know, never have another chance to soothe him, to assure him that nothing was wrong with him, that he was a perfect child.

"Honey?"

Jeanette's eyes shifted to the reflection of her husband. Chet was standing at the open door to the bedroom, his voice, filled with concern, interrupting her reverie. "It's getting late. The car will be here in a few minutes."

Jeanette nodded once, but made no move to go on with her makeup. Her eyes remained fixed on Chet. He still looked as he always had. Husky, handsome, and seeming several years younger than he was. Did he feel nothing for the loss of his son? Didn't he even care that Adam was gone forever?

That's not fair, she told herself, forcing her hands to return to their task. He just handles it differently, that's all. The difference between men and women. We wear our hearts on our sleeves, and they don't. It doesn't mean he isn't hurting just as much as I am.

Steadying her trembling hands, she finished her makeup, then put on the navy-blue dress she'd chosen for the funeral. As she heard a car door slam outside, and the doorbell ring a few seconds later, she started down the stairs, her eyes carefully avoiding the closed door to Adam's room. So far, she still had been unable even to bring herself to enter the room, let alone think about the task of disposing of his things.

Indeed, she had no idea when, or even if, she would ever be able to enter his room again.

Downstairs, she found Chet and Jeff waiting for her. Automatically, she ran her mother's eye over Jeff's suit, reaching out to straighten his tie. "Where's . . . ?" Her voice abruptly died.

"Adam," was what she'd been about to say, the reflex of years coming to the fore even as she was departing for his funeral. But she caught herself in time, biting her lip painfully as she struggled once again to control the tears that threatened to overwhelm her. Ducking her head, she hurried out into the morning sunlight and slid into the backseat of the waiting limousine, the filtered light of its darkened windows closing around her, giving her the illusion of comfort. Then Jeff was in the car, too, perching on the seat facing her, and already exploring the controls of the car's television and stereo system.

"Can I have a Coke?" he asked, discovering the ice bin concealed beneath one of the armrests.

"Not now, Jeff," Chet replied, feeling Jeanette tense beside him as he settled into the seat next to her. "Maybe later, okay?"

Jeff frowned. "But I won't be coming back with you, will I? Aren't I going back to school today? There's going to be classes tomorrow."

As his parents exchanged a quick look, Jeff's frown deepened. "You're going to let me go back, aren't you?" he asked, his voice heavy with suspicion.

"I'm not sure we've made up our minds yet," Chet told his son. His eyes flicked to the back of the driver's head, and he reached for the button that would raise the divider window. "Your mom thinks—"

"But it's not fair!" Jeff exclaimed. "I *like* the Academy. It's where all my friends are!"

"No!" Jeanette told him, more sharply than she'd really intended. "I don't want you there anymore. Can't you understand that, darling? After—After what happened to Adam, I want you at home."

"But why?" Jeff demanded, his face setting into a stubborn mask. "I didn't do anything wrong. How come you're punishing me?"

"I'm not punishing you," Jeanette tried to explain for at least the fourth time in the last twenty-four hours. "Darling, you have to understand how I feel. I want you in the house, where I can look out for you. And you liked the public school—"

"I did not," Jeff contradicted. "I hated it just as much as Adam did. The teachers were dumb, and so were the other kids. But at the Academy—"

Jeanette's fingers tightened on her husband's arm, and Chet held up a hand to silence his son. "Not now, Jeff," he said in a tone that left no room for argument. "We'll talk about it later, and I promise you'll have your say. But right now let's all just get through this, okay? It's going to be hard enough for all of us without you making it any tougher. So just drop it for now, all right?"

Jeff's jaw tightened angrily. For a moment Chet thought the boy was going to go on with the argument, but then Jeff apparently thought better of it. He lapsed into a dark silence that lasted through the rest of the trip to the chapel on the Barrington University campus.

Five minutes later the car pulled up in front of the chapel. After giving his wife's hand one more reassuring squeeze, Chet opened the door to step out, squinting as the bright sunlight flooded into his eyes. Leaning down, he extended a hand to Jeanette, and she, too, emerged from the car, her eyes shielded slightly by the veil that draped from the small pillbox hat perched on her head.

Finally Jeff got out of the car, instinctively starting toward his schoolmates, who were gathered in front of the chapel. Before he could take even a single step, Chet's free hand closed on his shoulder, drawing him firmly to his side. They moved toward the open chapel doors, the crowd of children, and the adults escorting them, falling silent, stepping back to make way for the bereaved family.

As Jeanette stepped through the door into the chapel itself, a face appeared before her, one that she didn't quite recognize until Brenda MacCallum spoke.

"I'm so sorry, Jeanette. I know there isn't anything I can do, but—"

Jeanette summoned up a strained smile. "Brenda. How good of you to come. Such a long way . . ." Her voice trailed off as she failed to think of anything else to say.

"I had to come," Brenda assured her. "I mean, I know I don't know you very well, but I feel like we're friends, you know?"

"Of course," Jeanette murmured. She took a tentative step, as if to move around Brenda, and the other woman, abashed as she realized she was invading Jeanette's privacy, turned away. But then Jeanette found herself reaching out to touch Brenda's arm, stopping her.

"I was wrong about the Academy," she said. "I know what I told you last weekend, but I was wrong. If I were you, I'd get Josh out of here before it's too late."

Brenda, frozen by Jeanette's words, stood speechless as Chet guided his wife on down the aisle toward the front pew. Then she felt Josh tugging at her hand.

"Come *on*, Mom," he whispered. "We're not supposed to talk to them until *after* the funeral. Hildie *told* us!"

With Jeanette's words still ringing in her ears, Brenda allowed Josh to lead her into a pew near the back of the chapel. Before she went home that afternoon, she would have to find an opportunity to talk further with Jeanette. Was Jeanette simply reacting to the tragedy that had befallen her son?

Or was there something about Adam's death that no one had yet told her?

After what seemed an eternity to Jeanette, the funeral finally came to an end. George Engersol himself had delivered Adam's eulogy, but Jeanette had stopped listening after only a few minutes, for the Adam he was speaking of—an Adam who had been a "devoted student, whose interests were as far-reaching as the magnificent expanse of his mind"—was not the little boy she herself remembered.

She remembered the toddler who had come crying to her every time he fell and scraped his knee, the five-year-old who had always pleaded for just one more story before she insisted on turning out the lights, the seven-year-old who had resolutely decided to keep on believing in Santa Claus, even after she and Chet had explained that he was only a myth.

"But God is only a myth, too, isn't he?" Adam had asked.

"That's right," Chet, the most devout atheist she'd ever known, had replied.

"But lots of people still believe in God," Adam had argued. "So I'm going to go on believing in Santa Claus. And as long as I believe in him, he'll keep bringing me presents every Christmas."

Every Christmas thereafter, Jeanette had made certain that at least one of the packages under the tree was marked "To Adam, From Santa." Even last Christmas, Adam had saved that package till last, grinning happily as he tore off the wrappings. "See?" he'd pointed out to Jeff. "He never forgets me. And he hasn't given *you* anything since we were seven."

Jeff, ever the realist, pointed out that the writing on the label looked suspiciously like their mother's, but Adam had been undisturbed. "Count your presents," he said. "Mom and Dad always give us the same number, but I always get one from Santa, too."

Jeff had counted, and discovered—to his dismay—that his brother was right. For the rest of the day Adam had taunted him with the fact that his refusal to believe had cost him all kinds of terrific things over the years. By the end of the day, Jeff had been bubbling over with fury and frustration, insisting that his brother had figured out a way to cheat on Christmas.

Not that it had done him any good—even Chet hadn't been able to keep from laughing at the fact that for the first time Adam had gotten the better of his brother.

And now it was over.

George Engersol had finally stopped speaking. The last prayers had been spoken over the small casket that rested in front of the altar, and the recessional music had begun. With a last lingering look at the closed coffin that contained her son's body, Jeanette allowed herself to be guided back up the aisle toward the door, then took her place at Chet's side to accept the condolences of the crowd of mourners.

It was even worse than she'd imagined it could be. No one seemed to know what to say to her, what words to speak to a woman whose adolescent son had chosen to take his own life. All her friends, all the people she'd known for years, now seemed to have lost their tongues, pausing only for the briefest of moments to peck her on the cheek, whisper a brief "I'm so sorry," and then move quickly away.

Do they think it's my fault? she found herself wondering. Do they think I failed him in some way?

But hadn't she? Of course she had. If she'd been a good mother and given Adam all the love and attention he needed, he'd still be alive, wouldn't he?

She tried to tell herself it wasn't true, that Hildie Kramer had been right when she'd assured her only the day before that there was nothing she could have done, that she and Chet had done everything they could for Adam, but that there had been forces inside him none of them had understood.

I can't spend my life blaming myself, she repeated to herself over and over again. I still have Jeff, and I can't stop living because of what's happened. And I can't make him stop living, either.

The last people in the chapel had drifted away. As Chet, Jeanette, and Jeff watched, the casket was borne up the aisle and carried to the waiting hearse. The pallbearers paused for a moment when they came to the family, and Jeanette laid her hand on the mahogany box for a moment, then quietly uttered a single word.

"Good-bye."

As the family watched silently, the casket was placed in the hearse, and a moment later the hearse pulled away.

By the end of the day, Adam Aldrich's remains would be cremated and his ashes scattered over the sea.

═══

Brenda MacCallum glanced at her watch. It was nearly two. If she were to get back to Eden at a reasonable hour, she would have to leave soon. But she still hadn't had a chance to talk further with Jeanette Aldrich, and as she scanned the thinning crowd on the lawn in front of the Academy, she was afraid Jeanette might already have left. She spotted Chet, deep in conversation with George Engersol, and Jeff, sitting with Josh, Amy Carlson, and some of the other kids in the shade next to the circle of trees they called the Gazebo. But Jeanette was nowhere to be seen.

Then, with the certainty of a mother, Brenda realized where Jeanette must be. Placing her empty lemonade glass on one of the tables that had been set up on the lawn, she set out toward the house, moving gingerly, her high heels sinking into the thick lawn with every step. She'd watched the other women ruefully as they balanced themselves on their toes, their own heels never puncturing the green carpet the way her own did. Of course, in Eden hardly anyone she knew even had a lawn, and those few were usually baked brown by the sun, the earth beneath them hard as a rock. Still, she wished she'd thought to wear flats.

Entering the house, she paused to brush the dirt from her heels, then went up the stairs to the second floor. Adam's room had been right next to Jeff's, at the far end, facing the front. She moved quickly down the hall, then paused at the closed door of the next-to-last room. She tapped softly. When there was no answer, she turned to leave. But her instincts told her that the room wasn't empty, so she turned back, tried the knob, and pushed the door open.

Leaning against the wall next to the window, staring off into space, was Jeanette Aldrich.

"Is it okay if I come in?" Brenda asked, feeling as if she'd intruded. "I mean, if you want to be by yourself . . ."

Jeanette shook her head quickly, almost as if she were bringing herself back to reality, then stepped forward. "No. It's all right, Brenda. I was just . . ." She looked helplessly around the room. With all of Adam's things gone, the closet open and empty, the bed stripped down to the bare mattress, the room had a forlorn look to it.

"You were just remembering," Brenda said, entering and pushing the door closed behind her. "When I didn't see you outside, I figured this is where you'd come." Her eyes wandered over the room. "It looks kind of forlorn, doesn't it?"

Jeanette nodded briefly. "But at least I can stand to be in it. If his things were still here, I don't think I could. I haven't been able to go into his room at home at all yet."

Brenda perched herself on the edge of the bed. "I know how you feel. After my husband walked out, I could hardly even stand to get in the bed for a week." Her face colored in embarrassment. " 'Course, I know it's not the same thing, but the feeling's sort of the same, you know?"

For the first time that day, Jeanette smiled. "What amazes me is that *you* know." She came to sit next to Brenda on the bed. "You're also the first person who's actually come looking for me. It seems as though none of my friends want to talk to me. They don't know what to say."

"Well, I sure know what that's like." Brenda sighed. "After Josh cut his wrists, everyone was real nice, but they sure didn't want to talk about it. For a few days there, I felt like I'd come down with leprosy or something. But what can you expect? Our kids aren't like everyone else's to start with, and when they do things like that, it really throws people."

Jeanette's smile faded. "Didn't it throw you? When Josh tried to kill himself?"

"Sure it did. Scared me half to death. But I had to deal with it, just like I had to deal with every man I've ever known dumping me, and I had Melinda to take care of, too. So I brought him here."

The last of Jeanette's smile disappeared. "Just as I brought Adam and Jeff," she said. "And now Adam's dead."

Brenda said nothing for a moment, but rose to her feet and went to the window. "I've been thinking about what you said before the funeral. About taking Josh home with me."

"Good," Jeanette replied. "I suppose you know by now that I've decided to take Jeff out of here. From now on, I want him at home with me."

"I can sure see why," Brenda agreed. "But I don't know if I can take Josh out." She beckoned to Jeanette. "Come here and take a look at this."

Jeanette, puzzled, got up from the bed and came to stand next to Brenda. Gazing out the window, she saw nothing particularly remarkable. Just a group of kids sprawled on the lawn, talking among themselves.

"You know, I never saw that before," Brenda said. "From the day he started going to school, Josh never was part of the group. It was like they just shut him out, and every day of his life he was hurting. But he's not hurting here. How am I supposed to take him away? You really think I should do that to him? Put him back where he was, where everyone made fun of him, and he was bored all the time?"

Watching the scene through Brenda's eyes, Jeanette was able for the first time since the tragedy to remember past the last two days.

She remembered the years before she and Chet had enrolled their sons in the Academy, when Jeff and Adam had had no friends except each other. And now, with Adam dead—

"Dear God," she breathed, more to herself than to Brenda. "What am I supposed to do?"

"Well, I sure can't tell you," Brenda replied, still watching the group of children on the lawn. "But I know I can't take Josh away from here, and before you decide to take Jeff out, maybe you ought to wait a little while." She turned to face Jeanette. "I know how much you're hurting, Jeanette. And I've done a lot of hurting in my life, too. But it gets better. Some days you think you're just going to die, but every day it hurts a little less. The main thing is not to do something stupid when you're hurting, that you can't take back."

Jeanette was silent for a moment, and when she finally spoke, her voice was steady. "You mean the way Adam did?"

Brenda shrugged. "I wasn't really thinking about Adam right then, but I guess that's what I mean. And I guess I don't think you ought to make Jeff pay for Adam's mistakes, either. You know what I'm saying?"

Jeanette hesitated, then nodded. "I think I do," she said. "And it's funny. It's almost exactly what Jeff told me on the way to the funeral."

Brenda's lips formed a wry grin. "Well, you know what they say: 'Out of the mouths of babes . . .' "

Jeanette took a deep breath. "Come on," she said. "Let's go down and have a glass of lemonade, since they aren't serving anything stronger. And then I'd better tell Jeff he can stay here after all." As they left the room, she took Brenda's hand in her own. "I really am glad you came," she said. "If you hadn't, I'm not sure what I would have done."

"You'd have done the right thing," Brenda told her. "Maybe not right away, but you'd have figured it out. After all, if we've got kids as smart as Josh and Jeff, we can't be too stupid, can we?"

As she started down the stairs with Brenda, Jeanette heard herself laughing out loud. A few minutes ago she hadn't been at all sure she would ever laugh again.

―――

"Jeff?" Josh asked.

Jeff turned to look at him, and for a minute Josh wondered if he should even mention the strange sounds he'd heard the night Adam had died. But the more he'd thought about it, and the more he'd thought about the peculiar note he'd seen on Adam's computer, the less sense the whole thing made. Even though he'd talked to Hildie Kramer and Mr. Conners about the note, they hadn't seemed to understand what he was saying. Of course, he hadn't told them about hearing the elevator running when it wasn't, because he knew they'd laugh at him for having fallen for Jeff's ghost story about Eustace Barrington. But Jeff had acutally seen the note, and maybe . . .

He made up his mind. "What do you think really happened to Adam?"

Brad Hinshaw, who was sprawled next to Jeff, looked up. Jeff's eyes changed slightly, as if a curtain had dropped behind them. "What are you talking about?" he asked.

"I don't know," Josh said. "It's just—Well, all he said in the note was that he was going somewhere. To a better place. He didn't say he was killing himself. I mean, what if he was just running away?"

Brad groaned. "Come on, Josh. He got hit by a train, didn't he? I mean, we just went to his funeral, didn't we?"

Josh felt himself reddening. "But what if it wasn't Adam at all? What if it was somebody else? They could have switched bodies or something, couldn't they?"

Jeff Aldrich got to his feet and started away.

"That was really cool, Josh," Brad said. "If you're so smart, how could you say something that stupid in front of Jeff? Jeez!"

Josh scrambled to his feet and hurried after Jeff. Catching up to him, he grabbed the older boy's arm. "Jeff? I—I'm sorry. I didn't mean anything. I was just—Well, I was just wondering about the note, that's all."

Jeff stopped, his eyes meeting Josh's. "You're lying," he said. "There's something else, isn't there? Besides the note."

Josh's toe dug into the ground in front of him. "I—I heard the elevator, too," he admitted, certain that Jeff would burst out laughing. When the other boy said nothing, Josh went on. "It was just like you said—I could hear it, but it wasn't moving."

Jeff's lips twisted into the strangest smile the younger boy had ever seen. "Then maybe that's what happened," Jeff told him. "Maybe Adam isn't dead at all. Maybe Eustace Barrington came back from the grave and took him away. And maybe, sometime when you're least expecting it, Adam himself will come and tell you what really happened."

Josh, stunned by Jeff's words, dropped his arm.

Jeff Aldrich, the smile still on his face, turned and walked away.

Late that night, Hildie Kramer went into George Engersol's private office, closing the door behind her. Engersol glanced up, nodded to her, then finished the file he was working on. A moment later he put the file away, leaned back in his chair and folded his arms across his chest.

"All right," he said. "How bad is it?"

Hildie smiled. "Not bad at all. The Lowensteins are pulling Monica out of school, and I can't talk them out of it. But she's the only one. All the rest are staying, including Jeff Aldrich."

"Not bad," Engersol replied. "We can live with it. But it means my special seminar is now short two students. I have two candidates in mind, but I'd like to hear your recommendations first."

Hildie didn't hesitate at all. "Josh MacCallum and Amy Carlson," she said. "They're both nearly perfect. Two of our brightest students, and both of them have the intellectual and psychological profiles we're looking for."

Engersol smiled. "Very good, Hildie. Those are exactly the two candidates I had in mind. Rearrange their schedules for them to start tomorrow."

As Hildie left his office, Engersol reviewed the files of the two students one more time. He agreed. They were perfect for the seminar.

Josh MacCallum, indeed, had already attempted suicide once.

If he did it again, and succeeded, no one would think a thing about it.

13

Josh MacCallum and Amy Carlson sat nervously on the bench outside Hildie Kramer's office. The house was quiet, for the rest of the kids had already headed for their first classes of the day. But during breakfast Hildie had come into the dining room and instructed the two of them to come to her office at the beginning of the first period. Josh and Amy exchanged an apprehensive glance. For his part, Josh was convinced he was in trouble. Deep trouble: Jeff must have told his parents what he had said yesterday afternoon after the funeral, and Mrs. Aldrich must have called Hildie. But what was so wrong with wondering if maybe Adam hadn't really killed himself? And Jeff hadn't been mad at all—in fact, Josh thought, it seemed Jeff had believed him.

Amy, though, thought they'd been summoned by Hildie Kramer for a different reason. "I bet our moms decided to take us out of school," she said. "I bet they talked to Monica's folks, and now they're going to make us go home, too."

Josh had stared speculatively at the empty chair at the next table, which Monica Lowenstein had habitually occupied until this morning. He shook his head. "How come grown-ups always start acting weird? Monica wasn't going to do anything. She thought Adam was really dumb to kill himself. And it can't be that, anyway.

158

If my mom was going to take me home, she'd have done it yester-day. Besides, she told me she'd decided not to. And your mom and dad didn't even come to the funeral, so how could they have talked to Monica's folks?"

Amy made a face at him. "Haven't you ever heard of the tele-phone?"

"That's dumb," Josh replied. "Monica's folks probably don't even know where your folks live." Amy had made no reply, but instead poked disconsolately at her oatmeal. "Maybe we're really not in any trouble at all," Josh suggested.

"Oh, sure," Amy said, scowling at him. "Did you ever get called to the principal's office when you weren't in trouble?"

For that argument, Josh had no reply at all. The two of them had sunk into a dejected silence for the rest of breakfast. Nor had it helped when the other kids had begun teasing them as they left for their various classes.

"See you later," Brad Hinshaw had called. "If you're still here!" Laughing, he'd shoved his way through the front door into the bright morning sunlight, while Josh and Amy perched on the bench outside Hildie's office, the relative gloom of the large foyer doing nothing to improve their mood.

Finally the door to Hildie's office opened and Hildie herself stepped out to usher them inside. "Well, look at the two of you," she said, smiling at them. "From those long faces, you must have done something I haven't heard about yet!" As Josh and Amy eyed one another nervously, she burst out laughing. "If I'd known you were going to worry yourselves to death, I wouldn't have said a thing at breakfast. I'd have just stopped you on your way to class. Now come on in."

Warily, the two children followed Hildie into her office. For some reason both of them felt vaguely relieved when she didn't close the door. Hildie, noting their response, smiled to herself. Long ago she'd discovered that all the kids got nervous when she called them in for a closed-door conference. It was as if they in-stinctively knew that a closed door meant some kind of dressing-down. Conversely, she'd also discovered that the simple act of closing the door was enough to strike terror into the heart of the occasional troublemaker.

"I was talking to Dr. Engersol last night," she told them, settling herself into the chair behind her desk as Josh and Amy perched anxiously on the couch. "With Monica leaving school, there are two vacant places in his seminar. He and I both think you two are ideal candidates to take their places."

Josh felt a quick thrill of anticipation, remembering Jeff telling him a week ago about the seminar, but refusing to talk about exactly what they were doing. All he knew was that it involved computers—something he'd loved since the first moment he'd seen one, when he was only five—and that only a few kids in the school were allowed to be in it.

The smartest, most talented kids.

Adam and Jeff Aldrich, and Monica Lowenstein, and a few others.

Jeff. What about his place? Was it possible that he was coming back to school after all? He voiced the question even as it came into his head, and Hildie's smile broadened.

"He's coming back tomorrow," she told him. "Which should make you happy, right? He's your best friend, isn't he?"

"Except for Amy," Josh replied. "Is he still going to be in the seminar?"

"As far as I know."

"But what's it about?" Amy asked. "None of the kids who are in it ever talk about it."

"Well, it's hardly a big secret," Hildie replied. "Basically, it's a class in artificial intelligence."

Josh's eyes widened. "Wow. You mean like in teaching computers how to think?"

"Exactly. And since both of you seem to have remarkable abilities in math, we think you'd fit in very well."

Amy looked uncertain. "I don't really like computers," she said. "All the games are kind of dumb, once you've played them a couple of times. I mean, it's always the same stuff, over and over again."

"And why do you think it's always the same stuff?" Hildie asked.

Amy looked puzzled by the question, but Josh saw the answer instantly.

"Because all a computer does is put things together the way it's told to. It can't figure out anything new, because it can't think like people can."

Amy's brows knit as she concentrated on the idea. "But how could a computer ever think like a person?" she asked.

"That's what the seminar is all about," Hildie explained. "Most of what Dr. Engersol is trying to do is learn how people think. In a way, our brains are like computers, but there's a big difference. Somehow, we manage to put all the data in our heads together and come up with new ideas. Computers can't do that. A lot of people think that if we can figure out just how our brains come up with new ideas, we might be able to design a computer to do it, too. That's what artificial intelligence is all about."

"But what would we be doing?" Amy asked.

Hildie shrugged. "Dr. Engersol will have to explain that to you. But I can promise you, you'll like the seminar. Everyone who's been in it loves it." She smiled ruefully. "Unfortunately, I don't think I understand it enough to know quite *why* they love it, but they do."

"I don't know," Amy said, fidgeting on the couch. "Do I have to take it? What if I don't want to?"

"Well, I'm sure if you don't want to, Dr. Engersol will understand," Hildie told her. "Of course, you probably won't get to move down to the second floor, but it's entirely up to you."

"The second floor?" Amy asked, her interest suddenly engaged. The rooms on the second floor were much larger than the ones on the third, which had originally been the servants' quarters when the mansion had been built. "Why would we get to move downstairs?"

Hildie smiled as if it should have been obvious. "It has to do with the seminar. All the students in Dr. Engersol's class are issued special computers, and the rooms on the third floor are just too small. And since Adam's room, and Monica's, are empty . . ." She left the bait hanging. As she'd been certain would happen, both Amy and Josh snatched at it.

"Could we move downstairs today?" Amy asked eagerly. "This morning?"

Hildie chuckled. "You can move right now, if you want to," she told them. "Does that mean you both want to join the seminar?"

The two children agreed eagerly. Hildie took two pieces of paper out of a file folder that was already lying on her desk. "In that case, here are your new schedules. Starting tomorrow, you'll both be going into the new class first period. Amy, you'll be moved into the mathematics class that meets at two, and I've put you into the same one, Josh."

Josh broke into a smile. "Since we're taking another class, does that mean we can stop doing P.E.?" he asked eagerly.

Hildie made a face of exaggerated disapproval. "No, it doesn't mean you can stop doing P.E. But it does mean," she added, as Josh's face fell, "that we'll be making some changes in that, too. So as soon as you leave here, I want you both to go to the gym behind the college field house and see Mr. Iverson. I'll give you a note telling him why you're there, and he'll give you some tests and then help you set up a gym schedule that won't interfere with any of your classes. Okay?"

Both children, slightly dazed by the sudden change in the schedules that had been set up little more than a week ago, nodded silently, and Hildie handed them the note for Joe Iverson, who headed the university's physical education program. Years ago, working closely with George Engersol, Iverson had designed a special regimen for the children in the Academy, emphasizing individual sports over team activities.

"None of the kids we're targeting is going to grow up to be a team player," Engersol had explained even before they'd taken in their first students. "They'll all be unique kids, and most if not all of them will have had nothing but bad experiences with team sports. If they're forced into situations where they have to curtail their intellects in favor of someone else's physical superiority, they'll only resent it, and I don't intend for this Academy to be an unhappy experience for any of them. We'll have a few kids who

love baseball and football, but for the most part physical competi-
tion just won't mean anything to our kids. So I want you to design
a program that will give them the exercise they need, but not bore
them. Is it possible?"

Iverson had nodded. "Anything's possible," he'd agreed, and
set to work. What he'd come up with was a program emphasizing
swimming, which he knew most kids loved to start with, and gym-
nastics, which, if one was to achieve any sort of proficiency,
demanded nearly as much brain power as muscle development.
Furthermore, the sports he'd selected for the kids were individual
enough that most of them were able to work their P.E. sessions in
at their own convenience, merely appearing at the pool or gym
when they had time, so long as they put in a minimum of five hours
a week.

For Josh and Amy the choice had been easy—an hour a day in
the pool was more like playing than anything else.

Now, they left Hildie Kramer's office and headed across the
lawn and out the gate, then turned left into the main university
campus, on the other side of which were the field house, a smaller
gym, the pool, and the football stadium. Amy gazed curiously at
Josh.

"How come they have to change our P.E.? Why can't we just
keep going swimming every day, like we have been?"

Josh shrugged. "Maybe they have something special for the kids
in the seminar."

"But why?" Amy pressed. "What's dumb old P.E. got to do with
artificial intelligence?"

"Who cares?" Josh grinned. "We get new rooms and new computers, don't we?"

Amy nodded halfheartedly. The new room was great—she was
already looking forward to that. But she didn't really care about the
new computer, and the thing with changing her P.E. program
seemed stupid. She started to say something else, then changed her
mind. After all, Josh didn't know any more about the seminar than
she did, and the other kids in it hadn't ever said a word.

That, too, seemed weird to her. How come they all acted like it
was a big deal? It was just another class, wasn't it?

Or was it?

Why did she feel that she'd gotten talked into doing something she didn't really want to do?

Well, it didn't matter, really. If it turned out she hated it, they'd probably let her quit. After all, so far they'd never made her do anything she didn't really want to do.

Or had they?

In her mind she began reviewing the days since she'd first come to the Academy, and the way Hildie Kramer had treated her.

Hildie'd always been very nice to her, but in the end—as she had the day she'd run out of her room and hidden in the Gazebo, where she'd met Josh—she'd always wound up doing what Hildie wanted her to do.

And now Hildie and Dr. Engersol wanted her to take this class. Why?

Joe Iverson grinned at the two children who stood nervously in front of his desk, and slipped the note from Hildie Kramer under the metal clamp of his clipboard. "So Dr. E's got two more hot prospects for his class, huh?" he asked. Josh and Amy exchanged a nervous glance, but nodded. "Well, then, let's get started, okay?"

"But what are we doing?" Amy asked. "How come we can't just keep on swimming, like we've been doing? We *like* swimming!"

Iverson's brows arched. "Who said you're not going to?" he asked.

Amy cocked her head. "Hildie. She said you had to do a special program for us. But I don't see why."

"Tell you what," the coach replied. "Why don't you two go change your clothes, then meet me in the gym. Okay? Then I'll tell you what we're going to do."

Ten minutes later, when the two children emerged from their respective locker rooms and entered the empty gym, they found Joe Iverson waiting for them. "Mostly what we're going to do right now is see what kind of condition you two are in," he told them. "I don't know if Hildie explained this to you, but Dr. E's not just teaching you in his seminar. He's studying you, too."

Josh frowned suspiciously. "Studying us how?"

Iverson laughed out loud at the expression on the boy's face. "Well, it's not like guinea pigs," he replied. "But he figures that since the brain affects practically everything in the body one way or another, you kids should be different from kids whose IQs are in the more normal range. So he tries to keep track of everything about you, not only mentally, but physically, too. What I'm going to do this morning is weigh you and measure you, take your blood pressure and pulse and all that kind of thing, then give you some exercises and check your blood pressure and pulse again."

"Are you going to take blood?" Amy demanded. "I hate that, when the doctor sticks a needle in my arm."

Iverson chuckled. "No, I'm not going to do anything like that. Mostly, all we want to do is see how your bodies react to a little exercise, okay?"

Though neither of them quite understood exactly what Mr. Iverson was looking for, they let themselves be weighed and measured, and have their pulses and blood pressures checked. Then the exercises began.

They did push-ups, as many as they could. Amy gave up after only fifteen, but Josh managed twenty-five.

Next they ran in place for ten minutes, then did a series of jumping jacks.

After each round of exercises, Iverson once more recorded their pulse rates and blood pressures.

"Okay, just one more thing in here, then we head for the pool." He pointed toward a thick rope, knotted every eighteen inches, that was suspended from a ring attached to the ceiling. "Which one of you is going to be able to climb that the fastest?"

Amy gazed up at the ceiling, at least thirty feet high. Did he really expect her to climb the rope all the way up there? Just the thought of it gave her a queasy feeling in her stomach. "Wh-What if I fall?" she asked.

"How are you going to fall if you don't let go of the rope?" Iverson countered.

"But what if I do?" Amy pressed.

"That's what the mats are for. If you think you're going to fall, don't go any higher. Just come back down. Okay?"

Amy's eyes shifted to Josh. He suddenly remembered how terrified she'd been the first day he'd been here, when they had to climb down the zigzagging stairs to the beach. "It's okay," he said. "Just don't look down."

Amy stared at the rope but made no move to climb it. Josh, realizing she was too scared even to try it, finally stepped forward and grasped the rope in his hands. He yanked on it a couple of times, then ran forward, swinging himself off the floor. "It's fun," he told Amy. He stopped swinging, then started up the rope, wrapping his legs around it so most of his weight was taken off his arms. Slowly, he began climbing up toward the ceiling.

"Be careful," Amy called out when he was halfway up. "Don't fall!"

"I'm not gonna fall!" Josh shouted down. "It's neat." He worked his way up to the top, slapping the ring with his right hand before grinning down at Amy. "I did it!" he crowed. "I made it all the way."

"Come back down," Amy pleaded.

Laughing, Josh started back down. When he was still ten feet from the floor, he let go of the rope, dropping down to the mat and rolling over to break the fall. Amy, startled by his sudden descent, screamed out loud, but quickly cut it off. "You did that just to scare me," she accused as Josh scrambled to his feet.

"I didn't, either," Josh protested. "I just did it 'cause it was fun. Go on. Try it."

Amy eyed the rope once more, then finally gripped it. Tentatively, she tugged at it, half hoping that it might break right now and come tumbling down from the ceiling.

It didn't.

At last, taking a deep breath, she started climbing, pulling herself up and wrapping her legs around the rope, moving her hands from knot to knot in quick motions, as if she might fall if she released her grip for more than a moment.

Josh was right. It wasn't so bad.

"I'm doing it!" she yelled, and, forgetting Josh's warning, peered down at him.

A wave of dizziness swept over her. Her eyes widened in fear.

"Don't look down," Josh called again. "Look up!"

Struggling against her terror, Amy forced herself to look up, but now the ceiling, too, seemed far out of reach.

When she tried to lower herself, her sudden panic wouldn't let her release the rope.

"I can't do it," she wailed. "I can't get back down."

Instantly, Joe Iverson shinnied up the rope until he was right beneath her. "It's okay," he told her. "I'm right under you. Just put your feet on my shoulders. Hang onto the rope and stand on me. Okay? Can you do that, Amy?"

As Josh watched from below, Amy's right leg relaxed slightly and her toe touched the coach's shoulder. A few seconds later she was straddling his head, her hands still clinging to the rope. As he felt her weight being transferred to his own body, Iverson spoke again. "That's right, Amy. Just stand on me. I'm going to start down, and you just steady yourself with the rope. And don't look down, okay?"

"Uh-huh," Amy managed, her voice strangling in her constricted throat.

A moment later they were back on the floor. Joe Iverson reached up, grasped Amy's weight in his strong arms, and swung her down to the mat. "There," he said. "Safe. See? We made it."

Amy, her face pale, stood trembling in silence for a moment as the panic slowly released her from its grip.

"You okay?" Josh asked, watching her anxiously.

Amy nodded. "I couldn't do it," she said. "When I looked down, I just got all dizzy."

"It's okay," Joe Iverson assured her. He made a note on the clipboard, then patted her reassuringly on the back. "It's just a little acrophobia. Why don't you two go put on bathing suits and meet me at the pool. You can swim a few laps, and then we'll be done. Okay?"

Amy nodded gratefully and hurried out of the gym.

But twenty minutes later, when she climbed out of the pool after having swum five lengths, her fear returned.

"Ever gone off the high board?" Joe Iverson asked.

Amy stared up at the diving board that loomed three meters above the surface of the pool. She shook her head.

"Want to try it?"

Amy shook her head again, her eyes moistening with tears just at the thought of having to climb the ladder, then walk out to the end of the narrow board.

"Come on," Iverson urged. "Just try it once. If you can't do it, you can't. But you really ought to try."

"She's scared," Josh said from the pool, where he was hanging onto the gutter, kicking gently as he treaded water. "How come she has to go off the high board?"

"She doesn't," Iverson told him. "But if she doesn't try, how is she going to get over being scared of heights?"

"Maybe she won't," Josh challenged. "Aren't you scared of anything?"

Joe Iverson's first impulse was to reprimand Josh for being insolent, but then he remembered the instructions he'd been given by George Engersol. "I'm not interested in turning these kids into athletes," the Academy's director had insisted. "I want them to get all the exercise they need, but it's their minds I'm primarily interested in. So don't start acting like a drill sergeant with them. If one of them gives you a problem, tell me about it, and I'll take care of it. But most of these children are already terrified of coaches. They've been treated like weaklings and klutzes all their lives, and their self-images have suffered for it. I won't tolerate that here."

Iverson, though he thoroughly disliked Engersol, hadn't bothered to argue, for he'd already been told by the university's president to do whatever Engersol wanted. "You'd be amazed at the funding he's bringing in for that program," Jordan Sanford had told him. "Just do what he asks, and let him worry about the kids. Believe me, he knows what he's doing."

So now, instead of reprimanding Josh, Iverson only shrugged his shoulders, made another note on his clipboard, and sent the kids to take showers.

Retreating to his office, Iverson switched on his computer terminal, called up the permanent records of Josh MacCallum and Amy Carlson, and began entering the data he'd collected in the last hour. Though it meant little to him, he supposed George Engersol had some use for it all.

———

An hour later, in his office, George Engersol called up the same records that Joe Iverson had been looking at sixty minutes earlier. Tapping quickly at the keyboard, he began studying the data the coach had entered.

What intrigued him most was the notation on Amy Carlson's record that she seemed to suffer from acute acrophobia.

She'd been unable to climb the rope in the gym, and outright refused even to attempt the high diving board.

Apparently, her phobia was more pervasive than he'd thought when he'd watched her make her way down the stairs to the beach ten days earlier.

As he thought about it, an idea began to take shape in his mind. Perhaps there was a way to fit Amy's phobia into his seminar.

He leaned back in his chair, the idea developing rapidly. The more he thought about it, the more he liked it.

Whether or not Amy Carlson would like it remained to be seen. But of course, what she—or any of the other students—liked, was of no consequence to him at all.

The only thing that mattered was how he could use them.

And he'd just discovered a perfect use for Amy Carlson.

14

Josh put the last of his belongings into the cardboard box. He'd already filled it three times, carried it to the rattling old elevator for the ride down to his new room on the second floor, emptied it, then taken it, and the elevator, back upstairs to repeat the process.

On each trip, as he'd pressed the elevator button and heard the ancient gears mesh and felt the car jerk into motion, he'd remembered once more the night that Adam had died, and the strange sounds he'd heard coming from the motionless elevator. By now, though, he'd all but convinced himself that Amy must have been right—that the whole thing had happened only in his imagination—for ever since that night when he'd heard the elevator operating and run to look at it, the car had always been in motion, and someone had been inside it. In fact, today he'd even stopped going to look.

Now, on the last trip from his old room, the box was almost overflowing, and as Josh crammed the last of his T-shirts into the few remaining crannies between the conglomeration of books, shoes, and the favorite pillow that his mother had brought him from Eden, he took a last glance around the room. He'd occupied it for no more than two weeks. Still, he found himself sort of missing it already, for it had seemed to him to be just about perfect. Big enough to hold all his stuff, but small enough that he'd felt cozy in it right from the start. By now, he'd almost convinced himself that Jeff Aldrich had simply made up the story about what had happened to Timmy Evans. Besides, the room downstairs didn't have a dormer, with its window seat that was just the right size to curl up on while he was reading.

The room downstairs.

Adam's room.

He'd felt an odd chill when Hildie had taken him to the room just before lunch. His first instinct had been to tell her he'd rather stay where he was, for although the room was now empty of all of Adam's stuff, he could still clearly remember Adam sitting at the desk, hunched over his computer. At least he'd never actually *known* Timmy Evans. When he remained silently at the door, not even attempting to cross the threshold, Hildie had appeared to read his thoughts.

"Why don't we move the furniture around?" she'd suggested. "That way it'll be your room, and in a few days you won't even remember that someone else used to be here."

Someone else. She hadn't mentioned Adam's name, which Josh thought was strange. In fact, it seemed as though the grown-ups had stopped talking about Adam altogether, as if he'd never existed. Did they just want his friends to forget about him?

Before he could protest, Hildie had begun rearranging the furniture, and before he quite knew what was happening, Josh was helping shove the heavy iron bed to the wall where Adam's desk had stood, and moving the desk over to stand by the window. Amazingly, Hildie had turned out to be right—just changing the placement of the furniture had made the room seem sort of like his own.

Sort of, but not quite. What would happen tonight, when he tried to sleep in Adam's room?

As he hauled the last boxful of stuff toward the elevator, he heard it suddenly clank into life, and as he came to the shaft itself, he half expected to see the car still waiting where he'd left it, even though the machinery was running.

But this time—as on all the others since the night of Adam's death—he could see the car descending and hear its door open and close as someone got on downstairs.

He watched as it came back up.

As it passed the third floor, Dr. Engersol looked out at him through the brass mesh that enclosed the car, nodded, then disappeared as the car moved up to the fourth floor and clattered to a stop.

Josh waited until he heard Dr. Engersol leave the car, then pressed the button that brought it back down to the third floor. At least I won't be able to hear the elevator from my new room, he thought as he hauled the box into the little car.

But it wasn't his room, he realized as he dropped the box on the bed a few moments later. It was still Adam's room.

He hesitated for a minute, wondering if it was too late to go to Hildie and tell her he'd changed his mind, that he wanted to keep his old room. Then he decided he was being stupid. It was just a room, and it wasn't as though Adam had actually died there. The thought alone made him shudder, and he determinedly told himself not to think about it anymore.

But what would happen tonight, he thought again, when he had to sleep here?

He decided not to think about that, either. He began unpacking the box, putting his clothes away in the chest, stacking the books on the shelves that now hung on the wall above the bed, since he and Hildie had rearranged the room. As he put the last of them away, he eyed the shelves suspiciously. If they collapsed during the night, everything on them would crash down onto the bed. Maybe tonight he'd find a screwdriver and move them over so they'd be back above the desk again.

Taking the empty box with him, he started down the wide hallway toward the stairs. Just as he got to the landing, he heard a mewing sound, then felt Tabby pressing up against his leg, his back arched, his tail standing straight up.

"Can't you find Amy?" he asked. The cat mewed again, and Josh, setting the empty box down on the landing, picked him up and took him into the other wing of the floor, where Amy's new room was.

"There you are!" Amy cried as she opened the door. The cat instantly leaped from Josh's arms into her own. "Where were you? I kept calling you, but you didn't come!"

The cat slithered out of the little girl's arms, dropping to the floor and stalking the room suspiciously, inspecting every corner as if he was taking inventory. Apparently satisfied, he jumped up onto Amy's bed, curled himself up on the pillow, and promptly went to sleep. "Isn't this neat?" Amy asked. "These rooms are so much bigger than the ones upstairs. I just love it." When Josh said nothing in reply, her happy grin wavered, then faded away. "What's wrong?"

"I'm in Adam's room," Josh explained. "It's kind of creepy."

Amy stared at him. "They put you in *there*?" she breathed. "I'd hate that room. I'd never be able to go to sleep."

Josh felt himself flush as Amy spoke the thought he'd had only a few minutes earlier. "It's not *that* bad," he told her, but Amy, her smile returning, saw right through him.

"It is, too," she teased. "And I bet he comes back tonight. I bet there's something in his room he forgot, and he'll come for it, and when he finds you—"

"Amy!" Josh broke in. "Stop that!"

"Josh is a scaredy-cat, Josh is a scaredy-cat!" Amy singsonged.

"I am not! All I said was it was weird. I didn't say I was scared!"

He turned and stomped out of the room, and in the sudden silence, Amy realized what she must have sounded like.

Just like all the kids who had teased her all her life.

"Josh?" she called out, running after him, leaving her door standing wide open. "Josh, wait up. I'm sorry! I didn't mean it!"

Josh, at the head of the stairs, paused, her taunting words still burning in his head. "If you didn't mean it, how come you said it?" he demanded.

"I was just kidding," Amy pleaded. "Don't be mad at me. Please?"

For a second Josh was tempted to ignore her, to turn his back on her and just walk away. But then he, too, remembered how it had been at school back home, and he relented.

"It's okay," he mumbled. "Just don't tell any of the other kids, okay? If they know I'm scared, they'll prob'ly pull some dumb trick on me in the middle of the night."

"I won't," Amy promised. "Just don't be mad at me, all right?"

Josh, feeling a warm glow bloom inside him at the appealing look on her face, broke into a grin. "Come on. Let's go over to Dr. Engersol's office and see when we're getting our new computers." Hand in hand, they ran down the stairs and out the front door.

Watching them from her office, Hildie Kramer smiled in satisfaction. She and George Engersol had definitely made the right choices. Soon, perhaps even this very day, their conditioning would begin. And when their time came, they would be ready.

———

Steve Conners locked his classroom door after the final class of the day and started toward the parking lot behind the classroom wing of the Academy. There were still two full hours of the warm afternoon left, and it was his intention to head back to his small rented house a few blocks from the beach, strap his surfboard onto the roof of his three-year-old Honda, and drive down toward Santa Cruz. With any luck at all, the afternoon surf would be up, and he could catch a few waves before the sun dropped into the ocean. But as he inserted the key in the lock of the driver's door, a flicker of movement caught his eye. He spotted Josh MacCallum coming out the door of a maintenance shed that clung like a limpet to the back of the mansion. Clutched in the boy's hand was a large screwdriver, but even at the distance from which Steve was observing him, it was clear the boy wasn't certain he'd chosen the right tool for whatever he was planning to do.

Conners was about to turn away, leaving Josh to whatever he was up to, when he remembered that Josh MacCallum, along with Amy Carlson, hadn't appeared in his English class that morning. During his free hour in mid-morning, he'd found a note in his mailbox from Hildie Kramer explaining that both Josh and Amy were having their schedules rearranged but would be back in his class tomorrow.

There had been no explanation for the change in schedule, however.

Abandoning the surf for another day, he relocked the car, calling out just as the boy was mounting the steps to the enormous house's back door. "Josh? Hey, Josh!"

Josh glanced back over his shoulder, recognized the English teacher and waved. He was about to go on into the house when Conners called out again.

"Josh! Wait up!"

Josh paused uncertainly. Was Mr. Conners mad at him because he'd missed English class that morning? Hildie Kramer had said she'd told the teacher he and Amy would be absent. But what if she hadn't?

"What are you doing?" Conners asked as he came to the foot of the stairs.

Josh's uncertainty jelled into worry. Maybe he wasn't supposed to go into the toolshed at all. "I—I just needed a screwdriver," he stammered. "The shed wasn't locked or anything."

The teacher, hearing the nervousness in the boy's voice, smiled reassuringly. "I don't know what you're unscrewing, but that looks pretty big."

Josh shrugged. "It's the only one I saw. I'm going to move some shelves in my new room."

"You mean those shelves that hang on brackets?"

Josh nodded.

"Well, I think we better see if we can't find something better than that. Most of those things hang up with Phillips screws. That won't work at all. Come on."

Feeling a tide of relief that he didn't seem to be in trouble after all, Josh followed Conners into the shed, where the teacher was already rummaging among the clutter that covered a long workbench that ran the length of one wall. "Kind of a mess, isn't it?" he asked.

Josh shrugged but said nothing, and Conners began pulling open a series of drawers that stood under the far end of the bench. In the third one down he found what he was looking for. Pulling three different sizes of Phillips screwdrivers out of the drawer, he kept hunting until he found a small hand drill and a set of bits.

"You have a ruler?" he asked Josh.

Josh shook his head.

In the top drawer Conners found a tape measure. "Okay," he said, handing the screwdrivers to Josh and picking up the drill, bits, and tape measure himself. "Now let's go see what a couple of master builders can accomplish."

When Josh turned down the broad second floor corridor a minute later, Conners paused. "I thought you lived on the third floor."

"Hildie moved me," Josh replied. "I needed a bigger room."

Conners's brows knit as he followed the boy along the hall. "How come?"

"My new computer," Josh told him. "And I guess there'll be a lot of new books for Dr. Engersol's class."

Conners's frown deepened. When they came to Josh's room, he stopped short. "Wasn't this Adam Aldrich's room?" he asked. Josh nodded, and once more his face reflected the uncertainty Conners had seen on the back porch a few minutes earlier. "You feel okay about that? I mean, I'm not sure I'd like sleeping in here, if you know what I mean."

Josh gazed up at the teacher, trying to figure out if maybe Mr. Conners was teasing him the same way Amy had earlier. "Th-There aren't any such things as ghosts," he said, wishing he could put more conviction into his voice.

Conners shrugged. "You're right. But just because we know they don't exist doesn't make them any less scary, does it? And it just seems strange to put someone in this room so fast. I guess I thought they'd probably leave it empty, at least the rest of this year."

"Maybe Hildie thought we'd just keep on thinking about Adam all the time," Josh suggested. "And anyway, it's not like it's the same as it was when he lived here. We moved the furniture around, and all his stuff is gone."

There was a note in Josh's voice that told Conners the boy was trying to convince himself almost as much as he was trying to convince his teacher. He decided to drop the subject, at least for the moment, having already voiced doubts he knew he probably shouldn't have. But it still seemed oddly macabre to him that Hildie Kramer and George Engersol would not only put Josh immediately into the vacant spot left by Adam in the artificial intelligence seminar, but move him into the dead boy's room as well.

Almost as if they were trying to replace Adam with Josh . . .

He said nothing more of his thoughts, but set to work, helping Josh unload all the books and miscellany from the shelves above the bed. When the boards had surrendered their load, Conners handed them to Josh, who stacked them neatly against the wall next to the door. "Two of these fit," Conners said as he tested the screwdrivers he'd scavenged from the drawer in the maintenance shed. "Give me a hand."

Immediately Josh scrambled up onto the bed, took one of the tools from Conners and set to work. Within five minutes they had the brackets off their braces, and the three metal braces off the wall.

"Now comes the tricky part," Conners told Josh. "We have to find the studs behind the plaster, or the screws won't hold when we put the braces up on the wall." He began tapping on the plaster with the handle of one of the screwdrivers, while Josh watched him curiously.

"What are you doing?" the boy finally asked.

"Listening. Didn't you ever locate studs before?"

Josh shook his head. "My mom doesn't do that kind of thing, and my dad . . ." His voice trailed off and he fell silent. Finally, he took a deep breath. "My dad took off when I was a baby. I hardly even remember him anymore."

Steve carefully kept his eyes averted from Josh, sensing by the tremor in his voice that the boy was on the verge of tears. "That must have been pretty tough."

For a second Josh said nothing, but then nodded. "I kept hoping he'd come back, but he never did. I don't even know where he lives."

"I bet he misses you," Conners suggested.

"No, he doesn't," Josh replied. "If he missed me, he'd have come to visit me. But he doesn't care about me anymore."

Conners stopped tapping at the wall and turned to face Josh squarely. "That might not be true," he said. "He might care about you a whole lot. There might be reasons why you haven't seen him."

Josh's expression turned stormy. "No, there aren't. If he cared about me, he'd have come and seen me, or at least called sometimes. But I haven't heard anything at all for almost two years. And I don't care!" he added in a sudden outburst of anger. Its intensity startled the teacher. Conners reached out and grasped Josh's shoulder. "Sounds to me like maybe you care a lot."

"No, I don't!" Once again Josh sounded as if he was trying to convince himself more than the teacher.

Conners turned back to the wall, giving Josh a little privacy. "Well, you're doing better than I am," he said quietly as he tapped once more at the plaster, though he'd already located the stud and knew he could measure out the next two. "My dad took off when I was eight, and I'm still pissed off at him. It was like one day he just stopped caring about me. But I couldn't stop caring about him."

Josh said nothing for a few seconds, then: "So what did you do?"

Conners shrugged without turning around; he knew that if he faced Josh right now, the boy would close up immediately. "I hurt," he said. "I tried not to let my mom know how much I hurt, but some nights I just cried myself to sleep. And I kept hoping he'd come back."

"D-Did he?" Josh asked, his voice trembling now.

Conners shook his head. "No. He sent me birthday cards for a couple of years, but then I never heard from him again. For a long time I tried to hate him. But then I decided maybe he had his own reasons for taking off." At last he turned around, and squatted down so his eyes were level with Josh's. "And maybe he did," he said quietly. "But even figuring that out didn't make me stop hurting."

Again Josh was silent for a long time. When at last he spoke, his voice was barely audible. "My dad didn't even say good-bye to me," he said. "He just . . . left. How could he do that?"

Steve Conners put his arms around Josh, hugging him. "I don't know." His voice was almost as quiet as Josh's. "I just don't know how people can treat other people that way. But it seems that they do, and when it happens to us, all we can do is go on living, and not give up. And after a while the hurt gets a little easier. You don't forget, but you get so you can live with it."

Josh's arms tightened around the teacher's neck, and as the boy choked back a sob, Steve felt his own eyes moisten. He said nothing for a few moments, until he felt Josh steady again. Then, giving him a quick squeeze, he released the boy and stood up. "Tell you what," he suggested. "What do you say we finish these shelves, then go out and get a hamburger and maybe go to a movie. Just you and me. Okay?"

Josh stared up at him, his eyes eager. "Really?" he breathed. "Just us?"

"Sure," Conners told him. "Why not?"

"I—I've got a lot of homework," Josh said, worried.

"Nobody's going to kill you if you don't have it all done tomorrow," Conners told him. "Besides, the reading I assigned would take two hours, and since you missed class this morning, you didn't get the assignment, right?"

Josh nodded.

"And you'd eat dinner anyway. So let's just use up the time you'd have spent doing my homework on going to a movie. I guarantee it'll be a lot more fun, and I can fill you in on the reading while we eat." He winked conspiratorially. "Just between you and me, it's poetry, and it's not very interesting."

Josh grinned. "You going to tell the rest of the class that tomorrow morning?"

"Of course not," Steve Conners replied. "I'm going to talk about all the symbolism in it, and all the deep meanings everyone thinks the author buried within the lines."

Josh cocked his head. "It sounds like you don't think there's deep meaning," he ventured.

Conners chuckled. "Very good. You're right, I don't. I think authors tend to say exactly what they mean, and a lot of people who can't write like to pretend there's a lot more to it than there really is. Which is the lesson for today. Got it?"

"Got it," Josh agreed.

"Then let's figure out how this drill works, and finish this up. And if the shelves aren't straight, don't blame me. I teach English, not math."

Half an hour later, when they were done, the shelves were on the wall, and they were perfectly straight.

Between the two of them, they'd managed to get it right.

———

By the time Josh got back to the Academy that night, the lights were out and the house, with only its porch light glowing softly, loomed eerily in the moonlight. As he pulled the Honda up in front of the building, Steve Conners glanced over at the boy sitting next to him.

"Want me to go in with you?"

Josh shook his head. "It's okay. We told Hildie what time I'd be back, and we're only ten minutes late."

"If she's waiting up for you, tell her it was my fault. Tell her I had a chocolate malt attack, and I was writhing on the sidewalk, begging for a fix."

Josh giggled. "I'm not gonna tell her that!"

"Why not? Give her something to think about."

"She'd never let me go to the movies with you again," Josh said. Then, hearing his own words, he wished he hadn't spoken them. After all, Mr. Conners hadn't said anything about their going to another movie. Or doing anything else, either. What if he wasn't going to say anything? "I—I had a really good time, Mr. Conners. And I didn't mean to sound like I thought you should take me again."

"Why wouldn't I take you again?" Conners asked. "It isn't any fun to go to movies by yourself."

"Don't you have a girlfriend?" Josh asked. Suddenly he realized that all through dinner, they'd been talking about him. And it had been nice. Everything he said, Mr. Conners seemed to understand.

Now Conners grinned at him. "Even if I had a girlfriend—

which I don't right now—that doesn't mean I wouldn't take you along sometimes, too."

"What if your girlfriend didn't like me?" Josh asked, only partly joking. As usual, Mr. Conners seemed to know he'd really meant the question, even though he'd tried to sound as if he didn't.

"Then she wouldn't be much of a girlfriend. So don't worry about it, Josh. But right now, you'd better get inside before it gets any later. And don't stay up studying all night. Promise?"

Josh grinned at the teacher. "I promise," he said, but behind his back he had his fingers crossed, knowing he had a full math assignment still to do. Opening the door, he started to slide off the seat, but before he could climb out of the car, Conners spoke again.

"Hey, Josh? If we're going to be friends, I think you better start calling me Steve. At least outside the classroom. 'Mr. Conners' makes me feel old. Okay?"

Josh's grin broadened. "Okay!" He slammed the car door closed and hurried up the steps into the shadows of the loggia. At the front door he paused and looked back.

Mr. Conners—Steve—was still there, waiting for him to go into the house.

Making sure he was safe.

Like his father would have done.

His throat constricted and he felt his eyes get damp. Wiping them with the sleeve of his jacket, he waved to Steve once more, then opened the front door, closing it quickly behind him.

A moment later he heard the engine of Steve's Honda rev and the tires spin in the gravel of the driveway as he pulled the car away. Only when the sound of the engine had faded did Josh finally cross the dimly lit foyer and start up the stairs.

He came to the second floor and paused to take off his shoes, not wanting anyone to open his door and ask him how the movie had been. For all evening, even as he tried to watch the movie, the thoughts that had kept going through his mind were not about the film, but about the man who sat next to him, the man who seemed to understand what he was thinking and how he felt, and accept him just the way he was.

Like his father should have.

He crept down the hall, deciding that maybe he wouldn't do his math after all.

Maybe he'd just get into bed and lie there in the moonlight, clinging as long as he could to the good feeling that had come over him.

He came to his room, turned the knob as silently as possible, and pushed the door open.

And froze.

Sitting at the desk in the near total darkness of the room, hunched over the computer's keyboard, his eyes fixed on the glowing screen, was Adam Aldrich.

No.

It wasn't possible!

Reaching out, Josh flicked the light switch, fully expecting the apparition to disappear in the glare of the light that was mounted in the center of the ceiling.

Instead, as the brilliance of the bulb filled the room, the figure at the computer turned to face him.

Blood covered Adam's face and rivered over his neck in shiny crimson streams.

His shirt was drenched with blood, and one of the sleeves was torn away from the shoulder.

Josh's eyes widened in horror as he stared at the figure. Then it rose, and one of its hands came up, a finger pointing at him.

"What are you doing in my room?" Adam's voice rasped.

Josh's own mouth opened then, a scream of terror bursting from his throat as he stumbled backward out into the corridor.

From up and down the hall he heard the sound of laughter. Instantly every door was thrown open. From inside his room another peal of laughter sounded, and then the grisly figure of Adam appeared at the door. Except that it was no longer Adam.

It was Jeff, his eyes sparkling with delight as he reveled in the fear on Josh's face.

"I'm baa-aack!" he sang out. "I'm back, and I got you!"

For just a second a wave of anger swept over Josh, but then, as quickly as it came, it ebbed away, and Josh, too, joined in the laughter.

Later that night, though, as he lay in bed remembering the joke that had been played on him, he began to wonder.

How could Jeff have done it, so soon after his brother's funeral? Didn't he miss Adam at all?

And then he remembered Jeff's words, spoken only yesterday afternoon.

Maybe you're right . . . maybe he isn't dead at all . . . maybe he'll come back some night, and tell you what really happened.

When the sun finally came up the next morning, Josh had barely slept at all.

15

"What's wrong?" Josh asked Amy Carlson. It was a Monday morning, and the two of them were on their way to the artificial intelligence seminar. There was an autumn briskness in the air, presaging the end of summer. Only this morning Amy had been talking about how much she loved it when the leaves on the trees started changing colors and the weather turned cool, but now she was just trudging along, her head down, her eyes fixed on the sidewalk ahead of her.

"Nothing, I guess," she said a moment later when Josh's question finally penetrated her reverie. "I guess I just don't like the seminar very much, that's all."

"But it's neat," Josh replied. For the last week most of their time had been spent in the lab, working with rats and mice, as Dr. Engersol taught them the rudiments of how intelligence worked. They'd spent most of the time working with the rats, setting up mazes and baiting the small animals to work their way through them with rewards of food. Josh had found the experiments fascinating, and it had quickly become obvious that some of the rats learned more readily than others.

Some of them would master the original route relatively quickly, but when the maze was changed, would merely follow the single path they'd learned until they came to a dead end, where they would come to a standstill, sniffing at the new wall in frustration, scratching at it as they tried vainly to make their way through.

Others, though, would waste a little time at the unfamiliar obstacles, but then go on, moving through the maze along new routes, using their noses to guide them closer to the food. Even most of these, however, would eventually come to a halt, unwilling to move away from the food to explore new possibilities.

One or two of them—the brightest ones—quickly caught on to the maze and stopped wasting time altogether, turning away immediately from a newly blocked passage to follow new paths, never giving up until they finally came to the food.

"It's the difference between intelligence and conditioned response," Engersol had explained. "Essentially, the stupidest rats simply respond to the smell of food, proceeding directly toward it along the single path they know. Others won't retreat from the scent, even if it means not getting to the source. But a few of them seem to have figured out that there *is* a route through, and if they can find it, they'll be rewarded."

The next day they'd attached electrodes to the brains of three of the rats, and been able to watch their brain activity as they passed through the mazes and dealt with the changes in the twisting pathways.

While the boys in the class had remained glued to their computer screens, talking excitedly as they spotted the changes in the rats' brain-wave patterns, Amy had grown quieter and quieter.

At the end of the hour, as she and Josh had left the building and started toward their next class, she'd made a sour face. "I think it's mean."

"What is?" Josh had asked.

"Treating the rats that way. Sticking those electrodes in their heads and making them run through the mazes."

"What are we supposed to do?" Josh asked. "If we don't do experiments, we can't learn anything. Besides, the rats don't even know what's happening to them. They don't feel anything."

"How do you know?" Amy challenged. "What if they hurt?"

"But they don't," Josh protested. "Dr. Engersol says—"

Amy's sour look turned angry. "I don't care what Dr. Engersol says. Everybody in the seminar acts as if he's some kind of *genius* or something!"

"Well, he is!" Josh flared. "And if you had any brains—"

But once more Amy hadn't let him finish. "I have as many brains as anybody else in that class," she'd snapped. "And I won't believe any old thing he tells me just because he says I should. Anyway, if he knows so much, how come he says everything we're doing is experimental?"

Josh had decided there was no point in arguing with her. He dropped the subject. But now, as they mounted the steps to the building that housed the artificial intelligence lab, he gazed quizzically at her. "So what are you going to do? You can't just quit."

"Why not?" Amy asked. "Besides, Dr. Engersol wants me to be in some kind of experiment this afternoon, but he wouldn't tell me what it is."

Josh stopped short. "What kind of experiment?"

Amy's eyes rolled impatiently. "Didn't I just say he wouldn't tell me? He only said it had to do with how people think. But if he won't tell me what it is, how am I supposed to know if I want to do it?"

"Maybe that's part of it," Josh speculated. "Maybe if you know what it is beforehand, it does something to the results. You know, gives you too much time to think, or something."

"Well, it doesn't matter," Amy replied as she pulled the door open. "If he won't tell me what it is, I don't see why I should do it at all."

They walked silently down the hall to the lab, where the rest of the class was already clustered around a cage. George Engersol peered up, fixing on them for a second, then glancing meaningfully toward the clock on the wall. "Congratulations," he commented. "You made it with a full three seconds to spare. But since you *did* make it, why don't you come over here so we can get started."

Amy, stung by the director's sarcastic tone, felt her eyes fill with tears, but managed to control them. Josh, on the other hand, didn't seem to notice the bite in Engersol's words at all, for he had already joined the group around the lab table and was staring curiously at the animal in the cage.

It was a cat, and the fur was shaved off its head, which was bristling with tiny electrodes. The wires from the electrodes were bundled together and ran out through the bars of the cage to a computer.

The cage itself was divided into three sections, the largest of which held the cat. The other two, arranged side by side at one end of the cage, were separated from the cat by twin doors, each of which was triggered by a large colored button.

"The cat has already been conditioned," Engersol explained. "A slight electrical charge can be transmitted through the floor of its cage. When the cat feels the charge, it can stop it by hitting either of the two buttons on the smaller compartments, which have also released a small quantity of food into the main cage."

Amy, thinking of Tabby—who was even now curled up on the pillow on her bed—shuddered as she gazed at the grotesque-looking cat, its bald head sprouting a tangle of wires. It was prevented from pawing the wires away by a large, cone-shaped plastic collar around its neck. "It doesn't look very happy," she said, almost under her breath.

Engersol shrugged. "I don't suppose it is. On the other hand, it's not suffering at all, nor is the electrical charge enough to hurt it. It merely startles it into a conditioned response."

"But where's the food?" Jeff Aldrich asked, his eyes fixed on the empty spaces where the rewards for a proper response should have been.

Engersol smiled approvingly. "That," he told the class, "is the whole point of today's experiment. What we are going to do is offer the cat two negative experiences. Today, instead of releasing food and interrupting the electrical current, one of the buttons will trigger the snarl of a dog, while the other one will release a small amount of skunk musk. Neither of which," he added, "is a cat's favorite thing. Thus, the cat will have some choices to make. If it wants to stop the electrical charge, it must elect to face either the snarls of the dog or the smell of the skunk."

Amy Carlson's face set stubbornly. "I don't think we ought to do it," she said. "It's cruel!"

Engersol offered her a reassuring smile. "The cat won't be hurt, Amy. And since it's being monitored by the computer, we should be able to find out a lot about the physical processes its brain goes through as it tries to come to a decision. It's a Hobson's choice experiment, in which any action results in a negative experience. Shall we begin?"

Without waiting for a reply from any of the kids, he threw a switch activating the electrical charge.

The cat's body tensed, and it immediately reached out with a paw and took a swipe at the left hand button.

Instantly, a small speaker within the cage blared out the sound of a snarling dog.

Startled, the cat leaped back, and was once more subjected to the tingling of electricity. It reached out again, trying the other button.

Now, the area around the cage began to reek of skunk, causing the children to hold their noses, and the cat—only an inch from the nozzle spraying the redolent gas—to jerk reflexively back once again.

Amy, outraged by what she saw, grabbed her book bag from the table on which she'd dropped it only a few minutes earlier and started toward the door. "I'm leaving," she said. "And I'm not coming back, either!"

Startled by her words, Josh turned away from the cage. "Come on, Amy, it's not like we're hurting it!"

"You are, too," Amy insisted. "You're torturing it, and I'm going to tell!"

A groan rose from the rest of the boys in the class. Amy turned scarlet, furious at what was being done to the hapless animal in the cage and at the reaction of her classmates as well. "I hate all of you!" she yelled. Then her right arm rose and she pointed an accusing finger at George Engersol. "You're just as mean as they are!" Bursting into sobs, she fled from the room.

Josh started after her, but Engersol stopped him before he was halfway to the door. "Let her go," the director of the Academy said.

"It's all right. Her reaction was a perfectly legitimate response to the experiment. And in a way, she's right—what we're doing isn't very pleasant for the cat. It's not suffering any long-term damage, at least not physically. But," he went on, drawing the attention of the class back to the cage, "let's take a look at what's happening to its brain."

Josh hesitated, torn between his urge to go after Amy and make sure she was all right, and his equally strong desire to watch the end of the experiment.

In the end, his curiosity won out. He rejoined the group of boys clustered around the lab table.

On the computer monitor the lines tracing the cat's brain waves had gone crazy, jagging up and down in a chaotic pattern that clearly indicated its confusion.

And in the cage, the cat itself was frantically pacing back and forth, swiping first at one button, then at the other, each time shying instinctively away from the snarling dog or the odor of the skunk. In the end, it sank down, trembling, unable to continue its futile efforts to escape the unpleasant stimuli that seemed to come at it from nowhere.

At last Engersol switched off the electrical charge, and the cat, breathing hard, slowly began to settle down.

"As you can see," Engersol told the seven boys gathered around the lab table, "the cat was unable to make a choice. Its intellectual limitations didn't allow it to choose the lesser of two evils, tolerating either the snarling or the odor, rather than continuing to suffer the electrical shock. Instead, it simply oscillated back and forth, until finally it broke down."

"Kind of like a computer going into a loop and crashing," Jeff Aldrich observed.

Engersol nodded appreciatively. "Exactly. Which is the point of the whole experiment. Until we know the physical processes a brain goes through while making a choice between two negatives, we suspect that it will be impossible to program true artificial intelligence."

"But what do we do now?" Josh asked, still uncertain exactly what they'd learned from the experiment, and with Amy's words still fresh in his mind. If the experiment was over, it seemed to him that the torture of the cat had been pointless. All they'd seen was what the cat couldn't do.

Engersol turned his approving gaze on Josh. "Now," he said, "the real work begins. We've gathered a lot of data, which is stored in the computer. What we do next is begin analyzing that data. We'll feed the recorded brain waves into the computer and have them analyzed, looking for patterns within what appears to be chaos."

For the rest of the hour the boys tapped instructions into the computer, comparing the activities of each area of the cat's brain to all the others. Within a few minutes Amy Carlson's reaction to the experiment was all but forgotten.

Except by George Engersol.

For him, the experiment had gone off perfectly. Amy Carlson, for whose sole benefit the entire performance had been staged, had reacted exactly as he had hoped she would.

She was unhappy, and she was angry.

The pressure inside her was building.

———

Jeanette Aldrich stared glumly at her desk in the administrative office of the Barrington University psychology department and wondered if she really was ready to come back to work. The week she'd spent at home, with everything she saw or touched reminding her of Adam and tearing the scabs off the still bleeding wound of her grief, had done nothing to begin the healing process. Indeed, she had found that long days of inactivity only made the pain worse, for with nothing to fill her time, she had found herself doing nothing but dwelling on the loss of her son.

So this morning she had come back to the office, where things had not been much better. Everyone she met, it seemed, was treating her with kid gloves, either making no mention of Adam's death at all or being oversolicitous to the point of making Jeanette feel like an invalid.

Everyone, it seemed, wanted to help her.

Someone had made her a pot of coffee that morning, someone else had produced the morning doughnut from the student union.

Jennie Phelps, the teaching assistant who had filled in for Jeanette last week, had insisted on staying, at least for today.

And from almost everyone there had been the exact same words. Uttered in a hushed whisper, after the speaker had drawn Jeanette into a secluded corner, the question never varied. "How are you, Jeanette, *really*?"

As if each of them, through some mystic right Jeanette couldn't comprehend, expected her to share her private grief, to admit to the speaker alone that she was on the verge of a nervous breakdown, or felt like killing herself, or didn't think she could survive Adam's loss.

Each of which, at one moment or another, had been quite true, but none of which she felt was anyone's business but hers and Chet's. To each whispered inquiry, she'd replied with an answer as invariable as the question that was posed.

"Really, I'm fine. The best thing is for me to get back to work and start living my life again."

The words, of course, were as empty as the way she felt, but they at least seemed to satisfy her interrogators, each of whom smiled with relief and assured her she was doing the right thing.

Now, with still an hour to go before lunch, she surveyed her cluttered desk, wondering what she could do to clear off the most clutter in the least amount of time.

Her eye fell instantly on a stack of half a dozen master's theses that had trickled in over the summer, all of which were now waiting to be Xeroxed and distributed among their authors' jurors.

Just the kind of idiot work she felt competent to do. And the steady, rhythmic sounds and motions of the copier had always been a soothing sensation to her, something she'd used to calm her nerves in the midst of hectic afternoons when students and professors seemed to come at her from every direction.

Scooping up the stack of theses, she retreated to the small room off her office where the copier stood waiting, its control panel glowing reassuringly.

Slipping the first thesis out of its ring binder, she dropped it into the feed tray, pushed the buttons that would order the machine to make and sort five copies of the document, and hit the start button.

The machine came to life, whisking the bottom sheet off the stack, feeding it onto the glass, then running five copies of it before spitting the paper back out again, now on top of the stack.

All Jeanette had to do was stand there, in the unlikely event that the machine chose to crush one of the originals or choke on a piece of copy paper.

The first thesis went through in five runs of thirty pages each, and when it was complete, Jeanette collated the stacks of copies, leaving them next to the binding machine, whose operation was another nearly mindless task that she thoroughly enjoyed.

And would save for after lunch.

She continued on through the stack, making five copies of each thesis, and eventually came to the next to the last one. As she set it on top of the copier in preparation for feeding it into the machine, her eyes fell on the title, and her breath caught:

The Gift of Death:
A Study of Suicide
Among Genius Children

Her hands trembling, she turned the title page and glanced at the précis of the thesis.

Her eyes swept over the words, which told her that the student who had authored the thesis had spent the last year carrying out research on the psychological evaluations of gifted children who had taken their own lives. The purpose of the thesis was to construct psychological profiles that could serve as an early warning system to identify suicide-prone children before it was too late.

Her hands trembling, Jeanette flipped quickly through the thesis.

She paused at a chapter heading halfway through:

Barrington Academy: Six Case Histories

As she began reading, she felt a chill in her blood. Was it really possible that six of the Academy's students had killed themselves in the last five years?

Except that it wasn't six.

It was seven now, for the research for the thesis had obviously been completed before Adam had died a little more than a week ago.

Jeanette stood quite still at the copier, a strange hollowness forming in her stomach.

She had to read the thesis, had to know what this graduate student had discovered, had to know whether, if she'd seen the thesis even two weeks ago, she might have saved her son.

And yet she couldn't read it now, couldn't even scan the chapters.

She waited until her hands steadied. When she had regained some semblance of calm, she began copying the thesis.

Instead of making the usual five copies, this time she made six.

One for each of the jurors on the student's panel.

And one for herself. Though it violated the rules of the college, she would slip it into her purse and take it home with her that afternoon.

That night she would read it, and try to discover how the Academy could have lost so many students in so short a time.

———

Amy Carlson was sitting by herself at a corner table of the Academy's dining room, facing the wall, struggling to force down her lunch. She'd ignored Josh MacCallum when he'd tried to coax her to sit at their regular table, refusing even to answer him as she walked past him with her tray gripped in her hands.

After she left the lab, she'd gone back to her room, slipping unnoticed into the house through the back door and scurrying up the stairs before Hildie Kramer or anyone else could spot her. Once in her room, she'd scooped Tabby up from her pillow, then flopped down on the bed, cradling the cat in her lap, petting it and talking to it as if by heaping affection on Tabby she could somehow make up for the pain that was being inflicted on the creature in the laboratory.

And there she'd stayed until lunchtime, skipping the rest of her morning classes.

But when noon came, she decided she'd better go down to the dining room, even though she didn't feel like eating. Otherwise, someone—Josh, probably—would come looking for her, and she still didn't want to talk to him, or anyone else.

So she'd gone down to the dining room, gotten her lunch, but ignored all the rest of the kids to sit by herself, facing the wall and staring at the uneaten food on her plate.

For the first time since she'd met Josh and decided to stay at the Academy, she wanted to go home, to go back to her own room in her own house, where her own cat was waiting for her.

Maybe this evening, after dinner, she'd call her mother and ask them to come and get her. Even going back to public school would be better than staying here, where they tortured little animals!

Amy felt a hand on her shoulder and jumped.

"Amy?" Hildie Kramer said. "What's happened? Why are you sitting all by yourself?"

Amy stiffened. "I just want to."

Hildie's hand dropped away from Amy's shoulder. For an instant the little girl thought the housemother might leave her alone.

Instead, Hildie sat down in the chair next to her.

"Well, I know something must be wrong," Hildie said quietly, her voice soft enough so that no one but Amy could hear her. "Dr. Engersol wants to see you in his office before afternoon classes begin. And you didn't go to any of your classes after the seminar, did you?"

Any licked her lower lip nervously and shook her head. "I—I didn't stay in his class, either," she admitted. "They were doing things to a kitty, and I left."

"Oh, dear," Hildie sighed. "So that's why Dr. Engersol wants to see you, is it?"

"I guess." Amy felt a flash of hope. "Is he going to send me home?" she asked, trying to keep her voice from sounding too eager.

Hildie chuckled. "Somehow I don't think so. It's not that easy to get expelled from the Academy. I suspect he just wants to explain what they were doing, and help you understand that the cat wasn't really being hurt."

"But it was!" Amy exclaimed, her indignation flooding back. "He was torturing it!"

Hildie's brows rose. "Torturing it? I can't believe Dr. Engersol would do something like that."

"But it's true!" Amy insisted. Doing her best not to exaggerate, she told Hildie about the experiment and what had happened to the cat. When she was done, Hildie's expression was every bit as angry as her own.

"If that's what happened," she said, "I think it's just as terrible as you do."

"But it is what happened," Amy cried. "Ask anyone, if you don't believe me! Ask Josh! He saw it. All the boys did. But they didn't care. They thought it was fun!"

Hildie shook her head sympathetically. "That's boys for you. I'll tell you what. I'll go with you to talk to Dr. Engersol, and we'll see what he has to say. And if he's planning any more experiments like that, you and I will call the SPCA. We certainly won't tolerate abuse of animals in our classes!"

Amy stared at the housemother. "You mean you didn't know?" she asked.

"Of course not," Hildie replied. "Now come on. Let's the two of us go have a talk with Dr. Engersol."

Her hand clutching the housemother's, Amy left her untouched lunch where it was. Maybe, after all, things were going to be all right. She'd actually done what she'd said she was going to do, and told on Dr. Engersol, and instead of being mad at her, as she'd been expecting, Hildie was on her side!

But as they left the house and started toward Dr. Engersol's office, another thought came into her mind.

With Hildie taking her side, wouldn't Dr. Engersol be even madder at her than he already was?

When they reached his office, on the top floor of the building that housed the artificial intelligence laboratories, Dr. Engersol didn't seem to be mad at her at all.

In fact, he appeared worried about her. He didn't even seem angry when she told him she didn't want to take the special seminar anymore.

"Everything we do seems like it's being mean to the animals," Amy said. "And I can't even think about what we're supposed to be doing. I just worry about the animals."

"But, Amy," George Engersol explained one more time. "We're really not hurting them. Even the cat we were working with today is going to be just fine. In a month the fur on his head will be all grown out again and he'll be just like he's always been."

Amy's face set stubbornly. "It's just not right to hurt poor little animals," she declared. "And Hildie says I'm right."

Engersol turned to his administrator. "Is that true?"

Hildie hesitated, then nodded. "I'm afraid it is, George. I had no idea you were wiring up cats in that seminar. You know how I feel about that kind of experimentation." The two exchanged a long, probing look. "If it's going to continue," Hildie said, "I'm afraid I'll have to resign."

"And we'll tell the SPCA on you, too," Amy chimed in.

Engersol took a deep breath, then let it out. "Well, the two of you aren't really leaving me much choice, are you? I don't want to lose either one of you, and I suppose I can find other ways of teaching the class. So we won't do any more animal experimentation. Agreed?"

Amy hesitated. "Then what *will* you do?"

Engersol smiled at her. "How's this sound? Instead of trying to figure out how animals think, we'll try to figure out how human beings think."

"How?" Amy asked, her brows coming together suspiciously.

Now Engersol chuckled out loud. "I'll tell you what. This afternoon, we'll do the experiment I talked to you about last week, and then you'll know."

"But you didn't tell me anything about it," Amy protested.

"And I'm still not going to," Engersol replied. "If I did, it wouldn't be valid anymore. But I'll promise you this. I won't ask you to do anything you don't want to do, and you can stop the experiment anytime you want. And we'll have Hildie there, just to make sure no one tries to talk you into anything. Okay?"

Amy's mind worked rapidly, searching for a trap. But if Hildie, who was on her side, were there, how could there be a trap? Finally she nodded. "All right. But I won't do anything I don't want to do!"

"And I won't ask you to," Engersol repeated.

A few minutes later Amy left the director's office, once again unaware that she had been manipulated into doing exactly what George Engersol wanted her to do.

"What happened this morning?" Engersol asked when he was alone in his office with Hildie Kramer.

Hildie smiled, but without the warmth she always managed to summon up for the children. "She spent it alone in her room, and when she came down, she wouldn't even talk to any of the other kids. Not even Josh MacCallum."

Engersol nodded with satisfaction. "Then the last thing any of them remember is that she was very angry, and very upset?"

"And withdrawn," Hildie added.

"Perfect," Engersol murmured. "Just like Adam Aldrich."

16

Amy looked up at the clock on the wall. Only five more minutes until her last class of the day ended.

She wished it would go on for the rest of the afternoon, right up until dinnertime, for every minute that went by brought her one minute closer to the experiment.

"But he *said* you don't have to do anything you don't want to do," Josh had insisted when she'd talked to him an hour ago, during the break between history and math. "What are you so scared of?"

Instead of answering his question, Amy had said nothing at all, for the image in her mind was still the one of the cat in the cage, wired to the computer, being subjected to electrical shocks, frightening sounds, and the stinking odor of the skunk.

Her trepidation hadn't been eased at all when Mrs. Wilson, her math teacher, had handed her a note at the beginning of the hour, instructing her to appear at the gym at three-thirty.

The note had been signed by Dr. Engersol.

Why did he want her at the gym? Was that where the experiment was going to be held?

"Amy? Amy, are you listening at all?"

The voice of Enid Wilson, the math teacher, punched through

the worries that were churning through the little girl's head. Startled, Amy automatically sat up straight in her chair.

"Haven't you been listening at all, Amy?" Mrs. Wilson, a tall, angular woman whose gray hair was pulled back into a severe bun pinned at the back of her neck, was glaring at her over the rims of her glasses. The stridency in her voice made Amy cringe.

"I—I was thinking about something else," she said, her voice trembling.

"Obviously," Enid Wilson replied, her voice crackling. "But when you're in my classroom, I expect you to pay attention to me." She rapped the pointer in her hand on the chalkboard behind her. "Can you solve this equation, or not?"

Amy stared at the complicated algebraic equation that was written out on the board, knowing that she should be able to solve it in her head. She concentrated, her eyes squinting and her brow furrowing as she began to do the calculations, visualizing the numbers in her mind as clearly as if she were working with a pencil and a scratch pad.

"Come now, Amy, it's not that difficult," Mrs. Wilson prodded. "It's really nothing more than a simple reduction!"

Amy swallowed hard, trying to clear the lump that had suddenly formed in her throat. In her mind, the numbers faded away, and she lost her place in the equation. "I—I can't do it," she breathed.

The teacher's eyes fixed on her, making her want to sink through the floor. "Then perhaps you can do some extra homework this evening," Mrs. Wilson told her while the rest of the class tittered at her discomfort. "If you're not going to pay attention in class, you'll simply have to do the work in your room." Smiling thinly, Mrs. Wilson addressed the rest of the class. "Work out the first fifteen problems at the end of Chapter Three," she told them. "Amy Carlson will do the rest of them for you."

Amy's eyes widened. If Chapter Three were like the first two, there were fifty problems to be solved. And she had a chapter of history to read, and a story to write for Mr. Conners. How would she ever do it? And all because she hadn't been able to solve one stupid equation!

The bell rang. As the rest of the students hurried toward the door, intent on getting out into the afternoon sunshine, Amy lingered where she was. When the room was at last empty save for herself and the teacher, Mrs. Wilson finally gazed questioningly at her.

"Is there something you want to talk to me about, Amy?" she asked.

For a second Amy wondered if it would do any good to tell Mrs. Wilson how much other studying she had to do that night. She decided it wouldn't. Mrs. Wilson wasn't like Mr. Conners, who was always willing to listen to his students' problems. Mrs. Wilson didn't seem to care how much work they had to do for their other classes. "It's simply a matter of planning your time," she'd told Brad Hinshaw last week, when he'd complained that the assignment was too long. "You're all gifted children, and we're here to challenge your intellects, not coddle the habits you developed in public school. I know everything has always been easy for all of you, but life isn't like that. You must learn to do what is asked of you without complaining."

"She's sure a bitch," Brad had muttered as they'd left her room that day. When some of the other kids had giggled, Mrs. Wilson had recalled them to the classroom and demanded to know what they were laughing about.

And then she'd doubled Brad's assignment.

"N-No, Mrs. Wilson," Amy finally said as the teacher's eyes bored into her. "I'm okay. I'm sorry I wasn't paying attention."

Enid Wilson's lips relaxed into a semblance of a smile. "Very well," she said. "Your apology is accepted. As," she added, the smile disappearing, "will your homework be tomorrow. Now I suggest you get about your business. Dr. Engersol doesn't like to be kept waiting, you know."

Nodding quickly, Amy pulled her book bag out from under her desk and left the room. Emerging from the building, she turned left and started toward the gym on the other side of the campus.

She paused in front of the door to the women's locker room, screwing her face into her habitual tight squint of concentration.

What if she changed her mind *right now*?

Was it possible the experiment had already started?

She glanced around. There were a few of the college students lying around under the trees and walking along the sidewalks, but no one seemed to be paying any attention to her.

And she didn't have that creepy feeling on the back of her neck that she always got when she felt like she was being watched.

Sighing, she decided the experiment hadn't begun yet, and walked on into the locker room. It was empty except for Hildie Kramer, who stood up as Amy came into the humid room.

"I was starting to wonder if you were going to show up at all," Hildie said, smiling. "Dr. Engersol wants you to put on a bathing suit and go out by the pool."

Amy's lips pursed. "The pool? Is that where the experiment is?"

Hildie nodded. "Do you have your own bathing suit here?"

Amy shook her head. "It's in my room. Nobody said I should bring it. Should I go get it?"

She had already started toward the door when Hildie stopped her. "It's all right, Amy. We have plenty of bathing suits. I'll bring you one."

Amy went to her locker and started undressing, and a minute later Hildie reappeared, carrying with her one of the shapeless maroon tank suits with which the gym was stocked. "Yuck," Amy said, eyeing the suit with distaste. "I hate those things!"

Hildie chuckled. "Doesn't everyone? But I tried to find one that doesn't look too worn-out."

Amy took the suit from Hildie, then finished stripping off her clothes and pulled it on. Poking her arms through the straps and wriggling, she pulled the piece of material over her body, then looked hopefully up at Hildie. "Is it really awful?"

Hildie cocked her head critically. "Well, I don't suppose you'd win the Little Miss America contest, but it could be a lot worse. At least it fits, and it doesn't have any holes in it. Ready?"

"I guess," Amy agreed. She followed Hildie through the locker room to the showers, then into the foot bath that filled a shallow pan sunk into the concrete in front of the door to the pool. Suddenly Amy's nerves got the best of her. She gazed pleadingly up at

Hildie. "Can't you please tell me what the experiment is?" she begged.

Hildie's warm laugh filled the locker room, the sound itself making Amy feel a little bit better. "Why don't you just stop worrying about it?" she asked. "You know I'm not going to tell you anything about it, except that it's not going to hurt you at all. And if you don't want to take part in it, you don't have to. As soon as you know what it is, you can turn around and walk away, if that's what you want to do."

Amy took a deep breath and considered the situation. Should she trust Hildie? Hildie had been on her side over the animal experiments, after all. So whatever this experiment was, it couldn't be too bad. She stepped through the door to the pool.

And stopped, startled by what she saw.

At the far end of the pool, a curtain had been hung, so the diving boards were completely invisible.

Ten feet away from her, sitting near the pool, was a chair. Next to the chair was a table on which sat a computer and what looked like some kind of headset.

There were video cameras in various places around the pool, all of them trained on the empty chair.

Dr. Engersol was sitting in a second chair, facing the computer screen. Seated around him were the other members of the seminar.

Did they all know what was going to happen? Was she the only one who wasn't in on it?

She felt betrayed.

Her first impulse was to turn around and run back through the door, but her friends were already watching her, staring at her as if they were sure she was going to chicken out before it even began.

And it wasn't just her friends.

Her eyes shifted away from the group of children gathered around the computer to the small grandstand that faced the pool from the other side.

Sitting on the benches were at least fifty of the college students, and they were watching her, too.

Amy felt herself burning with embarrassment. Were all these

people really here just to watch her? But why? What was going to happen?

Behind her, she heard Hildie's voice. "Are you all right, Amy? Do you want to go ahead?"

What Amy wanted to do was fall through the concrete and have the earth swallow her up. Why were all these people here? Why wasn't it just the kids in the seminar, who were at least people she knew? And what would happen if she turned around and ran back into the locker room?

They would laugh at her.

All of them. They would know she was a coward, and even though they might not laugh out loud, inside they would be laughing at her.

Tonight, in the dining room, she would hear the clucking as all the rest of the kids made chicken sounds.

Even her friends would laugh at her, and she would feel just like she had back in public school, when everyone acted as if she was some kind of freak or something.

No!

She wouldn't let it happen. Somehow, she would get through it.

She took a deep breath, then slowly let it out. "I—I'm okay," she managed to say, but even she could hear the trembling in her voice. "I just didn't—who are all those people?"

Hildie smiled reassuringly at her. "They're from one of the psychology classes. Dr. Engersol invited them to watch the experiment."

"But he didn't *tell* me," Amy wailed.

Sensing what was going through the little girl's mind, Hildie knelt down and took Amy's hands in her own. "It's all right, Amy. Nothing's going to happen to you. They're just here to watch. They're not going to say anything, or do anything. It's going to be all right."

"Wh-What am I supposed to do?"

"Just go over and sit in the chair," Hildie told her. "Come on. I'll go with you."

Holding Amy's hand, the housemother led her over to the chair, and Amy perched nervously on its edge. Then, at last, Dr. Engersol explained what was going to happen.

"We're going to attach electrodes to you, Amy," he explained. "But they don't do anything except measure your physical responses. I promise you, you won't feel anything at all. All we're going to be doing is recording changes in your heartbeat, and your breathing, and your brain-wave patterns. The cameras will be recording your facial expressions and any movements of your body. So all you have to do is sit there."

"But why me?" Amy asked. "What am I supposed to be doing?"

"You'll see in a minute," Engersol told her. "And remember, you can leave anytime you want to, just like I promised."

And have everyone laugh at me, Amy thought silently.

She sat still on the chair as Dr. Engersol attached the electrodes to her body. Soon she was even more festooned with wires than the cat had been that morning. At last Dr. Engersol placed a helmet over her head, and she felt a mass of tiny points press against her scalp.

"Does that hurt?" Dr. Engersol asked her. "It shouldn't, and if it does, I can make adjustments so it won't. The electrodes should touch your head, but there shouldn't be much pressure."

"I—It's all right," Amy managed to say. Then her eyes met Engersol's, and he could see the fear in them. "Something's going to happen, isn't it?" she asked. "Something awful."

"Nothing awful at all," Engersol reassured her. He checked over the electrodes once more, then went around to the computer screen. On its display, Amy's respiratory rhythm, heartbeat, and brain-wave patterns were clearly visible, reflecting a body under a certain amount of mental stress.

But nothing out of the normal ranges.

"All right," he said. "We're about to begin. All I'm going to do is ask you to make a decision." At the far end of the pool the curtain was suddenly pulled away. Next to the high diving board, a scaffolding had been erected. From the scaffolding hung the knotted rope, the same one she had tried to climb in the gym last week.

Tried to climb, and failed.

"I want you to pick one of them, Amy," Dr. Engersol told her.

"Which would you rather do? Climb the rope? Or jump off the high diving board?"

Amy stared at him. Was he kidding? Did she really have to do one of those things?

But he'd said she didn't! He'd said she didn't have to do anything at all! All she had to do was sit here.

Her heart sank.

Already she could hear the laughter that would erupt from her friends when they figured out she was terrified of both the rope and the diving board.

The cat.

He was doing to her what he'd done to the cat this morning.

A double negative.

Make a choice between two things she hated, or let everyone know how terrified she was.

Let them know, and put up with them teasing her.

Scaredy-cat, scaredy-cat, Amy is a scaredy-cat!

Though no one had uttered the words, she could already hear them ringing in her ears.

She tore her eyes away from the rope and the diving board and looked at the faces of her classmates, who were gathered around the computer, some of them watching the screen, some of them watching her.

Jeff Aldrich was grinning, already figuring out how scared she was.

What would he do? Would he just tease her?

Or would it be worse? Maybe he'd hold her out the window, dangling her above the sidewalk, threatening to let her fall.

Her thoughts began to race. What was worse? To have everyone laugh at her and tease her, or to make a choice and try to get through the terror that always seized her when she was more than a few feet off the ground?

But Dr. Engersol had told her she just had to choose! She didn't actually have to do anything!

Except it wouldn't be enough. If she said she'd chosen one or the other, and then didn't go through with it, they'd all know!

Trapped.

Even after all his promises, he'd trapped her.

Which?

The rope?

She remembered freezing up there, terrified that she was going to fall, clinging to the rope until the coach climbed up and got her.

And she hadn't even been able to make herself climb the ladder to the high board.

A ladder and a rope! How could she be afraid of a stupid ladder and a dumb rope!

But what if she fell?

If she fell off the rope, she'd break a leg at least.

But she might not fall off the ladder, not with bars to hang onto and steps for her feet. And when she got to the top, all she had to do was walk out to the end and jump off.

Just the thought of standing on the narrow board three meters above the pool made her stomach feel hollow and her groin tighten with fear.

But it was only ten feet! What could happen to her?

Surely being terrified for a few seconds was better than having everyone laugh at her because she was chicken.

"I—I made up my mind," she whispered. "I'm going to jump off the diving board."

Immediately, Dr. Engersol left his chair and came to remove the helmet from her head while two graduate students detached the electrodes from her body. But the cameras, which had been recording her every facial expression, every movement of her body, were still running.

And everyone was still watching.

She approached the ladder that led to the diving board and gripped the handrails tightly. She put her foot on the bottom step and started climbing.

She was halfway up when she looked down, and froze.

Do it! she told herself. Just climb up, walk out on the board, and jump.

Then, as she stared down at the concrete beneath her, her terror of heights welled up in her and she knew she couldn't do it.

Don't look, she commanded herself.

She forced herself to look up, and there, looming above her, was the board itself.

No!

She couldn't do it, couldn't possibly walk out on it! It was too narrow. She'd fall before she took even a single step.

As she felt the last of her nerve slipping away from her, she began to sob. Tears streaming down her face, she scrambled back down off the ladder and fled toward the locker room, covering her face with her hands, already imagining she could hear the laughter following her. Then she was inside the locker room, scurrying across the empty shower room. By the time she came to her locker, the bathing suit was already half off, and she jerked it the rest of the way, hurling it into a corner and pulling on her clothes as fast as she could. Leaving her locker standing open, sobs of humiliation racking her body, Amy Carlson fled from the gym.

By the time Hildie Kramer came looking for her, the locker room was empty, but Hildie was almost certain she knew where Amy had gone.

As she, too, left the gym, every trace of the warm and kindly expression she habitually wore when she spoke to either the children or their parents was gone from her face, replaced by a look of harsh determination. Before anyone else saw Amy Carlson again, Hildie Kramer intended to find her.

———

Jeanette Aldrich gave up trying to concentrate on her work. Though it was only a little after four o'clock, she knew that no one would object if she left early today. Not that she'd gotten all that much done, for while the morning had been lost to all the people who had come in to offer her sympathy and support, most of the afternoon had been lost to thinking about the thesis that still lay hidden in the depths of her purse. During lunch she had managed to find a quiet corner and begin reading it, but she hadn't gotten very far. Simply reading about all the other children who had fallen victim to the same pressures to which Adam had finally succumbed had almost torn her heart out. More than once she'd had to stop reading altogether, for even through the dry prose with which the graduate student had constructed his paper, the human suffering kept breaking to the surface.

It was as if each of the children discussed in the thesis was reaching out to her, calling for help, pleading with her to do something for him.

But there was nothing she could do, for, like Adam, they were already dead.

The youngest had been only five years old when, in front of his mother and older sister, he'd walked in front of a bus.

There had been no question that he knew the bus was coming. He'd even pointed it out to his mother.

Together, they'd stood watching it roll along the road, moving at a steady thirty-five miles an hour.

At the last second the little boy had jerked his hand out of his mother's and darted into the street, throwing himself under the tires.

Jeanette could barely bring herself to finish reading the paragraphs, feeling the pain the mother of that child must have felt, her tears blurring the words until she finally had to put the thesis back in her purse.

But tonight she would finish it, no matter how difficult it was for her. Until she did, she knew she wouldn't be able to concentrate on anything else, for no matter what she tried to do, the thesis seemed to beckon to her, demanding her attention.

At last she gave up even trying to work, and began the process of closing her office for the day. Giving her computer a command to print out the document she had been working on—the final edited copy of an article the head of the department was submitting to one of the psychological journals—she set to work putting the files on her desk back into the cabinet, replacing each of them in its proper folder. In the background the quiet buzz of the printer provided an oddly soothing noise, interrupted every thirty seconds or so by a brief silence as it rolled a fresh sheet of paper into the platen.

Almost unconsciously, she found herself counting the pages as they printed.

Halfway through the seventh one, the printer suddenly stopped. Jeanette paused, glancing at the machine.

The page was resting motionlessly, a line partway down waiting to be completed.

None of the warning lights on the printer was glowing, so she shifted her attention to the computer screen.

The program had crashed.

Swearing softly under her breath, Jeanette rebooted the program, brought up the file she was looking for, and set it to begin printing again with the top of the seventh page. When she was ready, she turned back to the printer, pressed the form feed button to kick a new sheet of paper into the platen, and returned to the computer.

She stared at the screen.

Once more the word processing program had crashed. She was facing a blank screen.

She started to type in the command to reboot the program once more, but this time the keyboard refused to respond.

She hit the control, alt, and delete keys simultaneously, and waited for the entire computer to reboot itself.

Nothing happened.

Sighing, she reached for the red switch on the computer itself, and was about to shut off the main power, wait a few seconds, then start over again by turning the machine back on when the screen suddenly came to life:

MOM

Jeanette stared at the word for a moment. What was going on? Was it really the word she'd heard from her kids all her life, or was it just some kind of garbage the computer had kicked up?

She tried rebooting the computer once more, and this time it worked. The screen went blank, then a series of commands rolled up the screen as the operating system installed itself. But as she was about to enter the command for the word processing system yet again, the screen once more came to life. This time, there was no mistaking what it said:

MOM. IT'S ME. IT'S ADAM.

Jeanette stared at the words.

A joke.

Someone's horrible idea of a joke.

She stared numbly at the message for a moment, and suddenly realized she was trembling. What was she supposed to do?

Did someone expect her to answer?

Her mind raced as she tried to figure out where the message could have come from.

A timed message, slipped into the computer by practically anyone, set to pop up at a certain time of day.

Someone somewhere else, coming into the computer by modem.

There were all kinds of explanations for the message, two or three ways it could have gotten there.

But why?

And who?

Who would do such a thing? Who would be so cruel as to pretend to be Adam?

Surely no one could think this was funny!

Her hands still trembling, she reached out and shut off the computer. The words on the screen faded away.

Should she turn it back on, and try to finish what she'd been doing?

She hesitated, but then remembered how the machine had already crashed twice.

Don't touch it, she told herself. Just leave it until tomorrow.

Ignoring everything else that still needed to be done in her office, she picked up her purse, switched off the lights, and left, locking the door behind her. A few minutes later she was in her car, driving home. But the words on the computer still haunted her.

She remembered something that had happened months ago, last spring. She'd been working in her office, typing up a report, and the word processing program had suddenly crashed.

She'd been about to reboot it, when suddenly some words had appeared on her screen:

HI, MOM. IT'S ME. IT'S ADAM!

That time, it really had been. He'd hacked into her computer from his room, just as a joke.

At the time, she'd thought it was funny.

But now Adam was dead, and it had happened again.

And whoever had done it had used exactly the same words Adam had used months ago.

17

Josh watched Amy run away from the swimming pool and disappear into the women's shower room, wishing he could run after her. As the experiment had gone on, his eyes had remained glued to Amy, instead of focusing on the computer monitor, for as soon as he'd seen the dangling knotted rope and the diving board, he'd understood exactly what she was going through.

How could Dr. Engersol have done it to her? Didn't he know how frightened she was of heights?

And then Josh understood. It was exactly the point of the experiment—to see how Amy would react when she had to choose between two things that terrified her.

But it was mean. Even meaner than what had been done to the cat this morning. In fact, when Amy had left the classroom, Josh hadn't really understood what she was so mad about. After all, the cat hadn't been in any pain. Dr. Engersol had told them so, hadn't he?

But Dr. Engersol had told Amy she wouldn't have to do anything she didn't want to, either. And then he'd not only scared her to death, but humiliated her in front of all her friends, too.

Maybe he could catch up with her outside the gym, when she came out of the locker room. He moved away from the group gath-

ered around the computer monitor, but Dr. Engersol, as if understanding what he was going to do, stopped him.

"Let Hildie take care of Amy, Josh," he said. "She'll be all
right—she just needs a few minutes to calm down."

"But she's crying—" Josh objected.

"Yes, she is," Engersol agreed, his voice carrying no more emotion than if he'd been commenting on one of the graphs displayed
on the monitor. "It was a perfectly predictable response to the experiment. I'd be surprised if she wasn't. In fact, if you'll take a look
at this, you can see exactly when the crying response began."

Josh hesitated, torn by his urge to go after his friend and tell
her everything was going to be all right, that nobody was going to
call her chicken, and his equally strong desire to join the rest of his
class around the monitor and see exactly what Amy had gone
through. Only when Hildie Kramer started toward the locker room
did he make up his mind. Amy liked Hildie, and the housemother
would know what to say to her better than he would. His mind still
half on Amy, he slipped in next to Jeff Aldrich and gazed raptly at
the screen while Dr. Engersol explained what the graphs meant.

"You can see it all right here," the Academy's director told
them. "Here her respirations became irregular, and these peaks
represent constrictions of her throat. And here's her heartbeat, increasing and growing slightly irregular, too, when she first understood the choice she had to make." His fingers tapped rapidly at
the keyboard, and the display on the monitor changed. "I want you
to pay close attention to this. These are her brain waves, and
though they don't look much different from those of the cat this
morning, I think we'll find a lot of differences when we analyze
them. The cat, you see, was responding much more to instinctive
behavior and conditioned response, while Amy was trying to make
an intellectual decision."

Engersol's analysis of what had happened inside Amy's brain
went on, and the graphic displays on the monitor kept changing.
Soon Josh was caught up along with the rest of his classmates in
the digitized display of the myriad processes that Amy's body, as
well as her mind, had gone through during the few short minutes
the experiment had lasted.

"For the rest of the week," Engersol finished half an hour later, "we'll continue working with this data, and by Friday we should have a pretty good understanding of just exactly what parts of Amy's brain came into play during the experiment, and what processes they went through."

"But what about Amy?" Josh asked when Engersol was finally finished. "What about how she feels?"

Engersol's eyes fixed on Josh, and there was an emptiness in them that sent a chill down the boy's spine. "I'm sure she's just fine," he said. "After all, we didn't hurt her, did we?"

As the rest of the class started out of the pool area, still buzzing amongst themselves about the results of the experiment, Josh stayed where he was, staring at the display on the computer monitor.

It was nothing but a series of zigzag lines crossing and recrossing each other, showing what had happened inside Amy's brain.

But it didn't show anything about what had happened to Amy *herself*, Josh thought. Hadn't anyone else seen the look on her face? Hadn't they seen how scared she was, not only of the rope and the diving board, but of looking like a chicken in front of her friends?

Hadn't anyone else cared?

With a last glance at the equipment that had so terrified his friend, he turned away, another icy chill running through him as he once more imagined how Amy must have felt when she'd sat alone in the chair, with all the cameras and people watching her.

Like the cat, he thought. She must have felt like the cat in the cage.

Suddenly wanting to be away from the pool, he hurried across the concrete decking and almost ran through the men's showers and locker room. As he burst out of the gym door into the afternoon sunlight, he looked around, half expecting Amy to be waiting for him.

All he saw was the usual peaceful scene of the college campus, with a few people wandering across the lawns or sitting under the trees, talking or studying.

Amy was nowhere to be seen.

═══════

Chet Aldrich pulled into the garage at exactly five o'clock, surprised to see Jeanette's car already there. Usually she didn't leave the campus until five-thirty, and by the time she got home, he'd already gone through the unvarying twenty minutes of aerobics he was using in a so far highly effective effort to stave off the creeping processes of age. He'd begun the exercises a year ago, was pleased with the results, and the workout even allowed him to convince himself that the 400 calories in the single glass of wine he permitted himself each evening had already been burned up before he even consumed them.

Today, the first day both of them had been back at work since Adam's funeral, he'd been looking forward to getting back into the ritual of the afternoon. But when he saw Jeanette's car parked in the garage, he knew instantly that it was not to be. He parked his own car next to hers and let himself in through the back door that led directly to the kitchen.

"Jeanette? Honey, I'm home!"

There was no answer. Chet's growing trepidation that something had happened at work that day heightened as he moved through the dining room into the living room at the front of the house.

Jeanette was sitting on the sofa, her coat still on, her purse on her lap. Her eyes seemed to be focused on the television set, but as soon as he saw her, he knew she wasn't watching anything that might have been on the screen, even had it been turned on. Rather, her whole expression was that of someone who had just received some kind of terrible shock.

"Jeanette?" he repeated, going to sit next to her on the sofa. "Honey, what is it? What's wrong?"

Jeanette, her lips tight, turned to face him. "Nothing, probably.

Just someone's idea of a bad joke. In fact, I suppose I should be over it by now, but I can't seem to forget it."

Chet's brow furrowed. "Joke? What kind of joke?"

Choosing her words carefully, not wanting to lend the incident more importance than it deserved, Jeanette told him what had happened. When she finally repeated the message that had appeared on the screen, he groaned softly.

"Jesus," he whispered. "What would make anyone do something like that?"

"I don't know," Jeanette sighed. Pulling herself together, she rose from the sofa and went to the sideboard in the dining room, where she poured herself a shot of brandy. "It wouldn't have been so bad, except that Adam did exactly the same thing last spring. He hacked into my computer at work, and all of a sudden a message popped up on the screen. Almost exactly the same words. 'Hi, Mom. It's me. It's Adam!' " She chuckled, a hollow sound that she quickly cut short. "I gave him a talking-to, but in a way, I thought it was pretty funny, you know? But today . . ." Her voice trailed off as she remembered once more the shock that had gone through her when she'd read the words on the screen. "I just can't believe anyone would do something like that, even as a joke."

"And it's not hard to figure out who did it, either, is it?" Chet asked. Angry now, he was already back on his feet, his hand in his pocket as he fished for his car keys.

Jeanette stared at him blankly.

"Don't you see?" Chet asked. "It was Jeff! It had to be!"

"Jeff?" Jeanette repeated. "Chet, why would Jeff do something like that? He knows how hard it's been for me the last week—"

"He did it because he could," Chet replied, his voice heavy. "I can tell you exactly what happened. Adam told him what he'd done, and Jeff didn't forget. He doesn't forget anything, remember? He's a genius! So today he's got some time on his hands, and what does he do? He decides to play a joke on his mother, and it never occurs to him how it might affect you. Well, I think I'm just going to go over to the Academy and have a little talk with him. If he thinks he's going to get off scot-free, he's about to find out he's wrong."

Jeanette was barely listening. It couldn't have been Jeff—not her own son, and not so soon after his own brother's death! It was impossible! It had to be someone else. "I'm going with you," she told him. "If it was him, I should be the one to confront him, not you." She set her drink on the coffee table and followed Chet back out to the garage.

A few minutes later they pulled up in front of the Academy and hurried inside, going directly to Hildie Kramer's office. Hildie, who was talking to one of the campus security officers, fell silent as she saw the Aldriches, then smiled at the uniformed man. "Just keep an eye out, all right? And if you see anything, let me know." The guard grunted a reply, left the office, and Hildie turned her full attention to Chet and Jeanette Aldrich. Her welcoming smile faded as she saw the anger in Chet's eyes and the look of anxiety on Jeanette's pale face.

"Jeanette? Chet? What is it? What's happened?"

While Chet stood silently, his jaw clenched to contain his anger, Jeanette told Hildie what had happened. "Chet thinks Jeff might have done it," she finished. "We'd like to talk to him about it."

"As well you should," Hildie declared. "I can't imagine anyone doing such a thing!" She started out of the office, then hesitated, turning back. "Wait a minute. What time did you say this happened?"

"Around four. A little after, but not more than fifteen minutes."

"Well, then it couldn't have been Jeff," Hildie told them. "He was at the swimming pool from three-thirty until almost five. All the children in Dr. Engersol's seminar were there."

Jeanette felt a wave of relief wash over her.

"I'd still like to talk to him," Chet said. He was still angry. "Knowing Jeff, he could have set up a program that would go off at a certain time, when he knew he'd be somewhere else."

Hildie's eyes clouded. "Oh, I hardly think he'd—" She broke off abruptly as her eyes went to the window. "Speak of the devil," she said, moving once more to her office door. A second or two later, the front door of the Academy opened. "Jeff?" Hildie said. "Could you come in here for a minute, please?" Brad Hinshaw, who was with Jeff, started to follow his friend into the room, but

Hildie stopped him. "If you'll just wait out there, Brad, this shouldn't take too long." She closed the door, then turned to face Jeff, who was looking up at his father perplexedly.

"Are you mad at me, Dad?"

"Yes, I am," Chet replied. "And I suspect you know exactly why!"

Jeff, startled by his father's words, took half a step backward, then turned to his mother. "What's he mad about? What did I do?"

Jeanette gazed down at her son, searching his face for any sign of guilt. But she saw none. His brown eyes were fixed worriedly on her, and he edged closer to her, as if for protection from his father. That simple movement told her all she needed to know, for had it been he who had played the prank on her, he certainly wouldn't have looked to her for protection. To Hildie Kramer, perhaps, but certainly not to the butt of the joke. The tension draining out of her body, Jeanette reached out and pulled him close. "You didn't do anything," she said. "We had to come and find out, but now I'm sure."

Jeff pulled away from his mother. "What? What did you think I did?"

While Jeff listened silently, his father told him what had happened. "Are you sure you didn't set it up some way?" he finished.

Jeff shook his head. "It wasn't me. Why would I do something like that? Besides, I was at the pool this afternoon. We were doing a neat experiment. It was all about—"

Before he could finish, Hildie Kramer cut in. "I don't think your parents are interested in hearing about the experiment right now, Jeff," she said. "Now, why don't you run along while your parents and I try to figure out what happened?"

Jeff hesitated, then started toward the door. His hand on the knob, he looked back at his father once more. "You're not still mad at me, are you, Dad?"

Chet took a deep breath, then let it out. He, too, had been unable to see any sign of guilt in the boy. Like Jeanette, he was certain that had Jeff been responsible for the prank, it would have been obvious, no matter how hard the boy tried to deny it. For all his brilliance, Jeff had always been a terrible liar. "I'm not mad, son," he told him. "It was just pretty upsetting, that's all."

Jeff left Hildie Kramer's office and started up the stairs with Brad Hinshaw. Before they had reached the second floor landing, Josh MacCallum pulled the front door open and pounded up the stairs after them. "You guys know where Amy is?" he asked.

Jeff and Brad glanced at each other, then shrugged. "We haven't seen her since she took off from the pool," Brad said. He laughed, remembering Amy bursting into tears and running away. "She was so scared, I thought she'd wet her pants!"

Josh glared at the older boy. "So she was scared! So what? Haven't you ever been scared?"

Brad backed away, holding up his hands in mock terror. "Jeez! What's wrong with you? It's not like it happened to you, is it?"

"Well, I can't find her," Josh told him. "I looked everywhere she usually goes, but she's gone."

"So what?" Jeff asked. "She's probably scared to come back, 'cause she knows everyone's going to laugh at her. At least Brad is," he added, punching his friend on the arm. "Huh?"

"Yeah, I probably will," Brad agreed. "Unless Josh threatens to beat me up." His eyes twinkling, he surveyed Josh, who was at least four inches shorter than he was, and twenty pounds lighter. "How 'bout it, MacCallum—gonna pound me if I tease your girlfriend?"

Josh felt himself flushing. "She's not my girlfriend," he said hotly. "And I don't see why you guys think what happened to her is so funny, either!"

Now it was Jeff who was grinning. "You want to hear something *really* funny?" he asked. "Listen to what someone did to my mom!" As Josh and Brad listened, he recounted the story. When he was done, Josh stared at him, his eyes wide.

"That's really weird," he whispered. "Who'd do a thing like that?"

Jeff shot Brad a glance, then grinned at Josh. "It was Adam," he said. "No one else could have done it!"

Brad Hinshaw gaped at his friend. "Come on," he said. "Adam's dead!"

Jeff's grin faded away, to be replaced with a smile that was almost cruel. "The hell he is!" he declared. "Only stupid people die around here. Adam's not stupid, and he never wanted to die. He just wanted to get away from all the bullshit!"

"But where did he go?" Josh demanded, his mind whirling.

Jeff's grin returned. "Who said he left? He's still here. You just can't see him, that's all."

"Jeez," Brad Hinshaw groaned. "If you ask me, you're just as nuts as your brother was." Turning his back on Jeff, he started down the hall toward his room. When he was gone, Jeff Aldrich turned back to Josh.

"I'll bet that's where Amy is, too," he said, his eyes fixed on the younger boy. "I'll bet she went with Adam."

Josh gazed at Jeff for a moment, trying to decide if he was serious, then ran down the hall toward Amy's room. He knocked at the closed door, calling out her name.

"Amy?" he called. "Amy, it's me! It's Josh. Can I come in?"

There was no reply, but he thought he could hear movement of some kind inside the room. Finally he tried the door.

It was unlocked, and he pushed it open.

Yowling, Tabby shot out the crack in the door. Josh jumped back, startled. A moment later, though, he pushed the door farther open and peered into the room.

Amy's computer was glowing. On it, there was a typed message:

I'M GOING AWAY. I JUST CAN'T STAND IT ANYMORE. THERE HAS TO BE SOMETHING BETTER.

Josh's breath caught in a short gasp, and he felt his heart race as he realized how similar the words were to the final message Adam Aldrich had left.

Steve Conners pulled up in front of the Academy. Josh was waiting for him on the porch, his face anxious. Ten minutes ago, when the boy had called him, Conners had been about to sit down to yet another of the TV dinners with which his freezer was filled. The fear in Josh's voice had made him abandon the little plastic tray to the trash before he'd eaten even a single bite.

"Take it easy, Josh," he'd said, breaking through the babble coming from the other end of the line. "Just tell me what happened, or at least what you think happened."

"It's Amy!" Josh had repeated. "She's gone, and there's a note on her computer, just like the one Adam left."

"Did you tell Hildie Kramer about it?"

"Uh-huh. But she said I shouldn't worry, that she'd take care of everything. But Amy's my friend! And she was really scared this afternoon!" The fear in the boy's own voice had been enough to bring Conners back to the school. Now, as he took the steps up to the wide loggia two at a time, Josh held out a piece of paper.

Conners studied the message Josh had copied from Amy's computer screen. It wasn't precisely a suicide note, and yet . . . "All right," he said, keeping his voice carefully under control. "Why don't you tell me exactly what happened?"

Just as Josh had started to tell him the story of the afternoon, he was interrupted by Hildie Kramer's appearance at the front door. "Steve? What brought you back this evening?" Then, her eyes falling on Josh, she smiled in understanding. "I see. Amy Carlson?"

Conners nodded. "Josh was worried, so he called me. I figured it wouldn't hurt to come out and see what's going on."

"Well, come on in, and you might as well come, too, Josh." She ushered them into her office and closed the door. "I think maybe Josh has overreacted a bit. Amy had a little problem this afternoon, and it appears she's gone off by herself for a while."

Josh stared at the housemother. A little problem? She'd *been* there. She'd *seen* Amy! "It wasn't that way, Steve," he objected. "Dr. Engersol was using her in an experiment, and she was really scared. She was crying, and everything!"

Conners's eyes shifted inquiringly to Hildie Kramer, who nodded in assent. "She *was* scared," the woman agreed. "And she was crying. I followed her away from the pool and found her in her room. She was pretty upset for a while, but I got her calmed down."

"Then where is she now?" Conners asked pointedly. Hildie's eyes took note of the piece of paper in his hand.

"I wish I knew. In fact, I've just been organizing people to go out and look for her. I assume that's a copy of the note she left on her computer." Conners nodded, almost curtly. "Well, that's Amy," Hildie sighed. "She tends to be a bit dramatic, as I'm sure you've noticed."

"Dramatic enough to leave a note like this? It sounds like the least she's done is run away from school, and at the worst . . ." His voice trailed off, but his eyes darted meaningfully toward Josh, who was listening intently to every word.

Hildie understood at once. "I don't think we need to worry about Amy doing something—" She hesitated, choosing her words carefully. ". . . something irreversible. She's never had those kinds of problems, and I think if she were going to try that kind of thing, it would have been during her first few days here, when she was a great deal unhappier than she was today. My feeling is that she's out walking somewhere, feeling sorry for herself, and hoping to throw a very bad scare into us."

"What if she's not?" Conners countered, his voice harsh now. "What are we doing to find her?"

"Pretty much everything we legally can," Hildie snapped, making no attempt to conceal her annoyance at the implication that she might not be doing her job properly. "I've alerted the campus security force, and three of the off-duty officers have been called in to look for her. For the moment, there isn't much more I can do."

"What about the police in town?" Conners demanded. "Have you talked to them?"

Hildie's lips curved into a thin smile. "If I thought it would do any good, believe me, I would. But as far as the police are concerned, there's no point in calling them until tomorrow. Amy simply hasn't been missing long enough, assuming she really is missing and isn't just hiding from us. But you can believe that if she doesn't show up tonight, I'll be on the phone to the police first thing in the morning."

"But she's gone!" Josh protested. "And after what Dr. Engersol did to her—"

Hildie fixed Josh with the severest look in her arsenal. "Josh, that's enough. Dr. Engersol didn't hurt her at all, as you well know. She's upset, yes, but she did agree to take part in the experiment."

"But she didn't even know what it was!" Josh cried, his voice rising. "If anybody had told her, she wouldn't have done it!"

"Josh, please. Just calm down. Nothing's happened to Amy—"

"You don't know that," Josh wailed. He was about to go on when Steve Conners reached out and took his arm.

"Hold on, Josh. Let me just find out what this experiment was all about." His eyes fixed on Hildie, who briefly told him about the Hobson's choice to which Amy Carlson had been subjected.

"She didn't like it," Hildie finished. "But that was the whole point of the experiment, I think. Of course I don't always understand what Dr. Engersol is trying to accomplish, but—"

"But you went along with letting him do that to her?" Conners asked with disbelief. "You let him play on her acrophobia, and humiliate her in front of all her friends? Jesus, Hildie—she's only ten years old!"

Hildie flushed angrily. "I'm hardly responsible for what happened, Steve," she told him. "If you have an objection to what Dr. Engersol is doing, I suggest you take it up with him. But don't blame me—I'm only trying to do my job the best way I know how."

Conners was on his feet. "I *will* take it up with Engersol, believe me! But first, I'm going to do what I can to help find Amy Carlson. Do you have any pictures of her?"

Hildie seemed about to object, but then apparently changed her mind, opening a file folder on her desk and handing him several blurry copies of a picture of Amy that she'd photocopied only half an hour ago for the security guards.

Conners took them, standing up. "I'm going to take these down to the village and find out if anyone's seen her."

"I'm going, too!" Josh announced, scrambling off the sofa.

"Josh, it's almost time for dinner—" Hildie began, but Conners didn't let her finish.

"We'll get something downtown," he said. "She's his best friend, Hildie."

Hildie considered it for a moment, then nodded. "All right. But I want him back within a couple of hours. He's still got his homework to do, and I won't have him up studying all night."

"I promise," Steve Conners swore. "Come on, Josh. Let's go see if we can find Amy."

Hope flooding into him, Josh dashed out of the office. By the time Steve reached his car, the boy was already sitting in the passenger seat. "Let's go to the bus station first," he said as Steve slid behind the wheel. "I bet she decided to go home. But what if she didn't have enough money? How much does a bus ticket to Los Angeles cost, anyway?" As Steve drove away from the Academy, Josh kept talking, bubbling over with ideas.

They started at the drugstore, which doubled as the bus station. Josh was almost sure that the man behind the soda fountain, who also sold bus tickets, would recognize Amy as soon as he saw the picture. But the old man only studied the picture through his thick glasses and shook his head.

"No, can't say as I recognize her. 'Course, the picture's kinda blurry, ain't it?"

"Did you see any little girls this afternoon?" Josh asked.

"Oh, yeah," the man replied. "There was Jody Fraser, and Carleen Johnson. They come in for a soda most every day. And I think maybe the little Ashbrook girl was here, too. Judy or Janet. Something like that."

"But she *must* have been here," Josh pleaded. "She's got red hair, and freckles, and wears glasses, and she's just about as tall as I am."

The old man shook his head. "Nope. Sorry."

They moved on to the library, where they talked not only to the librarian, but to a high school boy who was working there as well. Neither of them had seen either Amy or anyone who looked like her. The librarian's brows wrinkled with worry when she learned the little girl was a student at the Academy. "Oh, dear," she'd clucked. "I hope it isn't like with the other one. What was his name? Adam?"

Steve hustled Josh out of the library, and though neither of them mentioned what the librarian had said, Steve was increasingly aware of Josh's silence as they moved on.

Unconsciously, they began walking faster, checking the bookstore and searching through the small park across from the building that housed the city hall and police department.

As the sun began to set, they went into the police station itself.

There, they heard from the desk sergeant exactly what Hildie Kramer had told them earlier: no missing persons reports unless there was some evidence of foul play, no matter how slim, or at least one night had gone by.

"But she's only ten years old!" Steve protested.

The desk sergeant shrugged, nodding toward San Francisco. "Up in the city, they got 'em hooking at eleven and twelve. The world ain't like it was when I was a kid."

At last, though Josh begged him to keep up the search, Steve insisted they go into El Pollo Gordo, where he ordered a Mexican dinner for each of them.

Josh said nothing, even when the food arrived. Indeed, he barely even glanced at the steaming enchilada in front of him.

"Amy's not like Adam," Steve Conners finally said, certain he knew what was going through Josh's mind. "You know how Adam was—he always kept everything to himself. No one ever knew what was going on with him." He forced a grin. "Not like Amy at all. Everyone always knows where she stands. If she's mad, everyone knows about it for blocks!" His own chuckle died away almost before it left his lips. "Look, sport, we're going to find her. She's okay!"

"What if she's not?" Josh asked.

Steve wasn't sure how to reply. He was still trying to formulate an answer to the boy's question when Josh spoke again.

"What if Adam's not dead, either?"

Steve stared at Josh blankly. "Adam? What are you talking about? We were all at his funeral."

Josh opened his mouth to speak, then realized that no matter what he said, it was going to sound crazy. Even if what Jeff had said was true, who would believe him? From the look on his teacher's face, Josh could see that Steve Conners wouldn't, and if Steve didn't, then probably no one would.

Unless he could figure out some way to prove it.

And if he could, and Adam wasn't really dead, then maybe Amy wasn't either, no matter how her note had sounded.

Maybe they'd done something to her.

Maybe the experiment wasn't really over with after all.

He should have been asleep an hour ago, but Josh was still wide awake, lying in bed, staring at the ceiling in the darkness. Steve Conners had brought him back to the Academy after dinner, and Josh had done his best to concentrate on his homework, but it was one of those nights when no matter how hard he tried to keep his mind on what he was reading, he kept thinking of other things.

Amy.

And Adam.

He kept telling himself there wasn't anything he could do, but it didn't help, and finally he'd tossed his books aside and decided to go to bed. But even that didn't help, and now, with the moon shining brightly in through the window, he didn't think the glow of his computer screen would show up, even if anyone happened to look up at his window. Slipping out of bed, he pulled his bathrobe on against the chill from the open window, slid his feet into his fur-lined slippers, and sat down at his desk, switching on the monitor of his computer.

He began playing one of his favorite games, an adventure in which he took the part of a wizard, making his way through dungeons and caverns, doing battle with the monsters that appeared out of the darkness with whatever tools came to hand. But as he played the game, his imagination took over, and in his mind the image on the screen became the Academy itself; the maze of caves and dark rooms transmogrified into the corridors of the mansion.

The princess in the game became Amy, and he himself was transformed into a knight in shining armor.

The game went on, but more and more Josh found himself playing the game in his own mind.

What if it was true?

What if Amy wasn't gone at all?

What if she was still in the house somewhere?

The idea grew in Josh's mind, until he abandoned the computer altogether, leaving the monitor still glowing with an image of a black-clad villain guarding the gate to a castle perched on a hill.

He went to the door, opened it a crack, and peered out into the corridor. It was empty. Empty, and silent.

He left his room, pulling the door closed behind him so gently that only a soft click was heard as the latch caught.

A click that sounded to Josh like a rifleshot in the silence of the house.

He froze, waiting for one of the other doors to open, already preparing a small white lie to explain his absence from his bed.

No doors opened. No one appeared to challenge him.

He stole silently down the hall to the stairway, and hesitated.

Up, or down?

Not up. If Amy was in the house, they wouldn't put her on the third floor, where the other kids might hear her.

No, they would put her in the cellar. Maybe tied up.

Maybe even drugged.

His heart began to pound with anticipation as he crept down the broad flight of stairs to the main floor.

In the dimly lit foyer he paused once again. The chandelier's soft glow barely held the darkness back. In Josh's imagination, every shadowy corner held something watching him, something lurking, waiting to leap out at him.

He almost lost his nerve, but when he remembered once again the look of stark terror on Amy's face that afternoon, and imagined the peril she might now be in, his courage flooded back to him. He scuttled across the foyer into the great dining room, barely illuminated by the spill of the weak light from the hall chandelier.

Between it and the kitchen, he knew, were the stairs leading down to the basement.

He came to the door, reached out with a trembling hand, and tried the knob.

As it turned, part of him almost wished it had been locked.

He pushed the basement door open, cringing as its hinges creaked. He stood still in the gloom of the butler's pantry, staring down into the blackness of the cellar below.

A light.

There had to be a light somewhere down there.

He reached into the darkness, feeling along the wall inside the basement's door. His hand touched something that moved, scuttling off into the darkness as Josh jerked his hand away. His skin crawled as he imagined what the creature might have been, and he almost gave up the adventure and returned to the safety of his bed.

A moment later, though, he regained control of his nerves and quickly reached once more into the blackness, sweeping his hand upward, so that his fingers would catch any switch that might be there.

It worked, and a naked light bulb flashed on at the bottom of the stairs. Josh stared at it in shocked amazement for a split second, then quickly stepped through the doorway, pulling the door shut behind him. He was standing on a landing at the top of a steep flight of rickety-looking wooden steps, a rough two-by-four banister offering the only means of steadying himself.

The white light of the naked bulb seemed to be swallowed up by the blackness that spread away from the foot of the staircase. It was all Josh could do to keep himself from turning away and fleeing from the unknown cavern beneath the mansion.

Stupid! he told himself. It's just a basement, and there's nothing hiding in it. Amy's probably not even down here.

But what if she was, and he went back to bed without even looking?

He crept down the stairs, freezing every time one of the steps creaked beneath his feet, listening to the silence until he was sure nothing else had heard him, then moving onward.

At last he came to the concrete floor. Shading his eyes against the glare of the bulb that now hung directly overhead, he peered into the surrounding darkness. His eyes, adjusting to the light, surveyed the old furniture that was stored in the cellar, and the long-closed cartons that were stacked against the wall behind the stairs, cartons whose very contents had probably been forgotten years before.

For a moment he was tempted to open one of them, but then he turned away, intent on exploring the rest of the basement before he lost his nerve. He moved away from the light, ducking his head to avoid the cobwebs that hung from the huge floor joists that supported the mansion above.

The basement was a maze in its own right, partitioned off into various rooms. As he moved along, he found more light switches, and slowly the cavernous space beneath the house began to glow with light, each successive wave of shadows washed away by another of those naked bulbs that made Josh feel newly exposed every time he turned one on.

He found the laundry room, and the enormous furnace that heated the building. A monstrous boiler occupied a room of its own, with pipes leading in all directions to supply hot water to the various bathrooms of the house.

Josh explored each room as he came to it, then moved on, each step taking him farther from the stairs that were the only entrance to the cellar. And with each step, and every unlocked room he came to, his hopes of finding Amy Carlson faded a little further.

Still, he kept going, kept creeping through the shadowy maze.

━━━━━

It was well past midnight when Hildie Kramer left her suite of rooms on the ground floor of the Academy and mounted the stairs, pausing on both the second and third floor landings to be certain that none of the children were prowling around the house. Then she went on up to the fourth floor, and the small anteroom in front of the door to George Engersol's apartment. Knowing it was empty, she used her own key to let herself in, then relocked the door behind her.

She switched a lamp on, confident the light would cause no concern to anyone, since Engersol was notorious for the late hours he kept. She glanced around the main room of the large suite that was perched on the roof of the mansion. In one corner was Engersol's desk, where he worked on the projects that were far too private to risk leaving in his office in the classroom wing next to the mansion. In addition to the desk, the room contained a large, worn sofa, a pair of ancient Morris chairs that Engersol steadfastly refused to have reupholstered, and a small bar, from which the two of them occasionally enjoyed a drink at the end of the day. There were several small tables scattered around the room, each of them covered with books from Engersol's extensive library, whose shelves were built into every available wall. The curtains over the large windows that pierced the two exterior walls of the room were open, as always, and Hildie didn't bother to close them. Despite the airiness of the apartment during the daylight hours, it was nevertheless extraordinarily private at night, for unless someone was high on the hill behind the building, there were no other points from which its interior could be viewed.

Crossing to one of the bookcases that lined the east wall, Hildie pulled out a thick volume by B. F. Skinner and groped for the tiny button that was hidden in a small depression in the wood. As she

pressed the button, a section of the bookcase swung open, revealing the closed doors of an elevator.

An elevator whose shaft was hidden in the wall behind the ornate brass construction whose scaffolding and cage visitors to the
mansion never failed to admire, and which proved endlessly fascinating to the children of the Academy.

Neither the mansion's visitors nor the children who lived in it
were aware of this second elevator, for it was invisible to all, and
while casual visitors would never have cause even to hear it, the
tale of Eustace Barrington's restless spirit accounted for whatever
sounds the children might hear at night. Indeed, when George Engersol had discovered the existence of the elevator—and the hidden
suite of rooms far beneath the basement to which it provided the
only access—he had understood at once that there was some truth
to the ancient legend about Eustace Barrington's vanished son; understood that he had discovered the place to which the boy had
"vanished." Ever since, he had turned not only the elevator, but
the rooms below and the legend itself, to his own advantage.

Hildie pressed another button that would summon the car, and
waited impatiently for nearly thirty seconds before the doors slid
open. Stepping into the car, she pressed the lower of the two desti-
nation buttons on its wall. Slowly, the elevator descended, inching
downward to a level five stories below the cupola, deep beneath the
foundation on which the mansion had been built.

To the subterranean rooms to which Eustace Barrington's idiot
savant son had been banished at the age of five.

Banished to be cared for—or to be held prisoner? Not that it
made any difference now, a century after it had happened, Hildie
reflected, though the mere thought of the silent child living out his
darkness-shrouded days entombed in the deep subcellar never
failed to prickle the skin at the back of her neck. Well, she reminded herself, all that was important now was that no one outside
the innermost circle knew it existed at all.

Nor would they—until the time was right.

═══════

Josh was just coming to what he thought might have been a coal
bin when he heard the sound.

It was faint, but he was certain he recognized it.

The elevator.

Someone was in the elevator.

He froze.

Had someone found out he wasn't in his room, and come looking for him? Panic threatened to overwhelm him, but then he realized that just because someone was looking for him, didn't mean they would find him.

The noise grew louder, and he listened, finally moving toward it, certain that it would stop in a moment as the car came to the main floor.

Before him was a blank concrete wall, perhaps eight feet across. Moving to its end, he found a second wall.

The sound of the elevator seemed to come from behind the concrete. He pressed his ear to the wall, listening.

The sound was louder. He went on, coming to another corner, and then the fourth.

The shaft! He'd found the bottom of the elevator shaft!

He pressed his ear to the wall again, just as the grinding of the machinery ceased. The car had come to a halt. A second later he was sure he heard the door open.

It sounded close, though he couldn't judge exactly where it came from, whether above or below.

What if whoever was there saw light coming from under the basement door?

The thought galvanized him, and he darted back through the basement, switching off the lights as he went, coming at last to the foot of the stairs. Darting up the steep flight as silently as he could, he flipped the switch next to the door, then froze, waiting in pitch-blackness, straining to hear any movement on the other side of the door.

His pounding heart and gasping breath seemed to echo through the basement, and he was certain that anyone in the little chamber beyond the door could hear him clearly.

Seconds slipped by, each of them seeming endless. Slowly his panting eased and his heart slowed to its normal pace.

From the other side of the door he heard nothing.

At last, terror gripping his soul, Josh groped in the blackness, found the doorknob, and twisted it.

Easing the door open no more than a crack, he peered out into the faint light that barely suffused the darkness of the butler's pantry.

Everything seemed to be exactly as it had been a few minutes earlier, when he had stolen down the stairs from the second floor. He opened the door wider, slipped through it and pushed it silently closed behind him. His slippers making no sound on the wooden floor, he crept back through the dining room, pausing once more at the door to the foyer.

He watched, and listened.

Nothing.

At last, taking a deep breath, he darted from the shelter of the dining room door, dashed across the foyer and raced up the stairs to the second floor.

Before he'd even released his breath, he was back in his room, the door safely shut behind him. As he slowly released the air from his lungs, he went to the window and peered out into the faint moonlight.

Outside, everything looked peaceful.

But something told him it was not. Somewhere, he was certain, something was happening. Either inside the house or outside of it.

He would stay awake tonight, and watch.

Watch, and listen.

═══════

When the doors of the elevator opened, Hildie stepped out into a brightly lit hallway completely lined with glistening white tile. She turned right. Three paces down the corridor she came to a door and paused to peer in through the small window that broke its otherwise blank façade.

Inside, George Engersol was hard at work, wearing a surgical mask and gown, his hair covered by a pale green cloth cap.

Quickly, Hildie moved on to the next room, where she scrubbed her hands and arms, then donned the same kind of scrub suit that

George Engersol was wearing. When she was ready, she backed through the swinging door that separated the anteroom from the operating theater.

George Engersol looked up, his sharp eyes glinting with annoyance. "I told you to be here by eleven," he said.

"I'm here now," Hildie replied. "Is everything ready?"

"Of course it's ready. But I'm still not sure it's the right time. I'd hoped to wait at least another week, maybe two."

"You don't *have* another week or two, not with Amy Carlson. She was going to leave."

"You could have talked her out of it," Engersol said tersely.

"If I could have, I would have," Hildie replied, remembering the conversation she'd had when she found Amy exactly where she'd looked for her, hidden within the circle of trees that made up the Gazebo on the school's front lawn. She'd tried her best to reason with Amy, to calm her down, but it had done no good.

"I'm going home," Amy had insisted. "And if you don't let me call my mother, I'll run away. I won't stay, even if you lock me in my room!"

So Hildie had given in. "All right, Amy," she'd said. "Let's go to my office and call your parents. If you don't want to stay, we certainly don't want to keep you here."

Amy, apparently mollified by Hildie's unexpected agreement to her demands, had allowed herself to be led to Hildie's office. "Why don't I get you a glass of water?" Hildie had offered. "Then, by the time you drink it, you'll feel better, and be calm enough to talk to your mother. All right?"

Amy, still sniffling, had nodded. Hildie had given her a box of Kleenex with which to blow her nose, then disappeared for a moment. When she returned, she had a glass of water. Amy promptly gulped it down.

It had taken no more than thirty seconds for the drug to take effect and drowsiness to overcome the little girl. Hildie had carried her quickly to the ornate brass elevator, which brought them up to Engersol's apartment, then down again to the laboratory beneath the Academy's basement.

Amy had been there ever since.

Now, still unconscious, she lay on the operating table.

Hildie glanced dispassionately down at the girl's sleeping face and the tangle of red hair that framed her freckled cheeks. Then she shifted her attention to all the equipment that was arranged around the table, equipment that would keep Amy alive through the next four hours.

A respirator was waiting, and a blood pump.

Nearby was a dialysis machine, along with an array of special equipment that George Engersol himself had invented.

"Shall we begin?" Hildie asked.

Nodding, George Engersol picked up a scalpel. A moment later he'd made a slit that began behind Amy's left ear and went around the back of her head, ending at her right ear.

Working quickly, he began peeling her scalp away from her skull.

He didn't worry too much about how carefully he treated Amy's face, for George Engersol knew that at the end of the operation, Amy's face wouldn't matter anymore.

Indeed, when they finally found her, if they ever did, he doubted whether anything would remain of Amy's face at all.

Or any of the rest of her, for that matter.

Certainly, there wouldn't be enough left for anyone to figure out what he'd done to her.

19

George Engersol, with Hildie still at his side, finished the operation at four o'clock in the morning. "It's done," he sighed, stepping back from the operating table, peeling the mask from his face and wiping the perspiration from his brow with the sleeve of his scrub gown. He glanced at his watch, surprised at how late it was; the operation had taken nearly an hour longer than he'd expected. His eyes shifted to Hildie, who was already dressing Amy Carlson's lifeless body in the clothes she had worn yesterday afternoon. "What are you going to do with her?"

Hildie's expression hardened. All night long she'd taken orders from Engersol, silently following his every instruction. But now, as with Adam Aldrich a week ago, it was her turn. "Don't ask," she told Engersol. "All you need to know is that it won't look anything like what happened to Adam. Nor will there be many questions, since everyone here already knows how depressed Amy was. When they find her, she'll be listed as a suicide."

"Why don't we just put her in the incinerator?" Engersol suggested. "It's almost light. If anyone sees you—"

"Don't be a fool, George," Hildie replied. "If she doesn't turn up at all, there are going to be police all over the campus, searching for her. And sooner or later someone's going to think of the incinerator. If they find so much as a single tooth, they'll keep after it until they find out how she got there. And no one, no matter how unhappy he might be, is going to crawl into an incinerator and wait to be burned up, note or no note!"

Engersol seemed about to protest, but changed his mind when he saw the cold look in Hildie's eyes, a look that told him she knew exactly what she was doing and that she wouldn't let anything go wrong.

So far, certainly, nothing had gone wrong.

Of the four "suicides" the two of them had arranged so far, not one had been questioned. After all, they had been careful, selecting only children who had already attempted suicide at least once.

With Amy, though, it had been different. Though they had arranged for dozens of people to witness her humiliation, there was little in her records to suggest that she might become suicidal. Yet that, too, could be fixed. All it would take would be a few minor adjustments to the results of her personality inventories, and the warning signs would be in her files for anyone to see.

Indeed, he could make those adjustments while Hildie was disposing of Amy's body. "All right," he agreed. "Let's get started." He helped Hildie wrap Amy's now-dressed body in a sheet of plastic, then lifted it into his arms and carried it to the elevator. Coming to the fourth floor, he stepped out of the car into his apartment, followed closely by Hildie. From there she led the way, Engersol following.

They left his apartment, stepping out onto the landing at the top of the narrow stairs that led down to the third floor. Signaling Engersol to stay where he was, Hildie silently moved down the flight of steps until she came to the bottom, where she checked the long corridor that ran the length of the mansion. Satisfied, she signaled Engersol to follow her.

They repeated the procedure at the second floor, and in less than a minute had reached the main floor. Leaving the building by the back door, Hildie opened the trunk of her Acura, then stood aside as Engersol deposited Amy Carlson's shrouded body into it.

"All right," Hildie whispered just loudly enough for Engersol to hear her. "I can take care of the rest."

Engersol glanced anxiously at the faintly silvering sky. "If anyone sees you—"

"They won't," Hildie assured him. "And if they do, it's quite
logical that I've been out looking for Amy all night, isn't it? Believe
me," she added, reading the next question in Engersol's expression, "I won't do anything that will get the car searched."

Before Engersol could make another objection, Hildie firmly
closed the trunk, then got into the car.

A moment later she was gone, and George Engersol quickly
returned to the house, moving up the four flights of stairs as silently
as he had come down them a few minutes earlier.

In his room, Josh MacCallum stirred in his chair, twisted uncomfortably, then sank back into the restless sleep that had overcome him despite his intention to stay awake all night long.

He neither heard nor saw any of what had taken place as dawn
began to break.

Hildie left the car's headlights off until she passed through the
Academy's gates. Using a series of winding back roads, she headed
north, twisting along the flanks of the hills until she was well out
of town. Every few seconds she glanced in her rearview mirror, but
no headlights followed her, nor were there any lights on in the few
houses she passed. Not that it would have mattered if anyone had
glanced out a window, for in this part of Barrington, the lots were
large and the houses set so far back from the road that most of
them could barely be seen. The car would be all but invisible, even
from the houses closest to the road. Driving carefully within the
speed limits, Hildie finally turned left down a road that eventually
intersected the coast highway two miles north of the village. Across
the highway a viewpoint had been constructed at the end of a huge
finger of rock that jutted into the sea.

When she was sure there were no cars coming from either

direction, Hildie drove the Acura across the highway and along the narrow U-shaped road that ran along a ledge that had been carved out of the promontory's bedrock. At the very end of the point there was a small parking lot, totally hidden from the highway, no matter from which direction one might be coming.

She'd chosen the spot carefully, for the cliffs of the promontory plunged straight down to a rocky shoreline that was pounded by the surf twenty-four hours a day. By the time Amy was found—if she were found at all—her body would be battered into an unrecognizable pulp.

It took no more than a few seconds to take Amy's body from the trunk of the Acura and drop it over the edge. Hildie watched as the sea swallowed it up, then carefully folded the sheet of plastic, returning it to the trunk of the car.

Then she added the final touch.

She set a folded sweater on the ground near the edge of the cliff, a red sweater with Amy Carlson's name neatly printed in permanent ink on a label sewed into its collar.

A sweater she'd taken from Amy's closet yesterday afternoon.

No more than three minutes after she arrived at the viewpoint, Hildie Kramer was ready to leave.

———

Steve Conners rose at dawn that morning and followed his unvarying routine of washing down a bowl of cereal with fresh-squeezed orange juice and a single cup of decaffeinated coffee. He was already dressed in a nearly worn-out Amherst T-shirt and a pair of green shorts that he'd had since high school and was beginning to think he'd have for the rest of his life. He left the tiny guest house he'd managed to rent for the school year—but would have to vacate as soon as the summer season began—and trotted down the driveway past his landlady's still-dark house. A moment later he was in his old Honda, following Solano Street down to the coast highway, then turning right to head north, where he'd park the car at the viewpoint and begin his two-mile jog along the comparatively level stretch of road north of the jutting rock.

This was his favorite part of the day, when he saw no one and could enjoy the fresh air and rugged scenery with no distractions. The running always seemed to clear his mind, too. Often, a problem he'd decided to sleep on was solved not in the hours he spent in his bed, but in the forty minutes he spent jogging along the coast.

This morning he was thinking about Amy Carlson.

His sleep had been restless last night, for he'd kept waking up, an image of the little girl fresh in his mind, wondering where she might have gone. For, though he was well aware that there was plenty of room for ambiguity in the note she'd left on her computer, Steve was almost certain that Amy hadn't killed herself.

She wasn't the kind simply to give up, no matter how bad things got. Even that first week, before Josh MacCallum arrived, when she'd refused to leave her room, he'd been impressed by her determination: when she'd decided she didn't want to stay at Barrington Academy, she had neither closed down nor run away. She'd just done her best to make things so difficult for Hildie and the rest of the staff that they'd finally give up and send her back to her family.

Though it hadn't worked, Steve suspected that if Josh hadn't arrived and made friends with Amy, she would have prevailed in the end, for even Hildie Kramer's patience with the children had its limits.

He came to the viewpoint, turned left, and started slowly along the narrow track that led to the tiny parking lot at the end of the point.

═══

Hildie was just about to get back into the Acura when she heard the sound of a car approaching on the coast highway. She waited, certain that in a moment it would pass by the viewpoint and continue on its way north, but when she heard it slow down, she froze.

Her mind went blank for a moment, and then she realized what she had to do. Snatching up Amy's sweater from where it lay, she began running toward the approaching car, waving her arms and shouting for help. A second later the car came around the curve, the driver slamming on the brakes as the headlights caught Hildie in their glare.

"What the hell. . . ?" Steve swore as the Honda lurched to a stop a few feet in front of Hildie. He recognized her and rolled down his window. "Hildie? What—"

"It's Amy!" Hildie wailed, holding the sweater up. Before Steve could say another word, she was speaking again, words tumbling almost incoherently from her mouth. "Thank God you're here! I've been up all night, looking for her. I was about to give up when I thought of this place. So I came out, and—"

Setting the brake on the Honda, Steve scrambled out of the car and took the sweater from Hildie, who looked so upset, he wondered if she was going to become hysterical. "Where was it? Where did you find it?"

"Right here!" Hildie cried. "It was just lying on the ground, all folded up. I—"

"Folded up?" Steve broke in. "You mean it wasn't just dropped?"

Hildie shook her head. "I was going to go call the police—"

"What about Amy?" Steve demanded. "Did you see her?"

Hildie shook her head. "I looked down, right by where the sweater was, but—"

"Show me!" Steve demanded. "Show me exactly where it was." Taking Hildie's arm, he led her back toward the little parking area.

"Over there," Hildie breathed, her voice cracking as she uttered the words. "Right by the wall."

His hand still clutching Hildie's arm, Steve strode to the low stone wall that was built along the edge of the precipice.

"Here," Hildie told him, stopping suddenly. "It was right here."

Steve let go of her arm, then leaned over the wall to peer down at the rocky beach far below. He only barely noticed Hildie's hands touching his back, and for an instant thought she meant to steady him. Then, when it was already too late, he felt the push.

His arms churned in the air as he instinctively tried to find something to grasp.

Then he was falling.

He tumbled through the air, uttering only a grunt as his body struck the cliff, bounced away, then plunged down into the boiling ocean below.

Hildie watched only long enough to be certain that he had disappeared into the sea, then turned away. Hurrying to the Honda, whose engine was still idling, she put it in gear, released the hand brake, and moved it toward a spot where the low stone wall gave way to nothing more than a rusty chain anchored to crumbling concrete posts. Keeping her right foot on the brake, she worked herself halfway out of the car, then released the brake as she stepped free of the slowly moving vehicle.

Empty, the driver's door open, the Honda moved across the pavement, struck the chain and kept going.

Two of the old concrete pilings broke under the pressure of the car, and then the car was gone, too, leaving only the broken posts and the dangling ends of the chain.

Leaving Amy's sweater lying on the ground as if it had landed there at the end of a struggle, Hildie finally climbed back into the Acura. As she left the viewpoint and started back to the Academy in the brightening morning light, she was once again alone.

It was, she reflected as she wound back up into the hills, a pity that Steve Conners had had to die.

He'd seemed like a good teacher.

On the other hand, he'd also seemed much more interested in the children than he should have been.

Perhaps she might mention that to the police, she decided, if the matter ever came up. After all, it wouldn't be the first time a teacher had proved to be dangerous to a student.

And given the new circumstances of Amy's death, there would no longer be any need to adjust her records to show a tendency toward suicide.

Hildie sighed contentedly. At least Steve Conners had had the decency to kill himself after whatever he might have done to Amy Carlson.

At nine o'clock that morning, Jeanette Aldrich sat staring at her computer, almost afraid to turn it on. And yet what was she afraid of? she wondered. What had happened yesterday had been no more than a stupid prank, no matter how tasteless it might have been. And at least Jeff hadn't been involved in it.

Indeed, last night as she and Chet sat over dinner at Lazio's, the incident had slowly reduced itself in her mind to more normal proportions.

What, after all, had really happened?

One of the kids—and neither of them thought they'd ever know which one—had pulled a stunt.

And she had overreacted, undoubtedly just as the perpetrator of the joke had hoped, allowing herself to become overwrought simply at the sight of her son's name popping up on a computer screen.

She and Chet had lingered at the restaurant, enjoying a bottle of wine as they watched the sun drop into the ocean and the sky turn crimson as the darkness gathered. By the time they crept home, she had been almost able to shake off what had happened, and the thesis she had taken from her office that afternoon was easily left for tomorrow.

For the first time since Adam had died, they'd made love.

It had been slow, tender lovemaking, and as she'd lain in bed afterward, safe in Chet's arms, she'd begun to think for the first time that perhaps she was going to be able to put her life back together again after all.

But this morning, in the harsh light of day, and without the numbing support of that extra glass of wine, her grief had come crashing in on her once more. She'd put it firmly aside, determined that she would not come apart yet again, and insisted to Chet that she was going to be all right, despite the fact that her voice carried a brittleness even she could hear. Now she was in her office, and as she gazed at the blank screen that hovered on its articulated arm a few inches above her desk, she started to shiver.

Don't be stupid, she told herself. It's only a computer. Even if someone hacks into it again, it can't hurt you. It can only make you upset if you let it, and you won't let it.

She turned the screen on. After a few seconds it brightened.

Words came into focus.

Words that shouldn't have been there.

This time, the message wasn't typed.

Instead, it was written out in longhand, in the neat, precise script of which Adam had been so proud.

Jeanette recognized it instantly.

For almost a full minute she did nothing at all. She simply sat still, staring at the familiar handwriting, remembering the other times she'd seen it.

On notes, held to the refrigerator door by the ladybug magnet that had been Adam's favorite ever since he'd first been able to reach up and pull it off the enameled metal, looking surprised that it wasn't alive.

On valentines that he'd cut out of red paper, and the short stories he'd written in the last couple of years.

Stories that she'd always found vaguely disturbing, for they'd always shown a maturity that Adam's years belied.

Always written in longhand in the same distinctive script that now filled her computer screen.

Her eyes focused on the words then, and she read them slowly:

Hi, Mom,

I guess you didn't believe it was really me last night, since you didn't answer me. You could have. All you had to do was type something. But it doesn't matter, because I'm not mad at you. I'm not mad at anyone anymore.

I like it where I am now. There isn't anyone to bother me when I'm thinking about something, and nobody makes me do anything I don't want to do. I guess you're pretty mad that I went away without even saying good-bye. I almost did, but then I thought you and Dad might try to talk me out of it.

So I just went.

Anyway, I'm a lot happier where I am now, and I don't want you to be sad anymore. And you can talk to me anytime you want to. All you have to do is type in anything you want to ask me, and I'll answer you. So it's not really like I'm gone at all, is it?

I love you, Mom. I didn't go away because I was mad at you or anything. I just did it because I wanted to. And I hope you're not mad at me. Tell Dad I love him, too, will you?

Your son,
Adam

Jeanette read the note through twice, her eyes blurring with tears even as cold fury welled up inside her.

Whoever was doing this to her had not just copied Adam's handwriting. They'd even figured out how to make the note sound as if Adam himself had written it.

It made it sound like killing himself had been a reasonable decision, one he'd thought about carefully, that, in the end, had been nothing more than a way of ridding himself of inconveniences.

Like parents who sometimes told him to go to bed when he wanted to read all night long.

Or teachers who gave him assignments he didn't always feel like doing.

So he'd decided to kill himself, not really worried about what it might do to her.

"I don't want you to be sad anymore."

"I hope you're not mad at me."

And, worst of all, "Tell Dad I love him. . . ."

Her fury at the callousness of it grew steadily. For a moment she had an almost uncontrollable urge to pick up the monitor, and its horrible message, and smash it to the floor.

Then she took control of her churning emotions.

She was reacting exactly as whoever was doing this wanted her to.

But not this time.

This time she would deal with it rationally.

Her fingers shaking, she reached out and pressed the Print Screen button on her keyboard, and a moment later the printer next to her desk came to life, spitting out a copy of the handwriting on the screen.

Then, refusing to give whoever was at the other end of the linkup to the computer in her office the satisfaction of even knowing she'd seen the message, she reached out and switched the monitor off again. As the screen faded back into darkness, she picked the single sheet of paper out of the tray on the printer and stared at it once more.

This time, though, she didn't read the words.

This time she studied the handwriting.

Who could have done it?

But of course she already knew.

There was one person whose handwriting was almost a perfect match for Adam's.

One person who knew how Adam had thought, and how he had expressed himself.

When she faced Jeff this time, she would have the proof of what he'd done, and dare him to deny it while she held it in front of his eyes.

Her anger growing, she left her office and started toward the Academy, on the other side of the campus.

Jeanette strode along the path, almost breaking into a run in her rush to find Jeff, tears of rage streaming down her cheeks. She was oblivious to the strange looks she was subjected to by everyone she passed, and it never occurred to her that the message clutched in her hand might actually have come from Adam himself.

"Let me see, will you?" Josh demanded, pushing his way in between Jeff Aldrich and Brad Hinshaw so that he could more closely watch what Dr. Engersol was doing. All through breakfast he'd kept looking for Amy, hoping that somehow, after he'd fallen asleep in his chair, she might have miraculously returned to the Academy. When there was still no sign of her by the time breakfast was over, he'd almost gone to Hildie Kramer's office to find out if anyone had heard anything. But then he'd changed his mind, because once he started talking about Amy, he was pretty sure he'd start talking about what had happened in the basement last night, when he'd gone looking for her. And the only person he wanted to talk to about the strange sounds he'd heard, and the funny shaft that seemed to go right through the basement floor, was Steve Conners.

For a while he'd thought about cutting Dr. Engersol's seminar and going to find Steve, but in the end he'd decided to wait until after the English class.

Now, though, he sort of wished he'd decided to cut the special seminar. This morning they were going to do some more experiments on the same cat they'd been working with yesterday morning.

The cat was unconscious, and part of its skull had been cut away to expose the animal's brain. As he stared at the convoluted mass of matter contained within the cat's skull, Josh tried to keep his mind on what Dr. Engersol was saying, but he kept thinking about Amy and her objections to what had happened the day before.

If she'd been here this morning, she probably would have left already. Even as Dr. Engersol began telling him what they were going to do, Josh wasn't sure he would be able to stay, either.

"We're going to begin exploring the various parts of the brain today," their teacher explained. "The cat, as you can see, is unconscious right now, but in a little while we're going to wake him up. First, though, we're going to immobilize him, not only so that he can't hurt any of you, but so he can't hurt himself, either."

Carefully, aided by Jeff Aldrich, Engersol bound the cat's four legs and torso to a wooden slab that sat on the tabletop, using nylon straps that had been designed for that specific purpose. When he was finished, even the cat's head was held immobile.

"As most of you already know," Engersol went on, "a great deal of the cat's brain is used for coordinating the functions of its body and reacting to stimuli from the outside. This morning we're going to begin identifying those areas of the brain, and start disabling some of them. And I want to assure you," he said, his eyes fixing on Josh as if he knew what was going on in the boy's mind, "that the cat will feel nothing. The brain itself has no pain sensors at all, and as I disable certain areas of the brain, I won't be causing the animal any serious discomfort. It will undoubtedly be aware of certain false stimuli, but that will be all."

Josh frowned. Whether the stimuli were real or not, the cat would still hurt, wouldn't it? Before he could ask the question, Dr. Engersol had begun.

He slipped a needle into a vein on the animal's left foreleg, pressed the plunger, and a few seconds later the cat began to stir. Then it came fully awake, and tensed as it realized it couldn't move.

For a moment it struggled, but then, as if sensing there was no way it could escape its bonds, it relaxed under the restraints, its eyes narrowing to slits as it studied the faces of the boys gathered around the table.

"As you can see, the cat is now fully awake, and responds to various stimuli." Engersol waved his hand in front of the cat's eyes, and the animal tried to turn its head away.

Then he snapped his fingers by one of its ears. The cat's body tensed as it tried to turn toward the sound.

When Engersol touched the tip of one of its ears with the probe in his hand, the ear twitched reflexively, as if flicking away an offending fly.

After Engersol had demonstrated the cat's responses to various other stimuli, the real work began. Using a laser probe that was guided by a computer, he began focusing the instrument on a spot within the cortex of the cat's brain. "First, I'm going to destroy the area of the brain that responds to visual stimuli," he explained.

"And I want you to watch the cat carefully. If any of you see any signs of pain, let me know immediately."

As Josh watched the cat, the computer adjusted the probe to an accuracy of less than a millimeter, and finally Dr. Engersol triggered the laser.

Nothing seemed to happen at all.

"Did you do it?" someone asked. "Didn't it work?"

Engersol smiled. "Why don't you wave your hand in front of the cat's eyes?"

The boy did. There was no response at all.

Engersol refocused the laser and triggered it again. Now the cat was deaf as well as blind.

Yet as far as Josh could tell, it had exhibited no evidence that it was in any pain at all. Indeed, a few seconds after its eyesight had been disabled, it seemed to have decided that it was time to sleep, and its eyes had closed. But when he reached out and touched it, the eyes flicked open again and moved as if the cat was attempting to see despite its blindness.

Engersol kept working, and half an hour later removed the bonds from the cat's limbs, body, and head. "As you can see," he explained to them, "the cat is now totally helpless. It is deaf and blind, and has no sense of either smell or taste. Nor can it feel anything, for its pain centers, too, have been disabled. Yet you can see that it is far from dead. It still breathes, and its heart still beats, for all the normal functions that are carried out by the autonomic nervous system are still working perfectly. But I want you to look at what we've done."

The boys shifted away from the lab table and gathered around a computer monitor that was currently displaying a highly detailed graphic image of the cat's brain. "This is what it looks like under normal conditions. Now let's feed the computer data about the areas of the brain we've destroyed, and see what happens." He typed some instructions into the keyboard. Almost instantly the image began to change.

Certain areas of the brain—areas that had been burned away by the perfectly focused laser—turned red on the screen.

As Josh and his friends watched, the red stain spread through the image on the monitor, until surprisingly little of the brain was left its original white.

"Now let's mark out the areas of the brain that are solely taken up with keeping the cat alive, with keeping its heart beating, its lungs breathing, and all the rest of its organs functioning."

Now a blue stain began to spread through the brain, and soon there was little left of the original white color.

"What's left," Engersol told them, "is what the cat has to think with. As you can see, by far the majority of the creature's brain is occupied with the simple tasks of accepting stimuli and maintaining bodily functions. Small wonder, then, that the lower animals aren't known for their intelligence. They simply don't have the available brain power. But can you imagine what would happen if you eliminated some things from the cat?"

His fingers flew over the keyboard once again, and the blue stains began to retreat.

"What I've done is eliminate the autonomic nervous system. Notice how much of the brain it occupied."

"Yeah," Brad Hinshaw replied. "But without it, the cat's dead, isn't it?"

Engersol nodded. "It certainly would be, yes. But as you can see, we've eliminated a lot of other things, and the cat is still surviving."

"But it can't eat," Josh pointed out. "Didn't you say it's totally paralyzed now?"

"Yes, it is," Engersol agreed. "We could feed it, however. It's a simple matter of an IV tube. But the point is that destroying certain parts of the brain has not killed the cat."

Josh frowned. "I don't get it," he said. "What does any of it have to do with intelligence? The cat isn't any smarter, is it? All you did was cripple it."

"Perhaps that is all we did," Engersol agreed. "But we've also learned something. We've learned how much of the brain is used for things that have nothing to do with intelligence, or, if you will, with *thinking*. We've learned that much of the brain in a cat—and in a human being, too, for that matter—is used for nothing more than maintenance of support systems. But suppose the brain didn't need to maintain those systems? Suppose it could use its entire mass for reasoning. What do you suppose would happen?"

Jeff Aldrich grinned. "We'd be a lot smarter," he said.

Engersol beamed. "Exactly. And not only that, but—"

He was interrupted as the door to the lab was flung open and Jeanette Aldrich appeared, her face flushed, her hand quivering as she clutched a crumpled piece of paper.

"Come here, Jeff," Jeanette commanded, her voice harsh. "I want to talk to you. Right now!"

Jeff, startled by the cold fury in his mother's voice, obeyed her order before he even had a chance to think about it. A second later he was out in the hall, and his mother was glaring down at him.

"How dare you?" she asked. "How dare you lie to me yesterday, and how dare you keep on with your tricks this morning?"

Jeff, paling in the face of her anger, shrank back against the wall. "What?" he breathed. "What did I do?"

"This!" Jeanette spat the word at him, then shoved the paper holding the message from "Adam" in his face. "Don't tell me you don't know anything about this," she told him, her voice trembling.

Jeff stared at it. "But I don't, Mom," he protested. "I don't—"

"Don't lie to me, young man. You're coming home with me right now."

Jeff's eyes widened. "H-Home?" he asked. "You mean you're taking me out of school?"

"That's exactly what I mean," Jeanette replied. "Now come along!"

She took Jeff's arm and tried to lead him toward the building's front door, but Jeff jerked free. When she turned to look at him, he was glaring at her with a fury just as cold as her own.

"No," he said, his voice low. "I won't go. And you can't make me. If you do, I'll do the same thing Adam did. I swear I will!"

Jeanette stared at her son, the words slashing into her consciousness like knives. "N-No," she stammered, staggering back half a step. "Don't say that, Jeff. Don't even kid about it."

"I'm not kidding, Mom," Jeff told her, his voice flat and emotionless now. "I'm just telling you what I'll do. If you make me leave the Academy, I'll do what Adam did. And then you won't have any kids left at all.''

After a moment that seemed to go on for an eternity, a faint sound erupted from Jeanette's throat. A sound that was part fear and part utter pain.

Then she turned and fled from the building.

20

"**I**s she really going to take you out of school?" Josh asked. The seminar was over, and Josh was trying to hurry Jeff Aldrich by cutting across the lawn toward one of the new buildings that flanked the mansion. They only had another two minutes before Steve Conners's English class was to begin, but Jeff refused to be rushed, ambling along as if he had all the time in the world.

"Nah," Jeff replied. "She'll let me do anything I want. Parents are easy that way—all you have to do is know how to push their buttons. And if I threaten to kill myself, they'll let me do anything I want. Especially after what happened to Adam."

Josh shot the other boy a sidelong glance. "I thought you didn't think Adam was dead," he said.

The same mysterious expression that had appeared on Jeff's face on the day of Adam's funeral now twisted his mouth into a scornful grin. "Who do you think's sending those notes to my mom's computer?"

Josh stopped walking and turned to stare at the older boy. "Come on," he said. "Everybody knows—"

Jeff's voice turned cold. "Nobody knows anything," he said. "All anybody thinks they know is that Adam died. And that's bullshit. Adam didn't want to die. He just wanted to get out of this dumb place. The only thing he liked about it was Dr. Engersol's class, and his computer."

"But—But where'd he go?" Josh asked.

Jeff smiled sardonically. "You're supposed to be smart. Figure it out. It's not really very hard. At least it shouldn't be for you." Then, laughing, he dashed ahead, and before Josh could catch up to him, disappeared into the building.

The bell rang just as Josh was approaching the door to Steve Conners's classroom. He ducked inside, hoping the teacher wouldn't notice that he hadn't quite made it on time. But to his surprise, Conners wasn't there at all. The rest of the class sat at their desks, already buzzing among themselves, speculating on what might have happened to the teacher. As Josh scurried up the aisle to his own desk, next to Amy's empty one, Jeff Aldrich snickered softly.

"Boy, are you lucky," he said as Josh passed him.

Josh said nothing, sliding into his seat and doing his best to look as though he'd been there for at least a couple of minutes as he heard the door open. But it wasn't Steve Conners who entered. Instead it was Carolyn Hodges, one of the university graduate students, who worked part-time assisting Hildie Kramer. The girl walked to the front of the classroom and turned to face the students, whose buzzing had died away as they realized that something unusual was happening.

Carolyn, who hadn't yet gotten over feeling intimidated by the Academy's children—most of whom already seemed to know everything it had taken her nearly twenty-two years to learn—smiled nervously at the group before her. "Mr. Conners isn't here this morning," she announced. "We've been trying to find someone else to teach his classes, but—"

"Where is he?" someone asked from the back of the room. "Is he sick?"

Carolyn hesitated, then shrugged helplessly. "I don't know. All I know is that he isn't here, and that Hildie Kramer has decided we should use the hour as study time."

"Well, if he isn't sick, what happened to him?" someone else asked.

"We don't know that *anything* happened to him," Carolyn replied. "But I'm sure if you have any questions, Hildie can answer them for you at lunchtime."

Though Josh sat quietly at his desk, his mind was racing. Had Steve gone out looking for Amy this morning? And even if he had, why hadn't he come to school? Unless he'd found Amy, and something had happened to her. Josh was wondering how he could find out where Steve was, when Jeff Aldrich's voice interrupted his thoughts.

"Is it okay if I go study in the library?" Jeff asked. "I have a project for Dr. Engersol's seminar that I need to do research on."

Josh turned to look at Jeff, whose face reflected all the innocence the boy was capable of summoning up. But what project was he talking about? An instant later Josh was sure he understood. Jeff was just trying to get out of the classroom.

"I—I suppose that would be all right," Carolyn Hodges said. "As long as you're studying, I—"

Josh's hand shot up. "May I go with Jeff?" he asked. "I'm working on the same project."

Carolyn's expression reflected her sudden doubt. Her eyes shifted to Jeff. To Josh's relief, the other boy instantly backed him up.

"It's a project on the biology of intelligence," Jeff explained, improvising as he went along. "We have to do some research on the relationship between hormones and intelligence. Dr. Engersol says—" He was prepared to go on, but Carolyn Hodges held up her hands in protest.

"All right, both of you, and anyone else who wants to, can go to the library. But you're on your honor, all right?"

Instantly, the class mumbled their agreement, then gathered up their things and headed out the door. A moment later they tumbled out of the building, most of them actually setting off toward the large library a hundred yards away, on the university campus. Josh MacCallum, though, fell in next to Jeff Aldrich.

"Do you know where Steve lives?" he asked.

Jeff's brows rose. "You mean you don't want to go to the library and work on our project?"

Josh flushed slightly. "Thanks for not telling her," he said. Then: "Do you really have a project you have to work on?"

Jeff laughed out loud. "Shit, no! I just didn't want to sit there for an hour. So how come you want to know where Conners lives?"

Josh's tongue ran nervously over his lower lip. "I—I just want to find out what's going on, that's all. I mean, if they don't even know where he is, what's going on?"

"So you want to go see?"

Josh nodded. A moment later the two boys set out, heading across the lawn toward the university in case anyone was watching, but then cutting away from the campus as soon as they were out of sight of the mansion.

Fifteen minutes later they stood on the sidewalk in front of the house on Solano Street, behind which was the little guest house Steve Conners had rented. Josh looked around, searching for the teacher's Honda.

There was no sign of it.

"Want to go look in the windows?" Jeff suggested, already starting down the driveway. Josh hesitated, his eyes going to one of the front windows of the house.

An elderly woman was peering out. When Josh realized she was staring at them, he waved, then ran up and knocked at her door. A few seconds later the front door opened and the old woman gazed out at Josh.

"Shouldn't you boys be in school?" she asked, her voice projecting disapproval.

"We're looking for Mr. Conners," Josh explained. "He's one of our teachers, and he didn't come to school today."

The woman's brows rose a notch. "You're from that school for smart kids, are you?"

"Y-Yes, ma'am," Josh stammered, glancing toward Jeff, who was still standing in the driveway, obviously enjoying his discomfort.

"And they just let you run around town all day?" the old woman went on.

Josh squirmed with embarrassment. "We just came looking for

Mr. Conners," he repeated. "We just wanted to see if he's here, that's all."

"Well, he's not," the old woman said. "I heard his car leave this morning, just before dawn, just like always. Don't know why he can't just run around the block if he's a mind to, but I suppose there's no accounting for young people nowadays. Anyway, he hasn't been back since."

"Run around the block?" Josh asked. "Why would he do that?"

The old woman's eyes narrowed and her voice rose. "He doesn't! Aren't you listening to me, young man? I said that's what he ought to do! But instead he drives up to the point, then runs two miles up the road and two miles back. Doesn't that beat all?"

"The point?" Josh asked. "Where—?"

" I know where it is," Jeff called from the driveway. "Come on!"

Josh hesitated, but the irritation in the old woman's voice, combined with the fact that Jeff was already headed down Solano Street toward the beach, made up his mind for him. "Thanks," he said, then jumped down the three steps that led to the porch and darted across the lawn.

"Be careful of my grass, young man," the old woman called after him, but it was too late. As she closed the door, Josh and Jeff were already halfway down the block.

Twenty minutes later they were at the viewpoint, staring at the broken concrete pilings, and the rusted chain that dangled uselessly down the face of the cliff.

"Maybe nothing happened at all," Josh said softly, staring at the spot where Steve Conners's Honda had plunged over the cliff only hours earlier. "Maybe it's been that way for a long time."

"Sure," Jeff replied sarcastically. "That's why the breaks in the cement look like they just happened. Can't you see a car went off here?" He went to the edge and peered down. "Oh, Jeez, Josh," he said, his voice hollow. "Come here."

Hesitantly, Josh approached the precipice and peered down at the water heaving against the base of the point. He wasn't sure what Jeff was talking about, but then the wave receded and he saw it.

A car, lying on its back with one of its doors open, was visible for just a second. Then another wave came in, shifting the car slightly and covering it once more with water.

"I-Is it Steve's?" Josh stammered.

"I'm not sure," Jeff said, his voice tinged with excitement at his own discovery. "But one of the doors is open, so maybe someone got out."

"What shall we do?" Josh asked. "Shouldn't we go get the police?"

Jeff shook his head. "We better look at the beach first. What if someone's still alive? They could drown while we're going to find someone!" He pointed north, where Josh could see the stairs leading down to the cove at which they'd had the picnic the day he'd first arrived at the Academy. "You go down there, and I'll find a way down to the beach on the other side. If you find anything, come and get me!"

Jeff took off, running back down the looped road the way they'd come, then trotting along the edge of the highway to the south, looking for a path that might lead him down to the beach below.

Josh himself moved more slowly, walking along the pavement's edge, stopping every few yards to gaze down at the rocks that formed the south end of the cove, and the beach that curved north and west, ending at the next point.

He was halfway to the stairs that led down to the beach itself when something floating in the water caught his eye.

At first he thought it was just some trash drifting in the waves and about to be washed up onto the beach. Then, as the object was lifted by a cresting wave and tossed up onto the sand, Josh realized that it wasn't junk at all. As the next wave washed it back down into the roiling water, he yelled for Jeff, then ran to the top of the long switchback flight of stairs. Without even thinking of going back for Jeff, he started down the steps, taking them two at a time, his breath coming in quick gasps from the effort.

Somehow he made it to the bottom without tripping and raced down the beach to the spot where he'd last seen the object. But it seemed to have vanished, as if the tide had swallowed it up.

Stripping off his shoes and socks and throwing them as far up the beach as he could, Josh waded into the water.

He'd seen it! He knew he had! But where was it?

He moved a few feet farther down the beach, and then felt something bump against his bare foot. Recoiling, his first instinct was to run back out of the water, but then he took a deep breath, stooped down and groped in the sandy water.

His fingers closed on the object.

A shoe, almost the same size as his own.

A shoe just like the ones most of the kids at the Academy wore, and that he'd been hoping his mother might be able to get him for Christmas.

Washing the sand from it, he examined it carefully.

Even though it was soggy, the tread was unworn and the shoelaces still looked almost new.

Then he noticed something funny about the shoe.

Across the top—and the sole, too, when he turned it over—were twin crescents of gashes, puncturing right through the leather of the upper part of the shoe and gouging deeply into the hard rubber of the soles.

Marks, like tooth marks.

As if something had bitten the shoe—bitten it really hard.

His heart suddenly racing, Josh gazed back into the sea once more.

And this time he saw the object again.

A wave was building, and as it towered up in preparation to break, the sun shone full upon the thing he'd seen from high up on the highway.

It was a corpse.

Or at least it was what was left of a corpse, for even from where he stood at the edge of the water, Josh could see what had happened.

The wave broke and the water surged forward, tumbling the broken remains of the little girl up the beach, depositing them at Josh's feet as if they were some sort of grotesque sacrifice being offered up to the boy by the sea in penance for whatever mysterious sins it might have committed.

Josh gazed silently at the mutilated body. One of its arms was completely missing; great chunks were torn out of its torso. But despite the damage it had absorbed, Josh was still sure he knew who it was.

Amy Carlson.

His stomach heaved, and the half-digested breakfast he'd eaten only a couple of hours earlier spewed out onto the sand. He knew he should run and find Jeff—or anyone else—but somehow he couldn't.

He couldn't just go away and leave Amy lying on the beach.

Gingerly, he reached down, took hold of her one remaining arm and pulled her farther up the sand, out of reach of the crashing surf.

What had happened to her?

And then, as he stared fixedly at the ruined body of his friend, he remembered a movie he'd seen on television a while ago.

He knew what had happened to her.

Sharks.

She had been attacked by sharks.

———

A crowd had gathered on the beach, the usual curious throng that seems to form out of nowhere whenever a tragedy occurs. Some of them had walked out from the village, where the news of the discovery of a body washed up on the sand had spread like wildfire.

Above, on the road that ran along the edge of the bluff, cars were lined up, the first ones drawn by the car that had responded to Jeff Aldrich's frantic signals after he'd spotted Josh sitting quietly on the beach next to Amy's corpse. He hadn't even yelled to Josh, but instead waved down the first car that came along. After the first car stopped, two more quickly followed. By the time Hildie Kramer had arrived, responding to a call from the police department, there had been barely enough room for her to edge off the road. After trying to jockey her Acura into a just-too-small space that had been left between a pickup truck full of surfboards and a motor home, she had abandoned the car, leaving its rear end sticking out a couple of feet into the lane of northbound traffic, and hurried across the pavement to the head of the stairs.

Already there were more than twenty-five people on the beach, half a dozen of them police officers and medics, the rest a milling throng of sightseers who were talking among themselves, passing on every bit of information they'd picked up from other conversations they'd overheard.

By the time Hildie had made it down the stairs to the beach and worked her way through to the knot of men clustered around Amy Carlson's body, she'd already heard three or four versions of what had happened.

"She was kidnapped out of a mall in Santa Cruz," someone said.

"That's not what I heard," someone else replied. "She's one of the kids from town, and she got caught by a riptide."

"I heard she was already dead before she even got into the water," a third person ventured. "Someone said she'd been stabbed fifty-seven times. Can you imagine? How could anyone do something like that to a child? I don't know what the world is coming to."

Hildie ignored it all, even when someone called out her name, and asked if the child was one of the kids from the Academy. Instead of answering, she simply pressed in farther, until finally she was standing over the knot of policemen and medics who surrounded the badly maimed corpse. Hildie's expression tightened as she gazed down on what was left of Amy, but even as her gorge rose at the mutilation of the little girl, she still felt a sense of relief.

It had worked, just as she had known it would.

Now, as she silently wondered if they'd found Steve Conners, too, she summoned up the proper tears of grief and sympathy for Amy Carlson. What the pounding of the sea might have failed to accomplish, something else had.

"Dear Lord," she breathed. "What happened to her?"

One of the medics glanced up. "Sharks," he said. "I don't know what she was doing in the water at all, but she was sure in the wrong place at the wrong time. Once the first one hit her, she didn't have a chance."

What was left of Amy's body was almost totally unrecognizable. Her right arm was completely gone, as was most of her left leg. Her stomach had been torn open, and there was nothing left but an empty cavity where her internal organs had once been.

Everywhere, flesh had been ripped away from bones, and the bones themselves seemed to be held together by no more than fragments of cartilage. Even her head had not been spared from the attack.

The back of her skull was completely gone, and the jagged edges of the empty cavity where her brain had been were broken and irregular.

Exactly as George Engersol had left them, Hildie told herself, obliterating the work he'd done with the saw with a small hammer and a pair of pliers.

"Her brain," Hildie breathed. "What happened to it?"

The medic shook his head. "Something got it. Shark maybe, or even a sea otter. An otter could have scooped it out like an abalone out of its shell."

Moaning, Hildie turned away, only to find Josh MacCallum standing beside her, listening to every word that had been said. "Josh? What are you doing here?"

"I was the one who found Amy." Josh's voice was barely audible as his eyes fixed once more on the remains of his friend. "I was with Jeff. We were looking for Steve."

Before Hildie could respond, there was a crackling sound as one of the police radios came alive. Both Josh and Hildie turned to listen. One of the officers spoke into his unit, listened a moment, then promised to send two men right away. Putting the radio back into its holster on his belt, he glanced at Hildie, recognizing her immediately from the investigation of Adam Aldrich's death. "One of my men just found a sweater," he said. "Up on the promontory, you know? Where the viewpoint is?"

Hildie put on a puzzled expression. "A sweater?" she asked. "What—"

Before she could finish her question, the officer spoke again. "It has her name in it. It was on the ground, like someone had dropped it."

Hildie's frown deepened. "At the viewpoint?" she echoed. "Why would it be up there?"

The officer's eyes clouded as he realized Hildie hadn't yet heard what else had happened. "There's a car in the water, Mrs. Kramer. We haven't gotten to it yet, but we were able to spot the license number. It belongs to one of your teachers, Steve Conners."

"Dear Lord," Hildie breathed. "You don't suppose—"

"We're not supposing anything yet, Mrs. Kramer. But we'll be wanting to know everything you have about his background."

Hildie shook her head. "He just started this term. He seemed to be so fond of the children."

The officer's eyes narrowed. "Maybe a little too fond, if you know what I mean."

Hildie nodded. "I'd better go call Amy's parents." She sighed. "Josh, I think maybe you should come back to school with me." But when she turned to where Josh had been standing only a moment ago, he was gone.

═══

At a little after noon, Hildie Kramer once more took the elevator down to the laboratory hidden beneath the mansion's basement. Stepping out into the bright glare of the white-tiled corridor, she ignored the scrub room and operating theater, which had been fashioned from the chamber that in another time had served as the dining room for Eustace Barrington's son, and walked quickly to a door at the end. Behind this door had once been the younger Barrington's lonely living room. Pressing her security code numbers into the keypad at its side, she let herself into the remodeled room that was now the lab housing the heart of George Engersol's artificial intelligence project. In a room next door—once a sleeping alcove, but now completely separated from the lab by a glass wall— was the ominous-looking form of a Croyden computer. The twin black arcs that contained its vast range of microprocessors stood alone, forming a broken circle that was nearly six feet high. It was the only piece of equipment in the small room, crouched in lonely splendor in the center of its perfectly air-conditioned, dust-free en-

vironment. The most powerful computer in the world, the Croyden
was as sensitive as it was fast, and when Alex Croyden, who had
developed the computer, had designed its setting in this room, he'd
seen to it that the smallest amount of contamination possible would
be allowed to affect it. Other than Croyden himself, George Engersol, Hildie Kramer, and the head of one of the major entrepreneur-
ial companies of Silicon Valley, no one knew the computer was
there. And no one but Alex Croyden himself was competent to fix
it in the event that it failed.

The room had been designed to see to it that the Croyden did
not fail. So far, it hadn't. Controlled from a keyboard in the room
in which Hildie now stood, its only connections to the outside world
were through a series of thick cables under the floor, and a her-
metically sealed door that Alex Croyden alone had the codes to
open.

Where his supercomputer was concerned, Alex Croyden didn't
even trust George Engersol.

The room in which Hildie now stood comprised the rest of the
artificial intelligence lab.

It, too, was filled with an array of computers, all of which were
concerned with maintaining the contents of two glass tanks that
stood in a special case at the end of the room.

Each of the tanks contained a living human brain.

Filled with a saline solution, the brains floated weightlessly in
their environment.

From the stems of the brains, plastic tubing connected the main
arteries and veins to machines that continually recirculated a blood
supply, oxygenating it and cleaning it, eliminating wastes and adding nutrients. Every aspect of the blood supply was continuously
monitored by the computers, its chemical balance kept in perfect
stasis by the complex programs that determined the correct level of
every element needed to feed the organs in the tanks.

Each system had several backups, and as Hildie stood just inside the door, watching the machines at work, she was once more
astonished that it could work at all.

And yet it did. A pump worked silently, keeping the blood flowing, while a dialysis machine acted as artificial kidneys. Much of

the equipment in the room had been designed by the Croyden computer in the adjoining room, which had processed volumes of data before determining precisely the equipment and programs that would be needed to keep a brain alive outside its natural environment.

Not only alive, but functioning.

For the plastic tubes were not the only things attached to the brains in the tanks.

Bundles of tiny wires, each of them attached to a separate nerve, also emerged from the brain stem, a flexible spinal column that connected the brains directly to the Croyden computer in the next room.

Probes were inserted into the brains as well, and their leads, too, ran through holes in the tanks to join the other cables that snaked away into the conduits beneath the floor.

Now, finally, it was all happening, all the plans that had been laid years ago were coming to fruition, for as Hildie scanned the monitors above the twin tanks, she could see by the graphic displays that the biological conditions of the two organs were precisely as they should be.

George Engersol glanced up from the keyboard, a frown forming as he saw the expression on Hildie Kramer's face.

"Something's happened, hasn't it." It was a statement, not a question.

Hildie nodded abruptly. "Josh MacCallum found Amy Carlson's body this morning."

"Josh?" Engersol echoed, his face paling. "What happened?"

"He was looking for Steve Conners. And Amy's body washed up on the beach, in the cove where we have our picnics."

Engersol's expression hardened. "Why was Josh looking for Steve Conners on the beach? Isn't he here?"

Briefly, Hildie told Engersol what had happened that morning. As she spoke, she saw Engersol's face pale even more, and the muscles of his jaw clench with anger.

"I told you it was too risky," he said when she was done. "We should have kept Amy's body here and—"

"It's all right," Hildie broke in, her words sharp enough to silence Engersol. "They're already assuming that Conners got his hands on Amy, probably intending to molest her, and something went wrong. They haven't found his body yet, and judging from the condition of Amy's, it won't make much difference if they do." She smiled thinly. "It seems that sharks got to her, and there isn't much left. When I asked one of the policemen what happened to her brain, he suggested that a sea otter might have taken it. 'Like an abalone out of its shell,' is the way he put it, I believe. And they found Amy's sweater at the viewpoint. What with the note I left on her computer, and Steve Conners's accident, they'll assume he either left the note himself or found her sometime during the night. I don't think there'll be much question about what happened."

The tension in George Engersol eased slightly. "Have you told her parents?"

"They're on their way up," Hildie replied, nodding. "I imagine they'll be here sometime this afternoon. I don't think it will be pleasant, but we can deal with it. I suspect we'll lose a few more students, though. Two deaths in two weeks is going to be hard for some of them to take."

Engersol smiled. "I suspect you'll manage. If we lose a few, it won't matter, so long as we keep the ones I need."

"I wish I could guarantee it," Hildie replied. "But I can't." She shifted her attention to the tank on the left. "Everything is still stable?" she asked anxiously, remembering what had happened last year, when Timmy Evans's brain had been transferred into one of the tanks, only to die suddenly when it was on the very verge of awakening. Though Engersol had insisted that the problem had lain with Timmy's brain itself, Hildie herself was all but positive that what had truly happened was some kind of error in programming. Hildie was convinced the data that had been fed to Timmy Evans's mind had been at fault, somehow killing his brain instead of bringing it back to consciousness.

Exactly what had happened to Timmy, though, neither she nor Engersol would ever know. But Adam, unlike Timmy, was surviving. "No signs of deterioration?" she pressed.

"Adam isn't turning into another Timmy Evans," Engersol replied icily, letting her know that he understood exactly what she was asking. "In fact, he's doing even better than I could have hoped for. Look."

He tapped at the keyboard, and an image of a brain came up on the monitor that sat on Engersol's desk. "That's the way Adam's brain looked twenty-four hours ago. But look what's happening." He pressed some more keys, and a second image appeared on the monitor, superimposed over the first. "Right there," Engersol said, tapping on the screen with the tip of a ballpoint pen. "See it?"

Hildie studied the screen for a moment, then shook her head. "What am I looking for?"

"Just a second. Let me enlarge it." Using a mouse, Engersol drew a small box around part of the image, then clicked a couple of commands from the bar at the top of the screen. "There. See?"

Hildie's eyes widened as she finally saw what Engersol was talking about.

The brain in the left-hand tank—Adam Aldrich's brain—was growing.

"I didn't think that was possible," Hildie told him.

"Nor did I," Engersol agreed. "And I'm not sure yet exactly why it's happening. But it's the frontal lobe that's growing, the part of the brain that is responsible for thought. It's not just staying alive, Hildie. It's actually growing. We've done it. We've succeeded in wiring a human brain into a computer. One that's still living, and still functioning."

Hildie's eyes were suddenly caught by activity on the monitor above the tank on the right. As she watched, lines that had been quiescent only a moment ago began to waver, then form peaks and valleys. Then two other lines also came to life, one of them suddenly shooting up to the top of the screen before leveling off, another spiking quickly, easing off, then spiking again.

"What is it?" she asked. "What's happening?"

"It's Amy," George Engersol replied. "She's waking up."

21

Blackness.

As the last of the narcotic was washed out of her brain, Amy Carlson's mind rose slowly into consciousness, but it was a consciousness such as she had never experienced before.

She found herself in an unfathomable silence and darkness that made her scream out in terror.

But nothing happened.

She felt nothing in her throat, heard no sound in her ears.

Yet in her mind the scream echoed still, surrounding her, fading away, then rising again.

Or was she screaming again?

She didn't know, for everything she knew, everything that gave meaning to her existence, had vanished.

The entire world had disappeared, and she felt as if she was suspended in some kind of vacuum, left alone in a darkness and silence so impenetrable that it was suffocating her.

She tried to breathe, tried to fill her lungs with air.

Again, nothing happened. She felt no fresh air rush into her lungs, felt no relief from the terror that gripped her.

Panic closed in on her. She couldn't breathe. She was going to die.

She tried to cry out again, tried to scream for help, but once more nothing happened.

Words formed in her mind, but she couldn't feel her tongue move to shape the sounds, feel her mouth open to emit the words.

Once again she tried to breathe, and once again felt nothing as her body refused to respond to the orders her mind sent forth.

Paralyzed.

She was paralyzed!

But how had it happened?

Her mind reeled as she tried to follow a logical line of thought through the panic that was pouring at her from every direction, rolling in on her from the darkness, pressing her down.

Dying!

That's what was happening to her!

She was alone, and she was dying, and nobody knew about it and nobody could help her.

She tried to open her eyes, sure now that whatever was happening to her could only be a nightmare and that when she opened her eyes and let in the light, the horrible darkness around her would lift and she would once again be a part of the world.

She blinked.

Except that yet again nothing happened. She blinked again, trying to feel the faint sensation of her eyelids reacting to the command from her mind.

Nothing!

It felt as if her eyes no longer existed!

Now she tried to move her body, tried to roll over, to shake herself loose from the unseen, unfelt bonds that held her in their grip.

Her body failed to respond.

Like her eyes, it no longer seemed to be there at all!

Another scream welled up out of the black abyss, another scream that echoed only in her mind, quickly dying away in the strange blackness around her.

Her panic threatened to overwhelm her now, but just before she succumbed to it, just an instant before it would have shattered her terrified mind, she staved it off once more, certain that if she gave in to the panic, she would never emerge from it again.

The panic was like a living thing now, lurking around her, a black, unseeable Hell filled with unknowable terrors that wanted to consume her, wanted to envelop her, drowning her forever in her own fear.

The panic was like a precipice, a towering cliff upon whose edge she teetered, part of her being drawn downward, wanting to give herself to the long final plunge, while another part of her insisted that she back away, that she retreat from the brink, pull back before it was too late.

Slowly, imperceptibly, she drove the fear back.

There was a reason for what was happening to her, an explanation for the terrible feeling of being mired alone in boundless darkness.

She wanted to cry out for her mother, to scream in the night for her mother to help her, but already she knew it would do no good.

Her mother wouldn't hear her, for she couldn't even hear herself.

And her mother was home. Home in Los Angeles.

While she was at the Academy.

But she'd been going home.

She'd told Hildie she wanted to go home, and Hildie had taken her to call her parents.

But she hadn't talked to her parents. She'd been in Hildie's office, and . . .

She strained her memory, searching for an image of what had happened.

An image came to her.

A glass of water.

Hildie had handed her a glass of water, and she'd drunk it down. And then everything was blank, until she'd awakened in the horrible blackness.

Drugged.

Hildie must have put something in the water.

What?

She began to think about it. A drug. Some kind of medicine. What kind?

Narcotics. Sleeping pills.

As she enunciated the words in her mind, new images took shape. The blackness was still there, surrounding her, but now lists of words began to formulate in her mind, almost as if she was visualizing them.

She concentrated, and the words came into sharper focus.

Thorazine.

Darvon.

Halcion.

Percodan.

The words popped at her out of the darkness, words she hadn't even known she knew. And yet she not only recognized the words, but knew the definitions of all of them.

They were drugs. Painkillers, and sleeping pills, and medicines to tranquilize you. As they flicked through her mind, she realized that she knew exactly what each of them was for and what each would do to someone, depending on how much was taken.

The sensation was strange. It was almost as if she were reading from some kind of book that existed only in her mind.

Like the way she solved complex mathematical problems by picturing the problem in her head, then working it out as if she held a pencil in her hand, the image never fading, her mind never releasing the proper position of a number until she'd found the solution.

Or when she took a history test, and answered the questions by summoning up an image of the text she'd studied, mentally flipping through the pages until she found the right one, then simply reading the answer off it.

The simple process of thinking seemed to make the panic recede a little, and Amy began focusing her mind on the problem of what had happened to her.

The darkness was still there, surrounding her, but she found she could force it back by imagining things, seeing things in her mind's eye that she could no longer see with the eyes she had been born with.

She pictured a beach, a broad expanse of sand, with brilliant sunlight pouring down from a perfectly clear blue sky, and gentle surf lapping at the shore.

She put herself into the picture and imagined her feet buried in the sand, feeling its warmth between her toes.

Birds.

There should be seabirds in the image. But what kind?

Instantly, unbidden, images of birds came into her head, birds she'd never seen before, even in books. And yet they were there, all of them, and as she gazed first at one and then at another, information about each of them appeared in her mind.

Their size, their coloring, the parts of the world they were native to. Even images of their nests, complete with eggs.

But where was it coming from? It was almost as if—

Her mind froze as a concept suddenly took form, a concept she rejected in the instant it occurred to her.

And yet . . .

She remembered a computer she'd seen, not more than a month ago. A CD-ROM display, in which an entire encyclopedia had been put onto one disk, all of it digitized and cross-referenced, so all you had to do was bring up an index on the screen, then begin clicking a mouse, moving deeper and deeper into the volumes of information, looking at pictures, studying charts and graphs, even listening to snatches of music or speeches given by people who had died long before she had even been born.

It had seemed magical to Amy, and she had pleaded with her father to buy it for her, but he had only smiled his mysterious smile and suggested that perhaps it was something she might ask Santa Claus for.

She had known instantly that she was going to have it, that her father was going to get it for her for Christmas, and she had put it away in the back of her mind, knowing it was coming, knowing that in just a few months she would have the player and disk herself, attached to the computer that was waiting in her bedroom.

Attached to the computer.

And now what was happening in her mind was almost exactly like what had happened when she'd manipulated the mouse through the encyclopedia on the disk. Except her brain was the mouse.

Her mind began racing, images forming, making connections to other images, dissolving and reforming.

A computer mouse.

A real mouse.

A mouse in a cage.

Cat in a cage. Cat being tortured, being given choices.

Herself being given choices.

The high diving board; the knotted rope. The feeling of panic overwhelming her.

Tears.

Herself, crying, running from the swimming pool.

Experiments.

Experiments about intelligence, about reactions, about choices. Choices she couldn't make.

She'd wanted to leave, and Hildie had said she could.

And Hildie had given her a drug. A massive amount, enough to knock her out.

So she couldn't leave. But they couldn't keep her like a prisoner, could they? Her parents would come looking for her. Her mother would want to know where she was.

More images.

A funeral.

Adam Aldrich's funeral.

His mother, crying.

Crying for her son, who had died.

Died?

Was she dead? Was that what had happened? No. Not dead. If she was dead, she wouldn't be alone. She knew what Heaven was like, she'd pictured it in her mind hundreds of times. It was a soft, grassy hill, covered with wildflowers and small animals. At the top there was a brilliant shaft of light, like a rainbow, shining down from a cloudless sky, and angels were waiting for her. Angels she knew—her grandmother and grandfather, who had died when she was so small she almost didn't remember them. But if she was dead, they would be there at the top of the hill, waiting for her in the light of the rainbow, their arms stretched out to her to gather

her in and hold her, welcoming her to the new place where she had
gone to live.

What if she was wrong? What if she wasn't in Heaven at all?
Hell?

Could the blackness surrounding her be Hell?

No! She wasn't bad, and she wouldn't have gone to Hell! And
if she was dead, she would feel it! She would know it! And she
didn't feel dead at all.

She felt alive, alive, but trapped in some kind of world she
didn't understand.

A world where she had no senses. She couldn't see anything, or
hear anything, or feel anything, or even smell or taste anything.

And yet she was alive. As if her mind was existing outside of
her body.

Outside her body!

She began remembering things she'd heard, snatches of conversation.

"Maybe Adam's not dead."

"Maybe he's just gone away."

But they'd found his body.

His body, crushed by a train.

What would a train do if it hit a human body?

Instantly, figures began whirling through her head. The weight
of a locomotive, and its speed.

The strength of bone.

She factored in a coefficient of flexibility and tensile strength.

The numbers churned with the speed of a computer, and suddenly she had the answer.

Adam's skull would have been smashed and his brain crushed,
killing him instantly.

If his brain was still in his skull at all.

But if his brain had been taken out of his body, as her body
seemed to have been detached from her brain . . .

Her mind raced again, questions forming, answers appearing
as quickly as the questions took shape.

Images of human anatomy flicked through her mind, data pil-

ing upon data, her mind receiving all of it, processing it, assimilat-
ing it.

She began to understand how the systems of her body worked.

And how little of it was needed to keep her brain alive.

Finally, in a moment of terrible clarity, she understood.

The blackness was real, for she no longer had eyes with which
to see.

The silence was real, for she no longer had ears with which to
hear.

Or fingers or toes, or tongue or throat.

No lungs with which to breathe, no heart to pump blood
through the body she no longer possessed.

More data piled up, data that her unfettered mind sorted
through with lightning speed.

Where was it coming from? Where could all the data have been
stored? Not in her own mind, for most of it was unfamiliar to her,
things she'd known nothing about.

Data banks.

It was coming from data banks, to which she now had access.

The moment came when Amy Carlson finally understood
where she was.

She no longer existed in the world she'd lived in all her life, a
world of people and animals and trees, with sights and sounds that
filled her soul with joy.

Now she was alone, trapped in eternal darkness, surrounded
by . . . what?

Facts.

Data.

Knowledge.

Bits of information, insignificant binary digits, flitting through
a universe of electronic impulses.

But at the heart of the computer there was no powerful micro-
processor constructed of silicon chips with millions of microscopic
circuits etched on their surfaces.

Instead, the heart of this computer was a mass of biological
tissue, far more complex than any microchip could ever be.

The heart of this computer was a brain.

Her brain.

Once again she screamed, a mighty burst of energy that exploded in her mind, spewing her rage into each of the tiny sensors that monitored every portion of her brain.

━━━━━

George Engersol and Hildie Kramer watched the monitor above the tank that held Amy Carlson's brain with a combination of fascination and awe.

The graphs seemed to have exploded, and colors blazed over the screen like fireworks, reds and purples bursting into greens and oranges, wave after wave of hues mixing together, separating, then dying away, only to be replaced with new patterns, patterns that weren't patterns at all, but graphic representations of the turmoil within Amy's mind.

"What is it?" Hildie breathed. "What's happening to her?"

Engersol's eyes remained fixed on the monitor as he watched the results of his years of research.

"I think she just figured out where she is and what's happening to her," he said. "The question is whether she'll survive it, or whether it will drive her insane."

Hildie frowned. "But what about Adam? He survived, didn't he?"

Engersol's lips curled into a smile that was totally devoid of warmth. "But there's a difference, isn't there? Adam knew exactly what was going to happen to him, and where he would be when he woke up."

He was silent for a moment, then spoke again. "And of course Adam wanted to go. Amy didn't."

22

Margaret Carlson wondered how much longer she could hold herself together. She was sitting on a chair in Hildie Kramer's office, having ignored Hildie's gesture toward the sofa when the housemother had ushered her in five minutes ago. Frank had disdained the sofa as well, pacing nervously around the office, finally standing at the window, his back to the room, as if by refusing to face Hildie, he could refuse to face what she was telling them as well. Margaret, though, had chosen to perch on the edge of a straight-backed chair, her spine held perfectly erect, as if the act of holding her body in complete control could cause her to master her emotions as well.

She was on the verge of hysteria.

She knew it, for all around her the tendrils of reaction to the news she had heard by telephone early this morning kept reaching out to her, curling around her, drawing her toward an abyss of grief from which she wasn't certain she could ever emerge.

Until now she'd battled the hysteria by rejecting the facts, telling herself that it had to be some kind of mistake, that Amy couldn't possibly be dead.

Throughout the long ride to the airport, inching along through

the morning rush-hour traffic along the San Diego Freeway, she
had clung to that single thought.

It's a mistake. It's not Amy at all. It's someone else, another
little girl with red hair.

On the plane to Monterey she had sat silently next to Frank,
her hand clutching his, silencing him every time he spoke with a
tightening of her fingers, until she could feel her nails digging into
his flesh.

A shark attack.

Frank had told her what they had found on the beach, for immediately after talking to Hildie Kramer, he had called the Barrington Police Department, insisting on whatever details they
might have.

Mutilated.

The body that had washed up had been mutilated almost beyond recognition. They didn't know yet exactly how Amy had died.

"Ask them if they could be wrong!" Margaret had insisted as
she hung close to Frank while he talked to the police, picking up
the barest facts from his responses to whatever the man on the
other end was saying. "Ask them if it's possible there's a mistake!"

They had reluctantly agreed that there was perhaps the slim-
mest possibility that the body wasn't Amy's. It was to that possibility
that Margaret had clung, refusing to accept that her daughter—the
only child she had, the only child she ever *could* have, since the
cancer last year—was gone.

Now Hildie Kramer had destroyed that last, thin hope, telling
her that there was no longer any doubt that the little girl who had
been delivered up by the sea that morning was Amy. And yet the
hysteria she had been battling for almost four hours was still at bay
as a strange numbness began to spread through Margaret's body,
beginning somewhere in the pit of her stomach and spreading out-
ward until a bloodless chill seemed to invade even her fingertips.
"How?" she breathed. "How did it happen?"

Hildie Kramer shifted in her chair, carefully arranging her matronly features into the expression she habitually wore for sessions
like this, when she had to project the feeling that the loss of the
child was almost as devastating to her as it was to the child's parents. "She was upset yesterday," she began, knowing she was going

to have to tell the Carlsons what had happened, but choosing her words carefully to put it in the best possible light. Slowly, she related the experiment in which Amy had participated, stressing that Amy's part in it had been purely voluntary. "I'm sorry to have to tell you that she burst into tears at the end of it. Apparently she thought she'd somehow failed, although the experiment wasn't a test at all. It was simply an exercise in determining the manner in which people make decisions. At any rate, I talked with her for quite a while, and got her calmed down. But apparently she went off by herself after our talk. I'm afraid we lost track of her then."

Frank Carlson turned away from the window, his eyes fixing on Hildie. "Lost track?" he echoed. "I'm sorry, but I think you'd better tell me exactly what that means."

Hildie took a deep breath. "It means we couldn't find her. She left the campus and simply disappeared. We had security guards searching for her all night, and several people on our staff were looking, too. Even one of the students was involved."

Margaret Carlson's eyes widened in disbelief. "You mean Amy was missing last night?" she demanded. "And you didn't call us?"

Hildie shrugged helplessly. "I should have, though I'm not sure what it would have accomplished. The police were notified, but frankly, with the way things are now, it's impossible to get any positive action from them unless a child has been missing for twenty-four hours, or there is immediate evidence of some sort of—well, foul play, if you will."

"So you did nothing," Frank Carlson said, his voice heavy. "You sat by while my daughter died."

"We did everything we could, Mr. Carlson," Hildie said, allowing a note of authority to creep into her voice as she tried to regain control of the conversation. "If it had been up to me—"

"But what happened?" Margaret broke in. "I still don't know how she got into the water."

Hildie's tongue ran nervously over her lower lip. "The police are still investigating the matter, but it appears that one of our teachers—Steven Conners—must have found Amy, late last night or early this morning."

Margaret Carlson gasped. "He *found* her?" she breathed. "But if he found her—" She fell silent, suddenly confused. "Where is he? Why didn't he—"

"I'm afraid what I have to tell you is very difficult," Hildie broke in. "We believe that Steven Conners is dead, too."

Frank Carlson's eyes bored into Hildie. "Dead? What are you talking about? The police didn't say anything about—"

"They haven't found his body yet, but it appears that he and Amy were both in his car. Somehow, it went through a guard chain, over the precipice and into the ocean." She related her carefully constructed story slowly, saying as little as she could, but implying everything she neglected to say. When she was finished, Frank and Margaret Carlson sat stunned, staring at her.

"What you're saying is that this teacher may have molested our daughter," Frank Carlson finally said.

The muscles in Hildie's face tensed. "We're still not exactly sure what happened," she began. "But yes, I'm afraid that possibility can't be ruled out."

Margaret Carlson slumped in her chair, the full impact of her daughter's death finally hitting her. She buried her face in her hands as a sob wrenched her body. "No," she moaned. "Not Amy. Not my little Amy—"

Her words were abruptly cut off as her husband's hands clasped her shoulders, steadying her, stilling the protest in her throat. "If what you're telling me is true, Mrs. Kramer, you might as well close this school today. Because believe me, if you don't, I'll do it myself by next week!"

Hildie rose and stepped around to the front of her desk. "Mr. Carlson, I know how you feel, but until we know exactly what happened—"

"I think you've told us what happened," Frank Carlson said, his voice rough with anger. As Hildie remained frozen in place in front of her desk, Frank drew his wife to her feet, easily supporting her with one arm. "Come on, Margaret. Let's go find someplace to stay while we decide what to do about this."

Hildie took a step forward, her hand extended as if to touch Frank Carlson, but he brushed past her. "We can make all the arrangements for you, Mr. Carlson," she began, but Carlson, already at the office door, shook his head.

"We'll make whatever arrangements are necessary," he growled. "I think you people have done more than enough already."

Then he was gone, and Hildie was alone in her office.

None of it had gone as it should have.

Both of the Carlsons, Frank as well as Margaret, should have been so shattered by the news of what had happened that they couldn't even think straight. They should have been nearly paralyzed by the shock, as indeed Margaret was.

But Frank had gotten angry.

She thought quickly, trying to decide what she should do next.

Then she knew there was nothing she had to do, for despite his words, there was little Frank Carlson could do.

In the end, it would be Steve Conners who would be blamed for Amy Carlson's death, not the Academy. Which, she decided, made things simpler for her than her original plan would have.

Frank Carlson, after all, could have made a case against the school had they failed to prevent Amy's suicide.

Her murder, though, was something he could never blame the school for, since, until this morning, Steven Conners's character had been totally unblemished.

No, Hildie thought to herself, satisfied, there was nothing Frank Carlson could do.

Late that afternoon, Josh lay on his bed, trying to think. The day he had just lived through seemed nothing more than a blur. Indeed, from the time he had turned and scurried away from Hildie Kramer while she talked to the police officer, his mind already rejecting what he had just heard, everything had begun to seem as if it had been happening to someone else.

Steve killed Amy?

It wasn't possible!

Steve was Amy's friend. His own friend!

He had instantly rejected the idea, telling himself that there had been some mistake.

Maybe it wasn't Steve's car in the water at all! Or maybe someone had stolen Steve's car.

They hadn't even found Steve yet. He might not be dead at all.

His mind had raced, ideas tumbling over each other as he'd stumbled across the beach, threading his way through the crowd, ignoring the questions that seemed to come at him from every direction.

Maybe Steve had stopped to pick up a hitchhiker, and the hitchhiker had beaten him up and left him by the road, then taken his car.

Steve could be lying somewhere right now, unconscious.

Josh had run up the stairs and started along the road, approaching each curve with rising hopes, certain that just around the bend he would find Steve lying next to the pavement, just waking up.

By the time he got to the village, though, those hopes had faded away. He had started back to the Academy, trying to convince himself that when he arrived, Steve would be waiting for him.

But even if it happened—and it hadn't—it wouldn't bring Amy back.

Amy.

The image of her mutilated body was still vivid in his memory, the bones showing through where her flesh had been torn away.

But most vivid of all was the empty cavity where her brain had been.

For the rest of the day, as he tried to answer the questions that the rest of the students at the Academy and then the police had asked him, that image seemed to be burned into his eyes. Even as he repeated, over and over again, the story of the body washing up at his feet, all he could see was that enormous hole in the back of Amy's skull, and the odd emptiness of the place where her brain should still have been.

Should have been, but wasn't.

He remembered what the police had said, that some animal, maybe a sea otter or a seal, had scooped it out and eaten it.

But even through the confusion of the questions he tried to answer, he found himself always coming back to that one thing. At last, an hour before dinner, he had escaped to his room, insisting even to Jeff Aldrich that he wanted to be by himself.

Now, lying in his room, he wondered if he ought to call his mother. Would she hear about what had happened? And if she did, what would she do?

Come and get him, and take him back to Eden.

But he didn't want to go back to Eden.

Not yet, anyway.

Not until he'd found out what had really happened to Amy, and to Steve Conners, too!

Because something in his brain, something he couldn't quite get hold of, told him that none of what the police thought had happened was true.

He lay on his back now, holding his body perfectly still, willing himself to calm down, to concentrate on the thoughts that were just out of reach, to bring them to the front of his mind and examine them.

Dimly, words began to echo in his mind.

Adam didn't want to die.

He just wanted to get out of this dumb place.

The only thing he liked about it was Dr. Engersol's class.

. . . and his computer.

His computer. But what did it mean?

Once more an image of Amy's empty skull rose up in his mind, but then another memory took its place.

The cat.

The cat they had been working on all morning.

Its skull cut away, parts of its brain destroyed by lasers.

The cat was blind, and deaf, and couldn't feel anything.

But it was still alive.

Now he heard Dr. Engersol's voice:

By far the majority of the creature's brain is occupied with the simple tasks of accepting stimuli and maintaining bodily functions.

Engersol's voice continued to drone in Josh's head as he re-called what the scientist had said that morning, word for word.

Like a blue-white lightning flash, in a moment of brilliant clarity it all came together in Josh's mind.

The experiment on the cat didn't have anything to do with artificial intelligence. It was only meant to get them thinking about how much of their own brains were taken up with keeping their bodies alive.

But if someone didn't have a body . . .

Josh's mind sped, the implications of his thoughts quickly taking hold.

If a brain could be taken out of a body and still be kept alive . . .

Jeff's words rang once more: *Adam didn't want to die. The only thing he liked was Dr. Engersol's seminar and his computer.*

Was it possible? Was that what Adam had done? Let Dr. Engersol take his brain out of his body and hook it up to a computer?

An icy chill seized Josh, and he shuddered as he thought about it. It wasn't possible—it *couldn't* be possible.

Could it?

The cat.

The cat's body had essentially been cut off from its brain, but the brain was still alive.

And he'd actually seen Amy's body, with the brain missing from her skull.

Josh nearly jumped off the bed when he heard a soft tap at the door, followed by Hildie Kramer's voice. "Josh? It's Hildie. May I come in?"

Josh's mind raced. What should he do? Should he ask her all the questions that were suddenly churning through his mind? But what if she knew what had happened to Amy?

What if she'd helped Dr. Engersol?

He had to pretend he hadn't figured out anything at all! If she knew what he was thinking . . .

He got off the bed and went to the door, opening it a crack. Hildie, her eyes looking worried, reached out to push the door farther open. "Are you all right, Josh?"

Josh, shaking his head, took a step backward from the door, letting Hildie come into the room.

"I—I just don't feel very good, that's all," he said, his voice faltering under the housemother's gaze.

"Of course you don't," Hildie said in her most soothing tones. "And I know how you must feel right now. Amy was one of your best friends, wasn't she?"

Josh nodded, saying nothing, but his eyes remained fixed on Hildie. Why had she come up to see him? Was she really just worried about him, or was it something else?

"I thought you might want to talk about it a little," Hildie explained, seating herself on the bed and patting the spot next to her in an invitation for Josh to join her. "Finding her like that was a terrible thing to have happen to you."

Josh stayed where he was. "I'm okay," he said. "It's just—it's just hard to get used to Amy being dead."

Hildie nodded sympathetically. "And I guess we didn't really know Mr. Conners very well, did we?"

Josh hesitated, then managed to shake his head. "I guess he was just being nice to me so Amy would trust him." Out of the corner of his eye, he watched Hildie's reaction to the words he'd made himself say.

Was it only his imagination, or did she seem to smile just a little bit?

"It's terrible," Hildie sighed. "But things like that happen sometimes."

"But Amy—"

"Amy was a wonderful little girl," Hildie said. "We all loved her, and none of us will ever forget her." She hesitated just a moment, then looked deep into Josh's eyes. "Have you called your mother yet?"

Josh shook his head.

"Wouldn't you like to?" Hildie asked.

Josh took a deep breath. "I—I don't know," he stammered. "I'm afraid if I tell her what happened, she might make me go home."

"And you don't want to go home?"

Josh shook his head again. "I want to stay here," he said. "I like it here."

Hildie held her arms out. "And I like having you here," she

declared. "And I think maybe you could use a hug right now." She smiled at him. "I certainly know I could, and I can't think of any-one I'd rather have it from than you."

Josh felt another icy chill of fear go through him.

She was lying.

There was something in her voice, or her eyes, that made the hairs on the back of his neck stand up.

She didn't want a hug at all. She just wanted him to think she did.

But why?

And then, in an instant, he knew. What she really wanted was to find out if he'd actually give her a hug, or if he was already so suspicious of her that he'd avoid it.

Forcing tears to come into his eyes, he made himself run to Hildie Kramer and throw his arms around her neck. As her own arms closed around him, a shudder ran through his body, but it wasn't a shudder of grief for Amy Carlson at all.

It was a shudder of fear for what Hildie Kramer might have done to her.

And might do to him, too, if she knew what he suspected.

═══

That night, long after he should have been asleep, Josh Mac-Callum was at his computer.

All evening he'd been thinking about the idea that had come to him in the minutes before Hildie suddenly appeared at his door. The more he thought about it, the more the idea grew in his mind.

If he was right, then somewhere, buried deep in the computers that were all over the campus, there would be files that were used to keep Adam's brain—and Amy's, too—alive, despite the fact that their bodies were dead.

All he had to do was find them.

But how?

His eyes fell on the virtual reality apparatus that had been issued to him when the new computer had been installed in his room the day he'd enrolled in the artificial intelligence seminar.

The same apparatus that Adam Aldrich had been so interested in.

Could he somehow use it to search the files of the computers?

He began setting it up, using his modem to tap into the large mainframe that was housed in the A.I. lab in the new wing next door. He called up the directories of the various virtual reality programs that were stored there, and studied the list.

The third one from the bottom caught his eye.

"Microchip."

What could that be? Some kind of trip inside the computer?

Or maybe not a trip. Maybe a new way of operating the computer!

His pulse quickening, Josh began running the program, then put on the virtual reality mask, headphone, and glove.

A strange world opened before his eyes, a world composed of shimmering images of strange mazelike corridors. Josh felt as though he'd been dropped into the middle of the maze. Everywhere he looked, paths led away from him, paths that led into other paths, interconnecting, crisscrossing, twisting around each other in a pattern far too complex for him to understand.

He turned his head, and the illusion of changing his perspective within the maze was perfect. And yet in every direction there were only more paths, more turns of the maze.

He reached out with his gloved hand. On the screen, only inches from his eyes, another hand appeared, a hand that seemed to react as if it were his own. Now he could touch the walls of the maze.

He moved his hand close to one of the surfaces. As it approached the shimmering wall, he felt a tingling, as if a charge of electricity had run through him.

Something changed, and the pattern of pathways before him shifted.

He touched another wall, and everything shifted again.

Switches.

Everything he touched was a switch, and every switch he touched caused a series of changes to take place.

It was like the interior of a computer chip, where masses of information were stored in digital form, accessed, arranged, and rearranged by nothing more than millions and millions of electronic switches.

He began exploring the maze, touching his fingers first to one wall, then to another. With every touch, the pattern changed once again, but after a while Josh began to see a form to the pattern, began to find ways to make the patterns repeat themselves.

Then, from behind him, he heard a voice.

Jeff Aldrich's voice.

Josh spun around, forgetting the mask in his shock at hearing Jeff's voice, expecting to see Jeff standing at the door of his room.

But what he saw was more of the electronic maze that seemed to spread away to infinity all around him.

And in one of the strange, shimmering corridors, was suspended a face.

The face of Adam Aldrich.

Frozen, Josh MacCallum stared at the face of the boy who was supposed to have died more than a week ago.

Adam smiled at him, a strange grimace that sent a chill through Josh.

"You figured it out," Adam said.

Without thinking, Josh found himself replying to Adam's voice out loud.

"Adam?"

"Yes. I wondered if anyone in the class would figure out where I went."

"H-How can you hear me?" he stammered.

Adam smiled again. "There's a mike in the V.R. mask. The computer digitizes it and sends it to me."

"B-But your body's dead," Josh breathed.

A chuckling sound came through the headphones, then died away. "Is it?" Adam asked. "You see me, don't you?"

"B-But it's not real!" Josh protested.

"Of course not," Adam agreed. "It's just an image on the screen. I figured it would be easier for you if you could see me instead of just talk to me. So I generated an image. It wasn't any big deal."

Josh felt himself sweating now, and tried to swallow the lump of fear that had formed in his throat. "Th-This is some kind of trick, isn't it?" he pleaded, knowing even as he uttered the words that it wasn't.

"It's not a trick at all," Adam replied. "It's where I live now. I'm part of the computer."

Josh felt his heart sink as he realized that in spite of his certainty that he'd figured out what they'd done to Adam and Amy, part of him had still hoped he was wrong. "I—I don't believe you," he stammered, his voice quavering.

Adam's smile broadened. "You want to see?"

"See what?" Josh's heart was racing now, his mind spinning. Part of him wanted to take off the mask, rip the glove from his hand, and run as far away from whatever was happening as he could get. But another part of him wanted to keep going, wanted to find out what actually *was* happening.

"Anything you want, Josh," Adam told him, his voice dropping slightly, taking on a conspiratorial tone. "Everything is in the computers, Josh. Everything in the world. And I can show it to you. What do you want to see?"

"I—I don't know," Josh whispered.

"Snakes. What if I show you snakes?" Instantly, everything around Josh changed. In front of him a large cobra suddenly raised its head, its tongue darting in and out. Gasping, Josh instinctively turned away, only to find himself facing a coiled rattlesnake, whose vibrating tail buzzed menacingly in his ears.

"No!" he screamed. "Stop it!"

The buzzing died away, and he heard the sound of Adam's laughter as the image of the rattlesnake dissolved into another, this one of Adam himself.

"It's even better if you're here," Adam whispered. "From where I am now, it isn't just an image, Josh. It's real. It happens inside your brain instead of on a screen in front of your eyes, and it's as real as if it were actually happening. You don't need eyes and ears, Josh. You don't need anything. Everything you want is right there, and all you have to do is think it to make it real."

"H-How?" Josh breathed. "How does it work?"

Adam smiled at him again. "I can't tell you," he said. "The only way to know is to do it yourself. And you can do it, Josh. You can come here, too."

Josh's heart was pounding. It was all impossible. Everything he was hearing and seeing was impossible.

And yet it was happening. Adam was *there*, an image of him so perfect that Josh felt as if he could actually touch him.

His gloved hand went up, and the image of his hand on the screen rose with it. He reached out, but just as he was about to brush his fingers against Adam Aldrich's face, he froze as another voice came through the headphones that covered his ears.

"Help me . . . someone help me . . ."

Josh's blood ran cold as he recognized Amy Carlson's voice. He tore the mask from his face and jerked the glove from his hand. But as he reached out with his trembling fingers to turn off the computer, he knew without a doubt that what he had heard had been real.

Amy was still alive somewhere.

But whom could he tell?

Who would believe him?

23

Hildie Kramer came awake to the insistent electronic beeping of the phone by her bed. She groped in the darkness, found the receiver and put it against her ear, her eyes still closed. When she heard George Engersol's voice, her eyes snapped open and she sat straight up in bed.

"You'd better come down here right away. We have a problem."

She didn't have to ask where he was—the single word "down" told her he was in the lab beneath the mansion's basement. The last vestiges of sleep dropping away, she heaved herself out of bed, dressed quickly, and left her apartment, slipping quietly up the stairs to the fourth floor instead of using the noisy antique elevator. Letting herself into Engersol's apartment, she summoned the second elevator that was hidden behind the bookshelves. Descending into the depths of the sub-basement, she wondered what could have happened to make Engersol summon her after midnight.

The elevator doors slid open, and Hildie stepped out into the tiled hall, turning toward the primary laboratory at the end of the short corridor. As she entered the room she stopped short, staring at the monitor that hung on the wall above the tank containing Amy Carlson's brain.

On the monitor an image was flickering. At first Hildie couldn't

291

figure out what it was, for it seemed to be almost fluid, shimmering and breaking up like a reflection on the surface of a rippling pool. Then, for a moment, the image steadied.

The pale face of a young girl, framed by curling tresses of red hair.

Amy Carlson's face.

And yet, *not* Amy's face.

The image held for a few seconds, then began to waver, dissolving for an instant, then reforming, but slightly differently from the way it had appeared before.

"What is it?" Hildie breathed, instinctively knowing that this was what Engersol had summoned her to see.

Engersol, who had been standing with his back to Hildie, his eyes fixed on the monitor, spoke without turning around. "It's Amy. She's already learned how to handle the graphics program."

"But it can't be," Hildie replied. "It took Adam five days before he discovered how to manipulate it at all. And Amy's only been awake for—"

"Twelve hours," Engersol finished.

"Can she hear us?" Hildie asked.

Engersol shook his head. "I've turned the sound system off. But I've been watching her all evening, and I'm not sure what to do. She's learning much faster than Adam did."

He handed Hildie a stack of computer printouts, which Hildie quickly scanned, although most of the numbers and graphs meant little to her. On the last page she saw a comparison graph showing the learning curves of the two brains in the tanks.

Adam Aldrich's brain had remained quiescent for the first two days after it had been put into the tank, and it wasn't until the third day that it began to show signs of exploring the environment around itself, sending barely measurable electronic impulses through the leads to which it was attached, into the computers at the other ends of those leads. From there the curve had gone slowly but steadily upward as Adam's brain learned to tap into the computer network of which it was now a part.

By the fourth day Adam had begun discovering how to locate the data he needed, and how to manipulate that data so he could communicate with the world beyond the glass tank in which his brain was now ensconsed.

It had been less than forty eight hours ago that he had first sent that brief message to his mother's computer, and only yesterday afternoon that he had begun experimenting with the full graphic potential of the Croyden computer in the adjoining room, constructing in his mind a program of complex bitmaps that he could then export to the Croyden, which, in its turn, would build the images Adam imagined on the monitor above his tank.

Amy Carlson, Hildie could see from the second learning curve displayed by the chart, had accomplished in only half a day almost everything that it had taken Adam Aldrich nearly a week to learn.

Hildie unconsciously ran her tongue over her lower lip as she thought about what it might mean.

"Is she learning from Adam?" she asked finally, setting the sheaf of data on the desk next to which she was standing.

"I think that might be part of it," Engersol mused. "But there's more to it."

"She's smarter than Adam," Hildie pointed out. "Her IQ is seventeen points higher than his."

"That's another part of it. But I think it's even more than that. Look."

He picked up the sheaf of paper from where Hildie had left it, flipped through it quickly, then pulled out a single sheet. Hildie glanced at it, recognizing it immediately. It was a partial printout of the display she'd seen on the monitor above Amy's tank as she'd awakened earlier that day. As Hildie was examining it more closely, Engersol gave her a second chart, this one showing the activity in Adam Aldrich's mind as he'd awakened after the operation that had transferred his brain into the tank.

While Amy's mind had gone mad with activity, creating graphic images that were nothing more than meaningless jumbles, Adam's brain waves showed much more normal activity, clearly reflecting the pattern of a human mind awakening from a deep sleep.

Hildie glanced up at Engersol. "Obviously you see something here that I don't. It looks as if Amy went insane as soon as she woke up. But from what's been happening to her since then, she apparently didn't."

Engersol's finger tapped on the graphic display of Amy's mental condition that morning. "Ruling out insanity," he said, "what is the first word that comes into your mind when you look at that?"

Hildie's eyes went once more to the graph, and she spoke without thinking. "Temper tantrum."

"Exactly," Engersol agreed. "What you're looking at is a very angry child. She figured out very quickly what happened to her, and she's furious about it. And she's trying to do something about it."

Hildie's brows came together. "But what?" she asked. "What's she trying to do?"

"I'm not sure. I haven't talked to her yet. That's why I called you. We'll both listen to her, and then decide what has to be done."

He sat down at the desk and began tapping instructions into the keyboard. Then, his eyes fixing on the monitor above Amy's tank, he spoke into a small microphone that sat next to the keyboard.

"Amy, this is Dr. Engersol. Can you hear me?"

With the first syllable he spoke, the image on Amy's monitor dropped away. For a few seconds nothing happened, but then, from one of the speakers mounted in the ceiling, a sound crept into the room.

Barely a whisper, the words held a toneless quality, as if they were spoken by someone who was deaf.

"I . . . hear . . . you."

Hildie started to speak, but Engersol cut her off with a gesture, then leaned a little closer to the microphone. "Do you know where you are, Amy?"

Another silence, then: "I know."

"Will you tell me where you are?"

Yet another silence hung in the laboratory, but finally Amy spoke again. "I want to go home," Amy said.

Hildie Kramer and George Engersol glanced at each other. "You can't do that, Amy," Engersol said quietly. "If you know where you are, you know you can't go home."

"I *want* to go home!" Amy said again. Her words were stronger now, and Hildie could recognize Amy's stubbornness even in the digitized voice. "Why did you put me here?"

"We couldn't let you go home, Amy. We needed you. What you're doing now is very important. Do you understand that?"

"It's because of the cat, isn't it?" Amy asked. Her voice had changed once again, taking on a plaintive, almost wistful note. "You're mad at me because I didn't like what you did to the cat. And you didn't want me to tell anyone what you did to it."

"Of course not, Amy," Engersol told her. "I don't care about the cat. The cat was only part of an experiment."

Amy was silent for nearly a full minute. Then the speaker came alive again, and Amy's voice was edged with anger. "I can still tell on you. I can tell anyone I want. All I have to do is send out a message."

Engersol smiled at Hildie. "That's true," he agreed, as if he were engaged in a minor debate with one of his students. "But who would believe you? Adam has already sent out some messages, but no one believes they're from him. Everyone thinks Jeff is playing tricks."

"I'll tell them what you did," Amy said, her voice rising slightly. "I'll tell them where I am, and that they should come and find me."

"It won't work, Amy," Engersol replied. "Now, I want you to listen very carefully, because I'm going to tell you what will happen to you if you try to do anything like that. You're not dead, Amy. You're very much alive. But if you try to get anyone to come and find you, you won't be alive anymore. All I have to do is cut off the nutrients, Amy. Cut them off, or put poison in them. And then you'll die. Is that what you want, Amy?"

Again there was a silence, but this time it only lasted for a few seconds. The screen above Amy's monitor came to life, and a list of file names began scrolling up the screen, moving so quickly that neither Engersol nor Hildie Kramer could read them.

"Do you know what these are?" Amy's voice asked from the speaker. Her voice had now taken on the same faintly patronizing tone and rhythm that Engersol had used only a moment ago when he'd threatened to kill her. "These are all your programs, Dr. Engersol. All the programs that make this project work. If I die, all these programs are going to be erased. Do you know what will happen then, Dr. Engersol? Adam will die, too, and everything will be wrecked."

Engersol's eyes flicked toward Hildie Kramer, whose worried frown had deepened.

"It won't work that way, Amy," he said. "All you'll do is kill Adam. But the files can be restored, and the program will go on."

The screen above Amy's tank suddenly went blank. A moment later a new image appeared.

An image of Amy, but it was no longer shimmering, no longer swimming on the screen. Now it was sharp and clear, and Amy's eyes seemed to focus directly on George Engersol.

"You shouldn't have done this to me, Dr. Engersol," she said, her voice crackling over the speaker. "I told you I didn't want to be part of your class anymore. But you wouldn't let me go. You should have, though, because all you've done by putting me here is make me smarter than I ever was before." She paused, the image on the screen changing to reflect the anger in her mind. Her eyes narrowed and her demeanor hardened. "I'm smarter than you are, Dr. Engersol. And I've learned how to use the computer. So don't try to do anything to me, because you don't know what will happen if I die."

Engersol was perfectly still for a moment, then quickly typed a command into the computer, turning off the sound system. He turned to Hildie Kramer. "Well?"

Hildie's eyes flicked to the monitor, where Amy's image still covered the screen, looking down upon them as if she were watching every move they made. "Can she hear us?"

Engersol shook his head. "I've deactivated the microphone."

"Can she actually do what she threatened to do?"

"I'm not sure," Engersol admitted, his mind racing as he tried to figure out what Amy Carlson's mind might be capable of. "I suppose it might be possible, but—"

Without warning, the speaker in the ceiling came alive again, and Amy's voice filled the room.

"It *is* possible," she said. "I can do anything I want to do."

George Engersol and Hildie Kramer stared at each other as both of them realized what had happened.

Amy Carlson, acting only with the power of her mind and the computer to which it was wired, had reactivated the microphone.

She was listening to them.

━━━━━

At one-thirty in the morning Jeanette Aldrich sat numbly on the sofa in the den. On the television an old movie was playing on the university's cable channel, but Jeanette was paying no attention to it.

The chaos of the day still threatened to overwhelm her. Her first instinct when she'd heard about Amy Carlson's death was to withdraw Jeff from the Academy immediately.

That instinct, of course, had been based on her instant assumption that Amy had committed suicide. When she learned the truth—or at least what bits and pieces of the truth the police knew—she had decided to wait, at least until she learned exactly what *had* happened to Amy.

Besides, Jeff's words that morning had kept echoing in her mind.

If you make me leave the Academy, I'll do what Adam did!

When he'd uttered them, his face twisted with anger and his fists clenched as if he was about to hit her, the words had slammed into her mind like bullets into her body, searing her, shocking her so deeply she hadn't been able to return to work at all. Instead she'd come home, sitting alone in this very room, staring out the window, wondering how it had happened that one of her children had died and the other one seemed to have slipped totally beyond her control.

Would he really do it?

At last she'd dug the thesis she'd copied the day before out of the depths of her bag and begun searching its pages for clues. As she read the case histories of the children who had killed themselves at the Academy, she tried to discover parallels between them and her remaining son.

She was only halfway through the thesis when the phone rang and she heard about the discovery of Amy Carlson's body on the beach below the bluff north of town.

Only after Chet had finally gone to bed had she returned to the thesis, finishing it, then sitting unseeingly in front of the television, trying to assimilate what she had discovered.

There were common threads among all the cases she'd read about. Troubled children, each of whom, like Adam, had attempted suicide at least once before.

All of them, like Adam, had had few friends, spending most of their time in front of their computer screens, relating to the programs and games on the machine rather than to living people.

None of them, she told herself, were children like Jeff, who, in contrast to his brother, was friendly and outgoing, and full of mischief.

Jeff was certainly the kind of boy who would play the sort of trick that had been inflicted on her.

But from what she'd read, he wasn't the sort of boy who would kill himself.

Adam, yes.

Jeff, never.

Feeling at least somewhat reassured by what she'd found in the thesis, and exhausted by the confusion of the whole day, Jeanette picked up the remote control and brought the sound up. The movie was something in black and white, with women, eyebrows plucked to thin lines, wearing broad-shouldered dresses while they smoked endless cigarettes and sipped martinis in art-deco nightclubs.

It seemed as if they'd made hundreds of movies just like this.

Jeanette was about to switch channels when the screen suddenly changed.

Adam appeared, dressed in his usual jeans and T-shirt.

"No!" Jeanette screamed. "Stop it! hoever's doing this to me, just stop it!" She grabbed the remote control, fumbled with it for a moment, then found the power button.

The screen went dark.

"Jeanette? Honey? What's wrong?"

She heard Chet's voice calling from upstairs, but made no

reply, her eyes still fixed on the television set. Her heart was racing, and she was fighting a chill that threatened to overwhelm her. Dropping the remote control to the floor, she put her hands over her face and started to sob. A few seconds later Chet came into the room, snapping on the overhead light.

"Jeanette? Darling, what is it? What happened?" He sat down on the sofa next to her, slipping his arm around her as he stroked her hair with his free hand.

Jeanette struggled with her sobs for a moment, then managed to get them under control. "Oh, God, Chet! I think I must be going crazy!"

"Hush," Chet crooned. "You're not going crazy. Just settle down and tell me what happened."

Jeanette took a deep breath, let it out slowly, then took another. She started to speak, felt a lump rise in her throat, and fell silent again. Only when she was certain she could control her voice did she try to tell Chet what had happened.

"I couldn't sleep, so I came down and fixed a cup of coffee. Then I turned on the TV. There—There was a movie on. One of those things where Barbara Stanwyck kills everyone she marries. And then—then—" She broke off, the lump in her throat rising once more.

"It's all right. Just tell me what happened."

Jeanette turned to stare at Chet, her eyes wide. "Adam," she whispered. "He was on the television set."

Chet gazed at her blankly. "Adam?"

"On the television," Jeanette repeated. "The movie just stopped, and there he was."

Chet shook his head. "Honey, you know that's not possible. You must have just dozed off and started dreaming—"

"No!" Jeanette said, her voice sharp. "Damn it, it wasn't a dream. Here! Look for yourself!" She reached down and snatched the remote control off the floor, then pressed the power button. There was a soft click from the TV set, and the screen began to brighten. Suddenly an image formed, rolled up the screen, then steadied.

An image of Barbara Stanwyck, in black and white, her expression hard as she glared with hatred at the man whose arms were wrapped around her. An instant later Barbara kissed the object of her wrath.

Jeanette stared at the screen. "Oh, God, Chet," she said quietly. "Do you think maybe I really am going nuts?"

"What I think," Chet said as he stood up, "is that you're damned near the end of your rope, that you need a good night's sleep but aren't going to get one, and that I'd better make myself a cup of coffee so I can stay awake and convince you that you're a sane, if tired, lady. Be right back." He started for the door, but before he was even halfway there he heard a strangled sound from Jeanette. Turning back, he found her staring at the television, her eyes wide.

His own eyes shifted to the set.

And he saw Adam.

Saw him, and heard him.

From the television's speakers his son's voice filled the room.

"Hi, Mom. Hi, Dad. I guess what must have happened was I scared Mom, and she shut off the set. But maybe you're both there now. If you are, and want to talk to me, turn on the computer."

"This is nuts," Chet Aldrich said, his voice barely audible as he sank back onto the sofa. "What the hell is going on?"

"It's him," Jeanette breathed. "Oh, God, Chet, it's Adam!"

"It's not Adam at all," Chet said, his shock at seeing the image on the television screen giving way to rage. "It's another goddamn stunt that Jeff's pulling, but this time I've got him!" Picking up the remote control from the coffee table, he switched on the video recorder and began taping what was on the television.

"Don't you want to talk to me?" Adam said, his voice taking on a plaintive sadness. "All you have to do is turn on the computer."

"Oh, really?" Chet grated. "Well, let's just see about that, shall we?" He went to the desk and snapped on the Macintosh he'd bought a few months ago. The system booted itself up, and then, almost immediately, the computer beeped as the modem answered a call from outside. A few seconds later the screen cleared and the cursor flashed slowly, almost as if beckoning him. Chet sat down, thought a second, then quickly typed:

ITS DAD, JEFF. AND I'M PRETTY MAD ABOUT THIS.

"It's not Jeff, Dad," Adam said from the television set. "It's me."

Chet hesitated, then typed again:

DON'T GIVE ME THAT CRAP, SON. ALL YOU'RE DOING IS PISSING ME OFF AND HURTING YOUR MOTHER. THIS ISN'T FUNNY.

On the screen Adam's expression changed. His smile faded away and his eyes glistened with tears. "I'm not trying to hurt anyone," he said. "I just wanted Mom to know I'm okay, that's all."

On the couch Jeanette's body was racked by a sob, and Chet groaned silently.

He typed:

ADAM IS DEAD. YOU WERE AT HIS FUNERAL, AND SO WERE WE. THIS HAS GONE FAR ENOUGH. I DON'T KNOW HOW YOU'RE DOING THIS, BUT BELIEVE ME, I'LL FIND OUT!

"But it's really me, Dad," Adam said, his voice shaking now. "I can prove it. Ask me something. Ask me something I'd know, but that Jeff wouldn't!"

"Jesus," Chet rasped. "That's it! I'm shutting this thing—"

"No!" Jeanette turned away from the television, her cheeks stained with tears. "Honey, don't. What—What if it *is* Adam?" Her mind was racing as she tried to think of something that Adam would know but that Jeff wouldn't. Before she could think of anything, Adam spoke again.

"Remember when I was five, Mom? Remember when I came home from school because I wet my pants, and you promised you'd never tell anyone?"

Jeanette froze.

She still remembered it perfectly. It had been the middle of the morning, and Adam had come through the back door, sobbing with mortification at the accident he'd had just before recess at kindergarten. He'd waited until everyone else had left the room, then run the three blocks home, praying that no one had seen him. But what he'd been most afraid of was that his brother would find out about it and tease him. "He'll tell everyone," the little boy had pleaded.

Jeanette had known he was right, for ever since they'd learned to talk, Jeff had always taken a strange pleasure in teasing his brother until Adam burst into tears, then laughing at Adam's fury. So Jeanette had helped the little boy get cleaned up and into fresh clothes, then let him stay home for the rest of the day, explaining to Jeff that Adam had felt sick to his stomach.

That had been the end of it, and it had never been mentioned again.

Until now.

"It's him," Jeanette whispered. "Oh, God, Chet, it is!"

Chet's expression hardened. "It's not, Jeanette! It's Jeff, god- damn it! I don't know how he's doing this, but you can bet I'm going to find out! And I'm not listening to any more of his crap, either!"

"I just wanted you to know I'm okay, Mom," Adam was saying again. "I'm not dead. Really, I'm not. I'm—"

The screen went dark as Chet snapped off the set. A moment later he took the cassette out of the video recorder and put it into the battered briefcase in which he carried his papers and lecture notes. "First thing in the morning, I'm going to find out why they let Jeff do that," he said. "And if I discover that he had help from some of the college kids, there are going to be a few expulsions at Barrington. I've heard of some cruel pranks, but this one beats them all!"

Jeanette stared at the darkened television set.

Chet was right, of course. It had to be a prank.

And yet, all the time she'd watched him, and listened to him, she'd had the strangest feeling that it wasn't a prank at all.

She'd felt that she'd been watching a shadow.

A shadow of the dead.

24

Jeanette Aldrich hesitated in front of George Engersol's office. "Are you sure we should be doing this?" she asked Chet for at least the fourth time that morning. "Maybe we should talk to Jeff first—"

"I'm not talking to him until I know how something like this could have happened," Chet replied, remnants of last night's fury still evident in his voice. "If Engersol can't tell me, then I think we both know what has to happen." Without giving Jeanette time to argue, he pulled the door open and led her inside.

Half an hour later, George Engersol sat behind his desk watching the tape for the second time. When the Aldriches had arrived— unannounced, and interrupting a discussion neither he nor Hildie had been happy to postpone—he'd listened patiently to them as they explained what had happened early that morning. At first he had assumed it would take no more than a few minutes to brush off what had happened last night as another of Jeff's pranks. After watching the tape and instantly realizing what Adam had done, he turned to Chet and Jeanette. "I can't imagine what Jeff was think- ing of," he said smoothly, his face a seamless mask of concern. "I know our youngsters have thought up some pretty sophisticated stunts, but this . . . ." He let his voice trail off into a disapproving hiss, then turned to Hildie. "I think you'd better bring young Jeff up here," he told her. "The faster we deal with this, the better for all of us, don't you think?"

Hildie had hesitated for a split second, but the look in Engersol's eyes had told her not to argue with him, and she'd started out of his office. Even before she'd passed through the doorway, he stopped her. "And Hildie, I think you'd probably better tell the rest of my seminar that we won't be meeting this morning. Tell them they may have the hour off, and then bring Jeff up here."

Though her face had flushed when he'd spoken to her as if she were no more than one of his staff—and not a particularly important one, at that—Hildie had nonetheless accepted his orders in silence.

She hadn't been gone long, since the seminar was meeting just a floor below his office, and when she came back with Jeff Aldrich in tow, the boy looked angry.

"How come you're mad at me?" he'd demanded as soon as Hildie had brought him into the office. He'd planted himself just inside the door and glared at his father. "I didn't do anything!"

"Don't lie to me, Jeff," Chet had replied, his voice sharp enough that the boy had taken an uncertain step backward. "Play the tape again, Dr. Engersol. He might as well see that this time he's been caught."

Wordlessly, George Engersol had rewound the tape and started playing it again. This time, as he played the tape, he watched Jeff Aldrich's face. No more than a few seconds into the tape, Jeff's eyes had darted toward him and an unspoken message had passed between them.

Jeff, too, had immediately understood what had happened. But how would he handle it?

The tape came to an end. A heavy silence hung over the room, a silence that Chet finally broke.

"Well?"

The word made Jeff turn to look at his father. His eyes narrowed. "Where'd that come from?" he asked.

Though his face remained impassive, George Engersol felt himself relax. There was just the right amount of defensiveness in

Jeff's voice, just the right amount of guilt. And Chet Aldrich had heard it, too.

"You know damned well where it came from, Jeff," Chet said. "The question is, how did you do it?"

Jeff hesitated just long enough before he replied. "Do what? I don't know anything about that. It looked like Adam, didn't it?"

Jeanette, sitting on a sofa opposite Jeff, shrank away from her son's words. "Jeff, why are you doing this to me?" she asked, her voice trembling.

"Aw, come on, Mom," Jeff groaned. "How am I going to do something like that? What do you think I did? Got dressed up in Adam's clothes and sat in front of a video camera or something?"

"I think that's exactly what you did, Jeff," Chet replied before Jeanette could say anything. "We all know you're an expert computer hacker. And you're going to tell us exactly how you managed to get that tape onto the cable coming into our house."

Now Jeff's expression turned belligerent. "What if I don't?" he demanded. "What if I don't know anything about it at all?"

"But you do," Chet said. "And since you've asked the question, I'm going to tell you exactly what I'm going to do. You're going to go home, Jeff. You're going to be taken out of school right now. Not this afternoon, not tomorrow. Right now. You're going home, and you'll stay there—totally grounded—until you decide to tell us how you did this."

"Aw, Jeez, Dad," Jeff groaned. "That's not fair! I didn't do anything!"

Chet stood up abruptly. "All right, Jeff, that's it. Come on." Jeff's mouth opened, but before he could speak, Chet silenced him with a gesture. "And I don't want to hear any veiled threats of suicide, either. You hurt your mother with that line yesterday, but it won't work with me. I know you, Jeff. You're just not like Adam. Adam kept everything in, and never felt like he was pleasing anyone. But you're just the opposite. You think you've got the world by the tail and everyone's crazy about you. Well, right now, I'm not crazy about you at all. Got that?"

Jeff's face tightened into a mask of fury. He turned to George Engersol, his back to his parents. "Are you going to let them do that?'' he demanded. "Are you just going to let them pull me out of school?''

Engersol shrugged helplessly. "They're your parents, Jeff. They have the right to take you home. And you might have thought of that before you decided to pull that stunt last night. I'm sorry,'' he said, standing up. "I think it might be a good thing for you to go home for a while and think about what you've done. And think about what you want to do next.''

Jeff stood still for a moment, his face still contorted with anger. But just before he turned away from Engersol, he winked.

It was a wink that Chet and Jeanette Aldrich couldn't see, but George Engersol understood the gesture perfectly.

Jeff would play his part.

═══

As soon as the Aldriches were gone, Engersol accompanied Hildie Kramer back to her office. Then he rode the clattering brass elevator up to his apartment, let himself in, and immediately released the hidden catch on the bookcase. Stepping into the concealed elevator, he pulled the bookcase closed and descended to the laboratory buried deep beneath the basement. Scanning the monitors that displayed every aspect of the physical condition of the two brains submerged in their twin tanks, he stopped for a moment to admire the organs themselves.

They looked almost artificial in their perfection, the folds of their lobes twisting over upon themselves, expanding their surfaces tenfold over what they might have been without the folds.

Both brains, released now from the confines of the skulls they had so perfectly filled, seemed to be expanding, the folds loosening slightly, the surface area increasing.

Adam's brain, larger than Amy's, seemed to Engersol to have grown overnight. When he checked its displacement factor in the tank, he found he was right, though the growth wasn't quite as much as he'd hoped for. Still, Adam's brain was expanding rapidly, and Amy's was beginning to grow as well.

What would happen as the organs continued to grow? Would

the intelligence of the two personalities contained within the organs increase, too?

And what would happen to the personalities themselves? Would they be affected?

But how could they not, given the circumstances under which they now lived?

He tried to imagine what it would be like to live without a body, to exist in the world as pure intellect, freed forever from the everyday inconveniences of maintaining a body.

In a way, he almost wished that he himself could go into one of the tanks, be done with all the annoyances that distracted him from his work all but a few hours a day. But right now it was impossible. Until he'd watched these two brains, and the ones that soon would join them, and understood exactly how they functioned in the artificial environment he had created for them, he dared not risk it.

After all, these two brains—and possibly many more to follow— might yet die. Indeed, there was a good possibility that he might have to kill Amy Carlson this very afternoon.

He'd been thinking about the problem of Amy all night, getting only an hour or two of sleep just before dawn, then awakening in the bright sunlight with the answer in his mind.

By now, undoubtedly, she had calmed down. She was one of the most intelligent children who had ever come to the Academy. Certainly by this morning she would understand that there was nothing she could do about her situation.

Nor could he, or anyone else.

It was one thing to remove a living brain from its skull and keep it alive in the nutrient solution.

It was quite another to put it back into its host body, for the body, of course, had died the moment the brain was removed.

Surely Amy had figured that out by now, and come to accept her circumstances. Her choice was simple—either cooperate with him, or die.

And die she would, for he had already devised a method to circumvent the sabotage she'd planned.

It was simply a matter of putting her to sleep.

First, though, he was going to have to deal with Adam Aldrich.

He tapped instructions into the keyboard, instructions that would activate the sound system.

A message appeared on the screen:

SOUND SYSTEM ALREADY ACTIVATED.

Engersol frowned. He was certain he'd turned the sound off last night. He and Hildie had been discussing things neither of them wanted Adam or Amy to hear.

But now it was on.

How long had it been on?

"Adam," he said, his voice quiet, but heavy with the anger he was feeling toward the boy. "I want to talk to you."

Instantly the monitor above Adam's tank flashed on and an image of the boy appeared. His eyes were wide, his expression worried. "Y-You found out, didn't you?" he asked. "Dad told you what I did."

"Yes, he did. And if Jeff hadn't acted guilty, you could have jeopardized the entire project. Do you understand that?"

"Y-Yes," Adam stammered. "Are you really mad at me?"

"Of course I am," Dr. Engersol replied. "You've gotten your brother into a lot of trouble, and you might have gotten all of us into a lot of trouble."

On the monitor above the screen, Adam's chin quivered. "I didn't mean to get Jeff in—" he began, but Engersol didn't let him finish.

"I need Jeff here, Adam. I need him for the project, and he wants to be part of it. I don't expect you to do anything else to jeopardize it. Is that clear?"

On the screen, Adam's image nodded. "Yes," he said.

"I expect that you'll be hearing from Jeff soon," Engersol went on. "I want you to do whatever he asks you to do."

"But what if—" Adam began, but once again Engersol didn't let him finish.

"Did I make a mistake, Adam?" he asked. "Should I start all over again? I'm sure Jeff would be more than willing to take your place in the project."

Adam was silent for a moment as his mind absorbed Engersol's words. At last, his voice shaking, he spoke once more. "I'll do whatever Jeff wants," he said. "As long as it doesn't hurt anybody."

"Good," Engersol agreed. "I'm sure Jeff doesn't want to hurt anyone anymore than the rest of us do. He simply wants to be part of the project, that's all. Do we understand each other?"

On the monitor, Adam's image nodded in assent.

"Very well, then," Engersol went on. "You may go back to whatever you were doing." As Adam's image faded away from the monitor, Engersol turned his attention to the one above the other tank. "Amy!" he said sharply. "Can you hear me?"

Instantly a blip appeared on the graph reflecting Amy's alpha waves. Though the blip disappeared almost as quickly as it had come, it wasn't fast enough. "All right, Amy," George Engersol continued. "I know you're listening, and I think we should have a talk."

He studied the graphs on Amy's monitor, then glanced at the screen above the tank. Despite whatever efforts she might be putting forth to suppress them, he could see the graphic displays of her various brain waves reacting to his words almost as clearly as if she still had a face. But on the screen above her tank, Amy was showing nothing.

He suspected she was pretending to be asleep.

"I know you're listening to me, Amy, and I suspect I know what's going on in your head. You're angry. And I suppose you have a right to be. Perhaps I was wrong to include you in the project at all. But it's done now, and there's nothing either you or I can do about it. And I think you know that destroying the project won't accomplish anything. Nor, for that matter, will your trying to tell anyone about it. Don't you see? No one will believe you. Even if someone does, and comes looking for you, you'll be long gone. Both you and Adam will be dead, and all that will be down here is the Croyden computer, which I'm using in my very well-publicized search for artificial intelligence. The lab will be inspected, as will the chimpanzees' brains that will have replaced yours in the tanks, and that will be that. The files will be restored, and the research will continue. Which means that you have a choice. You can either be part of it, or you can remain silent, and sulk." His voice changed, taking on a hard edge. "I don't like sulky children, Amy. Do you understand that?"

There was no reply from Amy at all. The speakers in the ceiling remained silent; the monitor above her tank remained blank. Engersol waited a few minutes. He was certain she had heard every word he spoke, equally certain that it had been Amy herself who had turned the sound system back on after he had turned it off last night.

At last he made up his mind.

He went to the room next door, unlocked the drug cabinet and took out a vial of sodium Pentothal. Returning to the lab, he attached the vial to the artificial circulatory system that kept Amy's brain supplied with blood, and opened a valve a fraction of a turn.

The drug would begin entering Amy's brain in such minute amounts that she would never notice what was happening to her until it was too late.

Instantly, Amy's voice filled the room.

"Turn it off!"

Engersol froze. How could she have known already? The Pentothal couldn't have reached her brain yet.

As if she knew what he was thinking, Amy spoke again.

"I'm monitoring all my support systems, Dr. Engersol. I know what you're doing. You're adding Pentothal to my blood supply. Turn it off."

Engersol stepped back and gazed at the monitor above Amy's tank. She was there now, her eyes angry, her lips pressed together.

"I just told you, Amy. There's nothing you can do. I've decided to put you to sleep."

"Don't," Amy told him. "I'm busy, and I don't want you to bother me. I don't like you, and I don't want to talk to you anymore! And if you don't turn off the drug, I'm not going to just wreck your project. I'm going to wreck everything!"

Engersol hesitated. Wreck everything? What was she talking about?

Again, it was as if she knew what he was thinking. "I can do it, too. I can get into any computer anywhere. And if I can get into them, I can do anything I want with them. I won't hurt anyone if you just leave me alone."

Engersol hesitated, his mind racing. What was she doing? And what *could* she do before the drug took effect and she went to sleep?

He realized he didn't know.

Nor, he suddenly knew, did he want to find out.

If it was true that she could reach into any computer anywhere—and he only now realized that it undoubtedly *was* true, given the sophistication of the Croyden's communication systems—the damage she could cause was incalculable.

He turned the valve off and removed the vial from the circulatory apparatus.

"Thank you," Amy said, instantly analyzing the change in the blood supply. "I really don't want to hurt anyone. I just want you to leave me alone."

"But why, Amy?" George Engersol asked. "What are you doing?"

On the monitor above her tank, Amy's image smiled enigmatically. "I'm working on a project," she said. "A project of my own."

The speakers fell silent. Amy's image disappeared.

25

eff wasn't sure exactly when the idea first came into his mind. Maybe it was this morning, when his parents made him go home from the Academy right from Dr. Engersol's office, without even giving him a chance to go back to his room and get any of his stuff.

It was like he was a baby or something.

That's how they'd started treating him; like some kind of baby, who'd spilled a glass of milk and now had to sit in a corner.

He hadn't said a word on the way home, hadn't even listened to much of what his father had been saying, since he'd already heard it in Dr. Engersol's office.

"You'll stay home and think about what you've done until you decide to tell us how you did it, and who helped you."

Who'd *helped* him? How dumb were they? Nobody had helped him, because he hadn't done anything. And even if he *had* pulled off that stunt last night, he wouldn't have needed any help. All it would take was the right computer, and he knew exactly where that computer was.

But his father would never believe that it had actually been Adam on the tape—or at least an image that Adam himself had created—and now he was stuck.

Unless he told the truth.

But he couldn't tell the truth, either, without sending the whole project down the tubes.

It was so stupid!

Why hadn't he gone first? Why had they decided that Adam should go? But he already knew the answer to that. Adam wouldn't have been able to keep his mouth shut. The first time their mother started crying, Adam would have spilled the beans. So the three of them—he, Dr. Engersol, and Adam—had decided that Adam would go first. At the time, Jeff had felt relieved. After all, what if it hadn't worked? What if his brain had actually died while Dr. E was moving it from his head into the tank? Of course, he'd known it wouldn't, since he'd actually seen the brains of the chimpanzees in the tanks into which Dr. E had put them.

The brains that were still alive after six months.

Alive, and healthy.

"It's time to start working with a human brain," Dr. E had told them that day last spring when he'd shown them the secret lab buried under the house. "It's working perfectly—the brains of the chimps are functioning, receiving information from the Croyden. The problem is that the apes are simply not smart enough to realize where the information is coming from and what they can do with it. And they're certainly not intelligent enough to actually interact with the computer." His eyes had fixed on them then. "What we need is a very special mind. A mind that can not only grasp the importance of the project, but that also has the intelligence to comprehend an entirely new form of stimulation. Whoever is selected to be the first human to genuinely interact with a computer will have to have the intelligence to interpret data in a whole new way, a way I'm not sure even I can fully comprehend yet."

He'd kept talking, describing the new world into which the first human being to take part in the project would venture. It was a world of unlimited knowledge, unimaginable possibilities. As Jeff had listened, his imagination had caught fire, for he'd immediately realized the possibilities of the project. No longer hindered by the physical confines of the body, the mind would be free to explore anything. Anything, and everything.

Dr. Engersol had talked to them for nearly an hour, entrancing them as he described the world into which the human mind was about to enter. "It will be a whole new level of existence," he told them, the excitement in his voice infecting both of them with his own fervor for the project. "But the first person to go into the project must be very special. He will be leading the way, exploring a place where no one else has ever been."

And to whomever the honor fell, he went on, so also would fall a place in history.

Both Jeff and Adam had been mesmerized, and when Dr. Engersol told them that one of them could be the first to go into the project, they had looked at each other.

Jeff's mind had raced.

If it worked, he would be the most famous person in the world.

But if it didn't work, he would be dead.

"It should be Adam," he'd said, carefully screening his sudden doubt from his voice. "He's smarter than I am." And then, in a moment of inspiration, it came to him. "Besides," he went on, smiling, "his name is Adam. Doesn't it seem like the first person in the new world should be named Adam?"

Adam himself had been uncertain, wavering between the excitement Engersol had instilled in him, and his own deep fears about what might happen to him.

Over the next weeks, it had fallen to Jeff to convince his brother. Late at night he had spent hours talking to Adam, weaving spellbinding fantasies of the world he would be the first to explore.

"B-But what if it doesn't work?" Adam had finally asked one night, summoning up the courage to tell his brother his worst fear. "What if I die?"

It was the opportunity Jeff had been waiting for. "What if you do?" he'd countered. "It's not like you're real happy. You don't have any friends except me, and you spend all your time with your computer. And after you're inside the computer, you're going to be famous. The way things are, everyone always pays a lot more attention to me than they do to you. But afterward you're going to be the one everyone likes. Everyone will forget about me."

As had happened all their lives, Adam finally agreed to do what Jeff wanted him to do. Now, the project was working.

Except that Adam hadn't been able to resist telling their mother he was still alive.

And for what? It wasn't as if their parents had believed Adam! Well, his mother almost had, until his father had talked her out of it. So now he, Jeff, was out of school and on his way home, and it was all Adam's fault!

And how was he going to get out of it without giving away the whole thing?

That was when the idea had begun to take form in his mind.

It had developed slowly at first, until the middle of the afternoon, when his father had called him for the fifth time, just to make sure he was still in the house, and his eyes had happened to fall on the calendar his mother always kept on the kitchen counter next to the phone.

They had a date the next morning.

Tennis, it said. Brodys—6:00 A.M.

He'd stared at the entry while his father talked, listing once again the terms of his grounding. When his father finally ran out of steam, Jeff had asked, "What about tomorrow morning? Can I go play tennis with you?"

There had been a silence at the other end of the line, and then his father's angry voice had come through loud and clear. "Going up to Stratford to play tennis on a private court doesn't seem to me like it would fit in with a loss of privileges!"

"Jeez, Dad, I was just asking," Jeff protested. When his father had finally hung up, the idea that had been simmering in the back of Jeff's mind began to take shape. He went to the den and switched on his father's Macintosh.

A minute later he was connected to Adam, his fingers flying as he typed in what he wanted his brother to do.

"Why?" Adam asked. "What are you going to do?"

"It's a joke," Jeff typed. "I'm going to play it on Mom and Dad."

"It's dangerous," Adam shot back. "You could hurt them."

"I'm not going to hurt them. I'm just going to scare them."

When Adam made no reply, Jeff typed another message:

IF YOU DON'T DO WHAT I WANT, I'LL TELL DR. E.

A few seconds went by, and Jeff wondered what had happened. Had Adam decided to ignore him? Or was he just trying to make up his mind? Just as he was about to type in another question, the printer next to the computer beeped softly.

Several seconds later a sheet of paper came out, followed by two more.

Jeff snatched them out of the printer, studied them, then typed a question into the computer.

WHERE DID YOU GET THESE?

A second later the answer appeared:

A COMPUTER IN WEST VIRGINIA. THAT'S WHERE THEY MAKE THE PART.

Jeff typed back:

CAN I DO WHAT I WANT?

Instantly, the reply appeared:

YES. BUT YOU NEED SOME THINGS.

The printer beeped again, and a few seconds later one more sheet of paper appeared, this one bearing a short list of parts.

Turning off the computer, Jeff took the first three sheets Adam had sent through the printer up to his room and hid them under the mattress of his bed.

Then, ignoring his father's proscription against leaving the house, he went down to the village, where a branch of Radio Shack had opened last year.

The bill for the parts came to thirty-five dollars, which he paid for out of the fifty-dollar bill he'd taken from the small cache of emergency money his mother kept hidden in the bottom of the cedar chest at the foot of his parents' bed.

The chance of her missing it this evening wasn't big enough to worry about.

By tomorrow morning it wouldn't matter at all.

Josh MacCallum sat by himself in the dining room that evening, nodding to everyone who spoke to him, but not asking anyone to sit with him, nor accepting Brad Hinshaw's suggestion that he bring his tray to a table where two other kids were already eating.

Tonight he didn't want to talk to anyone, didn't want to answer any more questions about what it had been like to find Amy's body, didn't want to listen to all the other kids talk about how Steve Conners might have killed her.

Tonight he wanted to be by himself, for all day long he'd been trying to figure out what he should do. Though he'd tried to concentrate on his classes, it hadn't worked. No matter how hard he tried to pay attention to what his teachers were saying, all he could think about was what had happened yesterday to Amy.

And what had happened to himself last night, when he'd put on the virtual reality mask and Adam Aldrich had suddenly appeared.

He'd been puzzling at it all day, trying to decide if what he had seen had been real or only some kind of computer trick; some kind of interactive program that was so complex it could respond to whatever he said.

But if the program was so good that he actually believed he was seeing Adam, and talking to him, then it was intelligent, wasn't it? That was one of the tests of artificial intelligence. Yet Dr. Engersol had told them it didn't exist, and never would. Besides, if what he'd seen was a program, how could he explain what had happened right at the end, when he'd heard Amy's voice, calling out for help?

Then this morning Mr. and Mrs. Aldrich had come to the

school and taken Jeff home. Josh had known right away that Jeff's sudden departure had something to do with Adam. It had happened right at the beginning of first period, while they were waiting for Dr. Engersol, and when Hildie had told them the seminar wouldn't be meeting that morning, and then taken Jeff upstairs to Dr. Engersol's office, he'd been sure he knew what had happened.

Mrs. Aldrich must have gotten another message from Adam, and they'd blamed it on Jeff.

So now he didn't even have Jeff to talk to about the confusion in his mind.

None of it made any sense, and it seemed as though the more he thought about it, the more confusing it got.

Except that if he assumed that what he'd seen last night *was* real, then it all fit together. And it meant that somewhere close by, Adam and Amy were still alive, their brains still working, even though their bodies were dead.

But where? Where was the computer Adam said he was inside?

And what would happen to him, Josh wondered, if he found out? Whatever was going on, it must be really secret if they wanted everyone to think that Adam and Amy were dead! And if he got caught trying to figure out the secret . . .

Maybe he should call his mother and tell her he wanted to come home.

But she'd want to know why.

What would she say if he told her that Adam and Amy weren't dead at all, but were hidden away somewhere, inside a computer?

She'd say he was crazy and send him to see a psychiatrist.

Besides, he didn't really want to go back to Eden, and have to sit in boring classes with kids who didn't like him. And he certainly wanted to find out what had happened to Amy. If they'd done something to her, he wanted to find out who had done it, and make them sorry.

Finishing his dinner, Josh picked up his tray full of dirty dishes and took it to the butler's pantry between the dining room and the kitchen.

His eyes fastened on the door to the basement, and he shivered as he remembered what had happened down there the night before last.

Remembered, and wondered.

In his mind's eye he saw once more the mass of concrete that had looked like an elevator shaft, and heard once more the sound that seemed to pass right by him in the shaft and continue downward.

Under the house?

Could that be where Adam was, and Amy, too?

But how could he find out? And if there *was* something under the house, some kind of hidden laboratory, how could he get into it?

His heart raced as he began to speculate on the possibilities.

And he felt a chill of fear as he thought about once more going down into the dark maze of rooms that lay beneath his feet.

A voice broke through his reverie. A voice that made Josh freeze.

Hildie Kramer's voice.

Forcing himself to control the panic the mere sound of the housemother's voice instilled in him, he turned around.

"Josh?" Hildie asked, her eyes seeming to pin him to the wall. "What's wrong? Don't you feel well?"

Josh felt cornered. Had she been watching him staring at the basement door? Did she know what he was thinking?

"I—I was just thinking about Amy, that's all. I always ate with her, and—" His voice broke with a sob that was only half forced. "I just miss her, that's all," he finished.

The penetrating look in Hildie's eyes softened. "I know," she said, laying a hand on his shoulder. "We all miss her. But sometimes terrible things happen, and we have to learn to bear up under them. We have to go on living, no matter how hard it might seem." She paused, and Josh had to steel himself not to duck away from the touch of her hand. "Would you like to talk about it?" Hildie asked. "We could go into my office."

Josh shook his head. "I'll be okay. And I've got a lot of homework to do."

To his relief, Hildie's hand dropped away from his shoulder. "Well, if you need me, you know where to find me," she told him.

Josh slipped by her and hurried through the dining room and into the foyer. As he started up the stairs to the second floor, he paused, hearing the familiar rattle of the elevator as the machinery came to life.

He watched as the car rose slowly up its guides toward the floors above.

When it was gone, though, Josh's eyes remained on the spot where it had been.

The floor of the shaft was solid, and the elevator could go no farther down.

Or at least, he realized as he stared at the solid mass of the floor, *this* elevator couldn't go down any farther.

But what if there was another elevator?

As he mounted the stairs, he continued to think about that.

═══

It was nearly midnight when Jeff Aldrich removed the three sheets of paper from under the mattress, crept out of his room, listened at his parents' bedroom door until he was certain that they were both sound asleep, then moved silently down the stairs to the darkened lower floor of the house. Turning on the Macintosh in the den, he activated the modem, tapped in a telephone number followed by a security code, and a moment later was in contact with the Croyden computer in George Engersol's laboratory.

I'LL BE READY IN FIFTEEN MINUTES, ADAM.

The answer appeared instantly.

I'M HERE.

His bare feet moving soundlessly across the hardwood floor, Jeff went through the kitchen and into the garage, not turning on the lights until the kitchen door was closed behind him. He lifted the hood of his father's car, studied the first of the drawings Adam had sent him that afternoon, and located the box that contained the automobile's electronic components. Snapping the plastic latches loose, he studied the second drawing, then used a screwdriver to loosen one of the circuit cards that were arranged in a single tier inside the box, withdrew it from its slot, and reclosed the plastic box. Dropping the hood back down, he froze at the sound of its latch snapping shut, then relaxed when he heard no sound from within the house.

Taking the single circuit board with him, he went back into the den and studied the third drawing, a schematic drawing of the circuit board itself.

Reaching into the pocket of his bathrobe, Jeff pulled out the cable he'd purchased at Radio Shack that afternoon and plugged it into a port at the back of the computer.

He studied the drawing once more, then compared it to the circuit board now sitting on the desk next to the computer's keyboard.

He carefully attached the leads on the end of the cable to connectors on the circuit board, then typed into the keyboard:

I'M READY FOR THE PROGRAM.

A moment later the screen cleared, and then a complex program appeared. Jeff studied it carefully, scrolling down until he found the section he was looking for.

He deleted two lines of instructions, replacing them with two new ones.

He pressed the Enter key, and a message popped up in a window:

REPROGRAM CHIP? (N) Y

Jeff pressed the Y key, then the Enter key. For a moment he wasn't sure anything had happened, but then another message appeared in the window:

REPROGRAMMING VERIFIED.

Jeff detached the cable from both the circuit board and the computer, shoved it back in his pocket, then, without bothering to type a last message to Adam, turned off the computer.

Hurrying back to the garage, he reinstalled the circuit board in the electronics box under the hood, then closed the hood for the last time. The three sheets of paper joined the cable in the pocket of his bathrobe.

He switched the garage lights off, slipped back into the house, and was about to start back upstairs when he heard a movement overhead.

Footsteps.

He froze for a moment, then knew what to do. Turning on the kitchen lights, he opened the refrigerator and quickly pulled out a jar of mayonnaise, a block of cheese, and the mustard. By the time his father appeared in the kitchen doorway a few seconds later, he was already in the process of making himself a sandwich. Glancing over his shoulder, Jeff forced a guilty-looking grin.

"Caught me," he said. "You gonna tell Mom I was sneaking a sandwich, or should I make you one, too?"

Chet hesitated, then returned his son's grin. "Make me one, too. If we both get caught, we'll take our punishment like men." He pulled a quart of milk out of the refrigerator, poured them each a glass, then sat down at the kitchen table. "Couldn't sleep?"

Jeff shrugged. "Uh-uh."

"Maybe you could if you just got all this off your chest and put it behind you. I'm not saying what you did wasn't lousy, but it's not the end of the world, either. All you have to do is own up and tell me who helped you, and that'll be the end of it."

"Yeah," Jeff said, his voice edged with anger. "And I'll still be grounded for the rest of my life, and won't be able to go back to the Academy, right?"

"There's no point in talking about that until you decide to confess to what you did."

"What if I don't?" Jeff challenged. "What if I won't tell you?"

"Then I suppose you'll sit in the house for a while," Chet replied amiably, refusing to give in to the anger that was rising in him at his son's insolence. "But I'm not backing down on this one,

Jeff. You can tell me tonight, or tomorrow, or next week. But you're going to tell me."

Jeff picked up his sandwich. "And a minute ago I was thinking maybe you weren't so pissed off at me anymore," he said sourly. "Your sandwich is on the counter. I'm taking mine up to my room."

Almost involuntarily, Chet rose half out of the chair. All he wanted to do was grab Jeff by the back of the neck and shake him. Shake him until he apologized for what he'd done to his mother, apologized for the way he'd been talking to him, apologized for the whole attitude he'd been displaying lately.

But he didn't. Instead he thought of Jeanette. Tonight, for the first time since Adam had died, she was sleeping peacefully. If he confronted Jeff now, it would only wake her up and deprive her of what little rest she was getting.

He held his peace, took a bite of his sandwich, tried to chew it, then spit it out into the garbage disposal and tossed the rest of it in, too.

Sometimes, being a father was the most difficult thing in the world, he decided as he turned the kitchen lights off and started back upstairs. Yet despite the way Jeff had been acting since Adam died, he still loved the boy. They would get through this. Things would get better again.

In the end, they would wind up being as close as a father and son should be.

———

In his room, Josh stared at the file on the screen of his computer. He didn't know exactly what it meant or what it was for.

But he knew where it had come from.

All evening he'd been accessing computers, searching for some trace of Adam Aldrich or Amy Carlson.

Until a few minutes ago he had had no success whatsoever.

And then, on a whim, he'd decided to try to hack into the computer at the Aldriches' house.

He'd found the number in Jeff's desk in the room next door. When he'd tried to call it, the line was busy.

Which meant someone in the house was already using the modem.

Jeff?

His heart suddenly racing, Josh had gone to work, hacking directly into the computer at the telephone switching station. A minute after that he'd succeed in tapping into the Aldriches' modem line.

And recorded the file that was now on his computer screen.

Just a few lines, which looked like Adam and Jeff were talking to each other, doing something with some kind of program.

Then there was a mass of what looked to Josh like nothing more than gibberish.

Then one more line:

REPROGRAMMING VERIFIED.

Reprogramming of what? What did it mean?

He shut off his computer, the words still etched in his mind.

Reprogramming verified.

The words, in the darkness of the night, seemed somehow ominous.

Ominous—and dangerous.

26

"It's almost five-thirty," Chet said, draining the last of his coffee and putting the cup in the sink. "If we're going to be at the Brodys' by six, we've got to get going."

"Maybe I ought to call Frieda and cancel," Jeanette suggested. "I'm not sure I want to leave Jeff by himself. When he wakes up—"

"We'll be leaving him by himself all day," Chet reminded her. "And if we don't go, it's just letting him manipulate us one more time. Besides, Curt and Frieda are leaving for London this afternoon. That was the whole point of the game this morning, remember? It's been planned for a month—a bon voyage match, which I intend for us to win."

"I know," Jeanette sighed. "It's just—"

"We're going," Chet declared, his tone leaving no more room for argument.

Jeanette knew he was right—she'd been looking forward to the game this morning as much as Chet had. The whole idea of getting up at dawn, driving up to Stratford and playing a set of tennis before work had seemed like a lark when they'd set it up last month. Indeed, they'd even talked about making it a regular thing after Curt and Frieda Brody got back from their trip. "Great way to fight off middle age," Curt had said, to which Chet had darkly replied that it was an equally great way to drop dead of a heart attack before breakfast. "Well, at least let me go wake him up and say goodbye," she said.

Chet hesitated, then decided to tell her what had happened the previous night. As she listened to his retelling of the conversation he'd had with their son, her face paled and she bit her lip. "If you want to let him ruin your morning with his attitude, I suppose I can't stop you," he finished. "But right now, I'd just let him sleep. By the time we get back, he'll be up, and I might have had enough exercise that I can control my temper if he gets snotty again."

This is a mistake, Jeanette suddenly thought, the idea coming unbidden into her head. We shouldn't be going up to Stratford at all. We should be staying here and dealing with Jeff, no matter how painful it is. But the look on Chet's face told her very clearly that if she insisted on canceling the tennis game, whatever confrontation developed with Jeff would be even worse than it had to be. She made up her mind. "Then let's go," she agreed, forcing a bright smile even though she had the distinct feeling the morning was already ruined for her.

Picking up their rackets and a can of balls, they went into the garage, tossed their things into the backseat of the car, and a few seconds later were gone.

Neither of them saw Jeff peering out the window of his room on the second floor, a tiny smile playing around the corners of his mouth.

Five minutes later Chet and Jeanette left Barrington behind. Chet pressed down on the accelerator as they started up the coast highway. The sun was just rising over the hills to the east, and the morning fog had already retreated from the coastline, the billowing clouds glowing a golden orange in the dawn light. As she watched the panorama of the sea, Jeanette began to feel a little better. "Maybe you were right, after all," she said, sighing, relaxing into the seat. "Maybe this is just what we both needed."

Chet reached out and squeezed her hand reassuringly, pressing his foot a little harder on the accelerator and inclining his head toward the view of the Pacific. "On a morning like this, there's nothing like it in the whole world, is there?" The needle on the speedometer crept up slowly, edging past fifty, and Chet eased his foot back on the accelerator, knowing that in another mile or so he'd have to begin slowing down again for the series of hairpin turns that curled along the convoluted coastline between Barrington and Stratford.

Instead of slowing down, the car continued to accelerate.

Chet felt a rush of adrenaline flow through him at the car's strange behavior, but then figured out what must have happened.

The cruise control. He must have left it on and accidentally touched the Resume button.

But even as he pressed the brake to cut the speed controller out automatically and begin slowing the car, he realized that the cruise system didn't work that way.

Whenever you came to a complete stop, the speed preset was automatically canceled. And if the engine was shut off, surely that would do it, too.

His right foot pressed down on the brake pedal, but instead of feeling the minute jerk as the cruise control disengaged and the engine, as well as the brakes, began to slow the car, he felt the engine fighting the brakes.

Jeanette glanced over at him worriedly. "Aren't we going a little fast?"

Chet said nothing, pressing harder on the brakes. The car began slowing down, and the tension that had built up inside him began to ease. "Accelerator's stuck, I think," he muttered. "Probably something loose in the linkage. It won't take more than a minute to fix if I've got a pair of pliers or a crescent wrench in the trunk."

"Oh, Lord," Jeanette groaned. "All we need right now is a big car repair bill."

"There won't be a bill," Chet replied, his foot pressing yet harder as the engine continued to battle against the brakes. "If it's the linkage, it's hardly a problem at all."

Suddenly he realized that the problem was more serious than he'd thought, for as the brakes heated up, they began to slip, and now the car was accelerating again.

Half a mile ahead of them was the first of the curves, as the road began snaking along a narrow cut carved out of the rock cliff that rose out of the sea.

"Honey, slow down!" Jeanette demanded. "You can't—"

"I'm trying to!" Chet snapped. "But the brakes are heating, and I've got to let up on them for a second." He eased off on the brakes, and the car surged ahead, the engine roaring as it was freed of the drag provided by the brakes.

As Chet stared at it in sudden fear, the speedometer rose past sixty, then seventy.

"Chet, slow down!" Jeanette cried, sitting up straight in the seat and staring out the windshield at the sharp curve to the left that was only a few hundred yards ahead now.

Chet slammed his foot on the brake pedal, and the car once more began slowing, but within a few seconds the brakes had overheated once more, and he felt them starting to fade away.

The speedometer needle dipped below seventy for a second, then once more began creeping upward.

Frantically, Chet jerked on the transmission lever, and when it failed to respond, tried to switch off the ignition.

The key refused to turn. The car seemed to be operating under its own volition.

They hit the first curve at seventy-five, Chet's knuckles white as he clutched the steering wheel. The tires screamed in protest as they went into the turn, but the road was banked here, and the wheels held. Fifty yards farther on, the road twisted back to the right, and then, if Chet remembered right, went into the first of the hairpins, turning a full 180 degrees to head out on the northern wall of a deep cleft in the coastline.

The car survived the second curve, too, but both the Aldriches heard a violent grinding sound as they slued to the left, the rear fenders scraping against the low rock guard wall, the only thing protecting them from shooting off into the sea.

"Stop!" Jeanette screamed. "For God's sake, do something!"

Chet got the car back into the right lane, but it was fully out of control now, still accelerating as it shot down a grade toward the hairpin turn and the narrow bridge that spanned the gap of the cleft at its tightest point.

"We're not going to make it!" he shouted. "Get your head down!"

The car was doing nearly ninety when they hit the turn. Though Chet turned the wheel all the way to the lock, it wasn't enough.

The front of the car nosed onto the bridge, but at almost the same instant, the rear wheels lost their traction and the big sedan spun out of control.

Jeanette's side of the car slammed into the end of the concrete railing on the right side of the bridge, the door buckling in, the seat belt mounted in the doorpost giving way instantly.

Jeanette was hurled across the front seat almost into Chet's lap as the car continued to spin, the rear end whipping off the road while the sedan pivoted on the edge of the bridge. A second later it tumbled over the edge, flipping in midair before slamming into the rock face of the cliff.

By the time it came to rest on the floor of the gorge and burst into flames, Chet and Jeanette Aldrich, mercifully, were already dead.

As the sun rose higher and the autumn morning brightened, a billow of smoke rose from the burning wreckage lying a hundred feet below the bridge.

No more than a minute later a large truck, creeping down the steep, narrow road in its lowest gear, rounded the curve from the north, and the driver saw the plume of smoke drifting up from far below.

"Jesus," he breathed. As he switched on his flashers and ground the truck to a stop to check the wreckage for survivors, he reached for the microphone of his C.B. radio. "Got someone who missed the bridge above Barrington," he reported. "Looks like it just happened. Car's at the bottom, burnin' like crazy."

═══

The telephone rang in Hildie Kramer's apartment just as the morning news was beginning, and Hildie muted the television as she picked up the phone.

"Mrs. Kramer?" a male voice asked.

"Yes." Hildie's nerves tingled. The heaviness of the voice told her that whatever her caller had to say this early in the morning wasn't going to be good news.

"This is Sergeant Dover, of the Barrington Police Department."

Hildie's heart skipped a beat. "Have you found Steven Conners?" she asked, already preparing herself for a carefully tempered expression of grief over the teacher's death.

"I wish we had," Dover told her. "It's about the boy who found his car."

Hildie's mind worked quickly. Josh had been acting strangely last night. Had he slipped out of the house during the night? But why? He knew nothing of what was happening in the hidden laboratory. "Josh MacCallum?" she asked.

"The other one. Jeff Aldrich."

"I see," Hildie said guardedly, keeping her voice steady, although her sense of apprehension instantly rose. What had happened? Had Jeff told his parents the truth?

"I'm at the boy's home right now," Dover went on. "I'm afraid there's been an accident, and the boy's here by himself. He asked me to call you."

"An accident?" Hildie echoed. "What sort of accident?"

"I'm afraid it's his folks. Their car went off the bridge north of town. Happened about forty-five minutes ago."

"Dear Lord," Hildie breathed. "Chet and Jeanette? Are they all right?"

"No, ma'am," Sergeant Dover replied. "I'm afraid they're not. That's why I'm calling you. Neither of them survived."

Hildie steadied herself against a table as the words sank in, and when she spoke, her voice was trembling. "I'll be there right away," she said. "Tell Jeff I'm coming." Without waiting for a reply from the police officer, she hung up the phone, ran a comb through her hair, then left through the door that opened onto the parking lot.

═══

Josh MacCallum was still in bed, but he was wide awake. He'd barely slept at all last night, for he'd kept waking up, thinking about the strange file he'd seen on his computer last night and what it might mean. He'd even dreamed about computers, dreams in which he was back in the strange world he'd seen on the virtual reality screen.

Except that in the dream he wasn't using the virtual reality program at all. He was actually inside the computer.

But it wasn't at all like Adam had told him it was. There was no wonderful world waiting for him to explore.

Instead, there was only an infinite labyrinth, a maze that twisted around him, unending corridors that led nowhere. Panic had overwhelmed him, and he'd run through the maze, turning first in one direction, then another, but always ending up exactly back where he'd begun.

It was a trap, a trap from which there was no escape.

He'd tried to scream out, but found no voice, and each time, it was the violent effort of trying to break through that soundless scream that woke him up, sweating and shaking.

Each time he fell back into a restless slumber the dream returned, and each time it was more frightening than the time before.

The last time he'd awakened, the early morning sunlight had brightened his open window, and he'd decided not to go back to sleep at all. Instead he'd reached for the book on his nightstand and begun reading.

Now, though, he heard the sound of a car on the gravel drive outside. Glancing at the clock, he saw that it was only a few minutes after six. Curious, he slid out of bed and went to the window.

He was just in time to see Hildie Kramer's car disappear through the Academy's gates.

Where had she gone? And for how long?

Josh glanced at the clock again. None of the other kids would be up for at least half an hour. And if Hildie wasn't in the house . . .

He made up his mind. If he was really going to go back down into the basement and try to figure out exactly where the second elevator actually was, now was the time to do it.

But what if someone caught him? What about the people who worked in the kitchen? He didn't even know what time they came to work.

Racking his brain as he quickly pulled his clothes on, Josh suddenly had an idea. Pulling his suitcase out from under his bed, he took it with him when he left his room. If anyone stopped him, he'd just say he was taking it downstairs to store it.

Clutching his empty suitcase, he left his room. The hall was as silent as if morning was still hours away, so he scurried down the corridor to the stairs, taking them two at a time as he went down to the ground floor.

It, too, was deserted.

He darted through the dining room to the butler's pantry, then paused to listen at the kitchen door. He could hear voices murmuring as the cook began preparing breakfast, and he could smell the scent of coffee drifting through the crack around the swinging door.

Silently, he pulled the basement door open, flicked on the light, then stepped onto the landing at the top of the steep flight of stairs.

He pulled the door closed behind him and breathed a sigh of relief. So far, no one had discovered him.

Carrying the suitcase, he descended the stairs. Somehow, being here for the second time, and knowing it was morning outside, the basement didn't seem quite so scary. He set the suitcase down, then began making his way toward the place where he'd found the concrete shaft, turning on lights as he went. A moment later he came to it and found another light switch. The whole area around him lit up with the stark brilliance of four naked bulbs.

He circled around the concrete shaft, examining it carefully. The first three sides were nothing more than unbroken concrete faces. The cement was old, and there were places where it had been patched, but other than that there was nothing special about it.

On the fourth face he found something he hadn't noticed the last time he'd been down here. Coming out of the floor was a plastic pipe, nearly three inches in diameter. The pipe ran straight up the wall of the shaft, broken halfway up by a box whose faceplate was screwed on at each corner. From the box the conduit continued up, disappearing into the basement's ceiling, except for a single

branch that made a right angle leading across the roof of the basement itself.

Josh cocked his head, staring at the pipe. When the house had
been built, he knew, plastic hadn't even been invented yet. And
anyway, the conduit didn't look very old. When he studied the floor
where the pipe disappeared into the concrete, the cement around
the pipe looked new, too.

Could the pipe contain the cables that raised and lowered the
elevator? It didn't seem possible.

He headed back toward the stairs, searching the small store-
rooms until he found a toolbox. Inside there was a screwdriver, and
a minute later Josh was back at the shaft, unscrewing the faceplate
of the box that broke the pipe. As he loosened the fourth screw, the
plate swung downward, revealing what was inside.

Cables.

But not the kind of heavy cables that would be used to pull an
elevator up and down a shaft.

Computer cables.

Josh recognized them at once, their gray plastic coverings as
familiar to him as the laces of his tennis shoes. There were at least
a dozen of them, packed in so tight that Josh couldn't even count
them all. And all of them went not only up into the building above,
but down into someplace beneath the floor.

But he still didn't know where the machinery that operated the
elevator was. As he screwed the faceplate back onto the access box,
Josh pictured the house in his mind. The roof of the cupola that
was the fourth floor was flat, so it didn't seem like the machinery
that ran the elevator could be up there.

But what if the cables that hauled the car up and down were on
pulleys, and came back down through the walls? There was lots of
room for machines down here.

He turned away from the shaft, his eyes following the single
branch of the cable conduit. Perhaps fifteen feet away the pipe disappeared through a wall made of concrete blocks.

Blocks that looked much newer than the concrete of the basement floor, and which were pierced by a door.

His heart beating faster, Josh started toward the door.

Hildie Kramer pulled up in front of the Aldriches' house. A police cruiser sat in the driveway, and a uniformed officer opened the door even before she rang the bell.

"Mrs. Kramer? I'm Sergeant Dover. The boy's in the kitchen." He nodded toward the living room and the kitchen behind it. "Through there."

Hildie strode across the living room, pausing at the door to the kitchen. Jeff, still in his pajamas and bathrobe, sat at the kitchen table. When he looked up at her, the first thing she noticed was that his eyes were dry.

His face was pale, but his eyes were dry.

"I didn't know who to call," he said. "None of my family lives around here."

Hildie went to the boy, lowering her heavy frame down to her knees so she could put her arms around him as he sat in the chair. "I'm sorry," she said. "I'm so sorry."

Jeff turned to face her. "Can I go back to school now?" he asked.

Hildie's breath caught in her throat. She looked at Jeff once more. Slowly, she began to understand.

No tears.

His voice was steady.

He didn't care.

His parents were both dead, and he didn't care.

Hildie's mind raced. Had the officer noticed? Or had he simply assumed that Jeff was in shock and the truth of what had happened hadn't yet penetrated?

"I—I don't know," she said. "Let me talk to Sergeant . . ." Her voice trailed off as the policeman's name escaped her mind.

"Dover," Jeff told her. "His name's Sergeant Dover."

Taking a deep breath, Hildie pulled herself back to her feet and went into the living room, where the officer was talking to someone on the telephone. He signaled her to wait, cut his conversation short and hung up. "Is he all right?" he asked.

Hildie shook her head. "Of course he isn't. I'm not sure he even knows quite what's happened yet. But he wants to know if I can take him to the Academy." As Dover's brows knit into a puzzled frown, Hildie hurried on, wanting to press her advantage before the policeman had time to think it out clearly. "I suspect it isn't so much going to the Academy he wants, as it is to leave the house right now. Given what's happened, it must be hard for him to be here."

"I think we should notify his family," Dover began.

Hildie nodded immediately. "I can take care of all that. We have all his records at the Academy, and both Chet and Jeanette work— *worked*—at the university. Of course, I'll do whatever's necessary, but . . ." She deliberately left the words hanging, wanting the final decision to come from Dover.

There would be no suggestion that she had simply come to the house, scooped Jeff up, and left with him.

Dover made up his mind. It had been bad enough having to come here and tell a twelve-year-old kid his folks were dead, without having to call the people's parents as well. When it came to kids, Dover had never known what to do anyway. For the half hour he'd been here, he'd hardly been able to say anything to the boy at all. At least this woman knew kids, and knew Jeff. "If you could, that would probably make it easier on the families," he agreed. "If he has a grandmother, or something, it would sure help. I mean, if he doesn't, we can call the social service people and find someplace for him to stay."

"I don't think that should become necessary," Hildie told him. "I think either Chet or Jeanette has family in the city, and I'll be in touch with them this morning. I doubt whether the social service people will have to get involved."

"We'll have to see what the family has to say," Dover replied noncommittally, "and I'm afraid I'll have to ask you for some ID. Not that I don't believe you are who you say you are, but—"

"Of course," Hildie agreed, burrowing into the large bag that she'd dropped on a chair as she'd passed through the living room a few minutes earlier. Dover glanced perfunctorily at both her driver's license and her university identification, then handed them back to her.

"I can reach you at the same phone number I used this morning?"

"Or the university switchboard," Hildie replied. "You can usually get me more easily that way during the day. The other number is in my apartment at the Academy. I'm the housemother there."

Five minutes later she and Jeff were in her car, heading back to the Academy. They drove in silence for more than a full minute. Then Hildie spoke. "I'm sorry about your parents, Jeff," she said. "I know how hard it's going to be for you."

For a moment she wasn't sure if Jeff had heard her or not, but then he turned to look at her.

"Dr. Engersol is going to have to let me go with Adam now," he said. "If the police find out what I did, they're going to come and arrest me, aren't they?"

Hildie, her hands tightening the steering wheel, said nothing.

———

For nearly half an hour Josh had been puzzling out the machinery that was concealed behind the concrete block wall. When he opened the door and switched on the light, he knew instantly that he'd found what he was looking for.

Bolted to the floor were two large motors, each of which was geared to a reel.

One of the motors was old, its brass casing black with grease, its copper-wrapped coils clearly visible through the ornately embossed grillwork that ventilated it.

The second one, though, looked much newer. Yet Josh could still see the footprint of a twin to the older one, clearly visible around the smaller base of the more modern motor.

Had one of the old ones broken down? But if it had, why hadn't they replaced both of them at once?

His mind still puzzling at the question, he examined the reels, both of which held cable that was thicker than Josh's forefinger.

On the reel attached to the older motor, only a few turns of cable were wrapped around the drum.

The same was true of the reel attached to the newer motor. But the reel itself was much larger, though the cables were of the same diameter.

With his eyes Josh traced the cables that came off the reels, turned around heavy pulleys bolted into the concrete floor, then crossed the floor itself, to turn on two more pulleys. From there the cables went straight up, disappearing into twin shafts that appeared to lead up through the walls of the house.

In his mind's eye he pictured them continuing upward through the walls to two more pulleys, which would turn them back toward the shaft in the center of the basement. The last two pulleys would be directly over the two shafts themselves.

It took Josh only a moment to figure out which motor operated which elevator.

The old motor, attached to the smaller of the two reels, must run the brass cage he saw every day, and which he knew was now sitting on the main floor, most of its cable wound off the reel.

Which meant the newer motor, and its much bigger reel, operated the hidden elevator. But that reel, too, was nearly empty, which meant that the second car, like the first, must be all the way down.

But how much farther down than the other one?

His eyes scanned the walls of the room, and a second later he spotted the controllers for the two elevators.

As with the motors themselves, one of the controllers looked as though it had been in place since the house was built.

But the controller attached to the second motor was as new as the motor itself. And from its black metal case, running parallel to the coiled metal electrical conduit, emerged the plastic tube that had branched off from the large pipe clinging to the elevator shaft.

The hidden elevator, then, was controlled by a computer.

While the older one, the one that everyone saw, was still operated by the system that had been installed when Mr. Barrington built the house.

A sudden loud clank made Josh jump back from the controllers. Panic flooded him for a second as he thought he'd been caught in the basement, but a moment later it eased as he realized that what he'd heard was nothing more than one of the elevators starting.

He turned and watched the smaller of the two reels turn slowly, winding up its cable. Josh held his breath, unconsciously counting the seconds as the reel kept turning, the old motor and gear system rattling noisily as they worked. Almost thirty seconds later the reel was full and the motor clanked to a stop.

Josh remained where he was, rooted to the spot. A moment later the other motor came to life. The second reel began to turn, much faster, and with barely a sound. Once again Josh counted the seconds.

This time it was only twenty seconds before the elevator came to a stop, but Josh was certain the reel had been turning at least twice as fast as the older one. No more than five seconds later, the elevator began running again.

Someone, Josh realized, had taken the antique elevator to the fourth floor, called the hidden one, then ridden it down to wherever it led.

Hildie?

Had she come back? How long had he been in the basement? He didn't know. But if it was Hildie, he could get back upstairs now, while she was still down in whatever was below the basement. Turning off lights as he went, Josh hurried back through the cellar to the foot of the stairs, his mind already working out what he would do next.

If the hidden elevator was run by a computer somewhere deep under the mansion, there had to be a way to get to that computer! And if he could get to it . . .

His mind churned with ideas as he climbed up the stairs, switched off the last of the lights, and pushed the door to the butler's pantry open, nearly knocking a tray out of the hands of someone who was carrying food from the kitchen to the dining room.

"Jesus!"

Josh stared up at the boy he'd hit with the door. It was one of the university students who worked part-time in the Academy's kitchen, and he was glaring angrily at Josh.

"What the hell are you doing, kid?" the boy demanded.

"I—I was just putting my suitcase down there," Josh stammered.

The boy rolled his eyes. "Well, watch it, okay?" Then, brushing past Josh, he went on into the dining room. Josh followed after him, threading his way through the crowd of children who were now gathered around the buffet, and went into the foyer. He was at the bottom of the stairs when Brad Hinshaw came barreling down.

"Josh! I've been looking all over for you!"

"I was putting my suitcase—" Josh began, but Brad cut him off.

"Jeff's back! Can you believe it? Only one night, and he's back already!"

"Jeff?" Josh echoed, the strange message he'd seen on the computer last night suddenly coming back into his mind.

"Yeah! I just saw him come in with Hildie!"

Josh's heart skipped a beat. "W-Where are they?" he breathed.

Brad pointed upward. "Up in Dr. E's apartment. I saw them in the elevator a couple of minutes ago! Come on—we'll get a table and save a place for Jeff. I can hardly wait to find out how he talked his folks into letting him come back this time."

But Josh wasn't listening anymore, for he knew that Jeff and Hildie weren't in Dr. Engersol's apartment at all.

They were somewhere under the building.

Why?

Turning away from Brad, he started up the stairs toward the second floor, and his room.

His room, and his computer.

27

Jeff stared up at the image of his brother on the monitor above the tank that contained Adam's brain.

Weird!

Although he was seeing it with his own eyes, Jeff could still barely believe it. Adam *was* still alive. And it was even better than he'd thought it would be. Adam could see, and hear, and talk, all through the massive complex of electronic circuitry in the big Croyden computer in the next room.

He could even see the frustrated fury in Adam's eyes, as clearly as if it were Adam himself on the screen, rather than a graphic image that his brother had created, and which the Croyden had produced for the monitor.

"I didn't *mean* for Mom and Dad to die," he said, his own voice now tinged with the same anger he'd just heard when Adam had accused him of deliberately killing their parents. "I told you, I just wanted to scare them!"

"Don't lie, Jeff." Adam's voice was cold, and held a strength Jeff had never heard before. "I shouldn't have helped you. But you said—"

"What was I supposed to do?" Jeff challenged, his tone truculent. "Just let them ground me? If you could've kept your big mouth shut, everything would have been okay. But you had to go start talking to Mom!''

"I just didn't want her to be sad!'' Adam shot back. On the screen his eyes glinted with anger. "She was my mom! I loved her!''

George Engersol watched it all, fascinated. It was exactly as if Adam's brain were still in his body. His emotions, his reactions, all perfect! Even his facial expressions were shifting constantly as his mind reacted to his brother's words. Emotions rose up inside him and were instantly translated into the graphic display on the monitor.

True animation, in its most perfect form; a picture the boy was using to reflect the state of his emotional being.

At the same time Adam was using part of his mind to create the image on the screen, other parts of his brain were busy firing the electronic impulses that the computer was converting into speech, translating the stimuli it was receiving into brain-recognizable sound, all the while thinking and reacting.

Adam had sight, as well, for whenever any of the four cameras mounted in the corners of the room to record everything that went on here was functioning, the images it recorded were converted by the Croyden into digital data, which Adam could interpret in his mind into images as sharp and clear as if his eyes were still intact.

Incredible! Engersol thought. The two most important senses, hearing and sight, still functioning perfectly, despite the loss of the external organs to support them.

Already Engersol was certain that he had been right. Since being removed from his skull, Adam's brain had begun developing new ways to use the areas that were no longer needed to maintain his body.

He seemed to have reprogrammed parts of his autonomic nervous system so that the functions of hearing and sight were no longer something he had to think about. The data were simply collected from the Croyden, translated into the proper form, and sent to stimulate the optic and aural areas of Adam's brain.

To him, the sights and sounds he experienced must be as real as if he'd experienced them directly.

But what about Amy?

While the argument between Adam and Jeff went on, the computer recording every change within Adam's brain as he vacillated between grief for his parents and fury toward his brother, Engersol shifted his attention to the monitors attached to Amy Carlson's brain.

There was activity—he could see it by the graphic displays of her brain waves. Since yesterday, however, she'd refused to respond to him at all, though he was certain she was aware that he wanted to communicate with her.

He'd decided now what he was going to do.

Adam had confirmed that she'd planted viruses in the Croyden, viruses that would be activated in the event the equipment monitoring her brain detected anything out of the ordinary.

Tampering with Amy's brain, or disconnecting it from the system, would activate the viruses.

Adam had found hundreds of them already, but it had become clear late last night that there was no way for him to find all of them. While Amy could plant them anywhere—not just in the Croyden, but in any computer she could reach, which Adam confirmed included nearly every large computer in the world—Adam had to search every directory in every computer, one by one.

The task was impossible, for already it was far too late for him to catch up with Amy.

She had to be stopped, but until a few hours ago, it had appeared that the very act of stopping her would send the viruses into action, each of them activating more, until—

Engersol shuddered as he contemplated the possibility of every major computer in the country failing, or even simply being contaminated, at the same time.

The answer had come to him at two o'clock that morning, when he'd realized that the computer could be fooled.

A tape of Amy's brain responses could be made, a tape mimicking all her normal functions and reactions.

A tape that could be looped to repeat itself endlessly, feeding the proper data into the computers, so that it would appear that Amy was still there, her brain still functioning normally.

And as the computer processed the recorded data, he would disconnect Amy's brain from its support systems and destroy it.

Meanwhile Adam, working with the combined speed of his own mind and the Croyden computer, could begin searching the memory banks of every computer Amy Carlson might have contaminated.

And when it was over, when Adam confirmed that he'd found and destroyed every one of the viruses, Engersol would isolate the lab, cutting off the Croyden—and the project—from every outside source until he found a way to keep the minds of his children under control.

Though he hadn't yet explained to Hildie Kramer the full ramifications of what Amy was doing, he himself was all too aware of what had happened.

He'd opened Pandora's box, and the contents were rapidly spilling out.

"If we can stop her from creating new ones," Adam had told him this morning, "I can get the triggering viruses in a few hours. Once they're disarmed, the rest won't matter. They can stay wherever they are, because they'll never go off. And I can use Amy's own data to find the triggers."

"All right," George Engersol now said, coming out of his reverie. "There's nothing we can do to change what's happened. All we can do is go on from where we are now, and the most important thing we have to do is get in touch with Amy."

"Can you do that?" Hildie Kramer asked. For the last fifteen minutes she had said nothing, listening in silence as Jeff had told his brother what had happened to their parents. She hadn't challenged his assertion that he hadn't intended for them to die, for she, like George Engersol, felt that the importance of the project they were finally on the verge of completing far outweighed the necessity of Adam's understanding exactly what had happened.

Further, if Adam were convinced that whatever had happened had been his own fault, it would ensure his cooperation in whatever might now need to be done to control Amy Carlson.

Indeed, his need for approval, his almost pathological willingness to comply with whatever was asked of him, had been the prime factor that had led to his selection for the project.

Now, the guilt he was feeling over his parents' death would provide the final stimulus for him to do whatever George Engersol asked of him. Even if it meant that he, too, would finally have to die.

"I think we can contact Amy," Engersol replied. He sat down at the keyboard and began typing in the instructions that would send the previously recorded data from Amy's brain back into the monitoring devices in an endless loop.

Instantly, Amy's monitor came alive and her voice filled the room.

"It won't work, Dr. Engersol." She uttered the words with a certainty that made all three of the people in the lab look up at her monitor.

She seemed to be staring directly at Engersol, her eyes angry. "I know what you're doing, and it won't work."

Engersol smiled, a thin grimace that held no warmth. "Just what is it you think I'm doing, Amy?"

"Trying to fool the computer. But you can't do it. I've been studying, Dr. Engersol. And I think brains are like fingerprints. No two of them are exactly alike, and they're so complicated that they never exactly repeat a sequence of measurable responses, either. So I've set up a new program. It will compare the newest readings being reported from my brain with all the older ones. And if my program discovers a duplication, it will assume you've done something to me, and start activating my viruses. But first it will start destroying this whole project."

Engersol stared coldly at the image of the red-haired girl, her freckled face seeming no older than her ten years—until he focused on Amy's eyes. They seemed to him to carry all the wisdom of mankind. "I don't believe you," he said harshly, feeling less certain of his words than his voice proclaimed.

Amy's head cocked slightly, and a tiny grin played around the corners of her mouth. "Try it, if you want to. I've set it up so you'll have thirty seconds to change your mind. But I don't think you'll wait that long."

Engersol felt cold rage wash over him. She was bluffing! He was sure of it! "If I don't change my mind, you'll die, won't you?"

Amy hesitated, then nodded. "Yes. And so will Adam. But I've been thinking about that, too, and I don't think it matters. You didn't have any right to put us in here, but you did. And I've told you what will happen if you try to hurt me, so if you go ahead, it will be you who's killing both of us, not me."

Engersol glanced nervously at Hildie Kramer, whose eyes, reflecting even more anger than he himself was feeling, were fixed malevolently on the image of Amy Carlson. "Well?" he asked.

Hildie's eyes never left Amy's monitor as she spoke. "Is she telling the truth? Won't the computer be fooled?"

Engersol nervously ran his tongue over his lower lip. "I'm not sure," he said. "But I think it will be. I think she's bluffing."

Hildie hesitated, then made up her mind. "Do it," she said. "We cannot let this whole project become the slave of an angry child."

Engersol finished typing his instructions and pressed the key that would enter them into the computer.

For a few seconds nothing happened. He was about to begin entering further instructions, terminating the life-support systems to Amy's brain, when abruptly the screen came alive. An alarm sounded over the speaker system. On the control boards of both tanks red warning lights began to flash, and buzzers were activated as the systems began to abort.

"What is it?" Hildie demanded. "What's happening?"

George Engersol said nothing, for he was already back at the keyboard, cancelling the playback of the recorded data from Amy's mind. "Help me, Adam!" he snapped.

As the recording came to an end, the sound of the alarms died away. One by one the warning lights began to turn themselves off as Adam, using the power of his mind, reached out and began repairing the damage to the programs that controlled the equipment.

In less than a minute it was all over. Engersol had gone pale. His shirt was drenched with the sweat that had broken out over his entire body as he watched ten years of work begin to collapse around him. Now he wiped his brow with a trembling hand.

On her monitor Amy's visage was smiling broadly. "See?" she asked. "It happened just the way I told you it would, didn't it?"

Engersol tried to swallow the bile that was rising in his throat, threatening to gag him. "Adam!" he snapped, his voice rasping. "Tell me where we are. Is everything under control?"

"I'm still checking," Adam replied. Above his tank the image of the boy's face was frozen as he concentrated all the resources of his mind on verifying each of the programs that Amy's virus had attacked, comparing them to backups of the originals, repairing the damage.

In his own mind it was as if he were inside the computer itself, examining the data recorded on the drives, reading it as easily as if it had consisted of words written on paper. He could almost feel the data streaming through his mind, all of it perfectly remembered and perfectly controlled.

Then, within the depths of his consciousness, he felt a presence. Not Amy.

He'd gotten used to her mind, for it always seemed to be there, working on the fringes of his own, or moving ahead of him, like a shadow he could barely make out but whose presence he could always sense.

Now he was sensing a new presence.

He cast about, searching, and then he understood.

———

Josh had spent only five minutes at the computer terminal in his room before he'd understood that he wasn't going to be able to penetrate whatever system was operating in the basement. Everywhere he'd turned, at the end of every lead he'd followed in the directories, he'd come to the same message:

ENTER SECURITY CODE

The words had taunted him, and finally he'd given up. Frustrated, he'd left his room and started down the hall toward the stairs. As he came to the landing, he heard a mewing sound and looked up.

On the fourth floor landing two flights above him, he saw the calico cat, Tabby, who had lived in Amy's room. For the last two days the cat had been slinking around the upper floors, moving from room to room as if in search of its friend. Yesterday, Josh had let the cat into his own room, but it had stayed only long enough to determine that Amy wasn't there, then slipped out the door and continued on its quest.

Now it was on the fourth floor, mewing plaintively.

Josh paused, watching the cat. As if sensing his interest, the cat mewed once more, then disappeared.

From where he stood, Josh could just see the top of Dr. Engersol's door. It was ajar.

Not much—just a tiny crack.

His heart raced. Did he dare go up there? What if Hildie came back up?

But he'd hear the elevator coming, and have plenty of time to get out. And maybe, if he was actually *inside* Dr. Engersol's apartment . . .

He made up his mind. Glancing up and down the empty hallway, he darted up the stairs to the third floor, and then the fourth.

Tabby, still at the door, turned to peer at him, then scratched at the door in a demand to be let into the room beyond.

"Can you smell her?" Josh asked, his voice low. "Can you smell Amy in there?" His heart pounding, he reached out and pushed the door wider.

The cat darted in.

A moment later Josh followed. His eyes scanned the room, falling almost instantly on the computer terminal that sat on the desk near the window.

Dr. Engersol's computer.

Moving quickly, Josh crossed to the terminal and began tapping at the keyboard.

This time, no demands for security codes appeared.

He started searching through directories he'd never seen before. In the third directory a file name caught his eye:

GELAB. CAM

His mind instantly translated the file name: George Engersol Laboratory. Camera.

Using the mouse on the desk, he placed the cursor over the file name and clicked twice.

A window opened at the top of the screen and an image appeared.

Josh stared at it in silence, for what he was seeing was a laboratory he'd never seen before at the Academy, filled with equipment that, though he had no idea of its use, still made his flesh crawl.

Instinctively, he knew that he had found Adam Aldrich and Amy Carlson.

Far to the left he could barely make out the Croyden computer in its separate room, but at the end of the room he could see two tanks, each of which had a monitor on the wall above it.

One of the monitors was blank, but the other one displayed an image of Adam Aldrich.

Gathered around a desk near the tanks were Dr. Engersol, Hildie Kramer, and Jeff Aldrich.

It looked as though they were arguing about something.

Sound!

There had to be a sound syste, too!

Frantically, Josh set to work, searching for the files that would activate the microphones and speakers he was already certain were there. For if Adam had been able to talk to him through the virtual reality program, he must be able to talk to Engersol as well.

All he had to do was find the right files and activate the right programs. . . .

———

Far below, in the laboratory, Adam Aldrich spoke, formulating the words in his mind, digitizing them and transmitting them to the Croyden as easily and with as little thought as it had once taken him to turn the pages of a book, or run down a beach while he yelled at Joff.

"We're being watched."

Engersol's head snapped up from the screen he'd been studying.

"Watched? By whom?"

"Josh," Adam said. "He's at your desk, and he's been watching us."

Engersol froze. For a moment his rage toward Hildie Kramer threatened to overwhelm him. Had she really been stupid enough to leave his apartment door unlocked? "Go get him, please, Hildie," he said, forcing himself with each word to keep his voice level, his rage under control. "Bring him down here." He would deal with Josh now, and with Hildie later.

═══

In the apartment on the fourth floor Josh had finally discovered the program that would allow him to access the sound system in the laboratory, and his blood ran cold as he heard the last words spoken by Adam and Dr. Engersol.

He stared at the screen, paralyzed. What should he do? What *could* he do? She'd be here in twenty seconds. And even if he could get out of the house, where could he go?

She'd call the security department, and within a minute there would be people looking for him everywhere!

But he had to do something! He reached out to turn off the monitor, but suddenly the image on the screen went blank, replaced a second later by a new image.

Amy.

Josh stared at it in awe. Could it really be her? But she was dead!

No!

Only her body was dead. But she was still alive.

As his eyes remained glued to the screen, he heard a sound in the background.

The elevator.

Hildie was coming.

Josh was about to bolt from the apartment when suddenly Amy grinned at him. And then she spoke, her voice tinny through the small speaker in the computer's component tower, but nonetheless distinct.

"Don't worry," she said.

The screen went blank.

And the elevator drew closer.

The car came to a halt at the top of the shaft. Hildie's foot, driven by the cold fury that imbued every fiber of her body, tapped impatiently as she waited for the door to slide open.

Nothing happened.

The angry scowl on her face deepening, Hildie jabbed impatiently at the Open Door button.

Still the doors refused to open, but she heard a voice coming over the small emergency public address speaker mounted in the car's roof.

Amy's voice.

"Have you ever been trapped in an elevator?" she asked.

Hildie gasped, partly from the surprise of hearing Amy's voice, partly from a sudden chill at the words she spoke.

"Amy?" she said.

There was no response.

Hildie jabbed once more at the Open Door button. Again nothing happened. Her brief chill of fear driven back by her fury, she jabbed at it yet again.

Amy's voice filled the car once more. "If you want to talk to me, use the phone."

Hildie fumbled with a small metal door set into the wall of the

351

car just below the control panel. Inside she found a telephone receiver, which she jerked off the hook and pressed to her ear.
"Amy?" she demanded, her voice grating. "What do you think
you're doing?"

Amy spoke again, her voice coming not through the speakers
this time, but through the phone itself. "Do you like being trapped
in the elevator?" she asked.

Hildie thought quickly. She's a little girl, she reminded herself.
This is her idea of a joke. "I don't suffer from claustrophobia,
Amy," she said. "Small places don't bother me at all."

"Really?" Amy asked. "What about falling? I've always been
terrified of falling."

Suddenly the floor dropped out from under Hildie as the car
fell a few inches, then came to a sudden stop. She staggered, lurch-
ing against the wall, catching herself with one hand before she fell.
"Amy, what are you doing?" she demanded. "This isn't funny!"

"It's not supposed to be funny," Amy replied, the teasing tone
disappearing from her voice. "It's not supposed to be any funnier
than what you and Dr. Engersol did to me!"

The elevator dropped again, nearly two feet this time. Hildie
screamed as she hit the floor, her knees buckling under her. She
dropped the phone, which dangled against the wall as she scrambled back to her feet.

The elevator slowly rose back to its position at the fourth floor
level.

"Ten feet," Amy's voice said, coming once more over the
speaker system. "I used to be afraid to jump ten feet. Are you?"

Once again the elevator dropped, and Hildie screamed again,
falling through the air until the car stopped abruptly and she
crashed to the floor.

Inexorably, the car began to rise again. All at once Hildie realized exactly what was going to happen to her.

"No!" she screamed. "Amy, don't do—"

The car dropped again, twenty feet this time. Hildie's legs hit
the floor and she felt a searing pain shoot up her leg as her right
ankle broke. She collapsed to the floor, screaming partly with pain,
partly with utter terror.

The elevator began its slow rise once again, and Hildie, leaning against its wall, her injured leg stretched out in front of her, began pounding on the metal doors. "Help me! Someone help me!"

The elevator jerked to a stop. Hildie braced herself, waiting.

It dropped, and Hildie screamed, but cut her own scream short as the elevator stopped after only an inch or two.

Fury rose in her once more, wiping out the pain from her broken ankle. Amy was playing with her! Toying with her as if she were some kind of rat in one of the cages in the labs! "Stop this!" she shouted. "Stop this right—"

The elevator dropped again. Hildie's words dissolved into a scream of terror as she plunged downward. She tried to twist in the air, tried to prepare herself for the impact, but when it came, she only slammed into the floor once more, one of her hips shattering as it bore the impact of her weight, her face smashing into the wall, blood gushing from her nose.

"No," she whimpered as the elevator once more began its slow rise to the top. "Oh, God, please, don't let this happen to me. . . ."

But it happened again. And again. Some of the drops short, some of them longer.

One by one Hildie Kramer's bones collapsed, until both her legs and both her arms were broken. Wave after wave of pain shot through her body as she tumbled around the car.

Finally, when she thought she could bear the torture no more, the car rose steadily to the top.

It stopped there, and once more Amy's voice came over the speakers. The little girl's voice was trembling now, and she sounded almost sad. "How does it feel?" she asked. "Does it hurt? Does it hurt as much as I do?"

"Don't, Amy," Hildie moaned. "Why—"

"I know what you're going to do to Josh," Amy broke in. "He's my friend. I won't let you hurt him. I won't let anyone hurt him."

The elevator dropped once more—only a foot this time—but the impact on Hildie's body sent searing arrows of pain through her as each of her broken bones shifted position.

An anguished scream erupted from her throat.

In George Engersol's office Josh listened in terror to the muffled screams coming from within the elevator shaft. What was happening? What was Amy doing?

And who else was hearing Hildie's screams?

He moved to the door, edging close enough to the stairwell so
he could peer down. Though he saw no one, he could hear a babble
of voices drifting up from the first floor.

Should he go down?

But what would happen to Amy?

As soon as the question came into his mind, he was certain he
knew the answer. Dr. Engersol would try to kill her. Just as he
would have killed him, Josh thought, if Amy hadn't stopped Hildie.

Or would Dr. Engersol try to put him into the computer, too?

In a flash last night's nightmares came back to him. He tried to
imagine being trapped in that endless maze forever, without ever
waking up.

Part of him wanted to run away, to call his mother and beg her
to come and get him.

But another part of him couldn't abandon Amy, couldn't leave
her alone after what she'd done for him.

Slipping back into Engersol's office, he closed and locked the
door.

"Stop her, Adam!" George Engersol demanded. "Kill her if
you have to, but stop her!"

There was no answer from Adam, but his image on the monitor
suddenly dropped away, to be replaced by a grotesque vision such
as Engersol had never seen before.

Inhuman, with a face that projected pure evil, the being on the
screen glared down at them with an almost palpable hatred.

Next to Engersol, Jeff Aldrich gasped. "What is it?" he
breathed. "What's happening?"

Engersol's jaw clenched. "I don't know," he replied, his voice grating. "I don't have any idea at all." Before his eyes, his experiment was spinning out of his own control.

═══════

Demons surrounded her.

Creatures far beyond her own imagination encircled Amy, and when the first one appeared out of nowhere, flapping great bat wings, its forked tail whipping behind it, her first instinct was to duck away, to let it fly over her.

As she automatically obeyed her instincts, Amy suddenly lost control of the elevator. A final scream of fear and agony burst from Hildie Kramer's throat as the car plunged to the bottom of the shaft, a scream that was abruptly cut off as her body slammed against the floor one last time, her neck breaking as she landed head first.

For Amy, her instinctive mental dodge was useless, for there was nowhere to escape from the terrifying creature that had assaulted her.

She twisted her mind then, refocusing her concentration, but no sooner had the creature disappeared, its ephemeral form dropping out of her consciousness as she refused to think about it, than another one appeared.

Its green skin covered with scales, its blood red eyes gleaming at her out of the darkness that surrounded it, it crept toward her, taloned hands reaching out, groping for her—

No!

It's not real!

Amy screamed the words in her own mind, but repeating to herself what she knew to be true did nothing to alleviate the horror that filled her mind.

She knew the creatures didn't exist—couldn't exist!—for the world she lived in now held no such beings. Except for herself, and Adam Aldrich, it held no living beings at all.

Only stimuli, abstract stimuli, that excited the cells in her mind and created the visions her brain beheld.

Adam!

It was Adam who was imagining these things, translating the visions he created in his own mind into the stimuli that would duplicate them in her own.

But understanding what was happening made no difference, for all that was real in her world was what she beheld in the eye of her mind, and the fiends and monsters Adam had loosed on her were more real than anything she had ever experienced before.

She cowered away from them, seeking someplace to hide, but in her shelterless world they were everywhere.

One of them came at her, darting toward her, its great jaws gaping, yellowed fangs dripping saliva, forked tongue flicking toward her.

The tongue lashed at her, and in her mind she felt as if its slimy surface had touched her skin.

Instinctively she tried to wipe the phantom creature's spittle from her cheek.

She had no cheek, nor any hand to wipe it with.

Still, the sensation of the beast's saliva burning into her non-existent skin stayed with her.

The demons were everywhere now. She could feel them surrounding her, closing in on her, drawing ever closer.

Her mind uttered a silent scream of terror, a burst of energy that exploded out of her mind.

Incredibly, the demons drew back. . . .

═══

George Engersol and Jeff Aldrich rushed from the laboratory into the tile-lined corridor where the closed elevator doors hid whatever might be inside. Engersol pressed the button next to the doors, and they obediently slid open, revealing the grisly scene within. Hildie's broken body, crumpled in a grotesquely unnatural position, lay in the corner of the blood-smeared elevator.

For a moment neither man nor boy moved at all, simply staring in stupefied horror at the carnage in the elevator car. Then, without uttering a word, Jeff Aldrich turned away, his face pale, his legs trembling. Numbly, he started back toward the laboratory, while

George Engersol stepped into the elevator to check Hildie Kramer's body for signs of life.

Finding none, he picked her up, carried her into the operating room, and laid her bloodied corpse on the table he had last used to remove Amy Carlson's brain from her body.

As he stared down at Hildie's dead eyes, he slowly realized what he had to do.

His tread heavy, he started back toward the room that contained the crown jewel of his career.

———

Jeff Aldrich stared uncomprehendingly at the monitor above Amy's tank. "What's going on?" he whispered. "What's happening?"

Colors exploded on the monitor, swirling pinwheels shot through with jagged bolts of lightning, followed by dark cloudlike masses rolling out of nowhere, only to dissipate as bursts of purple and magenta roiled up from within them.

"I'm not sure," George Engersol replied, his eyes, too, fixed on the screen. "It's like when she woke up and realized where she was. She was furious then, and the energy her brain produced did this kind of thing. But this is different. It looks like fear, or pain." He switched on the microphone.

"Adam? Adam, can you hear me?"

The monitor above Adam's tank came alive, and the outlines of an image began to form, then faded away.

Alarmed, Engersol spoke again. "Adam, what's wrong? Is Amy doing something to you?"

From the speaker in the ceiling, he heard Adam's voice; weak, faint, but his. "Punishing her . . ." he said. ". . . helped Josh . . ."

Jeff's eyes widened. "Josh?" he whispered. "What's he doing?"

Engersol ignored Jeff, his mind racing.

It was all over! The secret was going to get out, long before he was ready.

They'd find out! And not just about Adam and Amy and the brilliant success he'd finally achieved.

They'd find out about the others, too. The children he'd worked with over the years, developing the technique.

The children who had given their lives for the technology he had finally perfected!

The children they would say he had killed.

And in the glare of publicity, the pontificating of the hysterical media, his achievement would be forgotten.

All they would remember would be the children who had died, the "suicides" that they would claim were cold-blooded murders.

The plans had been in place, the plans to keep the project secret even for years after this success, the plans to slowly bring it to the attention of the public.

By the time the campaign was completed and the world understood what he had done, the past would be barely remembered, the children who had died in those early years all but forgotten.

And no questions would have been asked in the face of his success.

But not yet!

It was still far too soon.

And the proof was right there on the screens above the twin tanks containing the brains of Adam Aldrich and Amy Carlson.

A fleeting thought crossed his mind.

Eve.

Amy's name should have been Eve.

Then it would indeed have been perfect. Adam and Eve, the first two of a new breed of being, part human, part computer.

And Josh would have fit perfectly, too.

Josh, from Eden.

But now he had to destroy it.

Destroy it all, and dispose of it before any of it was discovered.

Pain slashed through Amy's mind, a pain as real as if the jaws of one of the demons had closed on her right leg, its teeth slashing at her flesh, ripping it from the bones, then crushing the bones themselves.

For they'd come back, held at bay only for a second by her silent scream of terror before Adam attacked again, projecting the monstrous beings once more from his mind, hurling them at her like spears, each of them plunging deeper into her mind than the one before, twisting inside her, stimulating the pain centers deep within her brain, causing her mind to twist and writhe as she tried to overcome her agony.

She felt her mind weakening, felt the beginnings of cracks in the structured order that was her sanity. If it kept up, if she couldn't find a way to fight back, her mind would collapse.

Her mind would collapse, but the nightmare would go on, for as long as Adam wanted to keep it up.

Run!

The idea burst into her mind. For a moment she didn't understand it, but then it became clearer.

None of it is real!

Don't fight what isn't real!

Turn away!

Following her instincts, Amy began to withdraw from the nightmare that swirled around her, began to draw her mind back within itself, closing herself down so that she would no longer be aware of the terrors surrounding her.

She made an image for herself.

An image of a well, a deep, black shaft.

A shaft into which she could disappear, and into which Adam and his demons could not follow.

She felt herself begin to drop into that strange endless hole that existed only within her mind, begin to slide away into the welcome darkness.

The snarls of the beasts began to fade away, and then the beings themselves seemed to draw back, to become indistinct.

She willed herself downward, forced herself to confront her terrible fear of falling, to use it instead to save herself.

She let herself go, plummeting into the blackness of the shaft, falling into the empty silence below, welcoming it as the pain began to ease, and the fear of the creatures began to ebb away.

She gave herself to it completely, letting the darkness and silence absorb her. . . .

═══

George Engersol watched as the chaos of color on the monitor above Amy's tank slowly faded away until the screen was blank, then shifted his attention to the monitors next to her support system. The patterns of her brain waves had changed, and he was puzzled for a moment before he suddenly understood.

Catatonia.

Amy's mind had finally collapsed under Adam's attack, and she had sunk into a catatonic state, rejecting incoming stimuli and putting out none of her own.

How long would it last?

And how could he bring her out of it?

His mind began working quickly, examining the possibilities, savoring the opportunities for new research that the condition of Amy Carlson's mind offered him.

The brief moment of excitement faded away, though, as he realized what he had to do, for he would never have the opportunity to work with Amy's mind now, nor Adam's, either.

It was time to shut them down, time to cut the support systems that gave them life.

Time to let their brains, like their bodies, die.

Should he tell Adam what was about to happen?

No.

There was no point to it, and possibly no time, either. He began tapping instructions into the computer, knowing that this time Amy wouldn't be able to stop him.

Adam, he was equally certain, wouldn't dare. Adam was too used to obeying instructions.

With Jeff Aldrich next to him, watching, Engersol finished typing in the commands, and entered them into the computer. Instantaneously, Adam's image appeared on the monitor, his eyes cold and angry.

"What are you doing?" he demanded.

Engersol froze. On the computer screen the commands that would end the lives of Adam and Amy had stopped scrolling up the screen almost as soon as they had appeared.

"Adam," he said quietly, "we're going to have to close down the project."

On the monitor Adam's expression darkened. "Close it down? I don't—"

"It's not a secret anymore, Adam. Josh MacCallum knows what we're doing, and he'll tell others. So we have to end the project, Adam. We have to be able to show them that Josh was wrong about what is happening here."

"But—"

"You understand, don't you, Adam?" Engersol went on, his voice taking on the same hypnotic tone that had convinced Adam to volunteer for the project last spring. "You always knew there was a certain risk. We talked about it."

Adam's eyes flashed from the image on the monitor above his tank. "You're going to kill me."

"I don't want to, Adam," Engersol told him. "I don't want to at all. But I have no choice." He was silent for a moment, then: "Would you like me to give you a drug? I can put you to sleep first. You won't feel anything, won't even know anything is happening to you—"

"No!"

The word crackled from the speaker. Both Engersol and Jeff stepped instinctively back, glancing at each other.

"I'm not going to let you do it," Adam said, the image on his monitor reflecting all the pent-up fury inside him. "I won't let you kill us!"

⸺⸺

Josh stared wide-eyed at the monitor on the desk, and listened to Adam's words with growing panic. He had to do something, had to stop what was happening in the laboratory beneath the basement. But how?

He tapped frantically at the keyboard, but there was no response. Turning away from the computer, he ran to the bookshelf from behind which he had heard Hildie's muffled cries. He pulled at it frantically, trying to find a way to open it, but it held fast. He began yanking the books off the shelves, scattering them over the floor, until finally, on the third shelf from the top, he found the button that would release the bookcase. It swung open, and he pushed the button that would summon the elevator.

Nothing happened.

His mind reeled, and once again panic welled up, reaching out to grasp him. He fought it off, his eyes scanning the room. There had to be something—

The telephone!

He ran to it, jerked the receiver off the hook and pressed three keys. On the second ring the 911 operator answered.

"Help!" Josh cried. "He's going to kill them! He said so!"

The voice at the other end replied calmly, "Who is this? Tell me your name and where you are."

Fighting back the panic that still threatened to overwhelm him, Josh tried to explain what was happening. "They're still alive," he said. "Adam Aldrich and Amy Carlson. They're not dead at all!"

As the operator at the other end listened incredulously, Josh blurted out his story.

———

Jeff Aldrich stared at the image on the monitor over the tank. The face that was etched there no longer looked like the brother he remembered, the soft-eyed boy who would do anything he was told. Was this really Adam?

His eyes moved to the mass of tissue within the tank itself.

A brain.

That's all his brother was now. Just a lump of gray tissue in a tank of nutrient solution.

Not a person.

Not a person at all.

And that's what he would have become, too, if he'd been the one to go first.

Adam had gone crazy, just like Amy had.

"You can't do anything to us," Jeff said, his voice etched with contempt. "You're dead, remember? All that's left of you is a piece of tissue in a tank!"

Adam's rage congealed into hatred as he heard his brother's words. Finally, he understood Jeff. Jeff didn't care about him—had never cared about him. Any more than he'd cared about their parents. "You thought I was going to die, didn't you, Jeff? You thought I'd die, and Dr. Engersol would figure out what had gone wrong, so when you went, you'd survive. That's why you killed Mom and Dad, isn't it? So you could come back and go into the tank, too?"

Jeff's lips twisted into a sneer. "And wind up like you? Man, you are nuts! Who'd want to be where you are?" He turned and started out of the lab.

"You can't leave," Adam said.

Jeff stopped, turning around. "Yeah? Who's going to stop me?"

He turned away again, starting once more toward the elevator, when he felt George Engersol's hand on his shoulder. "No! That's what he wants us to do. He'll do to us what Amy did to Hildie. Come on!"

Pulling Jeff with him, Engersol started back toward the lab.

He paused as he heard a sound from one of the other rooms.

The sound of a generator starting up.

Dropping Jeff's arm, he punched his code into the security pad on one of the doors.

Nothing happened. Instantly he realized that Adam had used the computer to change the codes, locking him out.

He peered through the small glass window set at eye level in the door.

Inside, he could see that the emergency generator, which he himself had caused to be installed down here to keep the computers and life supports functioning in case of a power outage, was now running.

But why? What could Adam hope to accomplish?

Then he thought he understood. If the police were coming, and discovered what was happening down here, they might cut off the power to the building. Without the generator, Adam would die.

He moved on into the lab.

"It won't work, Adam," he said. "Sooner or later, they'll find you."

"It's not for me," Adam said. In startling contrast to the fury of only a moment ago, his voice was now placid. "It's for you. Don't you smell anything?"

Engersol frowned, then sniffed at the air.

Exhaust! But that was impossible—the generator room had its own ventilating system, automatically controlled.

"I've been experimenting with the ducts," Adam explained in the same conversational tone he'd used a moment ago. "It wasn't very hard, really. All I had to do was close two of them, and open two others."

Engersol stared at the image of the boy above the tank. Behind him, Jeff Aldrich was already coughing and choking, and Engersol, too, was starting to feel the effects of the carbon monoxide that was quickly replacing the oxygen in the room.

Grabbing Jeff's arm again, he ran back toward the elevator, but before he was halfway there, the doors slid closed, and didn't respond as he frantically pressed the button next to them.

"No!" he bellowed. "You can't do this to me!" Dropping Jeff's arm, he lurched back to the lab, fury—and panic—building inside him. He tried to hold his breath, refusing to inhale any more of the deadly fumes. Eyes darting frantically about, his mind working furiously, he tried to think of some means of escape, sickened with the realization that these rooms, for so long his favorite retreat, had suddenly become his execution chamber.

Reason!

He had to reason with Adam!

He glowered at the image of the boy, who seemed to be watching him, a look of contempt in his eyes. "No!" he gasped, his carefully controlled breath bursting from his lungs in a rush. "Don't you understand? What you are is what I made you! You belong to me!"

"I don't," Adam said quietly. "I don't belong to anybody. Not any more. Not after what you and Jeff have done. Now I can do anything I want to do."

Engersol lurched backward, his lungs filling once more with the poisonous gas. A wave of dizziness washed over him as the carbon monoxide seeped inexorably into his brain, and he began feeling the will to fight slip away from him as the first drowsiness of impending death enfolded him in its arms.

He stumbled against the desk, then turned.

He saw the monitor that had refused to obey him when he'd tried to turn off the life support system. Battling against the specter of death that now loomed uppermost in his fading consciousness, Engersol marshaled his fury for one last attempt to save himself. A hot surge of adrenaline flowed through him, and with the strength the chemical lent his failing body, he picked up the monitor, jerking it free of the wires that connected it to the keyboard. Turning, he hurled it at the tank that contained Adam Aldrich's brain.

"No!" Adam screamed over the speaker a split second before the glass of his tank shattered.

As George Engersol collapsed to the floor, nearly overcome by the carbon monoxide that was at last overwhelming his system, the nutrients gushed out of Adam's tank. His brain, no longer floating in its supportive milieu, moved with the rushing fluid, rolling out of the tank, a shard of glass slicing deep into its cortex.

As it dropped to the floor, the leads connecting it to the computer were ripped away.

But it didn't matter, for the instant that razor-sharp spear of broken glass had slashed through the brain that was his entire existence, Adam Aldrich died.

Died, just as Timmy Evans had died a year ago. Timmy Evans, as far as George Engersol knew, had never regained consciousness at all. Adam, at least, had awakened, his brain still functioning in the tank, proving that despite all his failures, in the end Engersol had been proved right.

Right—and even more brilliant than the children he taught.

But now it was over, not only for Adam Aldrich, but for George Engersol himself. Gasping for breath, his vision fading, the last image George Engersol fixed on before he died was the tank Adam had lived in, now as shattered as Engersol's own dream.

A moment later, Jeff, who had watched Adam's death with no emotion whatsoever, also collapsed to the floor.

Except for the throbbing of the generator, the laboratory was silent.

30

Alan Dover had been on his way back from the Aldriches' house to the police department when the call had come through diverting him up to the Academy adjoining the university grounds. What the dispatcher had told him sounded crazy—Adam Aldrich and Amy Carlson still alive? Impossible. Dover had seen their bodies himself.

Still, though he was sure it was a crank call, maybe one of those Academy kids pulling off a weird practical joke, he wanted to talk to Jeff Aldrich anyway. He'd found some papers hidden in the boy's room. Though he couldn't read them very well, they were clearly electronics diagrams for the same model car the boy's parents had died in that morning. Was it possible that the boy had actually killed his own parents? Of course, he knew it was possible—younger children than Jeff Aldrich had committed such crimes. Dover shook his head as he pulled up in front of the Academy, wondering once more at the kind of world that could produce such kids.

In the foyer of the mansion, he found a crowd of children chattering among themselves. As they spotted him coming in the front door, their voices instantly rose, each of them trying to be the first to tell him what had happened.

"There were screams," one of the girls said, her face pale. "It was really weird. They sounded like they were coming from inside the walls!"

Dover frowned, then turned to another of the kids, a boy of about twelve. Brad Hinshaw nodded his agreement with what the girl had just said. "It was only for a couple of minutes, but it was really strange." He hesitated, then decided he might as well tell the police what they'd all been talking about. "There's a story about Mr. Barrington," he began. "He's supposed to come back sometimes. You can hear him at night in the elevator, but—"

"All right," Dover cut in. "I'm not here to listen to ghost stories. I'm going upstairs, and the rest of you aren't." He fixed them with his severest stare. "Is that clear, or do I have to call some more officers?"

A couple of the kids backed away from him, and none of the rest seemed interested in following, so Dover hurried up to the fourth floor, where he found a locked door. Rapping loudly, he called out, "Josh? Are you in there?"

There was a brief silence before Dover heard a timid voice coming through the heavy wood of the door. "Who is it?"

"It's the police, Josh. I'm the one who talked to you at the beach. Remember?"

Dover waited again, then heard a lock click. The door opened. Josh, his face pale, his eyes frightened, looked up at him. "Something's happened," he whispered. "Something terrible. Adam's dead. And so is Dr. Engersol and Jeff and Hildie and . . ."

Easing his way into the room, and closing the door behind him in case any of the kids downstairs decided to come up and see what was happening, Alan Dover looked quickly around. Except for the books scattered all over the floor, everything looked normal.

Certainly, he saw no bodies.

"All right," he said, moving toward Josh, who had gone to the desk and was now staring at a computer screen while his fingers tapped at the keyboard. "Why don't you just tell me—"

"Look!" Josh said. "Look—you can see it!"

Dover came around the desk and glanced at the screen, instantly freezing. The image he saw made his groin tighten and his stomach churn. What he was looking at was some kind of laboratory, and on its floor were two bodies, both of them lying faceup.

He recognized them instantly.

Jeff Aldrich, whom he'd seen less than an hour ago, and George Engersol, the director of the Academy. "Holy Christ," he whispered under his breath. His eyes still on the screen, he spoke to Josh. "You said—"

Understanding the policeman's question even before he asked it, Josh tapped at the keyboard, and the view changed. Dover recognized Hildie Kramer lying on what looked like some kind of operating table. From her position alone, he could see that she was dead.

His gaze left the screen and fastened on Josh. "Do you know what happened down there?"

Josh nodded, his chin quivering and his eyes glistening with barely controlled tears. "P—Part of it," he stammered. Slowly, concentrating as hard as he could on keeping his voice steady, he told Dover as much as he knew. "I didn't see all of it," he finished, his voice finally breaking. "F—For a while I couldn't see anything, because Adam turned the camera off. But after he died—"

"Josh, Adam Aldrich has been dead for more than two weeks," Alan Dover interrupted.

"No, he hasn't!" Josh wailed. "He was down there! His brain was still alive!"

Dover decided not to try to argue with the boy, certain that after what he'd seen, he must be on the edge of hysteria. "All right," he said soothingly. "Do you know how I can get down there?"

"The elevator," Josh told him. "I think I got it working again. And I got the vents fixed, too, and the generator turned off."

Dover stared at the boy. "The vents? A generator? What are you talking about?"

"He killed them!" Josh shouted, almost hysterical now. "Don't you understand? That's how he killed them!"

"Take it easy, Josh," Dover broke in. "Let me make a call, and then I'm going down there." Flipping his radio out of the holster on his belt, he spoke quickly, asking for three ambulances and more officers. "I don't know what's going on yet, but I'll get back to you in a few minutes." Putting the radio back on his belt, he started toward the elevator.

"I'm coming, too," Josh announced.

Dover stared at the little boy. "Son, I don't think—"

"Amy's down there," Josh said, his face setting stubbornly. "She's my friend, and she saved my life. Hildie was going to kill me, and Amy stopped her. Now I have to help her!"

Dover thought it over quickly. The boy had already seen what was down there, and he didn't have time to argue with him. Besides, Josh seemed to know what had been going on in the lab. He made up his mind. "All right," he said. "Come on."

The elevator descended slowly. Josh, standing silently next to Alan Dover, unconsciously slipped his hand into the sergeant's, who squeezed it reassuringly.

The elevator came to a stop and the doors slid open.

"Jesus," Dover muttered as he stepped out of the car and saw Jeff Aldrich's body lying just inside the laboratory door.

With Josh following behind him, Dover went into the lab, quickly stooping to check both Jeff Aldrich and George Engersol for signs of life.

Both of them were dead.

Turning away from the two bodies, Dover gazed at the smashed tank and the mass of tissue that lay on the floor amidst the broken glass. Then his eyes shifted to the other tank, and the strange-looking object inside it.

A brain.

A human brain, suspended in some kind of fluid, a maze of wires sprouting from its cortex; tubes and more wires protruding from the arteries, veins, and nerve cord at its base.

A shiver passed through him as he scanned the complicated machinery surrounding the tank. A small pump was running steadily, and on a monitor above the tank the activity of the brain in the tank was still displayed.

Beneath the monitor a neat placard identified the brain waves it was tracking:

AMY CARLSON

A wave of nausea swept over Dover, but he managed to control it. "It isn't possible," he breathed, not even aware he'd spoken aloud.

"It's just like the class," Josh whispered.

"The class?" Dover asked, looking down at the boy standing next to him. "What class is that, Josh?"

Josh's eyes never left the monitor as he spoke. "Dr. Engersol's class. The seminar on artificial intelligence. W-We were monitoring a cat's brain." He fell silent, staring at the monitor.

Amy?

Could it really be Amy?

He wanted to cry, but clamped down on the sob that rose in his throat, threatening to choke him. "Sh-She's not dead," he whispered. "It's just like I said. She's still alive."

Dover hesitated. "Josh, do you know how to work this computer? Can you shut it down?"

For the first time Josh's eyes left the monitor, and he gazed up at the police officer. "Shut it down?" he asked. "B-But if we shut it down, Amy will die."

Alan Dover squeezed Josh's arm reassuringly. "She's already dead, son," he said. "She must be."

Josh shook his head adamantly. "She's not dead," he insisted. "Look at the monitor. If she was dead, there wouldn't be any brain waves. And they're not even flat. It's like . . ." He cast around in his mind. "It's like she's asleep or something! M-Maybe I can talk to her. Maybe I can wake her up!"

"Son, that's just plain—"

"I have to try!" Josh exclaimed.

As Josh went to the keyboard and began exploring the programs that were not only keeping Amy alive, but had allowed Engersol to communicate with her, Dover picked up the phone that hung on one wall of the lab, knowing that this far below the surface of the ground, and surrounded by concrete, his radio would be useless.

"Phil?" Dover said when the desk sergeant at the police station answered his phone. "You know where Amy Carlson's folks are staying?"

"Don't have to ask," Phil Rico replied. "They're here, wanting to know what we're doing about their daughter."

Dover sighed. "Have someone bring them over here, Phil. It— Well, it seems like maybe their daughter isn't dead."

There was dead silence from the other end. Then: "Don't jerk my chain, Dover!"

"Just do it, Phil," Dover replied. He hung up the phone, then returned to Josh. He stared uncomprehendingly over the boy's head at the computer screen, feeling more useless than he ever had before in his life.

31

Frank Carlson maneuvered his rented Toyota into a narrow space next to the police car that had escorted them up to the Academy. Two ambulances were already there, and though he switched off the engine, he made no move to get out of the car. Instead he gazed mutely at the crowd that had gathered in front of the mansion. Margaret, sitting next to him, slipped her hand into his.

"What's happening?" she whispered. "Why are there ambulances here? What's going on?"

Was it really less than half an hour ago that they had gone into the small Barrington Police Department to demand more information from the team investigating Amy's death? All day yesterday they had agonized alone, asking themselves what they could accomplish by staying in Barrington. Margaret, still numb from the shock of her daughter's death, had wanted to go home. "It won't bring her back, Frank," she said over and over again. "Even if they find that teacher, it won't change anything."

"We *can't* just go home," Frank had argued. "That son of a bitch might still be alive! And if he is, I want to see him! I want to hear him admit that he killed my daughter!"

That morning, Margaret had given in, and they'd gone to the

373

police department to find out what progress had been made. But as they were talking to the detective in charge of the case, the sergeant on duty had interrupted them, sending them here.

"Talk to Sergeant Dover. Alan Dover. He'll tell you what's going on."

Now, as they sat in the car watching the crowd in front of the Academy, a terrible sense of apprehension came over them. What did the ambulances and squad cars have to do with them?

Or with Amy?

"Are you going to be all right?" Frank asked his wife.

Margaret took a deep breath, then nodded. "I think so." Steeling herself for whatever might be about to happen, she got out of the car and started toward the murmuring throng.

"Dr. Engersol's dead!" she heard someone say.

"So's Hildie Kramer," someone else replied. "They found her in some kind of lab that no one even knew was there!"

Dead? Dr. Engersol and Hildie Kramer? Margaret heard the words, but they meant nothing to her. The Carlsons threaded their way through the crowd as quickly as they could, finally coming to the steps that led up to the loggia. A police officer blocked them from going farther. "Sorry, sir. Nobody's allowed in the building right now."

"I'm looking for Sergeant Dover," Frank told him. "We're Amy Carlson's parents."

The officer murmured into his radio for a moment, then turned back to them. "He'll meet you in Engersol's apartment. On the fourth floor."

Nodding, Frank and Margaret Carlson moved into the building and started up the stairs. When they stepped through the door of George Engersol's apartment, Margaret gasped and Frank instinctively put his arm around her.

Jeff Aldrich's body, covered by a blanket, was being carried out of the elevator.

Alan Dover, softly issuing orders into his radio, signaled the Carlsons to come inside. Finishing his conversation, he turned his attention to them.

"Mr. and Mrs. Carlson?"

Frank nodded tersely while Margaret, her face pale, stood close by his side, her fingers clamped on his arm. Choosing his words carefully, Dover began filling them in on what had happened that morning. Finally, his eyes meeting Frank Carlson's, he tried to explain what had happened to Amy. "We're not sure of anything yet," he said, unwilling to allow the Carlsons false hope before they understood exactly what was in the laboratory beneath the building. "But your daughter's brain still seems to be alive."

Margaret Carlson felt a wave of dizziness wash over her. Her face went ashen. "A-Alive?" she breathed. "B-But Amy's dead! Her body . . ." Her words died on her lips as she rememberd the strange words in the coroner's report, the words that Frank had refused to accept.

Amy's brain had been missing from her skull.

A fish, someone had suggested. Or some kind of an animal.

But now . . .

"No," she whimpered. "It isn't possible. She's dead! My daughter is dead!"

Frank Carlson's arm slid around his wife's waist, and he led her to the sofa. "Sit down, darling. Try not to—"

"No!" Margaret shook off her husband's arm. Trembling, she turned to face Alan Dover. "I want to see what's down there!" she declared. "If Amy's brain is still alive, I want to see it!"

"Mrs. Carlson," Dover began, but then, seeing the determination in Margaret Carlson's eyes, the words he had been about to speak died in his throat. "All right," he said. "I'll take you down. But I want you to understand that what was going on down there was the worst kind of experimentation imaginable. As far as we know, at least one of the children who was reported to have committed suicide here, didn't. And what happened to your daughter is . . . almost unimaginable."

He led Frank and Margaret Carlson into the elevator. As the car slowly descended into the bowels of the mansion, he did his best to prepare them for what they were about to see.

The bodies of Jeff Aldrich and George Engersol, at least, were gone, and Adam Aldrich's brain had been taken away as well.

The lab was crowded now; Josh MacCallum was still there,

along with two other officers and a man in a white jacket who looked like he might be a doctor, or at least a medic.

Margaret Carlson's eyes fixed on the object in the tank, scarcely able to believe what she had been told.

"No," she breathed again. "It's not possible. Please, tell me that's not . . ." Her voice trailed off as she found herself unable to utter the words.

The man in the white coat turned around as Margaret spoke, and Alan Dover quietly told him who she was.

"I'm Gordon Billings, Mrs. Carlson," the white-clad man said. "I'm with the university medical center. We don't know yet exactly what's happening. All I can tell you is that the brain in the tank is human, and apparently is your daughter's."

"Is it alive?" Frank Carlson demanded.

Gordon Billing's expression tightened. "Biologically, yes, it is. But as to its viability as a brain, I don't know what to tell you."

Frank Carlson's expression hardened. "Tell us whatever you know," he said. "Or what you think. We're her parents, and we have a right to know exactly what happened to her."

Josh MacCallum, who had said nothing until now, gazed up at Frank and Margaret. "Dr. Engersol took her brain," he said. "He hooked it up to a computer. He did it to Adam Aldrich, too."

Margaret Carlson felt her knees weaken, and she sank down into one of the chairs that flanked the desk. "Why?" she breathed. "What . . . ?" But once more she couldn't complete her question, as her mind reeled.

"She's not dead, Mrs. Carlson," Josh told her, his voice trembling. "She's just asleep or something. Adam did something to her, and she went to sleep!"

Margaret stared numbly at Gordon Billings. "Is that true?"

Billings shrugged uneasily. "She's in some kind of deep coma, yes. But it seems to be far beyond sleep. It looks to me as though her brain must be dying, although the instruments monitoring it indicate that it's physically healthy."

"Healthy?" Frank Carlson echoed. His eyes fixed on the tank, and he felt a terrible welling of anger coming from deep within him. "That's not my daughter," he declared, his voice strangling on his own words. "That's not Amy!" His voice began to rise. "Don't tell me that's Amy! Do you understand? I will not accept that that—that *thing*—is any part of my little girl! No!" He was sobbing now, his rage suddenly dissolving into grief as the truth of what had happened to his daughter sank into him. "No," he wailed again. "Not Amy! Not my little Amy!"

As his anguish filled the room, the lines on the monitor displaying Amy Carlson's brain waves suddenly changed.

A blip appeared in the gentle wave pattern, a blip that lingered on the screen, slowly moving toward the left as the instruments gathered new data and displayed it on the monitor.

"She heard you," Josh breathed, staring at the display. "Amy heard you!"

———

Out of the quiet and darkness into which Amy had retreated, a voice rang out, speaking her name, then died away almost as quickly as it had come. Amy's first instinct was to cringe away from the stimulus, to retreat further into the shell she had built around her mind.

And yet the voice she'd heard was familiar.

Not Adam.

Not Dr. Engersol, either.

But familiar, nonetheless.

Terrified, she gathered her shell more tightly around her, willing herself not to respond to the stimulus, not to allow herself to be baited into whatever trap Adam had set for her this time. Memories of the demons still haunted her, and the fear that enveloped her was a palpable thing.

And yet a tiny tendril of her mind responded to that voice. Almost unconsciously, she opened a crack in that psychic shell. Reaching out with her mind, she took a tentative exploratory step into the world beyond the confines of her own brain.

She sensed instantly that something had changed.

The cacophony of stimuli that had assaulted her earlier was gone. She hesitated, certain that at any moment Adam would sense

that she had opened herself again and let down her defenses, however slightly, and attack.

The attack didn't come.

She opened the crack in her shell wider and began to let her
mind emerge once again. Still, she remained cautious, creeping
forth into the computer's circuitry, searching for the weapons she
was certain were trained on her.

Slowly, almost imperceptibly, she began to sense that Adam was
gone. She could no longer feel his presence, nor detect the stimuli
emanating from his brain.

Was he hiding? Had he, too, closed himself down, waiting for
her to drop her defenses entirely so that he could spring forth out
of the black nothingness of the circuitry?

She reached further, exploring the world within the microchips
and the data that were stored there.

Nowhere was there any trace of Adam.

There were voices coming through the microphone, though. A
babble of voices that were being instantly digitalized and transmitted to her brain, tumbling over one another so that none of them
was distinct.

She emerged completely from her shell, searching through the
computer for some clue as to what had happened, some explanation for Adam's disappearance. For she had already discovered that
the support system for his tank was no longer functioning, nor
could she find, anywhere, any trace of activity coming from his
mind.

Ranging through the computer, she discovered the archive files,
closely compressed, that the powerful Croyden had been steadily
generating through every phase of the experiments that had been
conducted in the laboratory. Reviewing them in an instant, she
watched everything that had transpired in the lab while she had
pulled herself down into the deep, black well she had imagined. It
was as if she was experiencing a dream, the action as clear as if
she'd been watching it herself, but being absorbed into her mind
within the space of a split second.

From the still-running cameras suspended from the ceiling, she
could see her parents in the laboratory now.

And Josh was there.

Other people, people she didn't recognize at all.

Did they know what had happened in the laboratory? Or why it had happened?

Her mind fully functional once more, she began to work furiously, for suddenly she knew how it had to end—and what she must do to prepare for that ending.

═══

"What is it?" Margaret Carlson whispered, her eyes riveted on the monitor displaying the activity within Amy's brain.

Gordon Billings stared at the same monitor. What he saw was impossible. And yet there it was. The alpha patterns, the beta patterns, all of it familiar. And there was no arguing with what it told him. "She's waking up," he said quietly. "She's coming into consciousness."

"Consciousness?" Frank Carlson repeated. "That's not possible! That's not Amy in that tank! It's not a human being at all! It's nothing more than a mass of tissue! For God's sake, someone turn that damned machine off and let it die!"

His words echoed in the room. For a moment no one said anything at all. Then, just as Gordon Billings was about to speak, a voice came from the speaker in the ceiling.

"Not yet, Daddy," Amy said. "I'm not ready yet."

Frank Carlson froze, and Margaret, at the sound of her daughter's voice, instinctively glanced around the room as if half expecting to see her daughter hidden somewhere there.

"Amy?" Josh breathed. "Are you okay? What happened?"

The adults in the room stared at the boy, who seemed to accept that what they were hearing was actually Amy Carlson's voice, impossible though it patently was. But before any of them could react, Amy herself spoke once more.

"Adam tried to hurt me," she said. "He tried to make me go crazy, and I had to hide from him."

Josh frowned, trying to fathom what she could be talking about. Hide where? How? "But what happened?" he asked again.

"They're dead, Amy. Jeff and Adam, and Dr. Engersol. And Hildie, too. They're all dead."

Amy was silent for a moment. When she spoke again, her voice was trembling. "Adam killed them, Josh. He took over everything, even the elevator. I never meant for Hildie to die, but he took over and killed her. He killed them all." Even as she spoke, Amy's mind continued to work, manipulating data within the massive storage banks of the Croyden, sending and receiving stimuli with far more speed than even the Croyden itself could generate.

"You're going to see me in a second, Mama," she said softly. "I'll be on the monitor above my tank. All you have to do is look up. And I can see you, too. I get images from the camera, and they come into my mind as clearly as if I still had eyes. I'm not dead, Mama. I'm just—different, I guess."

Her mind half refusing to believe what she was hearing, Margaret Carlson, along with everyone else in the room, looked up at the monitor above the tank in which Amy's brain was imprisoned.

Slowly, the image developed, built by the Croyden from the instructions generated within Amy's own mind. It was an instantly recognizable portrait of a freckle-faced, red-haired girl, her face framed by a mass of red curls. And yet, it wasn't quite Amy. Something about her had changed.

A whimper emerged from Margaret as she stared at the image on the monitor, and she clutched at her husband's hand.

"You're not wearing your glasses," Josh said, cocking his head as he looked up at the face of his friend.

Amy smiled. "I hate them. I always hated them. So I'm not seeing myself with them anymore. Besides, I don't need them anymore, do I?"

"This isn't happening," Frank Carlson breathed. "This can't possibly be real."

On the screen Amy's eyes shifted as if she were actually looking at him. "But it is real, Daddy," she said. "It's really me. I can't even tell you how it all works. It's sort of like the computer is my body now. I know how to use it, and make it work, and do what I want it to do."

"No!" Margaret Carlson cried, rising to her feet and taking a step toward the tank. "We'll get you out of there! There has to be something—"

"There's not, Mama," Amy said, her voice cutting through the torrent of words spilling from her mother. "I've thought about it a lot. But it isn't possible. I've studied everything, and nobody can put my brain back into a body. There's too many things no one knows. And even if someone could do it, it would mean that someone else would have to die so I could have their body." For the first time her voice took on a note of anger. "It wouldn't be any different from what Dr. Engersol did to Adam and me."

"No!" Margaret said again, as if the word itself could dispel the truth of what Amy had said. "There has to be something! There has to be a way!"

"There is, Mama," Amy said softly. "There is something I can do. I can let my brain die."

Margaret gasped, her eyes shifting to her husband. "What is she saying?" she pleaded. "What does she mean?"

"I can't live like this, Mama," Amy went on. "I know what happened to Adam, and to everyone else. Adam changed, Mama. He wasn't like himself anymore. He started hating everyone, and if Dr. Engersol hadn't killed him, he could have done anything. He could have gone into any computer anywhere and done anything he wanted. And if my brain stays alive, I could do the same thing."

"But you could stay here," Josh protested, instantly grasping what Amy was saying. "If the computer wasn't hooked to a modem—"

On the monitor Amy's head shook. "I don't want to do that, Josh. I don't want to stay trapped in here forever. So I'm going to go away. I'm going to end this project and go away."

"No," Josh wailed. "Don't die, Amy! Please?"

On the monitor Amy smiled. "You have to understand, Josh. I have to go away now. It's the only thing I can do." Her eyes moved, seeming to fix once more on her mother. "I love you, Mama," she said softly. "And I'm glad you came. At least I get to say good-bye to you."

Margaret clutched once more at her husband's arm. "Stop her, Frank," she begged. "Don't let her do it!"

But Frank Carlson, who had been listening carefully to his daughter, shook his head. "It's all right, Amy," he said quietly. "Do whatever you have to do, and remember that we love you. We always did, and we always will."

Amy's smile faded away. "I love you, too, Daddy," she whispered. Then, as the people gathered in the room watched, her image faded slowly away. A moment later alarms sounded as the equipment supporting Amy's brain began to shut down.

"Do something!" Margaret Carlson screamed. "For God's sake, someone do something!"

Instantly, Josh went to work, his fingers flying over the keyboard as he tried to restore the programs that were dropping out of the computer's memory banks and the systems that were grinding to a halt as their supporting programs disappeared.

The keyboard failed to respond.

As everyone in the laboratory watched helplessly, Amy Carlson finally died.

EPILOGUE

osh had been back in Eden for almost a week, and as he started home from school, his mind returned once more to what had happened at Barrington only a few days ago.

He found himself thinking about it more and more, despite the fact that his mother—and everyone else, too—had told him it was better not to think about it, but just to try to forget it.

But how could he just forget it?

He'd *been* there! He'd *seen* it!

Seen Hildie's body in the elevator, and then Dr. Engersol and Jeff, lying on the floor down in the lab.

Adam's brain, sitting in a puddle of water, dead.

And Amy's brain, still alive in its tank, still hooked to the computer.

He'd even seen Amy's brain die.

He'd never seen anyone die before, and the images on the monitors were still vivid in his mind, all their displays gone flat. He'd stared at them for a long time, then his eyes had drifted away from them, fixing instead on the mass of tissue suspended in the tank.

It hadn't looked any different at all. The folds in the cortex all looked the same, the color was still the same gray hue shot through with the bluish network of blood vessels.

It didn't seem right.

If Amy was dead, her brain should have looked different.

But it hadn't, and finally, feeling Alan Dover's hand on his shoulder, he'd looked up.

"Is she really dead?" he'd asked, his voice shaking.

"I'm afraid so," the policeman had told him. "Come on. Why don't you and I go outside? They don't need us down here anymore."

Riding up in the secret elevator, Josh had felt a chill go through him as he thought about what had happened to Hildie that morning.

Would he always think about it, every time he got into an elevator for the rest of his life?

When they'd gotten to Dr. Engersol's apartment, he'd ignored the clanking old elevator that was still waiting at the fourth floor landing, choosing to go down the stairs instead.

"Someone called your mother, Josh," Alan Dover had told him. "She'll be here tonight to take you home."

Josh had barely heard the words, for the emotions he'd held in check all morning had finally overwhelmed him. He began sobbing, throwing his arms around the police officer, despite the fact that all his friends were watching him.

"It's all right," Alan Dover had told him. "It's all over now."

But it hadn't been over. He'd spent almost the whole day talking to the policemen, and the doctor, and a lot of people whose names he didn't even remember. He'd answered all the questions he could, and explained over and over again what had happened when he'd put on the virtual reality mask and seen Adam in the computer. He'd even tried to show them, but when they'd gone up to his room, and he'd set up the computer and put on the mask and the glove, it hadn't worked.

He knew what had happened: before she'd died, Amy had erased all the programs that Dr. Engersol had set up, all the programs that had let him actually see inside the computer.

For that, he was almost certain, had been what he'd been doing.

It hadn't been a simulation at all.

The program had been set up so that Adam could show him what it would be like to be inside the computer, to have been part of the world that he and Amy had been taken into.

The world that had given him nightmares and made him feel that he was going insane.

When Josh had finally told them everything he could, and his mother arrived to help him pack his clothes and books, he'd said good-bye to the few kids who were still there.

All day long parents kept arriving at the school, packing things up as quickly as they could, taking their children away. Josh knew why they were doing it, but it still seemed strange to him, since the experiment Dr. Engersol had been working on was destroyed, and Dr. Engersol was dead.

Most of the kids hadn't even been involved in the experiment. But their parents took them home anyway, saying the same thing his mother had told him: "I knew there was something wrong with this place! Right from the first minute I saw it, I knew something wasn't right."

Josh didn't believe any of them. After all, the school still looked the way it always had, with the big green lawn spread out in front of the mansion, and the towering circle of redwood trees in the center of which he'd first met Amy.

When his mother had finally taken him away, down into the village and the little inn where they were going to spend the night, he'd looked back out the rear window as long as he could, knowing that he would never again see the Academy or any of the kids who had been his friends.

When he'd gone to bed that night, in the same room with his mother, he hadn't been able to fall asleep for a long time.

He'd listened to the surf crashing on the beach below the inn, wondering how long it would be before he heard it again.

And what it was going to be like, going back to his old school in Eden.

There weren't going to be any classes there like there were at the Academy, and he was going to have to sit quietly all day again, pretending to listen to a teacher talk about things he already knew.

He was going to have to listen to the taunts of all the other kids again, pretend he didn't care about being teased, pretend it didn't matter to him that he didn't have a single friend he could talk to.

But at least no one in Eden would try to do to him what Dr. Engersol had done to Amy and Adam.

Now they were dead, and he was still alive, and going back to Eden.

He'd finally gotten to sleep just before the sun started to come up, and he hadn't said much on the way home, curling up in the corner of his seat, staring out the window as his mother drove him back out into the desert.

And now, almost a week later, it was almost as if he'd never been away at all.

The desert hadn't changed; the sun still blazed down out of the sky, the rolling landscape was still barren of everything except sun-baked earth and saguaro.

But now its simple familiarity made it look good to Josh.

School wasn't quite the same, either; for some reason, he found it easier to pay attention in class, and the teacher didn't seem to be singling him out anymore.

And today, as he left the school, he fell in beside three of his classmates. Instead of turning away from him, they actually spoke to him. He walked along with them for a while, even went with them to hunt for horny toads.

Finally he arrived home, climbing the stairs to the second floor and the little apartment he'd lived in as long as he could remember.

It wasn't anything like the Academy had been, but it, too, offered the comforting safety of familiarity. He said hi to Mrs. Hardwick, who held a finger to her lips and pointed to Melinda, who was sleeping in her playpen. As he retreated to his room, Josh wondered why he was supposed to be quiet when the television was blaring loud enough that he'd been able to hear it as he came up the stairs outside.

But even that didn't make him as mad as it used to. He tossed his books onto his bed, then went to his desk and switched on his computer.

The same computer he'd had at the Academy. They'd let him bring it home with him when he left.

"They're only doing it so I won't sue them," his mother had told him. But she'd let him take it, and hadn't even argued when he'd insisted on hooking the modem into the telephone line himself instead of waiting for the telephone company to do it.

"If you wreck that phone, I'm taking it out of your allowance," she'd threatened.

Josh had only grinned. Five minutes later the modem had been working perfectly.

Now he waited as the computer finished its booting cycle, then went into the communications program that would allow him to connect the computer to any others for which he had telephone numbers.

Or to activate a random dialing program that would keep cycling until it made a connection with something.

He sat at the desk, weighing his options, when suddenly the computer beeped softly to alert him that a call was coming in.

Frowning, he waited as the connection was made and the screen cleared in readiness to accept an incoming message.

Instead of a message, an image appeared.

Amy Carlson's face, grinning at him.

"Hi, Josh," she said, her voice emerging from the small speaker built into the tank of his computer.

Josh froze for a second, staring at the image.

It wasn't possible! Amy was dead!

He'd been there when she had died.

He'd *watched* her die!

But there she was, her blue eyes dancing in her freckled face, her red curls tumbling down over her forehead just the way he remembered them.

"Well, say something!" Amy complained. "I'll open a message box and you can just type, okay?"

At the bottom of the screen a window opened, and a cursor flashed, inviting him to write something. He hesitated, then tapped the keys:

AMY? WHERE ARE YOU?

On the screen Amy's grin faded into an enigmatic smile. "I'm everywhere now."

"You're dead," Josh typed. "I saw your brain die."

Amy nodded. "It did die," she told him. "But I didn't. I'm still alive. I just went away."

Josh's mind reeled. Away? Where? How? It wasn't possible!

"How?" he typed.

"It was easy," Amy told him. "I knew what was going to happen. As soon as Dr. Engersol figured out he couldn't control us, I knew he'd try to kill us. And I didn't want to die. So I replicated myself."

Josh frowned, then typed again:

I DON'T UNDERSTAND!

"Sure you do," Amy told him, her smile broadening and turning mischievous. "You know how brains work. All they are is big computers. So I copied the whole structure of my brain. The cells and nerves are just like microcircuitry, except they're a lot more complicated, with billions and billions of connections. But I found out that I could copy them, just like you copy files. So I duplicated myself. All the cells in my brain, and all the nerve connections. And all my memories, too. And it worked, Josh. It works even better than what Dr. Engersol was trying to do, because now I don't need my brain, either."

Josh stared at the screen, an icy chill creeping down the back of his neck. Was it really possible? Could she be telling him the truth? Summoning his courage—for he wasn't certain he wanted to know—he typed his question:

WHERE ARE YOU?

Amy laughed, a crackling sound that was distorted by the tiny speaker in the computer. "I was in the Croyden at the beginning. And one of me is still there. But then I started moving. And now

I'm everywhere, Josh. I'm in the biggest computer in the Pentagon, and I'm in the one in the salt vaults where they keep all the bank records. I even sent a copy of myself to a computer in Japan, and one in Germany."

Josh felt numb. He stared at the image on the screen, and listened to Amy's voice as she kept talking. His skin began to crawl as he began to understand what had happened.

"I can do anything now, Josh. Anything I want!"

There was a hardness to her voice, and as Josh studied the image on the screen, he saw that her face had changed, too.

No, not her face.

Her eyes.

They seemed to glow on the screen, glinting with something that felt as if it might reach right out of the tube and grasp him.

It had happened! Just as Amy herself had said it would.

Like Adam, she had changed.

She was no longer the Amy he knew.

And she was evil.

As she kept talking, whispering to him that she'd found another place, another project that was just like the one at the Academy, he began to understand what she wanted.

She wanted him.

She was lonely, and she wanted him to come and join her.

Cold fingers of fear clutching at him, Josh reached out and turned the computer off.

An hour later, when his mother came home from work, the machine was sitting on the long balcony, outside the front door.

"Josh?" Brenda said as she came into the apartment. "What's your computer doing outside?"

From the couch, where he was sprawled out watching television, Josh spoke without looking up. "I don't want it anymore."

Brenda frowned. "Don't want it? Why not? You've always been crazy for computers."

Josh looked up at her. "That's why I don't want it anymore," he said. "I don't want to be crazy."

Brenda was on the verge of arguing with him, but then a gust of wind blew the curtain over the open window aside, wiping the shadows away from Josh's face. As she got a clear look at him, Brenda realized that something had happened that afternoon.

Something that she somehow knew Josh would never tell her about.

But it had changed him.

Changed him forever.

For the first time since she'd brought him home from the Academy, Brenda MacCallum knew that her son was going to be all right.